PRAISE
GAIL HAREVEN

"This contemplative inquiry into the nature of love speaks across cultures and introduces a compelling new Israeli voice to English-speaking readers."

—*Publishers Weekly*

"Witty and compelling, [Hareven] will leave American readers . . . pining for more."

—Jessa Crispin, NPR

"Sometimes one has the experience of reading a book and just falling in love with it—because it is so well written, so moving, it gets into your soul. That was my experience when I read *The Confessions of Noa Weber.*"

—*Ha'aretz*

"[A] masterly written and translated story. Highly recommended."

—*Library Journal*

GAIL HAREVEN

Translated from the
Hebrew by Dalya Bilu

LIES, FIRST PERSON

OPEN LETTER
LITERARY TRANSLATIONS FROM THE UNIVERSITY OF ROCHESTER

First edition, 2015

Library of Congress Cataloging-in-Publication Data: Available upon request.
ISBN-13: 978-1-940953-03-8 / ISBN-10: 1-940953-03-0

This translation was made possible by the Institute for the Translation of Hebrew Literature.

This project is supported in part by an award from the National Endowment for the Arts.

ART WORKS.
arts.gov

Printed on acid-free paper in the United States of America.

Text set in Fournier, a typeface designed by Pierre Simon Fournier (1712–1768),
a French punch-cutter, typefounder, and typographic theoretician.

Design by N. J. Furl

Open Letter is the University of Rochester's nonprofit, literary translation press:
Lattimore Hall 411, Box 270082, Rochester, NY 14627

www.openletterbooks.org

LIES, FIRST PERSON

PROLOGUE

You should never believe writers, even when they pretend to be telling the truth. Everything that's written here is pure fiction.

My husband urged me to make this clear at the outset if I intended to tell this story. The version he proposed was somewhat different, as a matter of fact very different, but in any case I promised him to write this introduction.

My husband Oded is a lawyer. He adores me, our children, and our way of life; and I, who love and respect him profoundly, am ready to accept his advice. And to dispose of any doubt let me stress:

None of the characters that appear here, myself included, are real. The first person is not my person, and the events recorded here never happened to me or to anyone I know.

The truth is that nothing bad was done to anyone, and I did nothing bad, and I was always as quiet as a mouse.

In short, the truth is that nothing happened at all.

Perhaps it only could have happened.

BOOK ONE
THE GARDEN OF EDEN AND WHAT CAME BEFORE

- 1 -

First of all we have to plant the Garden of Eden, because without the Garden of Eden there is no serpent; without the boughs of the apple tree to hide in, the serpent is nothing but an eater of dirt, of no greater significance than a snail or a worm.

Therefore, let there be a Garden of Eden!

And in fact, why "let there be"? There was a Garden of Eden. The Garden of Eden existed. Because why shouldn't I call what I had a "Garden of Eden"?

Let's begin with a Sabbath day of unutterable sweetness. The smell of figs bursting with ripeness, in the enclosed garden of the house. Clouds sift the gold of the sun through the leaves of the grapevine hanging over our heads. Oded rolls a Sabbath cigarette from the grass he's been growing in pots ever since our sons grew up and left home. On weekends he likes smoking a joint or two, and for me, a non-smoker, he pours a glass of wine. I roll the glass between two fingers and observe the rays of the sun refracted in the liquid red, and my husband, relaxed, rubs the bottle against my upper arm, sliding the glass over my tiger face. Twenty-six years we've been together, and his enthusiasm for my tattoo has not waned, and it seems it never will. If not for him I would have had this totem surgically removed a long time ago, because there is no fear in the Garden of Eden, and a woman has no need of a totem to brandish. But Oded loves my tiger face, and I don't want to deprive him of anything.

The Garden of Eden. A muezzin calls the faithful from inside the Old City. We don't understand the words, and we enjoy the sound of the voice rising and gathering in the distance. The golden Sabbath time stretches out around us without a point of reference—perhaps it's morning now, perhaps it's twilight—people whose lives are as good as ours don't need points of reference.

Our financial situation is comfortable, some might say excellent. The firm in which Oded is a partner with his father is stable and successful. Money is saved, property accumulated, and if my husband should decide or be obliged, God forbid, to stop working, neither we nor our sons will want for anything.

The hand that casts the dice blessed us with two healthy, handsome, clever, and sensible sons. Within a few years they will both do well, each in his field, and in fact are doing well already. Nimrod in Atlanta, as an exchange student from the Israel Institute of Technology. Yachin is also in the United States, in Seattle at the moment, overseeing some project of the aviation industry. When Yachin was born I was twenty-one, Nimrod is less than two years younger than his brother, and I was happy with them both and thankful that I had not given birth to daughters.

My body is intact and strong and still able to take pleasure in the very fact of its existence. Without difficulty I carry baskets full of the earth's plenty from the market, and cook meals without effort for twenty or thirty of our friends.

My appetite for sleep is as voracious as that of an adolescent girl: ten, sometimes even twelve hours a day. Sleep tastes sweet to me, on no account should my greed for it be seen as a sign of depression.

My husband is in the habit of introducing his wife as a writer, and this is one of the few things about him that annoys me. Writing a column in the newspaper doesn't make a person a writer. I have had two offers to collect the columns of "Alice in the Holy City"—both by reputable publishers—for a book, and I turned them both down, even though my husband and my sons were very keen for me to accept them.

Oded, who mainly reads detective stories, tends to admire "literature" and "writers" in general whereas I, who read a lot, know what good literature is and how it incites the mind, and I have no pretensions to being what I am not. I was fond of my puppyish Alice, I enjoyed most of our walks round the city together, but I am not persuaded that her adventures are worth a book. The "Alice" columns enriched me with lively encounters and gave me a measure of fame too modest to arouse the envy of the gods—and this is no doubt another element of our happiness.

Paradise. Wine and pot, grapes and olives. Actually, no olives. We don't have an olive tree in our garden. Figs. A fig tree. And a good man planted underneath it. Successful sons. Professional satisfaction. Friends. Perfect weather, and a heating-air-conditioning system that protects us when the weather is less than perfect.

Who or what did I forget?

Menachem, Chemi, a patient patriarch, in his old age at least, whose health is also excellent.

Rachel, my blue-eyed mother-in-law, a practical angel with a beaming face.

Shaya, my father, whose flowery letters from Italy I didn't keep.

My sister Elisheva, who has gone to ground somewhere in the American Midwest.

And my dead mother.

When she deserted us I was too young to understand that my Garden of Eden would only grow on orphaned ground. I was young and raging, I raged a lot, until in the course of time I got over it. There is no room for rage in Paradise, and if a little surliness appears from time to time, it quickly disappears again. And thus on our languid, wine-drenched Sabbath day we experience no painful feelings. We mostly experience gratitude toward the invisible hand that allotted us a vine and a fig tree, and even more so gratitude to ourselves, for even if we didn't plant them, we knew how to tend them and make them thrive.

Leafy shadows dance in the light breeze. The taste of wine in my mouth, and in the air the fragrance of figs flavored with pot. The cellphone rings in the Garden of Eden, and his voice rises from it, the person who, for most of my life, I have been trying to forget.

"His voice" I say, but the truth is that I didn't recognize the voice. The phone rang, I thought of letting it ring, but on the screen I saw that it was an overseas call, and even though we had spoken to the boys earlier in the day and I didn't think it was one of them, I answered the phone, because overseas calls can't be ignored.

He asked into my ear "Can I speak to Mrs. Brandeis?" He spoke in English, even though he knew Hebrew and I knew him as a Hebrew speaker.

I replied: "Elinor speaking."

"Hello, Elinor." He said my name—and only then: "This is Aaron Gotthilf."

I didn't utter a word and for some reason I didn't hang up, either. Mutely I held out the phone to my husband, who took it immediately and refrained from asking me "What?" or "What's up? Who is it?"

I heard: "Oded Brandeis speaking," and then a long speech on the other end of the line. I saw Oded narrowing his eyes, absent-mindedly putting out his unfinished joint, and then very aggressively: "My wife has no desire to talk to you. This conversation is unwanted and I must ask you not to call again."

Quick to react, he jumped in between us, but too late; the reaction came too late. Aaron Gotthilf had searched for and found me, he knew my private phone number and my married name, which had often, too often, appeared in the newspaper. His thoughts were occupied with me, his desires pawed me, and he could do it again whenever he wanted to.

I went on sitting when Oded got up to stand behind me and put his arms around me, but I didn't lean back.

"What did he say?" I demanded. The embrace that restricted my movements made me feel uncomfortable.

"It seems he's on his way to Israel," Oded sounded apologetic, "it seems that some idiots or other have invited him to a conference. He said that he'd very much like for you to agree to meet him. And I say, listen, Elinor, what I say is this: I say let's just forget about him, let's forget about this phone call. That man and his conference—they're not relevant to anything."

"Did you understand what he wants?" I removed one of his arms from my breasts.

"What he wants? I don't know. He was . . . not exactly equivocal, cautious I'd say. He mentioned his grandchildren, he has a couple of grandkids in New York. You know what, I think, yes, I think that somehow he wants a connection with us. However incredible it sounds, he wants a connection. He repeated twice that he's already an old man."

"I don't want to hear it," I said and removed Oded's other arm. "It's not relevant."

"No," he echoed, "that person is no longer relevant."

"Stop calling him a person," I corrected him. "He's not a human being at all, and I don't want to hear anything about him because it's got nothing to do with anything. Just remember that I'll never, ever, not even when he's dead, forgive him for existing."

- 2 -

Oded says that I brought up the rape the first time I went out with him. But I remember clearly that the subject didn't come up on the first date, only on the third, and argue that his memory is changing the order of events for dramatic effect. In any case, there is no disagreement between us regarding the scene that followed.

I told him whatever I told him—not much—and then I said: "That's it. That's what happened. Just don't think that I'm going to tell you anything more about it, go into details, I mean." And he, in obvious confusion, replied: "Sure. Of course." And then he asked me: "Why?" Because what else could he say?

"First of all because it's my sister's rape, not mine, okay? That's the first thing. And apart from that . . . Never mind."

"Apart from that—what?"

"Forget it."

"No, tell me."

"Apart from that you're a man. Can you honestly tell me that you never fantasized about rape? Can you tell me that your imagination never wanted, even a little, to look and see? That's not a real question, so you don't need to answer it."

It wasn't fair. It wasn't fair at all. Oded Brandeis, salt of the earth, black belt in the gifted students track of the University High School, graduate with the distinction of a paratrooper commando unit, volunteer in a legal clinic in the Negev—Oded Brandeis was offended.

We met during the end-of-year exams, and the guy took the evening off to drive me to a spot on top of the Mount of Olives where he had only taken one girl he loved before. He brought a pique blanket for us to sit on and a bottle of white wine, and offered me the nocturnal view as if it belonged to him and he was free to give it away for nothing.

If people in this world got what they deserved he would have given me my marching orders on the spot. After jumping on him like that I deserved to have him cross me off the map. But in our world people don't get what they deserve, and the sudden ferocity of my attack didn't prompt him to get rid of me, but somehow made me more interesting in his eyes. Later on, when he dropped me off outside my apartment next to the market, I apologized, and he accepted my apology like an aristocrat: he made the broad, sweeping gesture of a man who can permit himself anything, even a crazy woman, even though it was clear that he was alarmed. Because not only was my ferocity intimidating, but my entire manner of speech. I said: "My sister was raped and she went mad"; "went mad" I said and not "was traumatized" or "suffered a mental breakdown."

The laws of attraction work deceptively: things are not what they seem. Beneath every marriage contract another document lies hidden, written in invisible ink that only time reveals, and with Oded and me time worked fast on what was hidden from sight.

When we met, Oded was about to complete his studies and was making up his mind whether to do what it was obvious to everyone he would do after he finished making up his mind: first, clerking for Judge Brenner, who was a friend of his father's, and from there straight to his father's office to take up his position as the third generation of the firm. But the third generation had, in his words, "second thoughts about the path," and his thoughts wavered between joining legal aid, changing to studying history, or maybe something else, even more revolutionary, exactly what he didn't know himself.

When he met me it seemed that he had found his rebellion: a rebellion with spiky hair, a tiger face on its arm, and the exaggerated halo of a kind of desperate kamikaze pilot. Everything about me looked romantic to him: studies leading nowhere in the English Literature department, missing classes, the day I forgot to get out of bed for an exam, the small literary prize I received for a dubious volume of poetry—most of the copies of which I succeeded in destroying in later years. My squalid apartment, the wall I peeled pieces of plaster off, the bits of plaster on the bed, the empty vodka bottles—everything seemed romantic, even my orphaned state was perceived as romantic. I was not the girl suitable to be taken to Friday night dinner with his parents, and precisely for that reason, only a little more than a month after we met, he took me to his parents' house.

Wise people, Menachem and Rachel, very wise. Is it possible that they read the message in the invisible ink? Did some intuition tell Rachel that the girl in the see-through green tank top with the chopped hair who bit her nails in public till they bled—this girl would give her two grandchildren within the space of three and a half years? And that she would always, always gratefully accept her help in raising them, to the point where their house and ours appeared to be one unit, whose rooms were only accidentally scattered around the town?

Perhaps they were nice simply because it was their nature, certainly Rachel's nature. And perhaps they considered that any opposition on their part would only fan the flames of their son's rebelliousness.

Whatever the reason, when I accompanied Oded's mother to the smell of the pot roast in the kitchen, she took the empty soup bowls from me and put them down, and then, with a twinkle in her eyes she stopped to admire my tattoo: she had never seen one close-up. How beautiful, like an artistic piece of jewelry, even more beautiful, more integrated, definitely more beautiful than jewelry—and with her little hand she stroked my tiger face.

"It suits your arm very well, but tell me, isn't it awfully painful to have it done?"

Suddenly feeling faint from the smell of the food I shrugged my shoulders, and she, without removing her hand, added something jovial about how much we women were prepared to suffer for the sake of beauty, perhaps it was a question of education, but what could we do? That's the way we were. She too would like to have a cute little tiger like mine, but she was too old already, and anyway she lacked the courage.

Oded sometimes jokingly claims that that I fell in love with his parents before I fell in love with him. Maybe this is true and maybe it isn't, but in any case, according to my mythological memory, on that Friday night I already lay down my arms. The cleanliness, the white cleanliness of the house acted on me like a drug as soon as I walked through the door. Without my noticing it made me feel disgusted by the filth of my own apartment, and what's more it made me yearn for something I had never had and of whose absence I had never been aware; for even before I took up residence in my squalid cave in the marketplace—in my parents' home, in the boarding school, in all the places where I had ended up, there was nowhere that was really clean, and it was only when I stepped into the quiet whiteness of the Brandeis residence that I could look back and be revolted, and only then did I begin to yearn for this new wonder.

The comfortable cleanliness, which was deep but not sterile, the vaulted white ceilings, the solid, welcoming wooden furniture—everything invited me to lean back, to close my eyes, and sail to a land where nothing bad had ever happened. And I closed my eyes and sailed to that Neverland, because after she had turned my tattoo into an ornament, Oded's mother went on calmly stroking me without hurrying to the stove. She traced the lines of the predator's face with her finger, touched the bared fangs, and in parting also gave its nose a friendly little poke. And with this gentle poke I fell asleep and I went on sleeping for a long time, until Aaron Gotthilf came back to ambush me and invade my dreams. For with the passing of time I had succeeded in banishing him from my dreams as well as my waking thoughts.

My lack of a mother and the absence of any other significant relations in my life were the main dowry I brought to my marriage with the Brandeis family. This was not a dowry to be admired out loud, but over the years we all came to appreciate its worth.

Free of parents, I relieved my father- and mother-in-law of the need to share the title "grandparents" with a pair of strangers, and gave them the gift of taking for granted the fact that their son and grandsons spent almost every holiday and Saturday with them. A picture in which they sit around the table with my pre-historic family is not one that I want to imagine. My father squirming and bragging and never still for a minute, the lock of hair stuck to his forehead growing greasy with effort. My mother raising her fair, plucked eyebrows, thin as a hair, in an exaggerated expression of amazement, and raising a hand to her operatically plunging neckline to feel her heart. Disgusting. I don't want to think about the disgust. For a long time I succeeded in not thinking about it, and I succeeded so well that I was close to believing that we are the masters of our thoughts.

- 3 -

Disgust is a cunning infiltrator; it's hard to keep its stealthy invasions at bay, and sometimes you have to recruit guards to protect you from them. The guardian of my soul against disgust was the idiotic Alice, the heroine of my newspaper column.

Alice appeared in my life when my sons were already in high school and empty pits of leisure began to yawn around me. The sentry of my soul appeared at the right time, a moment before my husband began to wonder where the artistic personality he had married, in his opinion, had disappeared to. Like a lot of other good things, the writing came to me as a result of a conversation with Menachem. Chemi collects books about journeys to Jerusalem. I sat on the comfortable window seat while he showed me an old-new addition to his collection to admire, and as I paged through it and examined the engravings I mused aloud that "you don't need to be a pilgrim to see this city through the eyes of a traveler," and in order to gild the lily of this pronouncement I added, "When you think about the history of Jerusalem, in a certain sense we're all only visitors here."

My family likes hearing remarks of this kind from me. Even though I haven't written a word for years, those dear to me continue to boast of me as a poet—including the sons I kept from reading my poems—and in their opinion, these are the kinds of sayings an artist is supposed to produce.

Chemi beamed at me, said that this was a very original view, and before taking the book from me to return it to the shelf, he set me a challenge: "Come on, Elinor, let's see you write something about Jerusalem, something short, from the point of view of a visitor. How long will it take you? Will a week be enough? Two?"

Menachem Brandeis knows how to direct others toward wanting what he wants. His son says that I have no idea how he used to tyrannize his employees and articled clerks. And how could I have any idea? In the family circle, not only have I never heard him raise his voice, I don't even recall him sounding stern.

Two days after the conversation with Chemi, Alice was already there. And when she appeared, I had no idea that she would be with me for years to come.

My Alice—she has no surname—was born and grew up in the fictional town of Coldstone in Alaska, and came to Jerusalem with one overriding obsession: to learn how to paint desert light. Why Alaska? And why desert light? Just because. Because that's what came into my head. With a pair of pigtails she came to me from a little town in Alaska to acquaint herself with a different light, and fell under the spell of a different city.

The first two chapters of her adventures—Alice enrolls in the Bezalel Academy of Art and Alice looks for an apartment in the picturesque quarter of Nahlaoth—were written in less than a week. A drawing teacher I met by lucky chance at exactly this time provided me with anecdotes about Bezalel; Nahlaoth I know very well. I had a basis in reality, and on it I began to elaborate the fantasy.

Over the years I composed hundreds of Alice episodes, but the characteristics of the heroine and the characteristics of the story remained as they were in the first two pieces that were written at the request-demand of Chemi: naïve and clueless, ignorant of our great stern beliefs, ignorant of the history and customs of the place, Alice from the realms of ice roams our streets, mostly our alleys, breathless with excitement, biting the tips of her braids, opening her eyes wide at the colorful sights she sees. Colorfulness is the key, and everyone who runs into Alice tends to see himself as colorful character.

"Are these real people? People you know?" Menachem asked when he finished reading my one thousand six hundred words.

"Partly. Not exactly. Partly yes. The Iraqi from the grocery store is quite real, as is the connection of the Armenian, Dakaan, to the Natural History Museum: the building was originally called the Villa Dakaan. Never mind. Most of it I made up. I was just having fun." I went to the table to take my pages, but Menachem put his hand over them. "The fact that you're talented goes without saying, but apart from being well-written, in my opinion you've hit on a gimmick here. Let me see what we can do with it."

I didn't protest. I was in Paradise. I was in the middle of the years of the Garden of Eden, and Alice was the kind of character you'd expect to meet among the trees. I enjoyed the company of this innocent, and from the moment she appeared I was in no hurry to get rid of her. My family was agog with silent excitement—Mom's writing, my wife's gone back to writing, quiet everybody. Even the boys didn't think that their mother was embarrassing them—and without an explicit invitation on my part, Alice began to accompany me almost everywhere I went, and like a Cocker Spaniel puppy she would urge me to take her out for a walk.

Menachem spoke to whomever he spoke to, sent off the material, and that same week I met the person who was then the culture editor of *The Jerusalemite* and explained the "gimmick" to him. As if I had intended a gimmick from the outset: Alice as a kind of reporter. She goes to real places in the city and interviews people, but her reports on them are only half true, and both of us are free to add fictional characters and fictional elements as the fancy strikes us.

Like Chemi, the editor too used words like "fresh" and "authentic." But at the same time he wondered about the possibility of libel suits. I promised him that there was nothing to worry about and that no such situation would come up. It wouldn't come up because the enthralled Alice saw nothing but good, and there was no way that anyone would be offended by her descriptions. In fact the opposite would probably happen: Alice would make the people she met see themselves as colorful characters and rejoice in the colorfulness of the world.

What I said without giving it much thought turned out to be true. In all her explorations of the city, innocently delighting in Jerusalem and all its inhabitants, Alice never offended or insulted a single soul. And something else happened too, which neither the editor nor I myself anticipated: over the years Alice acquired a circle of fans who set out to follow in her footsteps, curious to meet the people she had met and to find the charm she had found, mixing the facts with the fiction in her stories. Did the embroiderers of the curtains in the Armenian Patriarchy really sing like angels as they worked? Had "Mister Soup"'s green soup really been served at the table of the King of Morocco? Did the stammering seller of textiles in Davidka Square really hide pearls of ancient wisdom among her broken words, and did a descendent of the House of Romanov really get on the number four bus to Mount Scopus every morning? And perhaps only Alice found wisdom, and only she recognized royal features on the face of an old woman with her head wrapped in a scarf?

It took eight columns for Alice to find her first apartment, and in all her searches she never tired of basking in colorfulness and wallowing in wide-eyed delight. A grumpy Kurdish wizard accompanied by a pack of stray cats offered her a room on Agrippas Street. A tamer of hawks, working as a peddler of soap in the market, tried to deter her from taking it.

She met a pair of giggling circus twins who enjoyed having a laugh with relatives who had departed this world, and a poker player smelling of mothballs who was practicing how to die without batting an eyelash—and every one of them, every single one, was a wonder in her eyes. Even the one-eyed organ tuner who tried to steal her galoshes.

All of them butterflies on the lawn, songbirds in the trees, the glitter of gold in the sunshine. Great is the garden of God, tweet-tweet, and wonderful are his creatures.

- 4 -

If I had taken her to my parents' home and allowed her to open her mouth about it, Alice would long ago have painted me a portrait of a "colorful childhood experience."

A modest family hotel in the neighborhood of Beit Hakerem, referred to by the father of the family as "my little Switzerland," two stories surrounded by pine trees, their scent filling the rooms. And who lives there? A father and mother and two daughters. Two little dolls. The elder blonde, the younger brunette, the former slow and the latter quick.

The mother's heart is weak, she spends most of her days in bed or in the little reception office, which is also suffused by a resinous scent. On the office walls hang landscapes and cityscapes—given by artist guests as mementos to the proprietors, who are happy to point them out and mention the names of the many artists and intellectuals who return year after year to their modest hostelry.

A Jesuit priest comes every summer to take part in archeological digs and teaches the younger daughter to play chess.

"The child is ripe for intellectual development," avers the scholar. "Ripe, ripe" concurs the father.

A Yiddish singer affectionately powders the nose of the giggling elder sister as the younger brings a cup of tea to the singer's room, and even gives the child a lilac perfume bottle in the shape of swan.

A pair of Belgian birdwatchers teach the little girls to look up at the sky. The young man's finger on his lips, signaling silence, the young woman's finger points upward. Their identical noses are sharp, as are their identical chins, and they both wear the same round, gold-rimmed glasses. Behind their backs the girls call them "the twins" and laugh.

A cloth cap on his head, the lock plastered to his forehead pointing like an arrow to one black eye, Shaya Gotthilf stands in the little kitchen and flourishes the omelet pan like a paintbrush. Fate and the need to earn a living have made him a hotel proprietor, and once in possession of the establishment he also gave it his name, but Shaya looks more like an artist or a scholar than a service provider.

An observer less inclined to enthuse herself than Alice would have pointed out that, when it came to service, Pension Gotthilf did not always meet conventional expectations—and that's putting it mildly. The omelet is fried in the cheapest oil, the chrysanthemums in the Armenian pottery vases should have been thrown out the day before yesterday, and the feel of the bed linen testifies to a long life and many launderings. The Arab maid in her embroidered dress does not clean well, and from time to time, when due to confusion or illness or some other temporary difficulty the mother forgets to pay her, Jamilla does not come to work at all. The dark-haired daughter rebels. The fair-haired one smiles her slow smile and languidly pushes the vacuum cleaner about, without reaching underneath the radiators that give off a weak heat.

You won't find luxury here—Alice would say—but the place has atmosphere. There is something about the house that closes one's eyelids like honey and invites all who enter it to daydream. And it seems as if the daydreams of the guests did not leave with them, but are still stirring between the stones: the dreams of those who came to Jerusalem to dig up the treasures of her kings and Temple, of those who came to find in it a crown for themselves, and those who sought to redeem it.

Squeals of laughter from the little girls in the courtyard. A deaf-mute acrobat is teaching them to catch and throw a ball blindfolded. The older girl's eyes are covered with a red scarf, the younger refused the blindfold but keeps her eyes closed and doesn't cheat. The pealing of church bells is heard in the distance and mingles with the closer chimes of the old grandfather clock in the library. Hundreds of volumes are collected in Shaya's library, available to anyone who wishes to consult them, and the girls' father would fix his eyes on whoever entered the room, as if he wanted to etch the picture of a person holding a book on his heart.

"My foundlings," Shaya calls his books, which for the most part were picked up after being thrown out in the street. Volumes in Hebrew, English, French, Russian, German, Hungarian, Romanian, Polish, and Serbian. Volumes in brown, gold-lettered covers in languages unknown to their loving owner, who could not bear the sight of a book abandoned in the street because its owner had died. "With me at least they have a home," says Shaya, a solemn note in his voice.

The hand of fate sent a refugee child, his mother's only son, to Palestine. A great love for an exquisite Jerusalem beauty set him down in this house in its bower of greenery. But the same hand might have acted differently, and it's easy to imagine a different Shaya: Shaya Gotthilf of Manhattan, sharp-witted journalist and thinker; Shaya Gotthilf the Dutchman; Shaya the painter; Professor Shaya Gotthilf expounding his wide-ranging views from coast to coast in America, often invited as well to the capital cities of Europe. Shaya has a rich imagination, he could easily see himself in any of these incarnations. And even though he does not elaborate on them, Alice reads his fantasies, swallows his illusions whole, and enthuses:

Anyone else with such prodigious talents would have felt constrained by these narrow hotel walls, but Shaya sees himself as lacking for nothing: abundance is an attribute of the soul, not something outside it. A hotel, however small, is an entire universe, and a lively soul will always find interest in it. To his elder daughter Shaya often says, "This is your real school," and he never scolds her when she plays hooky from her regular school.

"More than once she came home from school with tears in her eyes," he says, without anger or bitterness, "but here, among people who know her and love her, here she can learn real things at her own pace, the way children used to learn once."

Shaya thinks that "the separation between real life and educational institutions is insufferable." But when his young daughter asked to go to a boarding school and even sat for the entrance exams without informing her parents, he gave her his blessing and with great effort also paid the fees. "Children are like plants," he explained. "If you water a cactus too much it will rot, while another plant receiving the same amount of water will shrivel and die. A parent, above all, must be a good gardener."

And perhaps he really should have been a gardener. For he quenches the thirst of his guests as well: with a glass of home-made cherry liqueur; with a word of wisdom; with an striking quotation. He dispenses his advice freely to the honeymooners from a kibbutz, to the guests of a festival taking place in the city, to the elderly immigrant whose stay is being paid for by the Jewish Agency until he finds a place of his own. Shaya only keeps his harmonica for himself and refuses to play it even when urged to do so. But on summer nights when the windows are open, a passerby in the streets of Beit Hakerem might hear a harmonica playing "A wandering star" somewhere in the distance.

I have been working with Alice for years and her ability to deceive can still surprise me; the naturalness with which she flutters her eyelashes and performs her legerdemain; draws our attention to a ball of dust under the radiator so that we won't notice the used condoms next to the bed. Knows that the superficial dirt distracts from the sordid filth, that admitting the existence of the dust creates the illusion of honesty.

Alice flits quickly past the reception office of the pension and leaves Erica, the mother, sighing over her "weak heart," as if she were some romantic nineteenth century heroine, to her fate. Six years, she states briefly, are the difference in age between her and the father. The couple claims six years, but the actual difference is nine. Alice, like everyone else, finds it easy to pass over the sickly mother and fill our ears with the pretentious ideas of the father.

Convenient to ignore the fact that one little daughter in a fancy dress hasn't been bathed for two weeks, and the other, suffering daughter, has been left to act as a servant in the house, crawling on all fours to gather up the muck of wet, used tissues.

Not a thought to little girls fraternizing unsupervised with strangers. Not a word about the parents' screaming quarrels with Jamilla, and not a word about the never-ceasing torture through which the two of them put each other. The man wants to sell the pension and the woman refuses: the pension is her inheritance, and her father, who put his whole life into it would turn over in his grave.

In private the man begs, implores, coaxes. Outside the range of hearing of the guests, but definitely within the hearing of his daughters, the man describes in glowing terms the personal and familial happiness awaiting them if they would only sell the house. The woman softens, agrees on principle to sell, but not now. Never now. Next year if everything is all right, after her health improves, after the price goes up, first they have to get another, more serious offer, first they have to get their affairs in order, and in any case it's impossible until after the end of the season.

Just because of her obstinacy we're stuck here. Just because of your mother's petty fears of moving without insurance certificates in hand. Wouldn't you like to live, girls, for example, in an artist colony in Italy? Or if it has to be a pension, then why not in Cyprus? You know that with the money the agent is already prepared to pay us, cash in hand, we could buy a little house exactly like the one on the postcard? Wouldn't you like to live in a little house like that with a veranda on the roof? Wouldn't you like a little donkey of your own to ride on? And if your mother doesn't want to go abroad—how about right here in Israel? A small apartment in Tel Aviv, facing the sea, wonderful winters, five minutes' walk to the theater and ten cinemas to choose from. Sitting in cafés with famous people passing by. There's no need to be afraid all the time. You have to know how to think big because it's the only way to succeed. Remember, children, what your father says, at least remember this: don't be afraid.

"My wife takes everything to heart," Shaya explains to the Jesuit when her wet sighs rise from the room.

"Your mother isn't sick, she's just sensitive," he reassures his daughters when the blonde one's eyes start to blink uncontrollably. "She has thin skin and little things penetrate it and give her heartburn. Tomorrow she'll be fine, and she'll take you to buy coats fit for a princess."

"Hysteria," pronounces the Yiddish singer calmly, "with her it's simply hysteria, we've seen it all before."

"Manipulations," whispers Gemma, the amateur painter from Verona, to her English girlfriend. "That's how she controls her husband."

"Problem with regulation of the spleen," announces the guest who claims he was a very great doctor in Georgia, and my father looks gratified as the three of us are given a picturesque lesson on the gall bladder and its effluents.

But no doctor confirms my mother's self-diagnosis, according to which she suffers from a sick heart. In one of the emergency rooms somebody once mentions "anxiety attacks." At the age of seven or eight I learn the word "hypochondria," but when I use it, my father scolds me for a crudeness he would not have expected to hear from his clever daughter. The soul, he tells me, is mysterious and as delicate as a spider web.

"Who are we and what are we to judge our fellows," he adds to the Jesuit who is sitting with us. And to me he continues: "What would help your mother is for all of us to go and live in Italy. For a refugee like me, everywhere is both exile and home, but for your mother's nerves, a quiet village in Italy would be best."

"Hypochondriac, hypochondriac, hypochondriac," I chant in spite of him after the two of them have left the table.

"Hypochondriac," I insist over the remains of their breakfast, which I have already made up my mind not to clear away.

When did my mother begin to treat herself with Digoxin? Who was the criminal doctor who prescribed Digoxin for a woman who was physically healthy? Did she swallow these pills for years in secret like a junkie, producing the terrible vomiting and irregular heartbeat that won her a bed in all the emergency rooms of the city?

"Doctors don't understand anything," she liked to say. Perhaps it was only after she understood what had happened to my sister that she began to use the drug seriously, because it can't be possible that she took it consistently for years, certainly not in lethal amounts, perhaps only one pampering pill from time to time, and straight to the hospital for a few hours of pleasurable care and concern.

"Do you think she took those pills to make herself sick, or that she really believed that she had a cardiac disease and that they'd cure her?" Oded asked me once, a long time ago. And he went on probing: "Do you think it was connected to what happened to your sister?" This was soon after we met, in the period when I was still running around and saying things to people I'd just met such as: "My mother's dead. She poisoned herself," and "My mother was a junkie, she killed herself with prescription drugs." I would say things like this and smile.

"Don't you get that I'm not interested in what it's connected to? That I really, really don't give a damn?" I growled at my well-meaning boyfriend. "That woman nearly ruined my life, that's what she did. So do you expect me to understand what went on in her head? There's nothing to understand and I don't want to go anywhere near her head. Or maybe you expect me to feel sorry for her too? Is that what you think? That I should pity her? Empathize?"

Oded didn't protest or argue. My love accepted it, like he accepted everything, without questioning or nagging. He simply let it go, he set my mind at rest, and cradled me until I learned to sleep for nine hours at a stretch to the lullaby of his no-no-no-I-shall-fear-no-evil, for he was with me.

•

My pigtail-sucking Alice is a perfect idiot and a chronic faker. She isn't capable of producing a single straightforward sentence, and her description of my childhood is, of course, completely false. That's what she's like, that's how I created her, and I take full responsibility for her falsifications and for the small pleasures they afforded me.

But what about my own account? Is it truer? More reliable? Was my childhood really as grim as I describe it? Were there no moments of grace in it? No dewy lawns of happiness?

You could say that I came out okay: I'm sane most of the time, functioning, and I raised two good sons well enough. By any accepted criterion I'm okay, and accordingly any reasonable person would assume that my parents did a few things right, and that there were presumably also a few corners of light in Pension Gotthilf. Because anything else is impossible. Impossible that there were no corners of light. Logic says there were. Perhaps later events cast their shadow backward, and perhaps this shadow makes me see my entire childhood as black.

Words of wisdom such as these were offered by Rachel, my mother-in-law, when we told her, only a little and in general, about my past—and what can I say? Maybe there was something good, too. Let's say there was. I'm prepared to admit that there was. But how does this good that may have existed help me, how does it help me if I don't remember any of it? What I do remember and know for certain is that from a very young age I began to calculate and calculate how long I would have to go on staying with my family until I could be free of them.

My mother, it seems, was not the only one who wanted to get away, and perhaps the need to get away is in my genes.

•

"Tomorrow your mother will feel better and the three of you will go to buy coats fit for princesses," promised Shaya, and the coats were indeed bought at the WIZO shop, even though it was the beginning of summer.

My father hoarded books, and my mother, Erica, collected theatrical clothes. Her sartorial inclinations always met my father's fantasies, and her closets were stuffed with exotic garments. The fair-haired elder daughter loved being dressed, and even as a young girl she adored having her hair combed. Her eyelids stopped twitching then, and her green eyes slowly closed, leaving slits like a cat's.

Alice described my sister as "slow," which was also the word used by our parents, as if they wanted and didn't want to say "retarded." But my sister wasn't retarded. Elisheva's movements were perhaps a little strange, the way she held a pencil awkward, and simple arithmetic exercises made her cry. And nevertheless, I am sure that today nobody would have kept her back a class in school or pushed her into the vocational track. Because, for example, in spite of her oddities, she loved to read, and not only books for girls but also, and above all historical romances: I remember her poring over old volumes of *Ivanhoe* and *Quo Vadis*. She read very slowly, it took her months to finish a book. When asked to read aloud she would pronounce the words with the exaggerated emphasis of a kindergarten teacher, and stress the wrong words in the sentence, but she understood what she read very well, and found interest in it; Elisheva learned English easily simply by listening to the guests, and she also knew how to recognize birds by their calls, which I myself never succeeded in doing; she remembered the names of people who had only stayed with us a single night; and after her breakdown, through her cracks, my sister shed a stream of statements that were terrible in their accuracy. "I'm your Jew," she said to me.

"What do you mean?"

"That I'm your Jew. So because you're a good person, you look after me and keep me from dying again. But what you would really like in your heart is for there to be no Jews. You won't let anyone hurt me, but in your heart of hearts you're revolted by me, for not being born like you."

A cold summer afternoon. My sister stands in the yard, wearing a red coat trimmed with fake black fur. Her eyes are covered with a dark scarf and she holds out blind hands to catch a rubber ball. Jamie the acrobat, a minor performer in the street shows of the Jerusalem Festival, speaks to her in English, with a Scottish accent she can barely understand—the acrobat is neither deaf nor dumb. The handicap is a whimsical fiction of Alice's—and Elisheva turns her body in the direction of his voice. My sister isn't laughing, neither laughter like the chiming of bells nor any other kind of laughter. Her fleshy shoulders are thrust forward, her hands stretched out stiffly, suspended in the air. A cold wind makes the clouds in the sky race, revealing and concealing the sun. Rays of light penetrate the swaying branches, touching and vanishing, and my sister's face is shadowed and illuminated in rapid alternation. Jamie and I and the branches, the shadows, and the sunlight don't stop moving for a second, and Elisheva stands rooted to the spot, waiting obediently for a sign.

"The firstborn daughter," Alice called her, and so indeed she was, my big sister, for a certain period of time, when we were still small. A difference of less than three years between us, and nevertheless she appointed herself the "little mother." Our parents were more concerned with the clothes we wore than with our personal hygiene, while she, to the best of her ability, insisted on bathing me and was often the one who put me to bed. "Little mommy" our parents liked to call her, and so did some of the guests, who saw how she held my hand on the stairs or gave me a square of chocolate after I finished my salad.

It didn't take me more than a few years to steal my sister's birthright; to put her in the shade with the skills I acquired, to skip a class, to sweep up all the highest marks, to rob her of any ability she might have developed and any true praise she might have won.

First I stole her birthright, and then I deserted her.

The quick daughter made haste to save herself and left the slow one behind.

I, the quick daughter, saved myself.

I deserted and abandoned my sister to her fate.

- 5 -

When Satan arrived in my parents' house, I was already in boarding school, and a feverish round of schoolwork and social activities gave me an excuse for cutting down my visits to a minimum. I was in Jerusalem, but the Jerusalem I was in was very far from the one in which I grew up.

Life in boarding school made my head spin with the range of possibilities it offered: interesting lessons, a history teacher who was particularly interesting, youth movements, a theatrical society, a writing club, stealing out and hitching rides, beer, kisses tasting of beer, political arguments, volunteer activities in the deprived neighborhood of Katamon, nocturnal excursions to the Old City and the churches of Ein Kerem, hesitant experiments full of self-importance with marijuana—I said yes to everything, I wanted everything, and every leap and every opportunity seemed to be the very one I had been waiting for.

I was surrounded by people who were as hungry and packed with energy as I was, and our hunger went on raging on the weekends and holidays too, which we were supposed to spend at home. We went on hikes, camped out and attended courses, and I did not refuse a single invitation: I spent Passover with a girlfriend on a kibbutz, and on Sukkoth I went to harvest olives at an Arab village. Every month or two I fell in love with someone else, a boy or girl whose uniqueness was always revealed to me in a flash. Amos, at the piano, singing songs by Georges Brassens. How could I have overlooked him before? Betty, cradling the face of a tiny boy who had cut his chin in the yard of the youth club in Katamon. Dror, declaiming Mark Anthony's speech in a British accent. Amichai, telling jokes all the way up the stiff climb to Massada without a single pant.

I was full of falling-in-love, and the love, like a moving spotlight, fell unexpectedly on one new object after another.

In order to visit my sister and my parents I had to walk for forty minutes on foot or ride on two buses for about half an hour. But for months at a stretch I didn't have the time. I didn't have the strength. I didn't have the energy. I wasn't interested.

But nevertheless, from my rare visits I remember the talk that preceded the arrival of the serpent from America: Your uncle, girls, the professor, the historian and commentator Aharon Gotthilf. Aaron he calls himself today.

"Uncle Aaron," my mother would say, taking care to flatten the "a" and drawl the "r" so that it would sound American. Uncle Aaron would arrive in December, when it was Christmas vacation over there. He intended to spend three weeks with us, but it was possible, very possible, that if certain things worked out as he hoped, he would stay longer.

Aaron was coming to attend his son's wedding in Jerusalem. It turns out—such a surprise, we had no idea—that he has a grown son, a son from an early marriage. Suddenly, now Uncle Aaron tells your father that he was once married to some Czech, a woman with serious mental problems. He met her when he was living in Paris. A sad story, very sad. Because the son grew up without him, and the mother, who didn't have a clue, sent him to a Chabad school, and what can you expect when you send a child to Chabad? The boy grew up ultra-Orthodox, came to Israel, didn't serve in the army, landed up in a black-coat yeshiva. Now they've arranged a match for him, and even though to this day he never had much contact with his father, he invited Aaron to the wedding out of honor for his father. That's one good thing that has to be said for those people, I have to admit: Honor thy father and thy mother. Aaron has another son who lives in New Mexico, about him we actually knew, we even told you once, his mother is a professor of archeology, she studies the Indians, and this son, who is your second cousin, treats his father very differently. Aaron told us that he isn't even prepared to come and visit him, even though he offered the mother to pay for the tickets.

Aaron came in December but they already started talking about him in the summer, in the wake of a surprise letter and a long, expensive phone call in which he renewed the connection with my father, his dear cousin. It occurs to me now that my parents described him in way that would have fitted nicely into one of Alice's idiotic columns:

I even remember my father defining him as "a classic Jewish intellectual" and a "colorful character on the personal level."

I don't remember him being spoken of before, but once the letter arrived, the talk began to bubble and the anecdotes about "Erwin, to me he'll always be Erwin"—overflowed to the paying guests as well. All my parents' acquaintances were required to bask in the glow of our uncle's glamour, whose glory could be assumed to reflect on his more modest relatives too.

My grandmother Sarah Gotthilf and her sister-in-law Hannah escaped from Vienna in November 1938, carrying in their arms sons who were intended to be the first but turned out to be the last. My grandfather was murdered in Dachau and his brother in Nisko, but we won't go into that here. The women crossed from Switzerland to Italy, where they spent six months in Genoa—judging by the way my father told the story it sounded as if they had set out on a tour of classical Europe—and then Sarah, who had contacts with the Zionists, obtained a certificate and sailed with her baby for Palestine, while the beautiful Hannah and her son Erwin—that's what they called him then—made their way to England.

Equipped with enthusiastic recommendations—her dissertation on Feuerbach came out in book form and Freud himself sent his compliments—Hannah Gotthilf found her way to the most interesting circles of the period, and in '47, two years after the end of the war, she married a well-known economist from Oxford who was also an aristocrat boasting the title of Sir.

As you may imagine, the son of Lady Hannah received the best possible education—the sciences, the arts, classical languages. His Hebrew was classical too, and at the age of twenty-one Erwin, who had in the meantime become Aaron, was already studying for a doctoral degree at the Sorbonne in Paris.

His reputation preceded him, wherever he went he stood out as an original thinker, and since the academic world in France before the students' revolution seemed fossilized to him, he didn't wait to complete his doctorate but took advantage of the first opportunity that presented itself to emigrate to America. There are mean-spirited dwarves everywhere. Pettiness and envy too are universal, but Aaron in his innocence believed that he would enjoy more intellectual freedom in America than in Europe.

The main subject of his studies was modern totalitarianism, and he shocked many people when he chose to focus on the writings of the Marquis de Sade. The Marquis, claimed Aaron, drew a dark, prophetic and amazingly accurate picture of modern tyranny.

The issues that engaged Aaron were always broad, too broad for the Procrustean bed of academia, and despite the high esteem in which he was held, the trailblazer also acquired a number of enemies. For three or four years it seemed to him that he had found himself a home in the University of Columbia, but for a man like Aaron every home is only a port from which to sail onward. In the wake of all kinds of slander that arose, he transferred to the University of New Orleans, and from there this Jew went on wandering to other stations and other ports.

Unlike those of his colleagues who secluded themselves in ivory towers, Aaron turned from the outset to the non-academic public as well. His articles were published in dozens of newspapers, and he made frequent appearances on television as well as on the radio. But Aaron was not the kind of sycophant who was only seeking popularity, and the things he wrote and said gave rise to more than a little opposition. The hippies considered him one of theirs, until he poured scorn on them in a stinging essay. A highly regarded Jewish journal flaunted him, until he insisted on publishing a paper on "Jewish murderers in the service of Stalin." The New York left, which in the past had attempted to embrace him, has not forgiven him to this day for a brilliant article analyzing their psychology. That's Aaron. A complex personality. Not an easy person, clearly. Not an easy man, but a deep one. Possessing a profundity you don't often see today.

Uncle Aaron's history was not always recounted from the beginning, sometimes my father expounded on a single chapter: Genoa, England, the title of Sir, the interesting circles of the period, the Sorbonne University in Paris, the Marquis de Sade, stations and ports. But I remember well how every chapter of the story concluded with the same words: deep, profound, complex.

"Aren't you sick of hearing about him?" I asked Elisheva. But my sister said that she was glad for Mommy and Daddy. She was glad because both of them were glad, and now that Daddy had a cousin he was sure to be happier, because family was good, and it was sad when somebody had a relative he didn't see.

If it had been voiced by anyone else, this sentence could have been interpreted as a complaint about my absence, but Elisheva never hinted, and I ignored the non-existent hint and the unuttered complaint and slipped away again to pursue my own affairs. If they were all happy, why should I question their happiness? And to my friends at school I threw out: "A cousin of my father's is coming, a British aristocrat or something, now they'll force me to come visit all the time, what a bore."

What room should they give him? My parents debated the question, and dwelled pleasurably on the subject right up to the eve of his arrival. First floor or second? Opposite the stairs or at the end of the corridor? Double or single? Our uncle would pay, he had made this an explicit condition, the income from three weeks was nothing to be sneezed at, but we had always preferred guests who came for a prolonged stay, and the ones who became like part of the family always received preferential treatment. If he preferred a double room, we would give it to him at the price of a single room. Number eighteen had a pastoral view, twenty-two was more modest, but he would have more privacy there, and for someone who was writing a book there was nothing more important: quiet and privacy, privacy and quiet—that's what our place gave its guests and that's what we could offer someone who had stayed in some of the most luxurious hotels in the world. Pay attention, girls, we won't disturb Uncle Aaron, and on no account will we impose ourselves on him. We'll spend just as much time with him as he wants to spend in our company, and we have to understand that he won't spend as much time with us as he might wish, because he's working on a book.

•

The business of the book was especially thrilling to my mother. From the intimate way she spoke about it you would have thought that he sent her drafts for her comments: Aaron will take advantage of his stay in Israel to go into the archives, but what Aaron's working on isn't just another piece of ordinary research. We know that this time it's something much more literary. Aaron has set himself a high literary challenge. Aaron is about to deal with something that nobody before him has even dared to touch. His book will present a historical angle that other people haven't had the courage to approach up to now. Aaron says that anyone who writes something so innovative has to expect a tremendous scandal after publication. And we, of course, are with Aaron. This is the small contribution that his family can make, and it goes without saying that we'll give him all the conditions he needs for his work. If Aaron decides afterward to mention that he began writing the book here with us in Jerusalem, fine, we're not hiding and we've got nothing to hide. A family has to be prepared to stand together even when there's a huge scandal, and we're not going to ask Uncle Aaron to hide anything either.

The excited anticipation improved my mother's health to no end. People quite often used to say to me "You have a beautiful mother"—and when I was very small I thought so too. By the time I was in grade school she already seemed to me embarrassingly affected—but shortly before Aaron's arrival I remember hearing such admiring remarks again. And I also remember my father saying: "Did you see how beautiful your mother looks today?"

The excitement took her almost every morning into the dining room, away from the account books, and from keeping account of expenses altogether. New glasses were purchased, both for cold drinks and for tea. And somehow she managed to persuade Jamilla to polish the ornamental samovar on the counter. In the evenings I know that she lingered to chat to the guests, smoking a slender cigarette, only one—she was permitted one little indulgence, who could deny her, life was short anyway—tapping off the ash with a finger freshly tipped with scarlet, gracefully inclining her chin, and waiting for another opportunity to insert Uncle Aaron into the conversation.

What was this special angle on history about which the professor was writing? To this Erica had no reply, and from the sly expression on her face it was hard to tell if she didn't know the answer or if she had promised to keep the secret. Only the subject may perhaps be revealed, revealed but not elaborated on: Aaron had taken it upon himself to write about Hitler. Yes, Hitler. Imagine the strength of mind required to tackle such a subject. A historian, and moreover a Jew, and with Aaron's personal background too, where did he get the courage? You'll agree, said my mother, that his strength of mind must be tremendous.

He arrived in December and extended his stay beyond what my parents had dared to hope, but more than three weeks passed before I saw him. It was morning, and I was standing in the little kitchen cutting up vegetables: cucumbers and tomatoes for a salad. Breakfast was served to the guests at seven o'clock. It wasn't yet seven, and he was already sitting in the dining room.

My father had gone out early to do some chores or other. My mother promised that she would finish getting dressed in a minute and come down to help me. Elisheva complained of stomachache, and I drew the curtains in our room and left her to rest in bed.

I stood and sliced vegetables; the tomatoes were a problem. My father was in the habit of buying crates of cheap vegetables, and the vegetables he bought were often too ripe or not ripe enough. Green tomatoes were easier to bury in a salad than those close to rotting, and that morning, I remember, the slices of tomato drowned in the juices on the board.

•

The tomato. From the point of view of its botanical classification a fruit, and not a vegetable: a flower-bearing dicotyledon, perennial plant of the family *Solanaceae*, native to tropical America. Thought to have been cultivated already in ancient Peru, but considered poisonous by Europeans who encountered it.

I have a lot more to say on the subject of tomatoes. I even know a song written in their honor, with a refrain which goes: Tomato, tomato / sing high, sing low / the song of the tomato / oh, the song of the tomato."

I am prepared to sing the song of the tomato. It needs to be sung from the depths of the chest, taking a lot of air. I am also prepared to provide information on the nutritional value of this vegetable-fruit, which would no doubt be of interest to the reader and contribute to the public health.

I'm ready to do a lot of things—to sing, to investigate, to lecture, but apparently I am not yet ready to introduce the serpent. I knew that I would have to prepare myself for his introduction, and now that the time has come, I am not prepared.

Because what I am supposed to say about him—what? And how am I supposed to do it? Should I focus on his body and describe his appearance, so that he'll come across as a "real person?" Should I mention, to make it more authentic, the cartilage of his gigantic ears? Let's say this: he was very tall, his long legs were stretched out in front of him, feet clad in moccasins, his one ankle rested on the lower calf of the other leg. He was tall and quite broad-shouldered, and although I thought of him as old, he looked a little like a movie star or some important politician. Not somebody in particular, but somebody. A persona. A persona on vacation, in a jacket with leather elbow patches.

Is that enough? For me it's definitely enough, and even if it isn't enough, how the hell am I supposed to remember exactly how he looked to me then, when all my memories are colored by what happened afterward? Am I supposed to fabricate a description of Satan in order to convince you that he exists?

He came. He was there, he sat there in the dining room—all these are facts. And I wondered in my embarrassment whether to wait for my mother or to go up to him and introduce myself, or not to introduce myself and simply to ask in a professional manner if he wanted tea or coffee. In any case the water hadn't boiled yet.

Is that important? What's important?

It's important that he stayed with us for almost six months, and that during this time he raped my sister consistently.

It's important that after he got her pregnant, he arranged for her to have an abortion and, immediately afterward, when she was still bleeding, he raped her again. He was turned on by the blood. And by her pain. Do I have to go into detail about that too? And why, exactly? In order to justify myself and what I did years later? In order to justify myself do I have to paint a close-up picture of my sister with a tear trickling down her round baby face? Or perhaps I should paint her holding a teddy bear, like in the pictures they publish in the papers to illustrate a story about child abuse? Elisheva didn't have a teddy bear. She collected make-up and little scent bottles, empty ones too, and she'd left her toys behind her a long time ago.

She actually had chubby cheeks, but at the time in question she suffered from adolescent pimples, which my mother forbade her to squeeze. She never had a lot of pimples, only a few, but for people like Alice it only takes a hint of that yellow pus to spoil the whole picture.

This story can be briefly told, the facts can be summed up as follows: he raped her consistently, but two years passed before she broke down. It happened when she was already in boot camp, and more time passed before she spoke about it, first to her psychologist in the mental hospital, and afterward to us. But up till then her weight gain and all the other symptoms of depression were attributed to her difficulties in school and her fear of the few matriculation exams that she sat for. We found this explanation convenient, and even when the psychologist invited my parents to come in for a joint session, they refused to believe it, at first anyway: my sister was crazy, and crazy people invent all kinds of things. To the important psychologist they said nothing, of course, they only made shocked noises, but I understood that they didn't believe it and I was the one who had to make them believe.

That's it, that's the whole story. Except that after I made them believe it, my mother took off with Digoxin, my father got on a plane to Italy, and I stayed with my sister until I couldn't stay with her another minute. And that's really everything.

Really everything?

When my mother came into the dining room, perfectly made up, she introduced me to my uncle immediately: "You haven't yet met our clever Elinor."

"Elinor and Elisheva," he said in his strange accent. "Two daughters. Eli and Eli." And then, as if playfully, he took my hand and lifted it to his mouth, and fixing me with a colorless stare under half-lidded, he kissed it.

- 6 -

Oded says that after that phone call from America it was hard to talk to me: that I kept uncharacteristically pressing him to tell me exactly what time he would be home, and when he was home he couldn't get anything out of me except for brief, laconic replies.

That's what my husband says, and it sounds logical—maybe that's how I behaved, but in any case Oded and I are in the habit of calling each other several times a day, that's what we've always done, and I really don't remember any excessive nagging on my part.

I assume we visited his parents, I don't remember any cancellations, and of course we didn't tell them anything about our dread. They both knew about my sister, that's to say they knew that she had been raped by a guest from overseas. That when it came out it broke my mother's heart, and that in the wake of all these horrors my father made haste to flee the scene of the crime and escape from the memories.

They knew about Elisheva's derangement too, and about how she returned to life in this world in an eccentric incarnation—I told Rachel all this, and she told Menachem soon after we met; and from time to time, once in a while, she would ask me how my sister was doing and if I heard from her.

I told my mother-in-law all kinds of things, and like Alice I directed her gaze toward the dust bunnies under the radiator so she wouldn't notice the real filth. Because I didn't tell her who had murdered my sister's soul. I kept this a secret and they, wisely, did not interrogate me. Perhaps they assumed that I didn't know his identity, perhaps they thought that his name wasn't important, but I had a good reason for keeping quiet, and it was clear to me why I held my tongue and why I ostensibly protected his identity.

The general impression I created, which I somehow tried to create, was that although the Gotthilf family was what they politely referred to as a "family with difficulties," it was "the tragedy" that caused us to cross the line into madness. And that but for "our tragedy" we would all have been a little strange, but nevertheless within the bounds of normality.

They received a daughter-in-law whose sister had barricaded herself in the toilets of Training Base 12 with a weapon, and whose mother, intentionally or unintentionally, had killed herself with prescription drugs.

They adopted a girl with a tattoo, whose father, according to her at least, was "unable to attend the wedding."

They embraced me as a victim, but how far could I stretch the limits of their tolerance? Even the tolerance of the tolerant, even the broad-mindedness of the most broad-minded has its limits, and a rapist in the family is going too far. They were generous to me. Generous to a fault, to the point of tears, bighearted and clear-minded and absolutely dependable, but at a certain point it was inevitable that even the bighearted and clear-minded would be assailed by genetic revulsion. And it was impossible, impossible that they would not be horrified by the amount of crooked genes that their daughter-in-law was bringing into the tribe. Presumably they would have refrained from outright opposition to the match, but I have no doubt that their dread would have found a way to express itself.

When he was four years old, my Yachin choked a playmate in preschool. Nimrod, at the age of fifteen, hid copies of *Penthouse* under his mattress: weren't these signs? Weren't they obvious symptoms of distortions in the nucleus of the cell? Long before my sons were born, I sensed that I would not have the strength to cope with this kind of dread in my benefactors, I would not be able to stand their revulsion. And after Rachel stroked my tiger-face, all I knew was that I yearned for her to touch me again.

So it happened that I hid his name, and so it happened that, after he came back again, Oded and I went on visiting his parents and behaving as if everything was as usual.

And many things were indeed as usual: the chronically enchanted Alice set forth on her weekly bullshit tour, visited the Ratisbonne Monastery, and was thrilled by the height of the ceilings and the charming stories of the Benedictine monk. I not only remember this column, I can even verify its existence in the archives. Saint Benedict, the founder of the Benedictine order, retired from the world to live in a cave. And Alice, who was curious about the spiritual experiences of the hermit, briefly considered going to look for a cozy little cave in the Judean desert: to taste the delights of spiritual seclusion for herself and to see the sun rise in silence.

Menachem, who was in the habit of phoning me every weekend to react to my column, remarked that "the story this time was both instructive and entertaining," and "I'm glad that your little Alice understood without having to experience it for herself that human beings are not cut out for solitude. As one of her greatest fans I wouldn't like to see her spending even a single day in a cave."

Nimrod and Yachin called, or we called them, as we did on a routine basis. We are a sociable couple, far from any kind of monastic seclusion, and it seems to me that we also had friends over for dinner.

As far as I can remember, I behaved as usual even though I was worried, but there seemed to be a growing disturbance below the surface, and I sensed that the disturbance was not in me, but in Oded. Now I think that if our relationship had not been beyond a doubt, I would have suspected him of having an affair. I did not suspect him, praise whoever deserves to be praised—in this instance presumably Oded and myself—but the signs of disturbance accumulated uneasily, even though it's hard to pinpoint them exactly. He looked at me too much and didn't look at me enough, meaning it seemed as if he gazed at me intently at the wrong moments, and looked away precisely when I looked at him. He listened when I spoke to him, but somehow he didn't listen in the right way, and even though he answered to the point, it seemed as if he was thinking about something else. His touches also felt programmed, and a couple of times when he kissed me it seemed as if he were obeying some instruction he had given himself. Another woman would have interpreted all this in one way only. I didn't know how to interpret it, and I waited. I was upset, and nevertheless I waited, because ever since that phone call from America everything around me was fragile, and also because I knew that in the end my husband would speak.

It took him almost two weeks, after the first rain fell, and perhaps it wasn't the first real rain of the year but only a summer shower, because it was still hot. We left the windows open, and with the fresh air that came in he said, "Elinor, there's something I should have told you before, it's just that I'm such an idiot I didn't know how. I received an email. That man sent me an email to the office."

"That man," he called him, and there was no need to explain who he meant. Innocent and blind as a puppy, my Oded expected me to ask immediately, "What did he write?" but I was unable to hear a word. The blindness, the wicked blindness of my good husband threatened me where I lived. And it was clear to me that if I didn't open my husband's eyes we would fall, fall deep underground: we had already begun to fall.

And so, instead of asking "What did he write?" I demanded: "When? When exactly did you get it? What's 'a few days ago'? How many days? What were you thinking? When exactly were you going to tell me? How dare you not tell me? By what right?"

Oded rubbed his brow and apologized again, and again admitted that he had behaved like a fool.

"But explain to me, explain to me what you were thinking? How could you come into the house every evening and know that you were going to lie to me?"

"Lie to you?"

"Not tell me the truth. What else would you call it?"

Oded's thick eyebrows bristled with all the rubbing, lending him the air of an angry troll. The bristling gray hairs did not suit the neatness of his close-cropped head, but I did not lick my thumb to smooth and straighten them.

"Sorry," he said. "Look at me, Elinor. Look at me. I'm truly, truly sorry. Try to understand, you were so upset by that phone call, I saw what it did to you, so in my foolishness I wanted to spare you."

"To spare me or yourself? Who were you really thinking of—me or yourself, that it would be unpleasant for you to tell me?"

"I don't see it like that."

"No? So how do you see it?"

"I told you, it was a mistake on my part. I made a mistake."

"You made a mistake because it was comfortable for you to let me live in an illusion."

"Do you really think that I felt comfortable?"

"Admit that you would have been more comfortable not telling me."

And so on and on, until I gradually calmed down, first to the sound of the pattering rain and Oded's quiet voice, and then to the touch of his hands on my face and the smell of his soap.

"Just understand," I said between his hands, "you have to understand that he's a snake, and that this is exactly how he operates. First he tried to talk to me, and now, after he didn't succeed, he's coming between us. Understand that when you don't tell me, it's like you're collaborating with him."

"No one can come between us. Nobody can do that."

"Okay. So now tell me," I said a little later.

"Tell you what?"

"Tell me what he wrote you."

My husband was ready for this part of the conversation, the forces of the salt of the earth were marshaled and ready. "Let's start with the good news, what I see as a good sign, which is that he sent the mail to me at the office and didn't try to phone again and speak to either you or me. Which tells me that he accepts there are limits he has to respect, and this, in fact, is how he began, by saying that he had no intention of troubling you. In English it sounds even more polite."

"Understood. But what does he want?"

"What does he want? That's harder for me to define. I'd say that he wants some kind of connection, don't ask me what or why.

He was careful of course, very careful in how he phrased it. Don't forget that he has no idea what you know, and certainly not what I know. He concentrated, in fact, on his book: he said that today he understands why a person might want to ostracize the author of this book. His main statement, as far as I understand, is that a lot of time has passed since he wrote it, and that today he himself has reservations about it, and not only privately, he has also publicly condemned himself. He even attached a link to some article of self-criticism that he wrote."

"Did you read it?"

"I had a look at it. I didn't want to go into all that stuff. What jumps out, in my opinion, is that at present he's on some new PR campaign, only this time the campaign is against the book. In the spring, as we already know, he's supposed to be coming here to take part in some international conference, and the title of his talk, as far as I remember, is the same title he gave to the article: 'My Mistake.'" What the man actually wants, I don't understand, but the explicit wish he expressed was that you would agree at least to hear him speak at the conference."

"You said he was coming 'here.' Is 'here' Jerusalem?"

"It seems so. Unfortunately. The bottom line: I think that what he's trying to tell us is that he's changed; that he is no longer the person you once justly called 'that Hitler." He claims not only the statute of limitations, but also repentance. I can only guess that he's hinting at something beyond the book."

"There's no such thing."

"As what?"

"As repentance. Everything he says, all his sophisms and rationalizations about limitations and repentance, are a load of crap. Elisheva doesn't have the luxury of wiping out the past and going back to what she was before. Hang on, I'm not angry at you, I'm not angry any more, it's just hard for me to hear those bullshit words coming out of your mouth. Repentance. The nerve of that man is something unbelievable. Can you believe that he had the nerve to call me and write to you? There's no going back from that either."

"I agree, I didn't say anything else," replied my glib attorney, and he was already standing in front of me to bring me too to my feet.

"There's no going back, so from here on you and I will simply go forward together."

- 1 -

I remember the clicking of the typewriter from room number twenty-two, the one at the end of the corridor on the second floor, the one that to the regret of my parents did not have a pastoral window, but ensured privacy. There, it appears, he began to write the cause of the scandal to which they looked forward, and there, in the privacy that was respected to an exaggerated, ritualistic degree, he conducted experiments on my sister. Once he made her crouch like a footstool at his feet, and forced her to remain in this position for hours without moving. And another time, when he had finished hurting her, he said that she had to understand how difficult all this was for him. If she thought that he had no feelings, she was a fool. He wasn't a psychopath, there were goals for which it was right and proper to sacrifice the moral sentiment, and "only history will judge the value of the work of literature to which our project gave birth."

The worst thing, she said, was when he talked to her. And also when he forced her to read aloud to him from the book. "The one he was writing? His manuscript?" I asked. No, she wasn't allowed to touch his manuscript when she cleaned the room. There were a lot of books there, but he always wanted one book in English. He would instruct her to read, and then sneer at her reading and do it to her. But there also times when he would first read aloud from it himself.

The things I know accumulated slowly: a statement here, a statement there. Sometimes she came out with something horribly coherent, but a lot of the time what she said was unintelligible. And I, choking on it, didn't know what was worse: when she spoke clearly I longed for vagueness, and when she was vague I wanted to shake her until she told me exactly what and how and when. Maybe with her psychiatrist she was different, but when I pressed her she was unable to answer, looking blank and stammering in reply to my questions.

Only when she was about to leave for the United States in her new incarnation, she revealed, as if by the way, the name of the book: *The 120 days of Sodom*. Because of the name she believed that she was destined to be tortured by him for one hundred twenty days, but the clue deceived her. She was tortured for longer.

He was a brutal, pornographic sadist, that's what he was. A filthy rat dressed up in sordid intellectual pretensions. He was something that I wouldn't even call human. A rat. A warped rat who decided he had it in his power to gnaw his way into the black box of Hitler and solve its riddle from the inside. Before he left he gave my sister a potted orchid. Elisheva put it on the reception desk, and there this gift remained until it died. I have no idea why I mentioned this now. I mention it because I remember. This detail of the white orchid I actually told Oded quite early on, but he wasn't very impressed by it; he only remarked that giving flowers seemed like part of the window dressing. But I knew, and kept it to myself, that the purpose of the orchid was completely different, and that in this final act of parting too, the Not-man meant to mock her. Like he did when he met me and kissed my hand.

•

When the book my parents had so eagerly awaited came out in America, Erica was already resting in her grave, my father was apparently resting with his lady love in Verona, and Elisheva and I were going crazy together in the renovated, three-and-a-half-room basement flat where my father set us up nicely before he deserted us.

I had no idea that the book had come out, or about anything else, except for the fact that I was responsible for a sister who, according to the official authorities, posed no danger to herself or others, and consequently did not need to be hospitalized.

Only months later, after I had put her back, not so nicely, in the hospital, I learned about the book from a newspaper article, and my first thought was: I hope they don't hand out newspapers in the psychiatric ward.

The article reported on a dispute between the literary editor and the owner of one of the big publishing houses in Israel. The owner wanted to bring out a Hebrew translation of *Hitler, First Person*, and the editor, it was reported, threatened to resign. Neither of the parties to the dispute agreed to be interviewed on record, but it appeared that they had given the reporter a broad overview of the reasons for the standoff.

Hitler, First Person, as may be gleaned from the title, attempts to present "an autobiography of the fiend." According to the blurb on the back of the English edition, the book was not a forgery like the so-called "Hitler Diaries," nor yet pure historical research, but rather "an attempt to deepen human consciousness by literary means" and by "a significant and chilling contribution to the self-knowledge of human beings as such." The book relies on hundreds of documents and historical research. It attempts to penetrate beneath the persona the Führer presented to the public, and shows the reader not the "real" Hitler, but Hitler as he might have been, and as he would have described himself if he had written a personal autobiography as a kind of complement to *Mein Kampf.*

According to the article, the controversial manuscript had been rejected by a long line of publishers in the United States, until it found one willing to bring it out, and but for the fact that two well known historians had violently condemned the book, it would probably have disappeared among the piles of trash written on the subject.

The growing campaign in denunciation of the book had given the author, Professor Aaron Gotthilf, exceptional media exposure, at the height of which he had been attacked at the entrance to a television studio by an elderly Holocaust survivor who tried to throw acid in his face.

Gotthilf, a controversial historian and a refugee from the Holocaust himself, stands by his opinion that giving voice to Hitler is not only a legitimate literary device that should be accepted in the framework of the principle of freedom of expression, but an important tool in advancing our understanding of the horrors of the twentieth century. "Hitler was a human being," he stresses, "and as such, he is not beyond the bounds of explanation." He adds: "To understand does not mean to forgive."

However, there are those who do not forgive Gotthilf for his book, among them our greatest Holocaust researcher, who described it as "a vile piece of filth not worthy of relating to."

Up to now the book has been translated into French, German, Finnish, and Italian, although it should be mentioned that the publishers who chose to bring it out in these countries are also regarded as marginal. Among the reactions to the book in France, the words "provocative" and "interesting" were used. In Germany, on the other hand, the book was widely denounced by critics.

The article also mentioned that the author chose to let Hitler tell his story only up to October 1938, a few days before Kristallnacht, and that some critics have argued that this choice plays into the hands, even if indirectly, of Holocaust deniers.

"It will soon become clear whether Gotthilf's fictional Hitler will be allowed to have his say in Hebrew too."

I tore the newspaper to shreds and threw it in the trash, poured the dregs of my coffee onto the scraps, and took the bag of trash out of the house.

I hadn't forgotten my parents' talk. I hadn't forgotten the sound of the typewriter, but for some reason I never thought about the book as something real that could actually happen. I never thought it would happen, too much had happened already.

All kinds of crazy ideas went around in my head, like writing to the publisher that I would kill myself if the book came out in Hebrew—because what other way did I have to preserve the fragments of my sister? But in the end I didn't even write a letter of protest from a concerned citizen.

I'll never know whether my mother meant to kill herself with her Digoxin games. I learned to live with the not knowing, let's say I learned, let's say I did, but one thing I do know today for certain: my mother did not pass on suicidal genes to me. I never really wanted to go away and die. I wanted other people not to be here.

When Elisheva broke down and was hospitalized for the first time, I was still in my senior year in high school and, surrounded by a protective wall of friends and activities, I spent most of my time at a relatively safe distance from the family.

When I banished her from our basement apartment to her second hospitalization I was already alone. Our parents had flown. My friends had joined the army, and I had been exempted from this obligation, too, which I had no possibility of meeting.

The way things turned out I didn't have a single soul I could talk to when *Hitler, First Person* came down on me in the kitchen like a ton of bricks. And after I destroyed the newspaper, not long after that, somehow or other I decided to live. Somehow or other, the decision was taken to live, live like crazy and as quick-sharp as possible. I left the apartment in Talpioth and threw myself giddily into to all kinds of stimulating experiments. I consumed quantities of alcohol, and men, and wild talk, and ups and downs at night and sleeplessness. One morning, after waking up alone in the Sheraton Hotel in Tel Aviv without remembering exactly how I got there, I snuck outside, and as I wandered the streets my eye fell on a tattoo emporium; I went in and had myself tattooed with my tiger face. It took two days to do it, and in between I fell asleep on a bench in the park among the smell of dog shit. All this isn't important now, and also irrelevant to *Hitler, First Person*, which I had started to talk about.

Three years after I met Oded and fell on him with false accusations, he traveled to London for the firm and there, between his real-estate negotiations, he was tempted to buy the book. He bought it, came home, and immediately told me. Presumably he believed that the act of confession would atone for the sin of voyeurism he had committed by reading it.

Alice had not yet been born then, but Yachin was lying at my feet on his baby blanket, and I was already pregnant with Nimrod, although I didn't yet know it—so my drive to attack had faded to a considerable degree.

"Where is it?" I asked.

"What? The book? I left it in the office. I thought you wouldn't want it in the house."

"You thought right. It's none of my business that you read it, I just don't have to hear about it," I said, and a minute later: "Okay. Now that you did it, you'd better tell me about it."

"I don't know what to tell you," he picked up our son and clasped him like a soft shield to his chest. "I'm not a big expert on literature. I didn't even finish reading it, it's over three hundred pages long, and I don't think I'll finish it."

"Is it that dreadful?"

"Dreadful?" My husband deliberated for a moment, and then pronounced the magic word, because of which, and only because of which, even though I have a thousand other reasons—I'll love him to the end of time. "Boring," he said.

I'm sure he didn't understand what made me burst out laughing and go on laughing, but my laughter infected him, and the two of us laughed and laughed until I slid off the sofa and he had to sit down on the carpet with Yachin.

"What did you say? Go on, say it again."

"Boring," he repeated.

"Boring," I bellowed. "Oded Brandeis, you're one of a kind. Hitler bores you."

Only when Yachin's face twisted and turned red did we calm down, even though we went on sitting on the floor. "So now explain to me, please."

"Look, I don't know, it's kind of banal. If it's supposed to be a mystery, if Hitler's a mystery, then I didn't get the impression it was about to be solved. I know this sounds a bit tasteless, but if I think of it as, let's say, a detective story, then up to now, up to the place I've reached in the book, I haven't understood the motive."

"Hitler's motive?"

"Yes. That's to say, there's all the usual stuff about the Jews, the vermin, and the cancer, there's a kind of paranoid person who believes in all those things—which, by the way, poses a certain problem, because if he's insane and honestly believes that the Jews are a deadly danger, then from the legal point of view at least, you could argue diminished responsibility. On the other hand the book presents his so-to-speak rational calculations with regard to political interests, and quite impressive political manipulations, especially after his relative failure in the 1933 elections, but all this doesn't add up to anything. In fact I hardly learned anything new from it. What I'm trying to tell you is that the book is actually banal: a kind of primary textbook for students who need to be provoked. Basic history for the lazy."

"And the first person?"

"What about it?"

"It doesn't bother you that Hitler speaks in the first person? Didn't you feel it was terrible to read 'I' when that 'I' is actually Hitler? The first person acts to create identification."

Oded thought for a moment; it was clear that until I asked the question it hadn't occurred to him.

"The truth is that I didn't feel like I was reading about Hitler," he concluded in the end. "I don't know how to explain it, but that Hitler somehow wasn't Hitler, not that I'm presuming to know who Hitler really was. So his father hit him and for some reason he brags about it. So he loved his mother and she died in agony and she had a Jewish doctor, so what does that prove? There could be all kinds of people who had things like that happen to them."

I thought he was finished, but he had something else to say, and in order to say it he had to put our son down first.

"Look, I don't have to explain to you why I was tempted to read it. I thought it would help me to understand something, you know, about that man and everything you went through."

"Yes?" I tensed.

Oded lowered his gaze and slowly rubbed his thighs. "Well, you know, because the author is a total pervert, somehow I expected his book to be full of perversions too."

"Yes?"

"From the little I know about history, he had enough material to base all kinds of pornographic descriptions on. The rumors about the single testicle," he blushed, "problems with normal functioning, obsessions, never mind, it doesn't matter, there are all kinds of theories, you know, but as far as I could tell, there's nothing like that in the book. It's true that I haven't finished reading it, but in the chapter I did read, he talks about some woman, Geli Rampal, he describes her as some chaste childish nymph who goes into the forest with him, and then, right after that, he blathers on endlessly about the purple velvet armchairs that he wanted to buy with her. Purple velvet armchairs! Can you imagine?"

"Yes?"

My clipped responses only increased his uneasiness, and nevertheless my husband persisted like a diligent schoolboy. He went on and on describing the book, and it seemed that his embarrassment prevented him from leaving out anything in the review he had prepared for me. My tenseness didn't go away completely, but at the same time I was overwhelmed by a kind of weariness that turned my "yes" into a mechanical murmur. It seemed that my previous wild laughter had exhausted all my wakefulness. Oded went on at length about the niece Geli Rampal, the affair of whose suicide wasn't solved or given any explanation for in the book, and at this stage I was hardly listening. While my husband unburdened himself by talking, my eyelids grew heavy, and it was only with an effort that

I kept my eyes open until he finished coming clean. I understood his need to tell me about his plunge into *Hitler, First Person*. I myself would have insisted on his not hiding anything from me. And at the same time, the longer he went on, the more I wanted him to get it over with and let me go. Yachin, who was teething, had worn me out during the day—a good reason to be exhausted. But why didn't Oded get to the point? He told me. I got it. We were done. Wasn't that the point? Weren't we done? How long was he going to go on lecturing me after he himself said that the book was boring. If it was boring, why didn't he stop? Why drag it out and mull it over.

I went on nodding. I went on muttering "yes" whenever I surfaced to listen. I remember the word "songbird" and after that something about suspect witnesses and that Hitler was well known as a cunning liar, and in any case you couldn't believe a word he said; and something about a statue of a horse, and about horses in general, but maybe I'm confused because why on earth should my husband have presented me with horses.

"In short," he said after shifting here and there, "it's a bad, shallow book out to create a sensation, but there's no German porno in it. And if I hadn't known it was written by a pervert, I never would've guessed."

"Yes, I understand." Sleep was already taking over me completely, and I still had to put Yachin down in his crib and lead myself to our bed. How was I going to drag myself there?

Aware of my situation at last, Oded stood up and pulled me to my feet.

"All I can tell you is that if I imagined that the book would help me understand something, I was wrong; I don't understand anything about that man." I should have asked him who he meant by "that man," but I was overcome by a fit of yawning and the pressing need to surrender to the tide of sleep and sink into the depths. Which is what I did. I allowed my husband, purified and clarified, to lead me to the bedroom. He put Yachin to bed and joined me. And enveloped by the clean white smell of the salt of the earth I slept dreamlessly till morning, and in the morning we spoke no more about the book.

Hitler, First Person was not translated into Hebrew in the end and it soon disappeared from the shelves of the bookshops. And nevertheless, it happened that people who knew my maiden name asked me if I had any connection to Gotthilf, the historian or author: hadn't there been some kind of scandal? Remind me, what was it exactly?

Years before the appearance of the pigtail-sucking Alice, I already knew that a partial truth was more acceptable than a lie, and I always answered: "I think he may be related somehow to my father, but I'm not really sure"—and changed the subject.

The book disappeared from the shelves in the bookshops, but not from the bookcase in which Oded had buried it in his office, and from which it came back to attack me six years later, after it had already faded from my mind.

This happened during the Passover holidays. Yachin was then almost seven and Nimrod had already turned five. We were in Spain. Chemi had decided that the family needed and deserved a vacation, and to the delight of all concerned he chose to take us to a charming hotel on top of a hill overlooking the Costa del Sol.

The weather was pleasant, Oded spent hours with the boys in the pool, Yachin was already able to hold himself above water with an energetic dog-paddle, and I, who don't know how to swim, spent the days reading, wandering around the village, and dozing in the mild warmth of the sun.

I was just a little drowsy when Menachem appeared in shorts and a shirt, set a chair beside my sunbed, looked down at my exposed face, and asked me the question about your-connection-to-the-historian-Gotthilf.

"To my regret, he's apparently some kind of cousin of my father's," the sun gave me an excuse to cover my eyes. "Sorry, one more relation I have no cause to be proud of."

My reply did not stop him, and he went on to ask me what I could tell him about the man.

"Hardly anything, in fact. I know that his mother got him out of Vienna at the same time as my grandmother escaped with my father, but my grandmother came to Palestine while they, I think, emigrated to England. What was his mother's name? Hannah, I think."

He was more experienced than I was in conducting interrogations, or perhaps he didn't mean to interrogate, but simply fastened his teeth on a subject he found of interest.

"And all those years you didn't have any contact with him? That's quite unusual, especially with people who suffered the common trauma of being refugees. None of the other members of the family, I understand, survived."

"I think he visited Israel once," I sank further into the artificial darkness of my arm. "I don't remember exactly. Maybe there was something like that. I think there was. Perhaps it was when I was already in boarding school."

"Interesting," he observed. The sounds of splashing and warning cries together with mild rebukes from my husband rose from the direction of the pool. "Interesting," his father repeated and put something down next to my thigh. "In any case, I'm curious to know what you have to say about this. I found it in my library in the office."

Menachem had the old-fashioned habit of wrapping the books he was reading in paper, so as not to stain them with his fingers—he had a collection of bookmarks too—and so, when he set the book down next to me and I finally opened my eyes, even though I should have realized at once what it was—for a moment I failed to do so.

"You're the expert on literature in our family, so take a look and let's hear your verdict."

With my face to the sun going down over the sea beneath us, I picked up *Hitler, First Person* and opened it.

"You want me to read it now?"

"Why not? At least have a look for a few minutes. As far as I can see you're not reading anything else at the moment. I'd like to hear what you think."

I could have told him that I didn't want to read about Hitler. I could have claimed that the book wasn't suitable for holiday reading and that he hadn't brought us to the pampering sunshine only to thrust us into the darkness with Hitler. I could have said all kinds of things to get out of it, the only problem was that I couldn't. Anyone who has once dwelled in the Garden of Eden will forever fear being cast out. And among the inhabitants of the rose-tinted heavens there must be more than a few fearful souls of those who, even in their previous lives were braver than me. Anyone who has tasted the honey of the leviathan and the milk of the pomegranates, will be terrified at the mere thought of exile. And only because of the fear of the flaming sword turning every which way, only because of my cowardice and my dread of the turning flame, only because of this and for no other reason I went on holding the book in my hands, and saw myself as compelled to read it.

•

Menachem went on sitting beside me, paging through a magazine, and appeared to be waiting for me to present him with a speedy report, and I stood up and raised the back of my sunbed. As I stood there I saw Oded coming out of the water, and carrying Nimrod quickly toward the showers. Yachin ran after them, and nobody came to me with a question or a complaint or a request for a kiss on a place that hurt.

The painted clay pots of plants hanging over the bar gleamed in the sunlight: the ladybugs painted on them, red against the yellow, were as big as the painted flowers. A pair of hotel employees walked past behind us chatting in musical Spanish: the tone of their voices was enough to tell me that that they'd finished work for the day and were on their way home. A third worker slowly and patiently unrolled a green net over the blue of the pool.

Chemi's imperial, bald head shone. He pored over his magazine with his lips closed, and in profile he looked like a statue of a man poring over a document. Menachem is the only person I know whose lips are never parted: neither parted, nor pursed. One lip rests on the other in perfect, unquestionable order. Once he had instructed me to read, he turned to his affairs, taking it for granted that I would do what was expected of me.

I learned to read at the age of four, and I read as easily as breathing. I have a BA in literature; in my prehistory I managed to write seminar papers with half a bottle of alcohol in my belly. I told myself that there was no reason I would not be able to read these pages that didn't belong to this place, or to me, or to Hitler, this text that didn't touch anyone or anything, and that I certainly would not allow it to do so.

I put on my blouse and skirt, again picked up the book wrapped in brown paper, and sat down to do as I was told.

The text opened with a boastful sentence. The narrator bragged that he had looked into depths where no one before him had dared to look. From there he launched into a description of a vision he'd had: an apocalyptic scene in the style of a science-fiction comic, or a description of killing fields in the World War I.

In November 1918, the speaker is in a convalescent home in Pasewalk, recovering from the effects of a gas attack—or perhaps from hysteria—and, blind as Tiresias, he prophesies the destruction of the world. Carcasses of horses. Scampering rats. Dogs falling onto piles of bodies. Steam rises from spilled intestines, steam rises from the earth, and everything is pervaded by an obscure evil.

Laughter rings without stopping in the narrator's ears, the poisonous ringing prevents him from sleeping at night, and he realizes that the laughter is the laughter of the Jews, and that the evil ever changing its shape is the Jews.

With this realization his vocation is revealed to him. From his earliest childhood he knew that he had a vocation, and from this moment his mission is clear to him: to choke the laughter.

The style of the writing seems portentous to me, bloated by the excessive and repetitive use of adjectives. My meager acquaintance with original texts written by Hitler did not enable me to determine whether the text in my hands was attempting to copy his style. I turned the pages. The narrator speaks about what he calls his "natural love of beauty." About experiencing the magnificence of the church festivals as a choirboy, about the sublimity of snowy mountain peaks, certain statues, and buildings. Almost three pages are devoted to his prodigious loathing of wood carvings, which is his opinion should all be burned.

I skipped to the "charms of friendship" with one August Kubizec, and the "monkey cages" of the schools that suppress the spark of genius in their pupils. The style had changed, and the hero now came across as a sensitive, rebellious boy, something along the lines of a Holden Caulfield kicking over the traces and protesting against suffocating adult hypocrisy.

More ambitious and robust than the hero of *The Catcher in the Rye* the adolescent boy confronts his father's iron will. He longs for the transcendence of art, the splendor of the opera, exalting torrents of music, and wherever he goes his horrified ears are infiltrated by the shrill, discordant voices of the Jews, which he, like Wagner, finds unbearable.

I went on, skipping forward and backward. Wherever I turned I found a narrator different from the one before, and with every new page the adjectives I had decided only moments before would describe my impressions of the text to Chemi became irrelevant.

Somewhere in the patchwork of the text I found myself in a green meadow strewn with flowers where an elegant and aristocratic lady was riding a white colt. And a little further on an elderly housekeeper appears, also aristocratic, her hair sprinkled with white. The angry adolescent is now replaced by a romantic novelist of an old-fashioned kind, and for a few pages it seems that this unbelievably archaic tone is taking over the story.

This impression lasted until the affair of the niece, where I stopped skipping and read right through.

She is a poor, fatherless teenager, and he, recently released from prison, carries her off to his eagle's nest. The canary receives private lessons and learns to sing. The pure voice of the young girl as she practices her singing at the end of the corridor enchants the hero, and on his return from his travels he occasionally finds the time to accompany her on a musical instrument.

One day the exquisite bird grows hoarse, and the doctor is called in to examine her and diagnose inflammation. Up to now everything seems more or less normal for the genre, if you ignore the identity of the first person narrator, as I succeeded—almost succeeded—in doing. But then, at this stage of the story, the narrator takes the flashlight from the doctor, and curious to know what lies hidden inside the golden canary, he too insists on looking inside. He takes hold of the seated girl's chin, shines the flashlight into the depths of her throat, and discovers a moist, gleaming tunnel spotted with white, apart from which there is "nothing there." There is nothing there. And since there is nothing there, nothing remains to distract him from his mission to purify the bloodstream and save Germany.

Oded didn't tell me about this scene. Perhaps he skipped it, perhaps he didn't understand its significance, and perhaps he read it and understood and decided to spare me. I put the book down and covered myself with the towel.

"So what does the literary expert say?" Chemi took off his glasses, ready to listen.

The last pages had numbed my ability to produce new adjectives, and this is apparently the reason why I answered weakly in Oded's words: "It's banal," even though as far as I was concerned there was nothing banal about the last scene. To this day I don't know if it was based on any historical source, or if this event of looking into the flesh and the subsequent conclusion that "there's nothing there" was concocted from start to finish in the author's black box.

"Banal?" the tone told me that I had to hurry up and rewrite my report. And to make himself clear Menachem added: "This abomination seems banal to you?"

"That's what your son said about it. That was his impression," I defended myself. But what is perhaps permitted to the son is forbidden to the daughter-in-law, who also happens to be related to the author of the abomination. Relationship by blood demands a far more vigorous denunciation, of a kind that will differentiate sharply between the daughter-in-law and the abominator.

"Oded's right, that's to say, in the sense that this text doesn't tell us anything new," I squirmed, "in the sense that it seems to be written for ignorant high school students who are too lazy to read history. But the attempt itself, the writing itself, the pretension itself—that's sick. The whole thing is so sick and so repulsive that I'm sorry I even touched it. It's sick."

Ignoring my feeble hints, whining tone, and huddling underneath the towel, Menchem picked up the book and got ready for the discussion he was intent on having. "So you can't tell me anything about this man?" he examined me again over his glasses.

"I'm sorry."

"Because if you ask my opinion, what your father's cousin did here is a hundred times worse, a thousand times worse, that what Nabokov did in *Lolita*. I'm surprised that you, someone who understands literature, didn't make this comparison yourself."

"Nabokov?"

"Nabokov. Because what is *Lolita* if not the justification of a pedophile and a rapist?"

It took me more than a minute to digest this entire sentence. Because what I heard at first was only "the justification of a pedophile and a rapist," and the words "pedophile and rapist" threw me for a loop, and made me think that Menachem either suspected or knew.

In the days when Elisheva and I were going insane together in our basement apartment in Talpioth, my sister developed a fantasy of being transparent: it seemed to her that all her privacy was leaking out, and that everyone who passed her could read her thoughts and see what was going on inside her. A feeling just like this took hold of me when Chemi started to talk about *Lolita*, because where did he get "rapist" from? Where if not from my own mind?

The next morning I was already able to tell him that he was making a big, if common, mistake in his reading of *Lolita*; that the book was pervaded by a consciousness of sin; that the utter ruin of Lolita is conveyed through the unreliable narrator, and that the reader together with Humbert Humbert are clearly aware of the fact that there is no restoration and that atonement is impossible.

That morning I already had the strength to get into general and comparative literature, but at that private moment next to the pool, what I mumbled to him was: "But Hitler wasn't a rapist." I imagine that he looked at me as if I were an idiot: I'm not certain, because under the threat of the flaming sword I couldn't lift my head and look him in the face.

"Fortunately for us," said Menachem, "the author of this abomination doesn't have one thousandth of the satanic talent of Nabokov. Just imagine if a really talented writer had written Hitler's autobiography."

"What does he want from me?" I wailed to Oded about two hours later, when we stood in the bathroom getting ready to go downstairs for dinner. "Just because I was once a Gotthilf, I have to prove to him that that crap makes me vomit? What does he expect me to prove? That I'm not a Gotthilf?"

Oded put a finger on his shaving cream mustache to signal me to lower my voice so as not to upset the boys.

"Apart from which," I went on in a lower voice, "even though your father is the nicest person in the world, let's not forget that he's a lawyer."

"What's that got to do with it and how is it relevant?" Asked my husband without taking his eyes off the mirror. I didn't know how it was relevant, but once I had begun, I went on unburdening myself, letting the words take over. "It means that he's not exactly Mother Theresa, either. Anyone would think that all the clients he represents are saints. What gives him the right to interrogate me like that just because I'm . . ."

My husband steadied his chin with one hand and with the other shaved off specks of foam, while setting the record straight for my benefit: Possibly, in my sensitivity, I had read his father's intentions correctly, or possibly not. And perhaps Menachem, who as I well knew had a lot of respect for my opinions, honestly wanted to hear what I thought about a book that had shaken him to the core. He often asked my opinion on books, after all. Oded was sorry for the unpleasant experience I had endured, and he was especially sorry to know that he could have spared me if he had only done the obvious thing and thrown the book in the trash instead of putting it in the bookcase in the office.

"And as for Mother Theresa, nobody is Mother Theresa, maybe not even Mother Theresa herself. Lawyers, in the nature of the profession, represent all kinds, that's true, but to the extent that I know my father, and to the extent that I know myself—neither of us is cut out to be a criminal lawyer."

I sat down on the lid of the toilet, and from there I raised my eyes to the handsome profile of my attorney.

"Do you think I'm completely crazy?" I asked meekly when he appeared to be finished.

"An interesting question," he shot at me. "I'll have to consider it."

"But do you think you'll still want to go on being with me?"

"Be with you? Let's see, I need time to think about it, but after the boys fall asleep I'll definitely check it out." He patted his face smugly with a towel, obviously pleased with himself and the charms that had enabled him to silence the howls of a madwoman so efficiently.

I imagine he said something in the course of the evening to his parents, or at least to his mother. Presumably he reminded them that any reference to the subject of my family upset me and "brought back the tragedy." Because after dinner my mother-in-law drew me outside for a breath of fresh air, and when we walked down the steep street she linked arms with me and said: "Menachem can sometimes be so tactless. Mostly it happens when he gets carried away by some intellectual question. When he gets started on one of his hobby-horses he can be as inconsiderate as a child, even though I don't have to tell you what a kind-hearted man he is. Over the years I've learned not to take it to heart. In married life it's sometimes best to keep quiet and overlook things."

- 8 -

My husband said there was no going back, that we had to look to the future, that the river would flow where it wanted, but the two of us would go forward together.

"There's no going back," my husband said to me after the bottom feeder had phoned me and sent an email to his office. He raised his chin and directed my eyes to the horizon, and all that was missing was a brass band playing a march in the background, so enthused was he by the future.

After he finished singing me his song about our future, my boy-husband of the beetling brows went to take a shower, while I went on sitting in the kitchen with a cup of tea and a mental image of a vice squeezing my head.

It was the second month of the Not-man's stay in our house, on a fine Saturday morning in the middle of winter. My mother came into our room and asked me to put on "something nice" and come down, because we were all going to have our photo taken with Uncle Aaron: and would I please hurry up, before the sky clouded over, and not detain our important guest who wanted to get back to work.

I didn't put on anything nice, but I went out to the garden as I was bidden. The endless fuss with which my parents surrounded our guest embarrassed me, but to be honest I have to admit that part of my embarrassment stemmed from the thought of how we must look to him. His manners were exemplary, but the hint of a curl in his lip sometimes made me wonder whether they weren't too perfect, as if he were playing a part and mocking us with a parody of a gentleman of the old school. Justice and honesty oblige me to admit that the supposed mockery hurt me, and that his opinion mattered to me. If I lie about this, I am liable to give the impression that I was wiser than my sister. I wasn't wiser than her, and on the few occasions that I met him, I was stupid enough to try to impress him with my cleverness. The apple doesn't fall far from the tree, and in my need to make an impression I was not so different from my mother. Among other things, I bragged about having read Kafka, and after he made a few remarks about "The Penal Colony," I found the story and sat down to read it again through his eyes.

Our mother sat on a cushion she had placed on the damp seat of the swing-bench, and he on a cushion next to her, his legs stretched out in front of him, his heels dug into the ground to prevent any rocking. My mother was wearing one of her fancy ensembles, a white dress with a white striped jacket; all that was missing to complete the picture was a frilly parasol. I don't remember what Elisheva was wearing, she was standing and waiting for me, fiddling with dad's Leica camera. Our father wasn't there. Perhaps he had already had his photo taken. Perhaps he had popped into the office to answer the phone. My sister's hair was loose and combed with a neat part down the middle, a pink flower stuck crookedly over her ear: perhaps it was a pin, perhaps a blossom plucked from one of the vases in the dining room. It's hard to remember. All I remember is a flower, and my guess is that our mother decorated her like this in honor of the photograph and our uncle.

If I had told Oded this, he would presumably have said that maybe I was right and maybe I wasn't. My sister liked dressing up, and among her treasures was a collection of pins, mainly enamel lapel pins: a Bambi, a giraffe, a glittering black cat—like little toys. So perhaps she had a flower pin too, and perhaps she stuck it in her hair on her own initiative.

At first I was summoned to the swing. When it appeared that the sun was behind us and threatening to spoil the photograph, we got up and stood under the cypress tree, and then our mother said that with the rhododendron behind us would be prettier, and we moved to the flowers. Looking bored with all these consultations and moves, our uncle complimented our mother on her eye for aesthetics.

We arranged ourselves for the photograph: man in the middle, mother on one side and daughter on the other, as demanded by both family and aesthetic considerations. And while the photographer focused the lens, the man put his arms around the mother and the daughter.

I won't say that he felt my breast. While it was happening I couldn't be sure. His hand groped up my ribs, a little above the waist, the fingers were outspread, and something, a raised thumb, moved and fastened itself under my armpit.

I'm not claiming trauma. I didn't experience any trauma, just a trivial and off-putting event. Every woman in the course of her life experiences ambiguous events of this kind.

My reaction to the thumb was instinctive. "Instinctive" I say; I latch onto instinct because I have no other excuse for what I did. Because what I did was this: I shook off his hand and stepped forward, took the camera from my sister, and said curtly: "I'll take the picture."

Our mother murmured "pity" and "souvenir," but my voice and expression were the same voice and expression that forced my parents to let me go to boarding school and to pay my fees: on my face—I know—was the same expression with which I ignored my mother's warnings that, if I left home, she would have a heart attack; the expression that even when I was a child would make her say ingratiatingly to the guests: "Sometimes that child frightens me."

"I'm not being photographed. I'm taking the picture," I repeated. And with these words I sent my sister to take my place.

And it could have been different. In retrospect it's clear that there was a different way, and not only one but several. The voice that knew how to talk could have said different things. The body was free to go and not to take the camera or her sister's place.

I don't want to exaggerate the importance of this picture. I didn't cause my sister to be raped, I know. It's very possible that the abuse began before, and in any case, even if I hadn't sent her into his hands, he would have abused her anyway.

My sister joined the line. She was photographed. I took the picture. That's all that happened. A matter of seconds.

I never saw the photographs. I assume my parents had the film developed. When my father made haste to sell the pension, property that had been accumulated for years was removed or thrown out in a few days, and it's possible that the evidence was thrown out with the garbage—in any case, what can you already learn from a photograph, and what can a photograph add to what I saw with my eyes?

Portraying an event that was over in a few seconds as a great drama is pointless, and in most cases is also a kind of lie: true betrayal creeps up slowly and lasts longer.

Traitors have hour after hour, day after day, in which they could choose differently.

Reality as it is, is never concentrated into one symbolic picture, and focusing the eye on a single picture is nothing but a literary device; an impudent sleight of hand, just like directing our attention to a bit of dust so we won't notice the other dirt.

No, I won't exaggerate the significance of this event or inflate its symbolism. It's true that after Oded told me about the intrusion of the snake, this picture stuck in my mind, that's true, but the mind is a capricious organ, and one of its caprices, one of its associative twists, certainly doesn't account for the entire unfolding of my plot.

Be that as it may, this was the picture I thought about, this was the one that stuck in my mind, and by the time Oded, fresh and pink, emerged from the shower, I knew what I had to do.

"I have to talk to Elisheva."

Tired from the day's work and the scalding water he likes to shower in, my husband confirmed I might be right, if that's how I really felt, and somehow it seemed to me that he hadn't understood what I said. "We have to warn her," I added, "if he found us, he might find her too. These days you can find anyone."

Only about an hour later, when his breathing turned into the breathing of sleep, I realized that he still hadn't understood, and I said out loud: "What I meant to say is that I'm going to go see her in America."

After my sister met her redeemer, converted to Christianity, and married, we lost contact. In the days when I was living in my lair in Nahlaoth I didn't even have her phone number, and it was only when I got married myself that a tenuous relationship with big intervals in time came into being between us.

In order to maintain the kind of telephone relationship I've had with my sons since they went to America, there needs to be common ground on which news can be exchanged: and the new Christian continent where my sister lived in her new incarnation was too far for me to be able to relate to it.

There was nothing that could be taken for granted between us, not even holiday greetings. Should I call her on my New Year? Was it still in some way hers? "Passover and Easter are the same thing," she promised, but how did I know when Easter fell, and what did you ask a sister preparing for Easter: do you buy ready-made *harosset* or make it yourself? And what was the point in talking about *harosset* in the first place? I didn't want to talk to her about *harosset* and most of the time I didn't want to talk to her about anything else, either. We had talked enough: the months when her demented ravings had held us in their grip, before she left for America, had apparently exhausted my strength to listen to her, and my life was full of other voices demanding my attention.

In later years, when the boys were already older, Elisheva, who from childhood had experienced difficulty in writing, discovered email as a means through which she was able to express herself in text. And since then every few months I would receive a well-written composition in English, whose lower margins were decorated with deer footprints. The person who composed these decorated compositions was a complete stranger, but in one of them I was informed of the birth of my niece Sarah, and this was already after it had seemed that my sister and her Barnett would not bring any children into the world.

Elisheva wrote that she was blessed, and that an entire lifetime would not suffice to give thanks for the grace of this fertility of which she was certainly unworthy. But even before the birth of Sarah she would enthusiastically list the blessings showered on her by God in every letter: the beauty of the autumn foliage in Illinois; a member of the church congregation who had ridden his horse into a truck and escaped unhurt. A checked jacket of Barnett's that had been lost and found by a stranger who became a friend—the hand of God was visible in all these things.

Under the personal supervision of a benevolent God and a benevolent husband, it was clear that my sister was in no need of my supervision, which had in any case been found wanting. I sent a box full of expensive gifts for the baby, my sister replied with exaggerated expressions of gratitude, and I deleted her reply just as I deleted everything else, and went back to tending my vine.

Nobody will ever know what my sister intended to do on the evening she locked herself in the girls' showers on base 12 with an Uzi. She probably didn't know herself, and I—who was away that week on a class trip, and only found out when I returned—definitely don't know.

I wasn't there during the four hours she locked herself in before she was persuaded to give up the weapon, I wasn't there when she was hospitalized, I didn't visit her in Kfar Shaul, and I wasn't present at the session when she told our parents about the abuse.

My role in this part of the story is that of the person who wasn't there.

Months later I heard from a graduate of the boarding school who was an officer on the base that "there were actually warning signs, the kind that are hard to ignore." Other girls complained that Elisheva didn't shower, that she slept in her uniform, that she was maddeningly slow, and that it wasn't fair for the whole unit to be punished because of one soldier. "It was hard to ignore," the officer said, but in the end everyone overcame the difficulty and succeeded in ignoring it.

She was nineteen when she enlisted. Height one meter fifty-eight, weight that rose with stubborn persistence to over eighty kilos. My parents attributed her obesity to the pressure of studying for her exams, and promised anyone ready to listen that in the army, with new friends and new experiences, her weight would go down of its own accord. I didn't even take the trouble to understand and relate to all this. I was busy with my own affairs, I had matriculation exams to prepare for. When I did go home my sister didn't stink. We shared a room, so I should know.

When it comes down to it, I don't think she has suicidal genes either. I believe that even in the swamps of hell, my sister never stopped hoping for a redeemer who would come and purify her. Later too, when both of us were locked into her madness, and I, in order to save my life, pushed her into the hospital—what she really wanted was to survive.

Our parents deserted, each in his own way, but our widowed father did not abandon his daughters without a plan: the one discharged from the army with disability benefits would continue her treatment and recover, perhaps she would even start studying something practical; whereas the other, who had skipped a grade and was in any case not yet old enough to be conscripted—she would register at the Hebrew University and get a degree. It would be a shame for a mind like hers to go to waste in the army, and as a student with an apartment of her own and a tidy sum of money set aside to pay for her studies—there was no doubt that this daughter at least was set to enjoy her life. How many students, after all, were as privileged as she was?

Our father found us a quiet three-and-a-half-room basement apartment in the neighborhood of Talpioth, and flew off to Italy—two years later he decided to let me know in an airmail letter that, prior to moving to Italy, he had not been in contact with Gemma and, in fact, in his terrible grief, hadn't even remembered that this former pension guest lived in the city of Verona, where he'd since settled down.

"A marvelous coincidence brought us face to face among all the thousands of people at the entrance to the arena," he wrote to me. "And even then I, like Job, doubted whether I was fit for a new life." I assumed that he was lying, but at this stage I had already cut myself off to such an extent that I only wondered why he had even taken the trouble to lie to me.

Later on he latched onto Elisheva's "new life" in order to justify his right "to devote the few years I still have left to try and create a little corner of peace and beauty." After that I no longer replied to his preening letters with their curlicues and circles for dots. I was revolted by his grandiose handwriting just as I was revolted by the words themselves, and I hoped that he would give up and leave me alone.

I registered in the English Literature department, and in this, and only this, the prophesies of the deserter came true: the clever daughter did indeed enjoy her studies. I enjoyed sitting in the lecture halls in an atmosphere of order and knowledge. I read a lot more than

I was required to. I loved the excitement of the carefully chosen words, and no less the theories that calmed the storm in a completely different language.

"The art of losing isn't hard to master," I would declaim when I stood up and when I sat down and when I went on my way. "The art of losing isn't hard . . ." I declaimed until it was almost an article of faith.

But Elisheva increasingly failed to acquire this faith. At first she stopped going to both her group therapy and her new psychologist. The first excuses she made were still couched in acceptable terms: a stomach ache, the worst heat wave in years, an ingrown toenail that turned every step into torture. But then, gradually, she stopped going out of the house, and her reasons grew weirder and weirder: People could see through her. The day was too fine. The light was too bright, everything was like glass, and through glass people could see everything. Didn't I understand? There were types. Like colors. Luckily I, her sister, was made of blue, because blue was the outside, the outside was blue and you didn't notice blue against the blue.

As soon as she started talking like this I understood that she meant that people could see the abuse on her, and I couldn't avoid the thought that in a certain sense she was right. Slow, dragging her feet, blinking even more than she used to, her large breasts emphasized by the sailor collars or the lace collars in one of the exotic costumes my mother had bought her, her fleshy shoulders making a kind of little hump under her blouse—the word "victim" was branded on her. And back when she still left the house from time to time, and went to the grocery store, visions of horror appeared before my eyes—a van slowed down next to my sister and started following her, a gang of teenagers accosted her and barred her way, at first as a game and then as something else—that kind of thing. And sometimes, because of these hallucinations, I went with her.

She spent her days in front of the huge television set that had accompanied us from the pension, watching children's programs. Staring at the screen, eating bread, bread and hummus, bread and chocolate spread. Slicing the loaf, and then as if absent-mindedly, rolling the slice into a kind of doughy sausage, dipping it in the spread, and cramming it into her mouth. Whenever I went out she would remind me in a fawning tone to bring her more bread, and even when I filled the freezer with loaves of bread she didn't stop. "What if you don't come back, what if you can't come back . . ." she would reply when I asked her for a logical explanation.

Every departure from the apartment and every return to it became a nightmare. Her eyes blinked at me anxiously from the armchair when I picked up my bag. Puppyish joy flooded her when I came in the door. Her attempts to please me. Her unintentional spite.

Once it occurred to her that if she dyed her hair black like mine, the black would help her. The idea became fixed in her mind, and after she repeated it again and again, I went and bought the dye and helped her color her hair. That night she went to sleep happy smelling of chemicals—shampooing with a lemon rinse failed to get rid of the smell, but at least she went to sleep and didn't keep me awake all night. She said she knew that in the morning everything would be different. And the next morning the same terrified eyes accompanied me to the door.

Most of the time I didn't know what to talk to her about, and I would babble on at random about whatever object came into my head: cheese with holes, cheese without holes, why did cheese have holes? Years before I invented Alice, I learned to inflate the figures of a bus driver and an old lady with a parasol, until they turned into colorful plastic dolls, which I brought my sister as a gift.

But sometimes I would go straight from the door to my room, and lock myself in until the next day.

For a few weeks I tried to read out loud to her from the list of required reading for the English Literature course. Comic passages from Chaucer, Shakespeare's sonnets, secular and religious poems by Donne, Dylan Thomas.

"After the first death there is no other," I pronounced. Elisheva didn't move, but my blood turned cold. I couldn't determine whether this conclusion of Dylan Thomas's poem was a promise or a consolation or a threat, but it was clear to me that it wasn't suitable, and in the days to come I was more careful and selective in my readings.

One night I read to her in a flat voice intended to put the poetry of the "Ancient Mariner" to sleep.

"Water, water every where / And all the boards did shrink / Water, water every where / Nor any drop to drink."

My voice was so dull that I myself stopped paying any attention to the words, and I went on intoning Coleridge night after night until in the end, not the same night, but out of the blue, one day in the kitchen, my sister informed me that "she didn't really like being read to."

A few days later, when I had finished swallowing the insult, I started reading my lecture notes to her, to which she didn't object. It even seemed to me that she was taking an interest, but I never knew for certain. And all the time I was afraid that my sister, the student with difficulties, was only trying to please me.

Her passivity drove me to despair. Most of the time she only spoke back to me when I hurled strong words of my own at her. And nevertheless one Saturday, when I was absorbed in writing a seminar paper, she came into my room and without any logical connection, asked if I knew whether Schopenhauer was "someone real who lived."

"Who?"

"Schopenhauer." She had always had an excellent memory for names.

"He was a German philosopher," I summed up everything I knew for her. "Why do you want to know?"

"I don't know. No reason," she replied noncommittally, and went back to the living room to knead her bread into dough. In spite of her disinterested tone I decided to see in the surprising question evidence of some mental awakening, which provided me with a reason to linger for an hour and a half in the library the next day. In the evening I brought my notes from "The Great Philosophers" into the kitchen and tried to tell her what I had learned, but she looked so blank and miserable that I stopped immediately.

"Why did you ask me about Schopenhauer if it doesn't interest you at all? I was stuck in the library for hours just because of you."

"I'm sorry. Forgive me."

"Never mind about forgiving you. What exactly got into your head?"

"Nothing. I'm sorry."

I looked at her, and only then, at a criminal delay of nearly twenty-four hours, I realized who it was who had entered her head. Because where else could she had heard about Schopenhauer? Certainly not in the children's programs on television. I knew, and I didn't want to know.

"All right, only next time don't ask me about things that don't interest you. If you're not interested—don't ask."

"Sorry . . ."

But there were also, of course there were, happier moments. One afternoon when I came home I discovered that she had prepared a surprise for me, she had taken all my trousers out of the closet and hemmed them all at exactly the right fashionable length. Or another time, when she embroidered a purple flower on my jeans by request.

One day she questioned me with untoward severity about the people I was seeing, and added that she hoped that I was "keeping company only with good people."

Sometimes she came out with funny, infantile sayings, such as: "You're a bread tiger. You're a tigress that goes out to hunt bread for us," and then for a moment it seemed the it was all a game, that the two of us had gone back to being little girls again, and she was only playing, and in a moment the game would be over.

But for the sleepless nights, perhaps I would have lasted longer than I did. But for the sleepless nights and for the malicious obsequiousness with which she innocently tortured me. How beautiful I was, how beautiful my hair was. Why wasn't I happy? Wasn't I happy to be so beautiful? Wasn't I happy not to be "one of the downstairs people?"

She referred frequently to "the downstairs people," and in the beginning I thought she was referring to our neighbors in the ground floor apartment opposite us. But of course she wasn't talking about them.

My sister never explained to me who the "downstairs people" were, as if it were self-evident to us and to the rest of the world, just as we all understood what a lamp was and what a table was.

"The upstairs people" were at liberty to go out whenever they wished, while even on the clearest and finest of days "the downstairs people" were sentenced to sit in a three-and-a-half-room basement apartment with the blinds down and watch old episodes of *Sesame Street*.

Wasn't I happy that from the day I was born and by my very nature I had not been sentenced to bring down the blind, or, more clearly, in words she never pronounced: Aren't you happy you're not like me?

And there was something else, and perhaps it was this that really finished me off: my role as the one who had believed her from the outset.

Weeks after the meeting during which, under medical confidentiality and the protection of the psychologist, Elisheva told them what had happened to her, my parents had not yet made up their minds whether their daughter was telling the truth. Whereas I, after hearing their abbreviated account, believed her at once, and later on, after she was discharged from the hospital, I found a way to prove it to both of them and to rub their faces in the truth.

Until I rubbed their faces in it, they said things like: "Not that we doubt what she says, but still, it's a fact that to this day no one has complained about him."

Or: "What sense does it make for a respectable man of his age, a man who never lacked for women—what sense does it make for such a charming man to molest a child?"

Things like: "From what we saw, and we can only judge from that, he treated her like a little lady. Don't you remember the orchid? And the way he stood up whenever she approached the table to serve him? And how patiently he tried to help her with her homework? Perhaps he exaggerated a little, and she was confused by his gentlemanly European manners? Perhaps she misunderstood him and began to develop all kinds of hopes and fantasies? Perhaps we sinned by thoughtlessness, by not imagining how a young girl like her was liable to interpret that kind of attention from an interesting man. We should have told him to behave differently with her. That was apparently our sin, that we didn't say anything to him."

And mainly they kept repeating, to each other and to me, pious declarations such as: "We shouldn't be in a hurry to judge. Everyone is entitled to a fair trial and we won't hold a kangaroo court here. Maybe all kinds of inconceivable things happened, but sometimes it takes time for the truth to come out. We hear what she says now, but in the future, after she gets well, who knows . . . ?"

But I, who made my judgment immediately and who had no doubts, succeeded in proving the truth of the one fact that they both tended in particular to deny.

This is what I did: Elisheva didn't remember, or perhaps she didn't know the name of the doctor to whom her rapist had taken her to perform an abortion. About which they both said to me: "What doctor would do such a thing without the father and the mother? Why would any doctor take the risk? And supposing something so shocking and inconceivable actually happened, wouldn't it be reasonable to assume that he would have taken her to some out of town clinic? Because according to what she says it took place here, in Jerusalem."

My sister couldn't tell us the name of the doctor, but one Saturday when the two of us were alone in our room, it turned out that she remembered the place where he operated on her perfectly well. Not the exact address, but a more or less exact description. Not a stone house, the outside wall covered in pale yellow stucco, a little street into which the taxi had turned from Palmach Street.

I took the Yellow Pages from the office desk, found a gynecologist who worked in Hachovshim Street, and in my father's presence, without our mother or Elisheva, I called the clinic. I told the secretary that it was Elisheva Gotthilf speaking, and that I wanted to make an appointment. "I already consulted him once, about a pregnancy," I added, and in the same breath I asked her to check and see if my medical file was there.

That's what I did, trembling all over, that's all, no more. And what I did was enough. Although even after the existence of the medical file was proved, they could, on principle at least, have gone on contorting themselves in additional doubts and hesitations. They simply no longer had the strength to keep up their denial.

When finally dispelled their doubts, our parents started to blame each other for what they called "our calamity"—"Your cousin," "Your refusal to sell this accursed place and get the girls out of here," "Your blindness," "All the times I begged you to sell. You know yourself how I pleaded with you." And so on, until Erica fled the scene with another bout of sickness.

I imagine that it was the confrontation with the truth that pushed her into the arms of the Digoxin. And I don't care. After years of hypochondria, at least she died of a genuine heart disease.

The important thing is that Elisheva couldn't avoid sensing their disbelief. Even though they never expressed it to her in so many words. And no less important is that from the outset she received my explicit and unconditional belief. I was the one who believed it all immediately, and this being the case, it was up to me to go on believing her: even when she talked about people who were blue, and days when the dangers outside were particularly grave.

Her wounded eyes never left me, begging for my belief, and I was incapable of betraying the belief that she begged for. This is my explanation for what happened in me, I have no other, and what happened was that gradually I began to see reality as if through her eyes, and even when I was sitting in class at the university, far from her, my eyes would seek out the "downstairs people" and separate them from the others: the boy with the big backside who jiggled his legs until the desk shook and couldn't stop; the girl whose facial skin was stretched in the direction of her ears by hidden screws. How did they dare go out on this fine day and come and sit among us?

I beat around the bush, sat myself in a classroom among strangers, and accused myself of trivialities, simply in order to put off admitting the most shameful thing of all. And the most shameful thing of all, the most despicable, is that drop by drop I absorbed my sister's beliefs until I began to see her as she saw herself, and for longer and longer stretches of time I put her in a different category from myself, as if she had been born into another race. She said that she was ugly, and I looked at her and saw ugliness. She believed that people like her shouldn't go out, and I was embarrassed by the thought of walking next to her in the street and being associated with her.

As sleepless night followed sleepless night I found myself turning into a creature made of blue, and into one of the "upstairs people." I began to see myself as being of a different substance, destined for a separate fate, naturally and essentially different from her sister-by-accident. It was a fact that I had been endowed from birth with a quick mind and a firm resolve. A fact that I knew how to say "I'm not having my photo taken."

I didn't see things like this all the time. There were also times of tender compassion and times when I was seized by a terrible, wrenching pity. There were definitely moments when I succeeded in conjuring up memories of a hand holding mine, and an older sister who insisted on bathing me. But these hours and moments grew fewer and fewer, and my pity for myself—sentenced as I was to live at close quarters with someone of her kind—increasingly filled the space left by that other pity. I was revolted by her flip-flops decorated with plastic flowers, by the movements with which she shook crumbs off her clothes, and by the way she came too close to me in the kitchen. I loathed the electric light in the apartment, the stupid sound of the television, and the pleas that stuck to me even when I went out. It happened that I cruelly refused to tell her when I was coming back.

And once it happened that I came home very late. It didn't just "happen." "Happen" means "happenstance." I deliberately came back hours late.

I don't remember how much vodka I downed in order to steel myself for this piece of cruelty, but I know very well that when I was already back in the apartment I crawled on all fours to the bathroom to vomit my guts out, and that the frightened Elisheva followed me like a shadow with a damp cloth and a glass of water. I told her that I had been attacked by a virus on my way home, "it's nothing, it's just a virus," and she of course believed me, because in our *folie à deux* we believed everything and the deal was mutual.

On fine days, on the clear days when objects shine as if they're under glass, on such days in particular I would imagine that I wouldn't return to the crumb-strewn gloom; that I would run away, go to Italy to scream at our father, put my sister on a plane and send her to him like a parcel. But until I broke, for those ten months—is ten a lot or a little?—I returned and returned, because I couldn't do otherwise. Today I say that my sister doesn't have suicidal genes, and that all her madness was directed toward survival, but then—what did I know?

- 10 -

When I informed my husband of my intention to go to America to see my sister, he immediately took me into his arms, assured me of my worth and the worthiness of my decision, and promised while combing his fingers through my hair to accompany me on the journey.

On the basis of everything I have said so far about the two of us and our relationship, I could have pulled an Alice here, adopted her style and written this chapter accordingly. Some of you would no doubt have believed it. People like swallowing sugar-coated rubbish. But that's not really the way things happened, and my husband's reaction was rather different, although I found sweetness in it too.

We were in bed, I announced, "I'm going to see my sister," and Oded put his hand on my thigh and without opening his eyes stated in the royal first person plural: "We're sleeping now, not talking." Even half-asleep he could be charming, and I smiled into the darkness of our bedroom and remembered to count my blessings, which included lying in my own beautiful home next to my own unruffled Prince Charming. I kissed his warm shoulder and let him sleep till morning.

Oded was then busy writing a complicated appeal—Menachem had begun to cut down on the hours he spent in the office—and in the morning he asked me to wait until Thursday at least before coming to any decision about the journey. "If you feel that you're ready for this, then obviously you should go, but after so many years when you haven't seen each other, the decision can wait for another three or four days." And I waited, not until Thursday, when he came home exhausted in the middle of the night, and not until Friday, when we had house guests, but until the Eden of Saturday afternoon, after the guests had gone. I didn't mind waiting. I was determined to go, and once I had made up my mind, making generous gestures to match my husband's didn't present a problem.

We sat in the living room; it was getting too cold outside, Oded smoked his Saturday joint and outlined the compromise agenda he had worked out for me. As much as he longed to get rid of the disturbance in our lives, my practical husband realized that getting rid of it completely wasn't an option. What was on the cards was only to distance the disturbance and minimize it until his wife saw things in a different light. With innocent cunning he tried to raise me to the heights of people of his ilk, people who were capable of seeing things in perspective.

Oded was obviously worried about my mental state and about what the meeting with my sister was liable to do to me, but he didn't talk about me, only about her, that it would be a mistake to suddenly shock and upset her by sounding an alarm that might prove to be groundless. He refrained from explicitly mentioning my own evident panic.

"She's your sister, it's natural for you to want to see her, it would be wonderful if you could improve your relationship with her, I'm one hundred percent behind it. But what do we know about her situation right now? We both hope and believe that she's fine, but we should take into account the possibility that if we come crashing down on her, from one day to the next, it might unbalance her." He snuck in the plural almost casually, "if *we* come crashing down on her," and without further discussion I accepted it.

I thought about the flight, about all those long hours in the air, I saw myself on the plane snuggling into that "we," and felt relieved. Once I had accepted the "we" my husband had slipped into the subject, other elements to be taken into account immediately made their appearance: with Menachem working fewer hours, Oded couldn't abandon the office until November at the earliest. We had sons in the U.S., and since we were already going there we should take the opportunity to stay on a while and visit them. "Perhaps you should write to Elisheva and tell her that we're coming to visit the children, and that we'd be happy to drop in on her on the way. That would be best, and then when she answers you, we can get some kind of indication and sense what her situation is. Let's talk to the boys and find out what their plans are. The four of us could meet somewhere, maybe Nimrod will want to come to Yachin in Seattle, we should check out the dates, maybe it'll even work out so that we can light the first candle of Hanukkah together. They say that Seattle is one of the most beautiful cities in the world." With talk like this, full of good sense and good taste, his feet on the coffee table, my husband redrew my trip as a family reunion with our sons. You had to know him as I did, to grasp that he was afraid. Not of the intrusion of the snake—in the land of the salt of the earth, a Black Belt isn't afraid of a snake—but of the women who, in spite of their charms, and perhaps this is their charm, tend to react without perspective.

I missed my sons, I longed to see my three men together, and even though I went on believing that I had to warn Elisheva, my sense of urgency was somewhat diluted by other feelings.

"Should we phone and wake the boys now, or should we let them sleep a little longer?" I asked. I moved the wine bottle and put my feet up on the coffee table next to my husband's.

•

Now that he had redirected the flight onto a routine tourist track, the trip began to take on the aspect he intended.

I sent my sister an email, and an hour after I sent it, an overjoyed deer-track decorated response arrived. We should come for as long as possible. She was delighted, Barnett was delighted, Sarah was so excited at the prospect of meeting her aunt and uncle at last. God had blessed the three of them. May God bless the two of us as well.

They had a spare bedroom in their house, but she and Barnett had decided to give us their bedroom, which was bigger and where we would be more comfortable. Did Oded have any dietary restrictions? Did I think he would like to go fishing? There was a beautiful lake a two-hour drive away, in November the weather was chilly, but it seldom rained, and if we dressed warmly we might be able to go to the lake anyway.

Oded remarked that perhaps it would be better if we found somewhere else to stay: "Look for some motel or nice bed and breakfast, if you can manage it without insulting her, I think we'll feel freer."

Elisheva wasn't insulted, or if she was she didn't show it. She sent another mail with a list of small hotels in the vicinity, which didn't boast of many attractions, but had one spectacular nature reserve, and also a fine little historical museum of the area. She was attaching a link to its internet site. Did I think we would like to visit it?

This was an Elisheva I didn't know; apparently it was time for me to get to know her. I began to think that perhaps there was a degree of truth in Oded's approach, and perhaps because the time was ripe, perhaps because of that too, I began to look forward to the trip.

•

Nimrod informed us that he would be able to drop in to his brother's for a weekend. Yachin said that he would be able to take the Thursday and Friday off from work.

Nimrod asked us to bring him coffee ground with cardamom from Danon's and not from the Old City, and Yachin said that we didn't have to bother bringing egg barley. Today you could get anything in Seattle, and in any case Mom shouldn't have to cook on her vacation. Did we ever have the chance to eat Vietnamese food?

The days filled with preparations before the trip. In the course of the years Oded and I had often flown together, to see buildings, people, art works, and animals. Planning the trip was always part of the fun, and as I planned and consulted and shopped and packed, the routine activity in anticipation of a well-earned holiday flooded me with an unexpected joy.

Should we fly via Atlanta or via Chicago? Land in Blooming-ton or Champaign? "Let's spend a fun day in Chicago," said Oded, and for the sake of this fun shortened our stay with my sister even further. "We'll take a look at Millennium Park, get some sleep, and in the morning we'll rent a car and get to their place relaxed and refreshed and without jet lag. Can you check out hotels in Chicago too?"

The serpent didn't disappear. He only settled into the dark of my belly like a parasite, and until close to the flight, with this sleeping parasite in my belly, I went on pursuing my usual activities. House-work and gardening, agreeable and less agreeable guests. Regular maintenance of my face and my body.

For a few days I sat in the National Library, and on the basis of the material I collected, I sent Alice on a three-column excursion in the wake of fictional and semi-fictional researchers into the Dead Sea Scrolls. People said that they were among the best columns I'd ever written. And a polite researcher from Bar Ilan University even wrote to me with a request for bibliographical references to the "riv-eting character of the man from the Freemasons," a character who was purely a figment of my imagination.

I brought the letter to Friday night dinner to entertain Chemi, and the patron of the braid-sucker from Alaska was as delighted by the fantasies of his protégé as I had hoped.

"You gave your Freemason yellow eyes," he remarked, "but since nobody in the real world has yellow eyes, I would have expected the

Doctor from Bar Ilan to understand that he was a fictional character. Interesting how people, even serious people, think that there is some secret about the Dead Sea Scrolls. The truth is that Alice's story was so successful that I myself almost began to believe that the Scrolls were written in a secret code."

Did we have windbreakers? We needn't worry if we didn't. My sister and her husband would be very happy to let us borrow theirs—what size was Oded? If we preferred to buy our own, we could find them here on sale. Barnett didn't like shopping much, but the little one adored shops, and if I liked, we women could shop till we dropped. What did I think?

What could I think? A foreign sister was showering me with a foreign love at the rate of two or three emails a week, as if I had done her nothing but good during all those years we were together, and as if we had never been together in our lives: she didn't write me a single word in the past tense.

Elisheva wasn't faking, no such doubt entered my mind for a minute, my sister didn't know how to fake, but what did I know about this American Elisheva? The tone of her American voice didn't sound as if it was addressed to me, presumably it was addressed to someone, but I had no idea who this person might be.

I was afraid of the past, naturally I was afraid, and I was very afraid of what I would have to tell her. And at the same time, as the emails accumulated, with all the diligent little plans, the historical museum and the nature reserve with the Indian name, with all the details about the hotels and the sales, my responses became increasingly soured by a feeling that was surprisingly similar to insult.

Above the decorative deer tracks my new sister was revealed as an organized woman. She went into detail more than I did. Her writing was orderly. If from time to time she still made spelling mistakes, her computer corrected them all.

Wasn't this what I wished for? Wasn't this exactly what I hadn't even dared wish for?

My new sister didn't remember my betrayals and the unkindness of my youth when I walked with her in the wilderness. She didn't resent me for all the times I abandoned her, and she didn't resent me for my collapse and the relief I obtained in the wake of the collapse.

What else could I hope for?

When I made up my mind to go and see her, as soon as the decision was made, I understood that I would have to prepare myself for different possibilities. But love like this wasn't one of them.

- 11 -

My collapse at the end of the period of the three-and-a-half-room apartment took me by surprise: like waking up in a hotel room without knowing why you were there or what had happened on the way. Until that afternoon I hadn't taken a collapse into account, and I had no idea that I was about to collapse.

It wasn't even an oppressively fine day. Just a rather dull day, neither winter nor summer.

I finished listening to my lectures and went to the administration office to hand in an application for a grant. They told me that the woman whose job it was to deal with the application forms would be back from lunch soon, but she didn't come back. I remember that her dereliction of duty gave rise in me to an illogical rage, but by the time I stopped in the center of town to buy myself a packet of *burekas*, the rage had subsided. I had only one beer in an old bar in

Rivlin Alley. I intended to take a bus home, but when I was already on my way to the bus stop, I suddenly felt I couldn't go on and I had to sit down for a minute.

I sat on the doorstep of a watchmaker shop on Ben Yehuda Street, and I went on sitting there, unable to get up. I didn't feel weak, I wasn't ill and I didn't faint, that wasn't it. I couldn't even say, "I don't feel well." The only thing I know is that my body detached itself from me, as if some thread through which the will transmitted its commands had snapped. At first, I remember, there was even something interesting about it, and I regarded the black sport shoes stuffed with my feet as a curious phenomenon—I thought that if I stopped paying attention to the phenomenon, the disconnection would go away. After a while I did indeed stop paying attention, and in hindsight it seems that I stopped thinking altogether.

Evening fell, I was aware that it was evening, shops closed, the watchmaker locked his door behind him and walked past me. Groups of entertainment seekers crowded the street. Near the square people were playing salsa music, and I went on sitting. Just sitting.

Any Jerusalemite coming to the center of town will always bump into somebody he knows, and at some stage, I have no idea what the time was, a friend from the prehistory of my boarding-school writing club walked down the street, and stopped next to me. She asked if everything was alright, and I answered with a "yes" that sounded alright to me, but she went on standing there anyway. Later on she told me that I didn't stop crying, and that was strange too, because I didn't remember any activity from my tear glands.

A friend of my friend happened by, they lifted me to my feet— once I was standing it transpired that I could walk—and together the two of them led me to the apartment of a third, an acquaintance who lived nearby; just a few buildings from there, a stone's throw, the fourth floor overlooking the street.

I climbed the stairs without difficulty, and when they asked me again what they could do to help me, I was already able to speak, and replied that I needed a phone because I had to get in touch with the municipal emergency services. This was the extent of my collapse. I, the competent, resourceful person who had figured out all on my own how to track down the gynecologist who had performed the abortion on my sister, said that I needed the "municipal emergency services," because my logic told me there was an emergency here and that it was urgent to contact the authorities in charge of dealing with it. And as I pronounced these words I felt a flicker of satisfaction with myself and with the logic that had started to operate again in spite of the emergency.

They gave me water, a lot of water, and by the time I finished drinking it I already knew that no municipality was going to rid me of my problem or take care of it, and I gave back the glass, thanked them kindly, and said that I had to go now. The three angels who had come to my aid wouldn't let me go. They went on questioning me until I found the right way to put it and confessed that there was a big problem with my sister; they fearfully inquired what kind of problem, and when I said "a psychological problem" their relief was evident. Not terminal skin cancer, only a mental problem, and there were people with expertise in solving such problems.

We settled in to tackle the matter in a purposeful manner. The name of the last psychologist who had treated my sister was Tamar Cohen, and in the telephone directory we found at least ten women with this name. We called the Talbiyeh mental hospital, and the person who answered the phone was unable to help us. We phoned the

Kfar Shaul hospital, and the person who answered the phone there remembered my sister, and helped us get in touch with someone in Talbiyeh who knew how to contact Tamar. All this took some time, and during this time the angels made toasted pita bread and tea with mint.

It was already quite late when I got hold of my sister's last therapist at her home number. Strengthened with tea, toast, and a sense of practical purpose, I was able to tell her that my sister was deteriorating, that I was alone with her, and that I was lost. And the three angels surrounding me nodded, confirming the correctness of my words and actions.

Until the therapist asked me if I thought there was a danger of suicide, I had no clear idea of what I hoped for from this conversation. Until this moment, the voice in the earpiece was only one of the concerned voices surrounding and supporting me and redirecting me between them. But with this question I was shocked into a hope that up till then had been out of bounds.

And from the moment that the hope struck me, from the moment it penetrated my mind, all thought of any other outcome became too dark to bear.

I didn't want to lie, but I said: "Our mother killed herself. Apparently she committed suicide. My sister must've told you."

This was the first time I ever spoke this sentence. In public. In the coming, crazy years, I used it to stun and shock until it lost its edge and I turned it into a joke, but the first time it wasn't addressed to an audience but only to the one person who could save me from the dark.

There were more questions and more answers, and then came the sentence I was dying to hear: "Can you bring her to me? We may have to consider hospitalizing her, for observation, at least." I explained again that there was no way I could make Elisheva leave the house. And I added: "And I can't be there all the time. I'm not with her now."

The therapist asked me to wait a moment, she went to consult her diary full of other people's troubles, and came back and said that she could come the next day, if we could make it early, at half past seven in the morning.

Three orderlies had to take hold of my sister in order to carry her to the car. The psychiatrist who signed the committal order had to inject her in the arm. I rolled up her sleeve . . .

That's not how it happened.

Tamar, the therapist, and I persuaded her to admit herself to hospital for observation, and Elisheva—who didn't want to go to hospital, tried to promise us that she would improve and that she could already feel signs of improvement—went quietly in the end. She packed her bag herself.

No three orderlies had to hold her by force, there was no need for an injection, none of that happened, but it could have happened, it could have, because if three stalwarts had been needed to distance her from me and to distance me from the dark—I would have let them do it. I think she knew it.

My sister was persuaded, and all the persuasion took place in the morning. That night, when I returned to our basement flat, I had only enough courage to tell her that both of us needed help, and that tomorrow morning her therapist would be coming to see us. I asked her if she wanted an omelet and if she would like to watch television with me, and when we were both sitting in front of the television screen, I muttered that I was exhausted and pretended that my eyes were closing against my will. And I sat like that until I was overcome by real exhaustion and really fell asleep. A few hours later, when I woke up, I discovered that she had covered me with a blanket.

My sister's final hospitalization lasted less than a month, during the course of which I visited her three or four times a week, and hardly stepped foot in our three-and-a-half-room basement apartment. I spent a few nights in my benefactor's apartment in Ben Yehuda Street, and after that other places were found.

After she went into the hospital Elisheva cooperated willingly with all her therapists, and when she came out her spirit had been renewed: not by the professional staff, but by another patient.

Barnett was in Talbiyeh for less than two weeks. That was apparently enough for him to rid my sister's mind of all manifest traces of Satan's presence and to instill in her the belief that he was the man intended to be her husband, and that she was intended—and therefore also worthy and capable—to be his wife.

When she returned to the apartment she no longer needed me and my presence. Barnett and his friends accompanied her when she applied for a passport and arranged for a visa.

The little I did was to buy her a suitcase, two days before she left. And after that we said goodbye.

- 12 -

The illusion of the family trip began to crack about a week before we flew. And at the same time the first mail arrived from Elisheva in which she made some kind of reference to the past.

My sister reiterated her excitement at the prospect of my expected visit, and said that she had been praying for it to happen for years, and that if it had been possible, she would have come to Jerusalem a long time ago. Many of the members of her congregation had visited Israel, some of them saved up and made a pilgrimage every year, and she couldn't describe the strength they drew from it. And she also added that she hadn't stopped loving me for a moment, that she and Barnett never stopped loving Jerusalem and speaking of it, and her words seemed to imply that Jerusalem and I were one and the same.

Both of them hoped that one day they would be able to visit, but they were still waiting for a sign that it was already possible. No doubt I understood that for Barnett Jerusalem was liable to be dangerous.

"Tell me more about your mysterious brother-in-law," requested Oded. For some reason he appeared to be more worried by the thought of spending time with her husband than by the meeting with my sister, but I couldn't tell him any more than he already knew.

Barnett Davis, a student of veterinary medicine at the University of Illinois, came to Israel with a group of evangelical pilgrims, and the holy city spoke to him. It spoke to him so loudly that he apparently started to hear voices. His initial symptoms were presumably attributed to religious exaltation within the bounds of the normal. But when the muscular round-cheeked blond man stood in the middle of Zion Square—not far from the place where I later collapsed, in the very same month—when Barnett stood there barefoot dressed in a *galabieh*, and prophesied about the city for two days straight, the members of his group decided that he had to be hospitalized.

Barnett was diagnosed as suffering from the "Jerusalem syndrome," in addition to which he was also suffering from pneumonia.

The hospitalization was brief. When I met him he was evidently embarrassed by the whole affair, and to the best of my understanding he saw himself not only as having gone out of his mind, but also as a sinner led astray by the devil. "I let myself be blinded by my vanity," he said to me. My loyal sister, on the other hand, saw things differently: "He was so full of that holy fire, that he couldn't stand having clothes on his body," she confided in me, and I, afraid of breaking the spell of the miracle that had been granted me, held my tongue and refrained from remarking that pneumonia gave you a fever.

The first time I met my future brother-in-law he came to our apartment alone. The second time he was accompanied by a couple of old ladies from his group—actually they weren't old, they just had gray hair, but then they seemed old to me.

It took a few days for me to realize that this deputation had come to ask me for my sister's hand. In the absence of other relations they hoped for my consent and blessing, and tried to supply all the information that a loving father and mother might have asked for.

Barnett's father, a dealer in agricultural produce, and a beloved member of his community, had suddenly passed away when his youngest son was a child of ten. His mother, a respected member of her community, supported her four sons by managing a stable where people from the surroundings kept their horses. Two of the sons grew up to become doctors, a third became a farmer, and Barnett, as I probably knew, was going to be a vet. From childhood he had known how to get along with animals. He had learned to ride before he learned to walk, and he had always enjoyed excellent health. In high school he had been on the football team, and today he served as a volunteer assistant to the coach. The intended lived with his mother, a forty minutes' drive from his university in Urbana. On Sundays, after church, he was in the habit of drinking a modest amount of beer, and outside the football season he spent a lot of time with those of his nephews who lived nearby: all three of them delightful children.

When they had finished introducing my intended brother-in-law to me, and thanking me for the wonderful tea I had prepared—that at least I did, made them tea—one of the ladies hesitantly approached the subject of religion. There were all kinds of Christians, needless to say, and they, as Christian women, were very well aware of the tremendous suffering, the terrible atrocities visited on the Jews in the name of our Lord. In their congregation everyone was very sensitive regarding this subject, and they never let anyone forget it. And so, even though they were Christians of a different kind, and she herself wondered whether those who had committed the atrocities were entitled to call themselves Christians at all, she would understand, understand perfectly, if I, as a Jewess, found it difficult to distinguish between one Christian and another. It would be inhuman and immoral to expect anything else.

I don't remember what exactly I mumbled in reply, presumably that I didn't judge people by the groups they were affiliated to, because what else could I say? But I do remember how the gray-haired auntie took off her glasses, wiped away a blue-tinted tear, and said that even though she shouldn't perhaps say what she was about to say, she would like me to know that she, as a Christian, felt a great need to ask for my forgiveness.

In my embarrassment I blurted out that there was nothing to forgive, and immediately corrected myself and said that she was not among those who needed to ask for forgiveness, and certainly not from me. The auntie replaced her glasses, even though there were still tears in her eyes, patted the back of my hand, and thanked me with a gentle smile "for being so kind and so understanding."

Politeness obliged me to thank them for their kindness to my sister: from the moment of her release from the hospital she had spent most of her time with their group.

Respect for my sister obliged me to at least make a show of reluctance to part with her.

But I behaved without politeness and without respect.

The five of us parted outside the front door. My sister went with the three evangelists to meet the other members of their group, and I went to hell.

I told Oded that what little I knew about Barnett, he already knew. "As far as I remember he's rather short, much shorter than you are, that's for sure. I don't have a picture of him, but Elisheva sent a photo of Sarah this morning. Come and have a look."

Sitting on a picket fence in denim overalls, shining wavy ginger hair and two front teeth missing—the little girl on the computer screen looked like the cheeky heroine of a children's book, or the star of a commercial for vitamins. She was as cute as they come, but it was almost impossible for me to grasp that she was family.

My sister became pregnant with Sarah when she was already over forty. Without her saying it in so many words, I understood that she had had difficulties in becoming pregnant, and I guessed, perhaps wrongly, that the problem was connected to what had happened to her. Rosemary's baby had been disposed of a long time ago, but the womb—so I imagined—had been damaged.

"Nice," Oded said looking at the picture, and massaged the back of his neck. "In the meantime it all looks very nice."

We told Menachem and Rachel that on our way to the boys in Seattle we would meet my sister, and on the Friday when we said goodbye,

Rachel hugged me and carefully said that she hoped I would find my sister in good health and that we would have a good meeting.

And Menachem said: "Enjoy the boys and the trip, and come back to us soon. I understand that Alice is taking a break, and two weekends without 'Alice in the Holy City' is more than enough. In all the negativity of the weekend papers a person wants to find a ray of light as well."

Two days before the flight, when I was downtown making final arrangements, I suddenly changed direction and completely cast off the illusion of the tourist vacation. In a last minute decision I went up to the men's office, and after greeting the secretary, without waiting to hang up my coat—I slipped into the library.

When I left the house to do some last minute shopping for the trip, I had no idea that I was about to do an about-face, no such plan entered my mind, and only when I was standing in a children's boutique to choose one more cute little garment for my niece, I was suddenly overtaken by a recognition of what was really ahead of us. Suddenly I couldn't stand the illusion of sweetness and light and the pretense. Things are not what they seem, and collaboration with deceivers is a crime.

I left the pile of sweet little dresses and blouses on the counter, and got ready to prepare myself - and perhaps also my husband—to confront reality. I had been cocooned enough, I had let him cocoon me enough, and I couldn't carry on like this.

Among the thick law books it wasn't hard to locate the single paperback. It was still covered in the brown wrapping paper in which Menachem had covered it a few years before.

A moment after I took *Hitler, First Person* from the shelf, Oded entered the room. My husband immediately recognized the book, and the welcoming smile died on his face.

"What are you doing?" he blurted, and then: "Aren't we done with that business yet? "

"What's the problem?" I looked him in the eye. "We have a long flight ahead of us, you know, I need something to read on the way."

My husband pulled up a chair and sat down on it with the ostentatious slowness of a long-suffering man. He was in the middle of the day's work. They told him that his wife had come, he popped out of his office to say hello, and was greeted by her crazy bitch version, smiling coldly as if to say, "Go on, let's see you handle this."

"Be serious. Talk to me seriously: I remember how reluctant you were when my father pressed you to read it."

"That's true."

"And you didn't want to go on reading it."

"No, I didn't want to. But apparently I've changed my mind."

"Elinor . . . Elinor, do you really seriously believe that that book is relevant to anything?"

"Why not? Why shouldn't it be relevant? What, don't you think Hitler is always relevant?"

- ß -

Flying is an inconceivable situation. When I sit in a plane, for moments at a time it seems to me that the movement of the metal through the air is nothing but a figment of my imagination. But precisely in this setting, within this inconceivability and between here and there, I succeeded in facing what had to be faced and doing what I should have done a long time ago.

The flight attendants served and cleared. Oded tried to make me read a new novel he had bought in the duty free shop. In front of us a baby cried and cried with earache. And I, strapped into my seat, the book on the tray in front of me, persevered in my task, even when we passed from light to darkness, and after the exhausted baby fell asleep, and after my husband gave up and switched off the light over his head and fell asleep.

I didn't read page by page. Submitting to the order imposed on me by this first person was out of the question. But chapter by chapter, skipping back and forth, I got through it anyway, and I read almost all of it.

On a second and calmer reading, without Chemi breathing down my neck, I realized how wrong Oded had been when he described it as "history for lazy students." Although it's possible that he wasn't really mistaken, and that he had wrapped the book in a disdainful definition simply in order to appease his wife.

No high school student could have learned history from this voice, which moved back and forth in time and mixed fact with fantasy. I am only familiar with the well-known bits of *Mein Kampf*, perhaps there were parts of this book that drew their inspiration from it, but I can say that it wasn't a manifesto along the lines of *Mein Kampf*. And as a one-time student of literature, I was struck again, this time more forcefully, by the lack of stylistic unity.

The stream of consciousness spoke in different voices that changed frequently, as if in the absence of some fixed "I": one minute it was that of a young boy gripped by self-doubt and criticism, searching for meaning, and sensitive to insult—the same Holden Caulfield with whom I was already familiar—and the next minute he was boring his readers with a bourgeois discussion of furniture. Certain paragraphs were sentimental to the point of parody—with the speaker unable to call simple things by their names—and others were full of obscenities. A pretentious philosopher gave way to a dry strategist, followed by a hurt child, a political cynic, an inspired Messiah, and a bully. Pedantry gave way to fantasy. The allusive dreams of a psychoanalytic patient were stuck onto speeches. An artist with a stereotypical sensitive and stormy soul was pasted onto an inarticulate, unfeeling brute.

The text was written in the first person singular, but the arbitrary changes of personality and style created the impression that it was not one but a number of people speaking, and therefore, in some sense, it was no one: a kind of entity that lacked permanence and solidity, that could be called by any name you chose to give it, that evaporated and evaded description by any fixed adjective. It wasn't Chemi's fault that I failed to describe the thing he put in my hands by the poolside that day on the Costa del Sol.

One of the many "I"s in the book suffers from an agonizing hypersensitivity of the senses: an ugly building, the discordant performance of a sonata, a stuffy office, all bring him to the point of fainting and the desire to put a bullet through his brain. But on the battlefield, in the stench of the trenches of the Western Front, the very same first person doesn't smell a thing, and even brags about reading Homer and feeling quite at home.

Another "I" burdens his readers with surrealistic memories and visions of death: animal carcasses and grinning skulls pile up in heaps. Living people, corpses and inanimate objects are all mixed up together, and most of the characters have no names. In this part of the text, and perhaps in the book as a whole, there seem to be more inanimate objects than humans.

One lengthy vision of a woman's body covered with "filthy snails" reminded me of something, and later on I remembered what it was: a drawing by Salvador Dali.

You couldn't call any of the narrators a necrophile, because the morbid interest of the "I" is focused mainly on the moments preceding death itself. The death in agony of "my poor, dear mother" is described in banal generalizations, but from this description the monologue passes directly to the horrors of the spring offensive at Arras where the "I" lingers at length next to a dying soldier from his company. And by the light of a hurricane lamp he observes like a scientist the seconds when life retreats and "death conquers my comrade."

The narrator hopes to see something there, some kind of revelation, he doesn't know what himself, and when he gets up and stands over the dead body of his comrade, he realizes that "there is nothing there."

This obscure conclusion is strengthened later on when the same apparent "I" goes on to observe dying enemy soldiers. He admits that the sight of their dying holds him spellbound. And years later, on the Night of the Long Knives, the narrator is unable to restrain himself from asking about the murdered men: did any of the executioners "see anything there"? The embarrassed interlocutor assures his Führer that nothing out of the ordinary was reported, and in the wake of this confirmation, the narrator is overjoyed, and confesses that he now feels as clean as a baby.

Looking into the void—says the first person—freed him from the cunning bonds of the devil.

"There's nothing there," the voice proclaims defiantly, and with the seductive swagger of a rock star he challenges his readers: "Who but me would dare to feel the pure terror of the void?"

Time and time again he fantasizes about clean ground and an unprecedented conflagration that would burn a thousand years and return its virginity to the soil. And at great length he prophecies a planet empty of human beings, where giant marble statues would take the place of the empty rotten flesh.

The first person decorated with a medal and two iron crosses is not afraid of being killed in battle, but for all his boasting, a constant dread of oblivion encircles him and threatens him like "a cloud of gas." Mocking laughter accompanies the continuing erosion of the void, the laughter returns again and again like a motif, until ringing laughter, erosion, and rot all seem one and the same.

A few of the first persons endure undoubted suffering. The reader is invited to pity the lonely, beaten, and haunted sufferer: the defeated soldier, the failed artist shivering in his poverty-stricken shelter, and especially the child, who is of course abused. But the expected empathy diminishes with the rise in the self-pitying pathos, and evaporates in the sudden transitions from self-pity to satanic pride, crude hectoring, or tedious lectures.

The hero is as proud of his suffering as his achievements, and points out among other things that at moments when others are overcome by hesitation, he alone understands that the choice is between existence and extinction, and in his genius and "the exhilaration of being backed against the wall" is able to turn defeat into victory.

On a number of occasions he compares himself to Jesus: in one place he says that death had him in its grip like Jesus, and like him he was destined to rise again, to resurrect others and to purify the earth. And in the fifth chapter, if I'm not mistaken, he threatens to expel the Jewish speculators from the Temple with a whip, just like Jesus.

The whip is also a motif: failures spur him into action like a whip. His voice lashes his audience in the beer cellar like a whip. A whip is thrust down the throat of a reporter from the *Munich Post* in a scene that seems very realistic. And in another scene, no less realistic, he beats his dog with a whip because if you don't master the dogs—the dogs will master you.

These are the whips I remember, but there were certainly more.

In one of the more coherent transitions the narrator, in his terror of the void, attempts to realize his existence in ecstasy. The ecstasy is born on the night when the boy "I" emerges from Wagner's *Rienzi* with his "faithful friend" and unfolds his "visions" to him with Linz spread out at their feet. He knows that he is destined to lead, and draws his strength from the friend and the city beneath him. Years later, during a course on "National Thinking" this formative experience returns to him before an audience of a few people, later on their numbers multiply, first tens and hundreds and then thousands and millions, and the roar of their blood "crystallizes in my flesh" into a single spirit, and silences the laughter. From now on—the narrator threatens—he is the only one who will laugh.

Art is ecstasy and ecstasy is art, he states, and as artist-actor he continuously teaches himself methods to summon the spirit and lift it from peak to peak and thrill to thrill, until it reaches the absolute realization, which is also oblivion. Loneliness vanishes when the "I" and the crowd become one, and it sometimes happens that "I come to the end of a rally so bathed in sweat that my underwear is dyed by the color of my uniform."

When he speaks of the mass rallies, the narrator ridicules the people he calls "the Jesuits," who eat the flesh of their savior and drink his blood. In a series of cannibalistic metaphors he describes how the flesh and blood of the destined redeemer is not consumed, but on the contrary: he is nourished by his audience and sucks his strength from them, until their voices emerge from his throat as one voice and their dreams unite within him into one idealistic vision.

The first person sometimes appears at three rallies on the same day, and declares that he is never tired. Youngsters like "my dear

Heidrich" sit around his table at night struggling to stay awake and trying to hide their exhaustion from him, while he, who is not deceived by their attempts, has no need to struggle: strength and movement are what create reality, and the strength that realizes itself in movement never tires and knows no mercy. It tramples those that stand in its way and grinds them to dust. One of the knights of his round table shows him a letter he received from a childhood neighbor, in which she pleads for mercy for her brother. Humanistic sentiment must be rooted out, is the leader's response. Pleas for mercy are the cunning venom of the parasites, and must be treated like the poison they are.

Does anyone complain of the ruthlessness of the sun as it moves along its determined course?

That's it. There were detailed, apparently reliable, descriptions too, of all kinds of political intrigues and maneuvers, and perhaps it was these that led Oded to describe the book as a textbook. I only encountered the word "rape" once: Europe could not be seduced with sweet words—wrote the first person—the bitch had to be raped. There was also some banal philosophizing, clichés such as: the morality of history is determined by the victors, and so on. I can no longer remember all the various incarnations of the so-called "first person," on some of them I dwelled, others I glanced through. But overall, the spirit of the text can be summed up in what I have described above.

It was a monologue by Satan; it was his apologia, and it concluded with a reference to the sun. This text, which through the use of the first person tried to turn me and all its readers into Hitler, this thing that turned Hitler's underpants into "my underpants" and stuck them to my skin—this thing was not written particularly badly, nor particularly well. It was beyond such literary judgments.

When I closed it I could not immediately find a name for it, and then the word came to me, loud and clear: the thing in my hands was unclean.

The plane had already begun its descent when I finished reading. "That's it. That's all," I said to Oded when he returned from the bathroom and threaded himself into his seat, glancing at the closed book on my tray.

But the pair of words "that's all" can be pronounced in different tones, and I repeated them over and over, and ran my voice over the entire spectrum, without knowing what exactly I meant, and what "that" was and what "all" was.

The words came gushing out of my mouth in a range of different ways—"you understand, you get it, you get it that that's all?"— until my husband put a silencing finger on my lips.

"I'm sorry. I'm sorry you decided to read it, I'm really sorry that you're allowing that thing get inside your head, and now of all times. We already decided that it was complete garbage. I can see what it's done to you."

"You're allowing" he said to me, assuming the existence of some other possibility. But it wasn't me who created a serpent, and it wasn't me who let it in to infect me.

"It didn't do anything to me," I said to him when he took his finger away. "Don't you understand, that it didn't do anything to me? That nothing got into me? You don't understand. You can't understand. Nothing got in, because it's nothing at all, it's empty. It's like a vacuum. That's it, that there's nothing there."

As I've already said, I had no idea what I was trying to say, but I know that with the words "there's nothing there" I started laughing quite hysterically, and a few minutes later we landed.

BOOK TWO
ELISHEVA

- 1 -

My husband said that he would need a stop over in Chicago to rest before the drive. I assumed that Chicago was part of the tourist game intended to calm his wife's nerves before being shut up in the car with her for four hours. Although I might have been wrong, and my salt of the earth was not so calculating in planning our trip, and all he wanted was to put off for a while the involvement with the religious cranks I was about to drag into his life.

In any case, neither of us had anything to complain about in Chicago. The woman who got off the plane laughing enigmatically found favor in the eyes of her husband, and Oded, as I have already said, always found favor in mine. Taking into account what lay ahead of us down the road, he suggested I book a room in the best hotel available—"If it's only for one night, why shouldn't we go wild?"—and I did as he said.

Five minutes after the bellboy left the room and shut the door behind him, I fell on the mini bar and straight afterward on the best of men. I was desperate to drown, and in my desperation I nipped the usual foreplay in the bud, until Oded rose up hard and shining to settle my mind, and then to settle it again, exactly as I wanted. I screamed for many waters to come and silence all the things that had no name, and my husband came and swept all the names away.

It was already evening when we decided that once we were already in Chicago we might as well go out to see the sights. And even when we went out and walked around we wanted no more than ourselves, our intoxication, and what we saw before our eyes, and we uttered only our own names and our names alone.

Oded, who had drunk only a little and whose delight in me knew no bounds, was not embarrassed even when I created a small scene in Millennium Park. A cyclist who had invaded the footpath came racing toward us and braked a few centimeters in front of me, and I grabbed hold of his handlebars with both hands and said right to his face and his dirty dreadlocks what I thought of him and his ilk. The stares of the passersby did no more than tickle me. I expressed myself in no uncertain terms and at length, and my husband made no attempt to stop me. My Black Belt stood beside me in silence, and after I finally let go and we went on walking he drew me to him and said only: "You know what, you're dangerous . . ."

A little after darkness fell we returned to the hotel, where we went on devouring each other with the concentration of people preparing for a great hunger.

Did we know that we were about to be expelled from the Garden of Eden? Something unknown and irrational—something unclean was invading our lives, and unthinkingly we tried to banish it by means of the irrational passion with which we were familiar.

The mutual conflagration died down in the morning, when Oded picked me up in the hired car at the entrance to the hotel; or more accurately I put it out myself with the aggressive coldness that overcame me and which I could not control.

I moved the seat back, preparing for the long drive ahead of us, pushed my bag under my feet, and asked in a casual, matter of fact tone: "Have you ever read *The 120 Days of Sodom*?

"Read what?" he asked, folding the road map and setting it in front of him.

"The Marquis de Sade." The name, and even more so the voice in which I said it, made him turn sharply to face me. It was the voice revealed to him on our first date—perhaps not the first, perhaps it was the third—when I first told him about the rape.

"Why would I want to read something like that?"

"I don't know. How should I know?"

My husband opened the map and folded it again. "I'm not interested in pornography," he said dryly. "You know me. *Playboy* is as far as I've ever gone, and that only when it came into my hands in the army."

"There are some people, learned people, who claim that he was the prophet of the twentieth century even more so than Kafka."

"In what sense?"

"Relations based on power, power is all that matters, total oppression, the complete absence of morality and hope. There are professors who see him as the great prophet of the gulag and the extermination camps."

"And that's what you want us to talk about this morning? The gulag and the Nazis?"

I didn't answer him: if he didn't want to know, we wouldn't talk. Fine. Nobody really wants to know, that's the system, and there's logic to the system. It exists for a reason.

"I understand that you have read it," he said when we were already in one of the slum districts in the south of the city, on our way out.

"Read what?" I asked maliciously.

"The great prophet of the gulag and the extermination camps."

"The Marquis de Sade. I may have read something once. A long time ago."

I read *The 120 Days of Sodom*, large parts of it anyway, in the university library. I read it there. The book was on the psychology department's "reserved" list, the ones you can't check out, and I sat in the library among the well-meaning psychology students, and in the exhausting neon light I forced myself to read the volume that, according to the stamps on it, had seldom been taken down from the shelves.

I read *The 120 Days of Sodom* because the Not-man had forced my sister to read it aloud to him, and because she had difficulty in reading, he read it aloud to her. That's why.

And mainly I read it because before he forced my sister, the Not-man almost tempted me to read it.

It was on one of my visits home, when with the encouragement of Erica and Shaya—"You know what our Elinor is studying now at school? They're studying Kafka"—we entered into a conversation, he and I.

I was well aware of the fact that the remarks made in a loud voice when I joined the table were directed at the guests sitting at the next table, and intended to feed my parent's self-esteem. I was aware of this, and the slightly amused expression on the face of the professor told me that he was aware of it too. The look he gave the high school student invited her to share in his amusement before the eyes and behind the backs and at the expense of the vulgar people who happened to be her mother and father.

He leaned toward me, singling me out from the others, and questioned me about what I was studying and what I thought about what I was studying. Shaya, I remember, tried to embark on one of his speeches about our-Israeli-education-system, but his cousin ignored him, and concentrated his attention on the clever daughter. He said that he was not familiar with the Hebrew translation of Kafka, and made some remark about translations into other languages. He asked me how I imagined Samsa as an insect—I shrugged my shoulders and replied "an insect"—and then he turned to the table at large and told them that Kafka had forbade any illustrations of the metamorphosis, because he wanted his readers to imagine the insect for themselves, each according to his own nightmares.

He said that he had another question for Elinor, and proceeded to ask me a question that I had not considered: was there any sense, in my opinion, in which "this petty clerk, Samsa" deserved the fate that befell him? I clearly remember this sentence with the "petty clerk" and the "befell him." The Not-man, perhaps I have already said, spoke impressive Hebrew. Embarrassed, I replied, "Obviously no one, even if he's a petty clerk, deserves to turn into an insect," and as far as I remember he took off from my reply to the Marquis, whose writings I might be interested in reading one day, and in whose opinion virtue could not expect a reward: in this world of ours the very expectation of a deserved reward was foolishness.

I think that the conversation was along these lines, perhaps it was a little different, but these were the main points, and once the name of de Sade was mentioned my mother raised the threads of her eyebrows and said: "Really, Aaron, our Elinor is still too young for such things," and Aaron replied: "Your mother is right. Your mother is always right," and smirked apologetically. And then, as if to relieve her embarrassment, he went on to play the buffoon and thumped himself a couple of times on the chest and said: "Forgive me, I am at fault. Mea culpa. Mea maxima culpa." And my mother giggled.

If he had informed me that he had works by the Marquis in his room, I would have followed him upstairs to borrow them. The Notman was interesting: far more intriguing than a Jesuit monk and an acrobat. And that same week, when I returned to boarding school, I was foolish and innocent enough to go to the school library and search the shelves for a book by the French writer de Sade.

If I had been asked, if I had spoken to anyone about it, I wouldn't have been able to point to any resemblance between *Hitler, First Person* and *The 120 Days*; no resemblance but for the piles of bodies heaped up by their writers: dead bodies in one, and copulating bodies in the other.

A different reader would have put them in two different categories. But I, even though I could see that the monotonous recording of the Marquis was obviously different from the elaborately detailed zigzags in style and consciousness of the First Person—nevertheless I sensed—more than sensed, it was as if I knew—that a single hand, a single entity, stood behind them both.

"Hand," I say, and "entity," but it wasn't really a hand. And it definitely didn't "stand." More accurately: a kind of buffoonish essence that seeped and soiled, a single fluid presence stealing in, changing one face for another.

Hitler, First Person remained in the garbage can of the O'Hare Airport, where I dumped it with a demonstrative flourish, to my husband's relief. But the person wasn't a person, and it had no boundaries, and the filth I had read penetrated and remained, with me and in me. I thought that I had to stabilize myself and confront the filth rationally and with my eyes open.

I thought: today I'm stable, stable and rational. Today it's different.

The more I thought about the First Person, the less rational my thoughts became, and the more difficult it became to fence them in or hold them in check. And it was impossible to explain any of this to the clean-shaven profile of the man by my side. Did I honestly believe that the Not-man was pursuing me and might still harm my sister? That's what the profile would have asked, that's the question my husband put to me, repeatedly and tactfully, and this rhetorical question is one that I wholeheartedly reject, because it has no right to exist.

This man, this First Person Hitler crushed my sister and destroyed what little dysfunctional family I had. But dysfunctional families have the right to exist too, and it's the only one I had. He came and crushed, and from the moment he reappeared, he haunted me, and I was indeed pursued.

- 1 -

It took us close to an hour to find our way out of Chicago, and when we got onto Route 57 I covered myself with my coat and fell asleep. Even during the most difficult periods, sleep was always available to me and it always came to me easily. One small step in my mind and I was already on the escalator carrying me to sweetness.

Oded kept quiet. I kept quiet. We drove south into plains of brown fields. Dry stalks of cut corn stretching to the horizon. Huge trucks. Road signs, a passing tractor, a bird of prey—in this yellow-brown limbo there was almost nothing for the eye or the imagination to take hold of. What could I do but sleep? I was nasty to my husband, and I knew that he would restrain himself and forgive me. The sun faded and paled beyond the flat gray expanse of clouds, and shortly before I fell asleep I was deceived into thinking that it was a full moon shining in the morning sky.

My sister lived in a town with a musical name, Monticello—"Limoncello" Oded called it jokingly—and not in Monticello itself but nearby, in a place we would be hard put to find by ourselves. After discussing it with my husband, who was confident of his ability to navigate anywhere, I arranged with Elisheva for her and her Barnett to meet us in the hotel where we were to stay, in a different town, a twenty minute drive from their home.

About thirty minutes after I fell asleep, Oded woke me up in the parking lot of a McDonald's in a quasi urban landscape. "Did you sleep a bit?" he asked in a relaxed tone and put a warm Styrofoam cup in my hand.

"I slept a lot. Did I miss anything?"

"Plenty. Especially a lot more corn. So, we're in Urbana, and because we got stuck on the way out of Chicago, we're a little behind schedule. If your sister is a punctual person, then they're already waiting for us at the hotel. I thought you'd want to wake up before we got there."

I rested my head on his shoulder. He removed the lid of my drink, and I smelled coffee and Styrofoam and the smell of my good luck's neck.

"I think everything's going to be fine. Even the weather is on our side in the meantime," said my good luck.

In hindsight I find a nice literary logic in the fact that my sister and I arranged to meet in the lobby of a hotel. We spent our childhood in a pension, many of our private experiences took place in its public space: wasn't it natural for our reunion to take place against the background of a similar décor? Wasn't it apt for the sisters to fall into each other's arms in a hotel lobby, and for their tears to mingle in precisely that place? Isn't that a pretty picture? My little pigtail-sucking Alice would have made a meal of it, and no doubt ended my story on this charming note. How nice it would be to conclude it like this, a decorative ending that massages the glands and gently strokes the heart. But to hell with the pigtail sucker from Alaska, and to hell with literature. The literary logic is false and the charm is a lie. I can definitely say that if Elisheva had lived in a normal place, Oded and I would have driven straight to her house, and that the reunion would have taken place there, not in any hotel reminiscent of any childhood pension.

Elisheva was a punctual person, and when my husband and I wheeled our suitcases into the lobby, she and Barnett were already waiting for us. At first I didn't see her, that is to say I saw someone, but not exactly my sister. All I took in was a flash of recognition and a rapid, familiar blinking, and a second later her coat exploded into mine. I think we stood there for quite a long time, in a bear hug, and I think that I closed my eyes. And when we disengaged our arms my sister said: "Oh my God, I'm so happy to see you! Thank you, thank you, thank you, my Lord, I'm so blessed."

That's what my sister said. In English.

When we disengaged our arms, I suddenly didn't know what to do. Barnett and I shook hands. The men shook hands, Oded went up to the reception desk to get the key, and Barnett insisted on taking my suitcase and accompanying us to our room. Did we want to rest? No need, the drive was very comfortable, apart from the exit from Chicago.

My brother-in-law suggested that the four of us go in their car, and although I still wasn't seeing very well, I could see that my husband had no desire to let go of the wheel. Somehow it was decided that we would take both cars, the men in one and the women in the other, and only when Elisheva opened the door of the gleaming pick-up for me, I realized that she was going to drive, my sister drove, and in fact how could she possibly live here without driving? Of course she drove, and moreover she was going to drive me.

Even before she took off her coat I noticed the change in her appearance, not exactly the details of the change, but mainly in what her body gave off. The woman who took the car keys out of her pocket was so different from the girl who walked down the corridors of the Pension Gotthilf with the bunch of keys in her hand, that they hardly seemed to be the same person. Without her coat I could see that she had grown thinner, and I was surprised that I hadn't noticed right away, because her face, framed in a stylish bob, had lost its roundness. I, who in my childhood had refused to eat, had grown rounder after my marriage, and after the pregnancies and births, in my twenties, I had started to wear a bra. Whereas my sister in the meantime had concentrated herself into a smaller body. Only her breasts under the blue sweater were still heavier than mine.

I complimented her on her appearance. "You look like a swimmer," I said and it was true, because her thick shoulders had taken on an efficient firmness that they didn't have before.

My sister smiled a gentle, grateful smile, which was familiar to me, and to my relief she began to speak to me in Hebrew. She said that while she didn't swim, she did quite a lot to keep fit: most of the people here engaged in some kind of activity, and Barnett had encouraged her in this, he was so supportive. So with all this support, she had started to run, at first only very short distances, later more and more, and today she could no longer imagine her life without it. Last Saturday Sarah's class had gone out for a country run, parents and children together, and she was so glad that she could take part and that her little girl had no cause to be ashamed of her.

Barnett's mother, she added, would take Sarah to school today, and later on, in the afternoon, Granny would bring her home to meet her uncle and aunt at last. I had no idea how excited the child was.

The men overtook us in the hired Chevrolet and disappeared around the bend in the road. The colors of the town we were passing through departed from the dreary uniform yellow of the road leading to it. Giant green trees rose high above the houses they dwarfed. Other trees blazed in autumn colors. The pavements were decorated with the red and orange of the fallen leaves, and a few orange pumpkins left over from Halloween grinned at us from doorways. Next to the street corner where the men had turned off, a huge plastic Santa Claus swayed next to a reindeer made of extinguished light bulbs lowering its head to the lawn.

"I have so many things to talk to you about," my sister said, and the old blinking gathered new wrinkles under her eyes. Her hair was dyed a darker shade than her natural color. A week before I had gone to the hairdresser to have mine dyed again.

Two little girls, one dark and one fair, which of the two is the prettiest—the grownups said—the dark one or the fair?

We drove and drove, and my sister did indeed talk without stopping, she talked like a tourist guide. This is Urbana, our big town. Our house is in this direction, in the north part of Monticello, there isn't much in the town itself, actually we only come here to visit friends. Everything you see to the right is part of the university campus. This is the football stadium, the baseball stadium is on the left. There, at the back, is the faculty of medicine and veterinary medicine where

Barnett teaches one day a week, and this is the learning dairy for the students, they moved it out of the town not long ago.

When we approached the fields of stubble again, I asked her to tell me about her life, what she did every day, and my sister shrugged her shoulders: "You know how it is, there's so much to do that you never get it all done." She kept house, she helped Barnett in the clinic, especially with the paperwork—ever since she had discovered computers it turned out that she was capable of even coping with the bookkeeping. She worked slowly—"You know how it is with me"—but Barnett never stops thanking her. With his support, her self-confidence had grown to such an extent that she even sometimes helped his mother with the paperwork for her business, which was the least she could do, because for all the urging and all the attempts, she was still afraid of horses, and she couldn't overcome this foolishness. Sarah, just like her father, sat on a horse even before she learned to walk, but this was apparently something you had to grow up with. Apart from all this, there was always community work: there were activities for the church and the Sunday school, there were sick people who needed assistance, and there was one disabled old lady, a wonderful lady, whom she assisted on a regular basis.

"So you're happy with your life," I said. My voice sounded artificial and stiff, but my sister didn't notice. "Happy? I'm blessed. I don't know why God saw fit to bless me with so much happiness."

- 3 -

A little house on the prairie, built of wood painted white, a chimney, and the triangular tower of an attic rising from its roof. Sheltered by luxuriant trees, with a squirrel trembling on a window sill and nibbling some orange vegetable. The kind of house children draw. And on the door a sign written in a childish hand: "Welcome Aunt Elinor and Uncle Oded."

A giant bulldozer had flattened hundreds of kilometers in this part of the planet. But in the place where my sister lived, on the outskirts of a little town with a musical name, the vegetation fenced off the horizon, and even hid the neighboring houses.

When we arrived the Chevrolet was already parked in the yard. My brother-in-law waved to us from the kitchen window, and an ugly old mongrel dog lying on the porch stood up to wag its tail in our honor.

"This is Soda. She's twenty-one years old," said my sister, and as she opened the door she added: "Did you hear that Daddy and his girlfriend adopted a puppy?"

As soon as we entered the house we were caught up in the inevitable exchange: were we very hungry?

"Tonight we're celebrating," Barnett announced. "But in the meantime there's lasagna for lunch. Should I make a salad as well? Will it be enough?" Were we cold? Would we like him to light a fire? What exactly were our sons doing in America? And how did they feel here? There were quite a few Israelis in Urbana, most of them connected to the university. A lot of Israelis did very well in the United States.

Oded talked about his work, and elaborated a little on the question of land ownership in Jerusalem and its political context: "The Holy City is a conflicted city."

I talked about "Alice in the Holy City" and my sister, in response, clapped her hands excitedly like a baby penguin. "So Daddy was right," she said. "Daddy always said that you would be a writer."

It was only when we laid the table that I dared to remark, and against my will my voice came out stiff and flat again: "So I understand that you're in touch with Shaya," and this time my sister registered the tone, and reacted with a look of alarm.

"Sometimes by email. More often since Sarah was born. I know how angry you are with him, because of how he left me with you and everything. You were such a heroine, I know how awful it was for you . . ." She fixed her eyes on her husband coming out of the kitchen and switched to English, and in the flood of English words coming out of her mouth everything sounded different.

In English her father was "a good man but weak, who never really recovered from all the sorrow he endured." Her father was an old man now—"we should be forgiving toward the old," my sister stated—and after Sarah was born, the old man wrote a really wonderful letter to them both, she'd been wanting to tell me about it for a long time. Among other things he wished Barnett that he would be a better father to his daughter than he himself had been to his daughters—"isn't that touching?"—and also expressed his confidence that he would be. Grandpa also sent his granddaughter an antique music box in the shape of a merry-go-round, which was one of her favorite toys. When the little girl arrived she would show me.

"I haven't forgotten," my sister said when we sat down at the table. "I know what a terrible thing he did to you and to both of us, but Daddy was never a strong person, and after Mother died, he was simply unable to function. It was so sudden. Nobody took her sickness seriously, and until the ambulance arrived, none of her doctors really listened to her or believed her. And neither did Daddy. So he must have felt . . ."

My sister's eyes filled with tears; later on I discovered that whenever our mother was mentioned, her eyes welled up like this, and my brother-in-law reached out over his plate to take her hand. As they held hands, my husband's leg moved under the table and lightly nudged my foot, but I withdrew my leg and looked down stubbornly at my lap. I felt enough, I felt too much, and my leg quickly drew back from an additional helping of feeling.

We were silent for a moment, not necessarily in embarrassment, and Barnett broke the silence by politely and rather shyly asking our permission to say a few words of prayer before we ate. With his hands clasped and his eyes closed my brother-in-law thanked God for the food before us, and went on to thank him "for bringing us Elinor and Oded who we always prayed to meet. May they take joy in us as we take joy in them. And may each of us find in this coming together what he wishes for and what he needs."

After that we ate lasagna.

Believable things order themselves. Those that are beyond belief have to be described in an orderly fashion: We drove, we arrived, we spoke. She said to me. I replied. And I shall try to record things in order: the first day with my sister, the second day, the third day—

There was no third day with my sister. I stayed in her unbelievable world for only two days, and after we parted, things became disturbed and disordered in the extreme. Not things—everything became disturbed and disordered, but in the meantime there was order: order and sweetness, bright sweetness and order, and unbelievable goodness poured down abundantly on the white wooden house on the prairies of Illinois.

It seemed that my sister was eager to present me with the entire contents of her life in the brief time we spent together, and the afternoon of the first day was crammed with introductions, here's a ginger tomcat and here's a she cat. This iron pot Barnett inherited from his grandmother, feel how heavy it is. Here, in the back, is the entrance to the clinic. Barnett doesn't actually spend much time there, he does most of his work on the farms. He bought those two peacocks last summer. He calls them his conceit. They're beautiful, that's true, but their screaming is really ghastly, and the worst of all is when they suddenly scream in the middle of the night. You'd think that such a beautiful bird would sing like a canary, but no. The Creator likes surprises.

If we go past the clump of trees over there, we'll be able to see the stream. The water's clean, in the summer Sarah swims in it with the dog, but now that Soda's getting old she's begun to develop an aversion to swimming. Perhaps they should get another dog for the child, take in a puppy like Daddy and Gemma did, but Barnett says that even though Soda's very tolerant with the cats, another dog in the house is liable to make her jealous and embitter her old age.

•

The house is crammed full of photographs. Group portraits with gleaming teeth. Children stiff in suits. Children in swimsuits decorated with medals on ribbons. Sports teams, one row kneeling and two standing. The boy Barnett on a horse. The adult Barnett on a horse. Sarah on a horse. Barnett with the baby Sarah on a horse. My sister carrying a white tower of a cake.

Bright testimonies to happiness as happiness ought to be hung in the living room and the bedrooms and even on the wall of the clinic. And because of this overload of family happiness it was only in the evening that I noticed the photographs of our parents, standing side by side on a shelf over the fireplace. They were photographs that I knew: the young Shaya, in faded half-profile, emphasizing the jaw muscle and exposing the weak mouth, holding a sheet of music, and directing his gaze obliquely upward.

Erica, about half my age, looks as if she has dressed up as an actress from the thirties: eyebrows thin as a hair. Eyelids shining with Vaseline. Mouth darkly painted. A perfect complexion and an exhausted expression. A wreath of babies-breath flowers on her wavy hair.

In the ugly, hasty days during which the place we called home was emptied of its contents—among gaping boxes, and furniture pushed aside and waiting to be sold, and cast off objects that nobody wanted; among heaps of dust, and scattered papers bearing footprints, and the stacks of Shaya's books sent in one lot to the shredders—in those hasty and ugly days, I paid no attention to the photograph albums. And even if I had, I don't think I would have taken a single photograph from them. But Elisheva in the depths of her grief and her sickness paid attention and took and hid. I suppose she hid, because in our basement flat, of that I'm certain, no photograph revealed its presence.

•

When we were finished with the house and the yard, we got back into the pick-up, and my new sister drove her guest to smear additional layers of paint on the picture of the little town in the background: this is Monticello's square, this is Monticello's café, this is its church—"not ours, ours is in Urbana."

And I was driven and escorted, and I nodded and murmured appreciatively, and expressed my admiration at the beauty of it all. And all the time I never stopped thinking about my blindness: how could I have failed to understand that my sister in the midst of her insanity was also mourning our mother?

The death of our mother was, as they say, a difficult event. It also led to a chain of events that were very difficult for me indeed. But even with all the difficulty, Erica herself—my mother the deserter, the perfumed narcissist who opened the door—I didn't miss for a moment.

And on the great days of a woman's life, her wedding day and the birth of her children, this woman said to herself that she was actually glad to be rid of her mother's lilac scent.

My father and my sister wept bitterly on our mother's grave, and I looked on skeptically at my father's impressive mourning and his gestures of grief, and closed my eyes to my sister's sorrow.

In any case, whatever I did and whatever I didn't do in the days of the basement apartment, the damage was already done, and it was irreparable. And the little I could do to repair it was to accept: to accept the fact that Elisheva missed our mother. My sister pined for the woman who had exploited and abandoned her, and absconded to her eternal rest when she could no longer deny her crimes, and all I could do was to accept it without challenging or arguing with her.

•

I promised order, and I shall now accordingly return to the proper order of things, where afternoon is followed by evening, an evening in which the white wooden house filled with guests.

"This is Mark, he works with Barnett at the university, Eve is his wife, a very dear soul. This is Iris, and Martha you must remember, she visited us when we were still living in our apartment in Talpioth."

One after the other they deposited their aluminum trays in the kitchen and came to shake our hands and inquire after the peace of Jerusalem. And then they stood around beaming brightly at us, because God loves the Jews, and because we came from the Holy City, and because I was the sister of dear Elisheva: I was the heroic sister who had taken care of her so devotedly after the tragedy.

For all these things they admired and loved us so much that the air grew steamy with love, relaxing tense muscles as in a sauna.

"I remember your special tea," Martha said to me and patted my shoulder.

Barnett's mother brought Sarah. Bearing a towering chocolate cake before her, the beautiful little girl greeted her uncle and aunt with self-confident courtesy, without a trace of shyness, and after her father relieved her of the cake she wrapped herself around us and listened with a frown of concentration to every word we said.

It occurred to me that our Nimrod, who was fond of children and got on well with them, would have fallen in love with his little cousin at first sight. And it was a good thing that Atlanta was far away, and he wouldn't have the opportunity to fall in love with her. Little children take in things that adults have no idea of. This was without a doubt a child who listened, and there was no knowing what she had heard from her parents and what might come out of her mouth even without her understanding what she was saying.

During the course of the years I had fed my children quite a consistent version of "our tragedy", so to speak—a difficult, but not dangerously poisonous story. A story you could cope with. A world you could live in, a picture of the world you could live with, the provision of which, like a meal and a shower, is no more than the basic duty a mother owes her children, and which every healthy instinct prompts her to provide.

Atlanta was far away, and no innocent remark would reach my son's ears to injure and agitate him.

More guests arrived: one of Barnett's brothers, tall and hollow-cheeked and not at all like him, and the son of another brother, and others as well. The women, without waiting for instructions, laid the table. Amid the buzz of conversation I heard my husband's voice talking about politics, and I saw people standing around him and nodding with expressions of sincere concern inappropriate to the occasion.

After making sure that all the guests were equipped with plates of food, my brother-in-law invited his mother to say grace, and once again the Lord was praised for the food and for "our very dear guests. You all know how Elisheva and Barnett longed to see them."

Later on in the evening the mother hobbled over to me. Mrs. Davis, a sturdy woman with lizard-like skin, her white hair tied up in a pony tail with a redundant and rather dirty velvet ribbon, gave me a clumsy pat on the shoulder. And almost immediately, without preamble, she said to me: "Your sister is a real treasure. Did she tell you that last Sunday she agreed to read to us from the Bible in Hebrew? Up to then we understood that she was shy and we didn't want to press her. But we're all so happy that she succeeded in overcoming her shyness: hearing the Psalms in Hebrew was an experience that people here won't forget. I just want you to know how much we all love her, and how much we all admire the way you cared for her. I have an eye for these things and I can see that you're a very special person."

Once again, the legend about my devotion and strength. I didn't know how to react to this falsification, whose source was without a doubt in my sister; my sister, who—and this too is certain—didn't have a clue that she was falsifying.

I muttered something to the effect that Elisheva had always been wonderful and that I hadn't done anything, and was immediately overcome by disgust. The expression on Mrs. Davis's face told me that she had interpreted my automatic disclaimer as evidence of the virtue of modesty. My father had been an expert in such affectations of humility.

"I also want to thank you for the accepting way in which you related to my son," she continued complimenting me in Americanese. "He told me how understanding you were when you first met in Jerusalem."

"It wasn't difficult. You have a wonderful son," I mumbled, because what could I say?

She agreed that Barnett was a good boy, but not everyone would have seen this when the child was in the throes of his crisis. "Thank you for being so non-judgmental and accepting. In the state he was in then, a lot of people would have had a hard time seeing who my son really is." She lowered her voice to a near whisper that sounded louder than a normal speaking voice in my ears, "And they would have been concerned, you know, about the genetic question. I hope your mind has been put at ease in this matter and that you've been informed that there have never been any cases of schizophrenia in our family: neither in mine nor in my late husband's."

I wondered what the horse breeder would have said if she had known that our genetic dowry included a suicide and a rapist.

For one wild moment I was tempted to tell her the whole truth about us, just to see how she would react.

"Barnett is a very special person," I said instead. And as I parroted this American cliché my palate sensed a taste of parody, and for a moment I felt a pang of guilt. Mrs. Davis was good to my sister, what right did I have to mock her? I didn't want to mock her, not even secretly to myself.

As far as I could judge, it seemed that the version Mrs. Davis had heard about the rape was similar to the one that my father-in-law and mother-in-law had heard from me. But unlike in our family, in the little white house on the prairie, the horror was simply registered as a given: a foal was born, the corn grew, the winter was late, one of our pilgrims went out of his mind in Jerusalem, and the wife he brought home with him was a victim of rape.

Because it was clear to me at this stage that not only her mother-in-law but everyone in the room knew everything about Barnett's hospitalization and also something about my sister's ordeal. The knowledge lay there in the room like the "Israeli salad' Elisheva had prepared in our honor, and the next day I received an explanation when we went for a walk in the park.

Elisheva, of course, hadn't divulged the details of the rape to anyone, but everyone in the room knew that she had been "sexually molested," and the whole congregation had heard about the breakdown of her family and the miraculous manner in which the Lord had brought about her meeting with the man intended for her.

"Imagine that somebody saves your life," my sister explained, "not only saves your life but really saves you, your soul. Wouldn't you want people to know about him and what he did for you? Think how ungrateful it would be to hide it. Our Lord Jesus raised me from the depths. Even if I lived for a thousand years, a million years, it wouldn't be enough to thank him. What kind of a person would try to hide such a miracle?"

Neither at that moment, nor at any subsequent moment was I tempted to enter into a theological debate with my sister and to ask her who had plunged her into the depths in the first place. Her face was radiant with a shy confidence, and I thought that "our Lord Jesus" as she called him had given her what no psychologist had been able to give her. I couldn't fail to be impressed by his power.

In a little village somewhere on the prairie lived a modest old couple whose fame had spread far and wide. They were known as "The teachers of love," and heartsick people came to them from the ends of the land to be taught the secret of the healing powers of love.

Many years ago the old man brought his wife to the village. He was very sick. She was wounded. Even the woolly sheep in the pen could sense her terrible pain, and whenever she stroked them they would bleat sadly under her hand.

But the man and his wife did not despair or sink into self-pity. Love is a balm that works slowly, and with endless patience they continued to brew their balm, until its effect became evident in them both. Their eyes grew bright. Their complexions grew fresh. The woman's figure grew shapely. Love covers a multitude of sins. And love covered all and ransomed every wound. And it shed its grace on their beautiful daughter, and on their neighbors, and on every living thing around them, and all their eyes brightened. Broken-winged songbirds began to sing again. Blind dogs regained their sight and frolicked in the meadows. A vicious thief who came to steal their cattle went to work as an orderly in the hospital.

"Love is a daily labor," the old woman instructs the lost youth who finds his way to their door. At the beginning of summer the youth ran away from home; in the course of his wanderings he heard about the "teachers of love," and one morning he simply knocked at their door.

"We do our daily work," the old woman said to him, "and the Lord performs his labor of love. As he did for me. Sit here, at my feet, next to the stove, and I'll tell you my story. You're old enough to hear it."

Far, far away in a little village, in a village where all the people are radiant, a magical old man and woman lived in happiness and love. Perhaps they are still living there to this day, and in this happiness our story concludes.

Nothing was concluded. What was concluded? How could it possibly end like this? The voice was the voice of Alice, coming to seduce me into this happy final solution. But it was as false and deceitful as usual, and my sister, even if she lived to be a hundred, would never say a sentence like: "Sit at my feet and I'll tell you my story."

The story wasn't over and done with, and even as the voice of the chronic enthusiast tried to seduce me into locking it up like this, I knew that it would go on twisting and turning in my guts. Not for a moment did I forget the mission on which I had come—a slithering snake, a poisonous Not-man was threatening to invade the walls— and even then I doubted the power of love to seal them.

My sister would go on living long after her fair hair went completely white. Amen. And I, the dark sister, whose duty is was to tell her—this time I would know how to protect her. I would protect her so that she lived a long and happy life and so that in her old age people would come from the ends of the earth to witness the miracle of the resurrection she deserved.

I will not allow my sister to be hurt again. I will not allow it—I swear. I am no longer what I was, I am not a child, I am not a fool, I have strength, and the past will not repeat itself. There will be no more harm done.

I repeated these things to myself. And even as I repeated them, my heart sickened and rejected the foreign transplant of the happy end.

•

But once again I'm losing the thread and getting ahead of myself. Because at this stage nothing had yet been explained to me—my marveling eyes saw only happiness—and at this stage it was still evening in the little white house: snatches of small talk sail through the air, someone puts on a CD of soul music. Out of the corner of my eye I saw Oded putting on his coat and going outside to talk on his cell phone. Elisheva, who had left the room to put her daughter to bed, came back and said that the child was asking for her aunt to come and kiss her good night.

Sarah's room was in the attic, and when I came in a ginger head rose behind a mauve net canopy, and a lively voice inquired: "So what are our plans for tomorrow?"

"Tomorrow you're going to school, after that you have athletic club, and now we're going to sleep," my sister replied and bent down to tuck in the blanket.

"I know, but what about after that?"

"We'll see."

"Will we have time to play?" The little face turned toward me and my heart contracted at the sight of its perfect innocence. "I know a game that you and Mommy used to play. Mommy taught it to me. You tie a scarf around your eyes and then you throw a ball and try to catch it." She seemed about to get up and demonstrate, and Elisheva gently pushed her back. "Goodnight, goodnight now."

"I know who taught you to play that game," said Sarah after we kissed her and turned to leave the room. The experienced mothers took no notice, but when we were at the door, a little voice full of satisfaction said: "I really do know. He was an acrobat, that's what he was. And you were both little and you were dressed like princesses."

- 4 -

After all these experiences, all this emotion, isn't it time for me to give myself and others a bit of a rest? Time to slow down and take a breath?

I could, for example, turn my gaze from people and their distraught passions and follies to the splendors of nature. I could rest my eyes on the natural miracle of the leaves, and their famous glories.

Leaves, how wonderful are the mysteries of the leaves: the green that year after year with the coming of the cold flames into shades of red on the trees. The crimson that dies into brown and yellow on the ground. The delicate skeletons of damp, transparent leaves—isn't this a work of art? The changing of the seasons, the carnival of colors, the invisible hand of the creator of the leaf—such things, they say, calm the mind. The tired head rests on a hill, the eye follows the complex dance of the clouds mating in the sky. The hand caresses clods of earth. Calm caresses the eyelids. Breathing grows quiet. Eyes slowly close and languidly open again. The sun goes down behind the trees and sets them on fire before it finally sinks. And a great consolation comes with the setting of the sun, a great consolation, because we know that tomorrow the sun will surely rise and shine again, and the dead will live again, and we can sense the cycle of life and death in its eternity. The stillness of nature in all its glory. Quiet, hush. How great is the glory that surrounds us, sublime beyond comprehension, and the silence of the falling leaves and the mystery of their beauty is mightier than all our noise.

Perhaps we should pause here to contemplate the magnificence of nature in this place, but when we left my sister's house it was already dark. Apart from the distant lights of the expressway we couldn't see a thing, and even in daylight I did not and do not tend to take an interest in the scenery. Nature in all its mystery and glory doesn't speak to me or tell me anything, apart from whatever is preoccupying my thoughts in any case.

My good Oded differs from me in this. My husband loves taking trips to the desert, he likes the silence and the quiet.

What he doesn't like, however, are the mysterious silences of his wife.

"Nice people," he remarked when my silence lasted all the way to the interchange. "It's quite strange to meet people who love Israel so much today. It seems as if nothing we do could make them speak a word of criticism against us." His wife kept quiet and he, in response, started to babble: "So yes, it's strange when you think about the kind of country we actually live in. But on the other hand . . . on the other hand, I wouldn't object to adopting a bit of their love, five percent, say, just as an antidote, because in contrast to these people you suddenly realize how exaggerated our self-hatred is: how we hate ourselves out of all proportion."

"At least you can't say that I lied to you," I blurted.

"You? Me?"

"I told you from the beginning that I had a crazy sister."

"Crazy?' he pronounced the word as if examining a new concept. "Do me a favor . . ."

"Do you mean the religious thing? So, as a Jew, even though I'm secular, obviously all that Christianity gets on my nerves a bit. Jesus was never our best friend. But if we're talking about believers in general: I know quite a few religious people from work, you know some too, and neither of us would say that a belief in God is a sign of insanity."

"Are you telling me you didn't see that she's crazy?"

"Not at all," he cut straight into the summing-up speech he had prepared for me, a speech he had definitely prepared in advance. "Look, I know something, I know a little about the hell she went

through. And the woman I met there is a woman who has completely, completely rehabilitated herself. Her life is full, she has a husband
and a lovely little girl. You can see she's a wonderful mother. If these
aren't measurements of sanity, I don't know what are. And apart
from all that, she seems to be happy. How many people can you say
that about? A lot of people could wish for a life like hers."

"Fine," I said shortly.

"What's fine?"

"Fine. You also read *Hitler, First Person* and thought it was a history book for high school students."

"And that's not legitimate?"

"Legitimate? No, it's not legitimate to not see."

"To not see what?"

"What's right in front of your eyes."

If he hadn't been so tired he would probably have left it at that
and avoided confrontation. He knew his wife. In most cases he
knew very well when to let sleeping dogs lie, and in general my
husband was an expert at the art of letting things be. But Oded was
exhausted. Before the flight he had worn himself out at the office. In
Chicago we hardly slept. On the way there, while I slept, he drove.
And despite all this, and despite the jet lag, my aristocrat had not lost
his civility and graciousness among the crowd of religious cranks
into which I had dragged him, and apart from one brief escape into
the yard, he had shown no sign of sulking.

Like a lot of other men, Oded tends to deny fatigue. And I think
that it was this denied fatigue which overcame his restraint and
good judgment, and which made him provoke me by asking if I still
believed that I should warn my sister. The resentment in his tone
revealed his opinion, which he immediately went on to explain, without waiting for my reply: My sister was happy, she had been beside
herself with joy to see me, so why ruin her happiness for nothing?

Who would it help, and how, exactly? What had happened had happened, what was done was done, and I knew as well as he did that no concrete danger was at hand. True, our insolent uncle had tried to make contact, but so what? If we were serious for a minute, we could agree that this did not constitute a real danger. My sister had found stability, after all she had been through—she was happy now, and anyone who took the risk of undermining that stability would be making a big mistake. You didn't spoil people's happiness, you didn't wake sleeping dogs, or cry over spilled milk—it would be both unfair and unwise to do so.

I leaned my head against the back of the seat, I looked into the darkness and I listened to my husband telling me that I was, in effect, not normal: seeing the shadow of mountains as wolves, about to terrorize my sister and pour cold water on her illusion of happiness. That I was not wise and not fair.

And he went on to interpret and rewrite the real meaning of my journey to me: what he saw as its hidden purpose and what in his innocent cunning he hoped that I would adopt as its purpose.

Estrangement between sisters was an unnatural and unhealthy situation, he said, especially when the women in question were fundamentally dear to each other. Families were always complicated. Sometimes people needed a time-out in their relationships, but he believed that by now I had matured sufficiently to renew the connection, and it seemed to him that the intrusion of that creep had simply provided me with a pretext to renew it.

I touched the frosty window and yawned. We had turned onto the expressway, which in fifteen minutes would lead us to the hotel and to bed.

The lighting on the road was meager and Urbana, which still lay ahead, was also in darkness. Ten o'clock at night, not even ten. People here went to bed early.

"We had a good day," said my husband. "You had a good day with your sister. Why spoil a good thing?"

It was time to speak. "Tell me," I asked, "did you get the impression that my sister is retarded?"

"What are you talking about?"

"Tell me."

I heard him take a deep breath. He opened the window a little to let the air in, perhaps to pray for patience before he answered me.

"Did I say anything or do anything to make you think that's what I thought? I don't think so. And no, Elinor, the answer is no. I don't think your sister is retarded. Apart from the religious business, which is beside the point, the impression your sister made was one of a pleasant and intelligent person."

"I'm glad to hear that you think so. I'm glad to hear this is your diagnosis, because a lot of people think or thought that my sister is retarded. And retards, as you know, can't make decisions on their own. I, as opposed to all kinds of people, definitely don't think she's retarded, and if that insolent creep, as you call him, if that creep has now emerged from the sewers to intrude on our lives, then to the best of my understanding, to the best of my understanding she has the full right to know. Just make up your mind what you think: either she's a retard who needs to be protected from the facts, or not. Just make up your mind and tell me if my sister has any rights."

He didn't make up his mind and he didn't tell me, and the last kilometers of the road passed by in silence. We drove into the town, passed more inflated reindeers and Santas, and didn't see a living soul until we reached the hotel.

By the time Oded had finished tidying the car and removing various items from the bags we had left there before, I was already in the shower, and by the time I emerged from the shower, he was already asleep. I slipped in under the blanket and waited. For quite a long time I waited, patiently and humbly, until my good, tired soldier turned on his side, and without waking up put his arm around me.

- 5 -

llerton Park is just the thing for souls seeking consolation in the glories of nature: for this purpose precisely, explained my brother-in-law, had the English garden been planted here in the first place, in the heart of the prairie.

A man named Allerton had planted it, and after he himself had found healing there, he had bequeathed his garden and estate to the community, so that anyone in need would always find consolation in it.

Kilometer upon kilometer of the glories of nature: trees and ferns and autumn leaves, etc., and in the heart of the park an avenue, and at its end a pagoda, where seekers of serenity could emulate the golden example of a statue of the Buddha.

Allerton Park, to which we had driven after dismissing the options of the historical-ethnological museum and the Urbana shopping mall.

I wanted a place where I could conduct a private conversation with my sister, and all the glories of the setting left me indifferent, even though Elisheva kept pointing them out to me: Look how tall that tree is. Quick, look over there, a wild bird.

My sister announced the objects to me as if she were out walking with an infant who needed to be taught to look and call things by their names.

The considerate men went ahead of us down the avenue, the tall one and the one who looked short next to him, and when they turned a bend and disappeared into the vegetation, I stopped and stood still.

"There's something I have to tell you," I said to her.

The toes of her shoes were a little scuffed: only when I had finished saying what I had to say I raised my eyes from them. "Oded thinks there's no need to tell you," I added straight to her face, which had already turned pink from the cold, "but I think that if he succeeded in tracing my cell phone, then there's a possibility, a faint possibility, that he'll find you too. So even if there's only a small chance, it seems to me that you have the right to know."

This time it was Elisheva who averted her eyes, turning toward me a cheek that still preserved a degree of childish plumpness. "He doesn't have to search for my address," she said. "I gave it to him."

"You what?"

"I sent it to him. I didn't give him my phone number, but once he has my address . . ." Her voice petered out. She blinked madly; yesterday I had noticed that she blinked a lot less than in the past, and now she seemed frightened again: frightened like a child caught red-handed, her profile trembled, and to my horror I realized that my sister was afraid of me. Of me, and not of the serpent. I wanted to shake her, to grab hold of her shoulders and shake her hard until it rid her of the unfairness, the shocking unfairness of being afraid of me.

I looked into the distance, all the way down to the end of the avenue, and only then raised my hand to gently touched her cheek.

"It's all right," I said. "Take your time. I understand. Sometimes when something frightens us, we almost want it to happen already. I know. Precisely when the enemy hides . . . sometimes the most terrible thing is not knowing."

What did you write to him? When did you write to him? Where did you get his address? And perhaps it wasn't just one letter but several that you wrote? And how did he keep his hold on you without my having a clue, without anyone having a clue, because it was inconceivable that anyone would know this terrible thing and not scream so loudly that it reached your idiot sister in Jerusalem, your blind and deaf sister, so that she could come and save you, snatch you away, lock you up if necessary, whatever was needed to separate you from this thing, who perhaps you hadn't only written to but also met, because he instructed you to meet him, and you didn't know any better and you could do nothing else, because one-hundred-twenty days of Sodom are never over? I know, I know how they're never over. Not even one day is ever over.

"It's all right," I repeated, gathering all my strength to stop the whirlpool sucking us in, demanding that we face what would come afterward: after she had confessed everything to me.

My sister inclined her head in a movement that signaled neither "yes" nor "no," and with a confused expression repeated that she had a lot to tell me, and for a long time now she had really wanted to tell me, but she wanted to so badly and there was so much to tell that she didn't know how to begin.

There wasn't a single bench to sit on in the whole park, only damp, freezing ground from the long nights. Elisheva seemed to be thinking the same thing.

"Will you be cold if we sit on the steps?" she suddenly came up with a solution.

We sat in the partial cover underneath the statue of the Buddha, my sister on my right, the green of the park in the background woven into the latticework of the pagoda. The bright red of a bird flitted past the white of the latticework, and Elisheva smiled unexpectedly and asked me if I remembered the Belgian birdwatchers, the ones we called "the twins," and who were actually husband and wife? They were funny, weren't they, with their pointed noses, and their binoculars? But thanks to them she had learned to pay attention to the birds, and perhaps thanks to them she had bought bird-feeders last year and hung them on the trees in the yard, when we got home she would show them to me. The winters here were hard, and for the little birds they were particularly difficult.

I tucked my coat in underneath me, Elisheva played with her glove, and I waited, my head lowered, for her to begin.

Her first years here hadn't been easy. She was like a person who had suddenly come into a fortune, a person to whom God had suddenly granted this fortune. A person who at first doesn't comprehend the extent of his riches. Who doesn't understand and doesn't really know how to live with such a great blessing, the likes of which he didn't know existed, and for which he was not prepared. Back in Jerusalem, when she was in the hospital, she had started to read the bible, and while she was still there she had accepted that God was her Lord, and that everything that was written, every word, was the truth. This was the first treasure that our Lord had given her: that he had revealed his gospel to her. But even after she had accepted the gospel of Christ, she still had a lot to learn, because she read slowly, and because she was, as I knew, "slow in general." Barnett didn't press her. He said over and over that everything in creation was the will of God, and that everything had a purpose, including her difficulties and his difficulties and the difficulties of both of them together. And she really knew even then, with her whole heart she knew, that God loved her, that he loved all his children, and God, who knew everything and saw everything, also knew how hard she was trying to understand what he wanted of her and how to give him all of herself, to give him her whole heart, which he had given her.

But even with this knowledge, even with all the love that God granted her, it still wasn't easy. People were wonderful to her. So wonderful and so generous. They were so generous in giving her the time she needed. And she really needed time to learn the simplest things: to drive a car, to get onto the expressway. To go to the bank, to be a wife. Because this, being Barnett's wife, being his mate, was one of the most difficult challenges in the inconceivable bounty that had been showered on her. The pastor's wife advised them to go to therapy, and they did indeed go to the psychologist Mindy found them, they went together and also separately. The therapy was yet another gift. Their therapist in Urbana had helped her more than all the others she had seen previously, not because the previous ones had been bad, most of them were good people and they had really tried to help her, but now the whole situation was completely different, because she was now able to receive the gift.

"My God who bore the cross with me and for me, Jesus Christ who subjected himself to suffering and to the most terrible humiliations to which a person can be subjected . . ." My sister's voice grew full. I dared to glance at her: her eyes were full of tears, and she blinked to get rid of them. "Jesus told me that I was clean, that he had cleansed me when he was crucified for my sake. When you realize this, that you have been purified and that you are pure, then you really are, from the moment you accept God you are no longer dirty, and after that you are open to receive his grace. And what happened was that I was opened to receive his grace, and all the other wonderful gifts that he in his grace granted me. Including the gift of psychotherapy."

The new psychologist helped her, as she said, "with the problems of self-image" that she had, and it also helped that she referred her to an additional specialist who diagnosed her particular learning disabilities: it turned out that she suffered not from a single disability, but from two syndromes combined, which clouded the diagnostic picture. The process took time, actually years, during the course of which there was an interval of nearly two years because the money she and Barnett could allocate to treatment ran out, but little by little she understood that "there are methods of coping with a problem like mine, methods developed by different people that can help me and a lot of others like me."

And then, with the new abilities she had acquired: "I also gradually internalized the fact that even if I'm not brilliant—I'm not stupid either, like I thought I was before."

I looked at her again; this time she saw me looking, and blushed and smiled at me without resentment, as if she was telling me a story that was all happiness.

And what did I do? I rested my cheek on my knees drawn up under my chin, and listened to my little big sister, this sister who many, many years ago had tucked me into bed. I listened until I was all attention and nothing but attention, and let the story cover me.

Long, long ago we had shared a room. Later on we shared madness and an apartment. In the times we shared she told me stories, but she had never been the heroine of any of the stories she told.

The red bird came back and perched on the lattice, and in a place with a red bird and a white pagoda anything is possible, if only for a moment—even entering into a story without any resentment in it.

•

The man and his wife longed for a child—"In the beginning Barnett would joke about persuading me to have four"—it seemed that God had blessed them with everything, except the child they yearned for more and more. The woman tried fertility treatment, five attempts failed, the money ran out, and the couple accepted that it was God's will directing them for the time being along another path.

"One of Barnett's sisters-in-law, a brilliant woman, is a professor at the university, and she often left her two little ones with us. Among the other problems I had with my self-image were quite a few fears about what kind of a mother I would be to my own children. That's another thing I worked on in therapy. But it turned out that these two kids were the ones who helped me most. Does that make sense? Then I didn't understand it, but it was as if God were saying to me: Be patient, before I entrust a new soul to your hands, we'll give you a course to complete. So I completed the course," her voice filled with an unfamiliar mischievousness, "and apparently nobody has any complaints about the results."

From the way my sister spoke it was clear to me that this wasn't the first time she was telling the story about the man and his wife, and presumably not only to herself. But from the moment she embarked on the story of which she was the heroine, from the moment she began telling this fairytale, with pauses in just the right places, I became a willing audience, happy to let her proceed at her own pace, to postpone the entrance of the snake, and put off everything I still had to say to her.

The nephews grew. Their parents found work in another country. The house emptied of children's laughter, and Elisheva went on waiting patiently for a sign from her God. "All the gospels say clearly that we mustn't be egoists, and that we shouldn't think too much about ourselves," she said to me, not as a stern sermonizer but like a serious, rather tired, little girl being tested on what the sermon said. "What the gospels try to teach us is to go beyond ourselves, beyond our private needs in order to serve others. When I was in therapy I thought a lot about myself, because that's what it's like in therapy, you know. But Barnett, and also our pastor's wife, both of them persuaded me that it was what I had to do in order to be able to serve our Lord better. And they were right . . . they were right. Because you see, after everything Jesus gave me, after everything, this was what I prayed for most: for God to show me how he wanted me to serve him."

The voice of the storyteller faltered, retreated, and died. It seemed that my sister's thoughts were wandering and that she wouldn't be able to lead her story to its happy end—and what would I do with this end? And what would I do after it? What could you do with something once it was done? Maybe it was better this way, without an end because that was, in fact, the truth, that it went on and was still going on, not for one hundred twenty days, but forever.

The hand playing with the glove clenched into a fist and then opened again, a hollow palm lying limply on her knee.

"Sometimes I thought that God hadn't completely forgiven me yet. That was hard for me," she said and I felt my insides tensing like a bowstring. "Because after the Valley of the Shadow of Death that Aaron put me through, somehow I believed . . ." She pronounced the name "Aaron" with the same simplicity as she had pronounced the names of the birds before.

"You remember how his typewriter clattered?" she suddenly asked. "You remember how we could hear it even downstairs? So all the time I knew that somehow it belonged to me too, the book about Hitler. That's what I knew, that the clacking belonged to those things he did to me, even if I didn't understand how. Even now I think, and Barnett says so too: there were so many victims in the Holocaust, all the people . . . the children who suffered, the mothers who lost everything, so why Hitler? Why about him? How come?

How come people don't know about all the children, why just about Satan . . ."

She knew about the publication of the book. One evening, about two years after she arrived in her little town—"We were still living in a different house then"—when she was taking clothes out of the dryer, she heard his name on TV.

For a minute she wasn't sure if it was his name she had heard. "You know, there are all kinds of people called Aaron, and even though I was stronger, I still wasn't so strong, so sometimes when people said "Aaron" or some name that sounded like it, I would suddenly panic as if it were him."

She went into the living room and "there was nothing there," in other words he himself wasn't there on the screen. But the newscaster described how Professor Gotthilf had been attacked when he entered the television studio of some other network: a woman, a holocaust survivor, who was lying in wait for him tried to spray his face with acid.

"I called my husband," my sister said. "But he was nowhere to be found. It was before cellphones, and without cellphones the situation was difficult. I know that if God hadn't been there with me . . ."

But this time my sister's God didn't abandon her, and the survivor who had tried to burn Aaron's face with acid didn't go away either.

"I thought about her a lot, all the time, in an obsessive kind of way, as if it was important to me to understand how she missed, if she had been standing closer maybe she wouldn't have missed. They didn't describe it on TV, how exactly it happened, but I put myself in her place and asked myself if I would've missed too. You see, I had this kind of fantasy that I was in her place and that I didn't miss, and in the picture stuck in my head I kept on and on burning his face. Let him burn, let him die. And then let him die again, but slowly.

Like in Hell. Where it goes on forever and you know that it will never end because Hell is the end."

I loved my sister. Am I permitted to say that I loved her in spite of the miserable way I treated her? I loved her. But I never loved her as much as I did at that moment, when she bit her glove, and at the same time I saw her going up in flames: she never even noticed when I put my hand on her knee.

And then she continued, in the same voice as before, in the same compulsive rush: "That was my nightmare, that I couldn't stop. As if there was no end to it, all the time I saw his face. And it's strange, because before that, before I heard about that old woman with the acid, I never thought about his face at all, as if I didn't remember it at all. And only when I imagined the acid, corroding, did I suddenly began to remember, and all the time that face of his, as if it were getting into my eyes. I wanted it to stop, I prayed, but it was as if my will didn't count, as if I was nothing, as if I didn't exist any more. And I wanted to exist. I already existed, God had brought me back to life. So I couldn't understand, I just couldn't understand why, how come God, who had been so good to me, was letting him haunt me, and poison my existence."

My sister kneaded and rubbed her forehead and her cheeks; there were no tears, she rubbed at her dry skin. "They sometimes say about God that he 'hides his face,'" she said, "it's a saying. But God's God, and he doesn't really hide his face, it only seems that way to us. Today I understand that God didn't abandon me even for a minute. That's absurd, because God doesn't abandon. Today I believe that he was only waiting for me to banish that other face, the face of Aaron that was hiding him from me. It took me time, it took me a lot of time to understand that that's what he was waiting for, and years before I gradually succeeded in getting rid of Aaron's face. But then, whenever I succeeded a little, I saw Jesus better. It's hard to explain in words, but every time like that when I felt his patience—how lovingly he was waiting for me—every time like that gave me a little more strength to move what was hiding him from me aside. Because without the love of God, I know, without his showing me his love, I would never have been able to get it out of me."

My sister prayed and her husband prayed: "And that helped me a lot too. He would ask for me to succeed in letting go of the acid and the pictures that had stuck in my mind. Because it was hard for him too, this poison that I had inside me. Because I—maybe I've said this before—hardly knew how to be his wife . . .

"I'm trying to tell you in one morning about years; I've been wanting to tell you all this for years. You know how much I missed you, and if only I'd known how to tell you before, so you wouldn't worry about me. I know how you worried about me all the time. And you're an angel, simply an angel for not being angry. How come you're not angry? But please understand, I know you understand: even if I had the talent, even if I knew how to write like you, at the time when all this happened—it was simply impossible to put it all down on paper. That's why I did something ugly and didn't keep in touch with you. After everything you suffered for my sake, I didn't keep in touch. But in my heart, in my heart inside me, I wish you could see straight into my heart, I always knew that one day you would come and I would tell you everything."

•

I put out a lying hand and took her hand, and she squeezed it with surprising strength. "Aren't you cold?" I asked.

"Are you cold?"

I was cold. The chill crept from the wooden steps through my coat and climbed up my spine. My back was stiff. But until I asked her about the cold, somehow I hadn't been aware of the discomfort I was suffering, and when I became aware, I felt no impulse to escape from it. So I was cold. So what? It was only my body.

"I don't want you to think that we were sad all the time, because truly we weren't sad, not at all," my sister said without letting go of my hand. "You know how it is when you clean the house, and then somebody comes in with mud on his shoes? So that's how I began to think about this obsession of mine to see Aaron burn. That it was like the dirt you have clean out of the house every day. What can we do? God gave us a house, and he also gave us the work to do. Barnett also began to see it this way, and sometimes we even laughed about it a little, just so you know. He would come home in the evening and ask me: 'Well, how did you get on with the cleaning today?' But then something amazing happened: little by little, it happened gradually, the house actually grew cleaner and cleaner until I hardly had to clean it at all.

"I was busy. The people here accepted me into their lives. Barnett found me all kinds of things to do, and suddenly I discovered that a day had passed without the obsession, and after that two days, and then more. It was like a miracle from heaven, can you understand what a miracle it is when your house cleans itself? When you wake up in the morning and know there won't be any dirt? Maybe just a little soot in the stove, but one wipe with a rag and, like in the commercials here, your stove is clean and you didn't even get dirty from the soot. How can you ever be thankful enough for such a miracle when you wake up in the morning? I know you're waiting for me to tell you what I wrote to Aaron. But in order to tell you, in order for you to understand, there are so many other things, so much to tell.

Because in my wish to thank God for the miracle he had performed for me, I began thinking and thinking what I could do to show him my thanks. And the fact is that I knew from the beginning, because this is the whole truth of Jesus, but it took me time, it took me time to be capable of it. And only with time I understood that if God had forgiven me, that just as God forgives us, just as our savior Jesus was the sacrifice that atoned for our sins, the sacrifice that God demanded from me—was for me to forgive Aaron."

Her grip on my hand loosened, she raised her face to the sky, and I didn't pull my hand away or take it back. To sit like this, only to sit still and let the incomprehensible words be heard. Without a movement, without an echo, without a single question, definitely without a scream. Because only thus, in this frozen state, in this lovely landscape in which I am nothing more than a detail, will it be possible to survive all this and get through it.

A bird twitters. A squirrel scurries past and suddenly stops dead for no reason. Hush, quiet. The fair, slow sister is speaking in a spate of words.

If necessary I'll be a squirrel frozen on the spot, or a transparent cloud in the sky. If necessary I'll be the step at her feet, because she deserves to have me at her feet, and this is what I deserve too: to be silent, to be still, to be as if I'm not there, because it's better for her, definitely better for my sister for me not to be there. For years I overshadowed her and for years she was silenced. This is her chapter, now she is speaking. From here on to the end I'll suspend myself and I won't interrupt her. The sister who thought it was urgent to rush to the rescue will no longer push in. The dark sister will be the audience only.

A transparent, barely perceptible cloud hangs in the sky. A squirrel bites its nail till it bleeds.

"I talked about it to my husband, and he had doubts. You know, Aaron never showed any sign of repentance. I'm not even sure if he understood what he did, though how could he not understand? After all, he's a learned man and he knew how to write a book. Anyone who can write a book must surely be capable of understanding.

"So however much we talked it over, Barnett still wasn't sure that it was the right thing to do. And when we went to talk to our pastor and his wife they both still had questions. Mindy—who's a very clever woman—Mindy told me that true forgiveness is a very high challenge, and before I took any steps, it was important for me to be sure that I could really and truly meet the challenge. Sometimes a Christian can deceive himself that he's forgiven, but his forgiveness is actually a kind of fraud, and God, who sees into our hearts, doesn't buy the fraud, even if the person who forgave really wants his fraud to be true. That's how she explained it to me and I'm sure her words were wise. But however much I looked into my heart, and examined it, I couldn't see any lie there. I hadn't yet forgiven. Not yet. But I was ready to ask God to help me to forgive. The four of us met a few more times and talked. We prayed together for understanding. And in the end what we understood was that it was forbidden to pardon someone who had no repentance, but what was possible, what I as a Christian could do, was to forgive Aaron as if on condition. That is to say, to tell him or write to him that if he was ever ready to confess what he had done to me, that if he succeeded in doing that, acknowledging his sin and admitting it and taking responsibility—if that happened, then he would have my forgiveness. That I would give it fully. And that's what I did in the end. That's what I wrote to Aaron. Not right away, but a few months after our last consultation, because we had several. I wasn't sure where to send my letter, and Barnett said that we could send it to the university. We didn't know if he was still working there, but Barnett said that even if he wasn't, they would forward his mail to him. He got the address for me, and then, once I already had the address, one evening I sat down and wrote the letter. It wasn't a long letter, and when I finished it, I asked my husband to read it and correct my spelling mistakes. And again something wonderful happened, you won't believe it, which is that I didn't have any spelling mistakes, not a single one, as if some invisible hand was guiding mine when I wrote it. That's what I felt.

"We went to bed. In the morning Barnett drove to one of the farms here, and I went with him. On the way I dropped the letter in a mailbox.

"I know that you want to hear what happened with the letter. That's what you asked me at the beginning, and in the meantime I'm talking and talking, and you with your patience . . . I'm so grateful to you. I'm sure there's a different way of telling it, but I don't know how to explain in any other way. So if you're worried, I know how you worry, I sent the letter and it was as if nothing happened. He never answered me. As if I had never written that letter. But the truth is, that in reality my letter actually changed things, it changed them a lot. Wait, I'll tell you.

"Barnett drove to the farm, and I went along. And while he was working I sat in the kitchen with the farmer's wife, but I was in a state because all kinds of things were going round in my head, including the things Mindy said to me. Even though I knew, I really knew that I wasn't lying to God, what she said stayed with me. My heart was beating so hard, like I'd been running, I could hardly speak, and so I left her in the kitchen and went out for a walk to try to calm down.

"I'm not a writer like you, I don't exactly know how to tell you what happened next: it was autumn, like now, before the leaves finish falling, when the trees are bright red, and the ones that aren't are green as can be. The sun was shining, a kindly sun, not a bit like the sun in Israel, and I simply walked in the sun, and as I walked I started to see the beauty, such beauty, and this beauty increased. You know how it is when beauty is like a pain, only the opposite? You go deeper and deeper in, and the beauty becomes like a wave that wipes out everything until there's nothing left but beauty.

"That's how it was for me, suddenly I started to see, to see how that beauty was really there, and how God had really given us such beauty, and how he was giving me the gift of seeing it. And my heart filled with the sun, as if the sun were honey on my heart, and I walked and walked with that honey, and suddenly I started to cry because I understood what it was that God had given me because I had forgiven. Because I had forgiven, I would always be able to see that green and that red of the autumn leaves, and now that my heart was full of sun I would never, ever have to remember what Aaron had done to me again.

"I had forgiven him the sin he had sinned against me, and then God had given me this gift of taking what had happened and making it go away. Because what Aaron had done, the things he did, the sin he committed against me—was like a dark prison where I had been locked up together with him, and then, when I forgave him, when I freed him of the sin, the prison was no longer there, and I was no longer a prisoner of the sin, and suddenly—beauty and sun.

"The prison guard had vanished, and he would never return because I had set him free. And that's it, that's it, there's no more guard to cover my eyes. It's not that I've forgotten, the memory hasn't been wiped out, but Uncle Aaron isn't important anymore, and he can't be important, and he'll never be important again. This was the grace that I suddenly understood.

"I walked for a long time. I don't know how long I went on walking in the fields, because the time that I walked was like years and also like a single minute, in which you suddenly see everything, and everything that exists is contained in that minute. At some point I saw Barnett and the farmer, and Barnett saw me and started walking in my direction. He was holding something white in his hands, and when he came close I saw he was carrying a lamb in his arms. You see, it wasn't the season for giving birth at all, and nevertheless a sheep there had given birth, and perhaps because it wasn't the season her lamb didn't want to come out and it got stuck, so that Barnett had to pull it out by force.

"So in the midst of all the beauty I see Barnett coming toward me with a wet lamb in his arms, in the midst of all the beauty . . . you understand what happened? No, how can you understand if I don't tell you? A year later Sarah was born. Exactly one year later. Even though I was past the age of child-bearing, like Sarah in the Bible, and both Barnett and I had resigned ourselves to being childless, God in his infinite patience and mercy gave us a child.

"That's it, that's one thing that came of the letter, and there's something else too, something I'm not sure about, I just think it's connected. We have a few friends who teach at the university. You met two of them. One of our friends teaches Jewish history and also helps with Hillel House programs—and he somehow remembered my maiden name. So a few months ago he asks me if I'm related to the Professor Gotthilf who wrote that evil book. And when I said yes, he told me that Gotthilf had published an article apologizing to everyone offended by his book and it had caused quite a sensation.

"I don't know anything, all I know is that the book and its evil— I know they're connected to the way he abused me. So I have this thought, maybe it's conceited of me to think so, that my letter is also connected to the fact that he's apologizing now. Maybe in some small way, even though he never answered me. And it may be too that this process began in him before. You know that he refused to sue that woman who wanted to spray him with acid? When I first heard this it just went in one ear and out the other. It didn't mean anything to me. Even when I wrote him my letter, and even when I consulted our pastor. But after this friend of ours told me about his article, and how he travels from place to place and appears in public and admits that he made a terrible mistake: after I heard this, I started to think that maybe it does mean something, that he could have sued that poor survivor but he didn't. Maybe already then he wasn't just Satan, and because he wasn't just Satan, the forgiveness I forgave him did change something, and what I wrote did count. It's just a thought I have. It's really not important, and for some reason it's not important to me to know. I don't need him to answer me, I don't even want him to. He can answer or never answer. The important thing is that even if he gets in touch again—never mind what he says—you don't have to be afraid for my sake. I know how you worry, and there really and truly is no need to worry any more. Even if the phone rings now. Even then.

"There are people who walk in darkness. I don't know why this is, but I know that he's one of them, like a bat that can't see in the light.

"He talked a lot, you probably remember. There was this thing that he talked to me all the time, and I didn't have a clue what he was talking about. As if he meant something by it but at the same time I never knew what he really meant.

"He'd be this way one day and that way another, different every time.

"Sometimes—it was as if it was some kind of joke of his, but perhaps he wasn't joking—sometimes he'd speak to me in a voice like a professor's, and in this voice he would say all kinds of things about a 'project.' About the 'project' and the thing that 'we're doing together.' As if it were all some kind of experiment and he was consulting a colleague. Never mind. It doesn't matter: but once, when I was very thirsty he suddenly brought me a glass of water and in that same voice he asked me a question that I didn't understand at all: if I agreed with Schopenhauer that pain was more real than pleasure. Does that make sense? And then he forced me to answer him, even though I didn't understand what answer he wanted from me.

"It doesn't matter now. It really doesn't. I'm just upsetting you, and I don't want to, I don't, because I don't even think about it any more, that story isn't in the least important. I only want you to know that when I wrote my letter, I told him that I am truly happy now, that's what I wrote to him. Because that's important, it is. You see, if someone is like a bat, then you have to tell him that there is such a thing as light, otherwise how will he know? So I wrote to him, and maybe, maybe what I wrote did have a little influence.

"I want to ask you, when we were small, were you afraid a lot? Because you know, even before Aaron I was afraid a lot, and I've only now stopped being afraid. I had all kinds of foolish fears, not only of school. You remember the pine tree that used to creak in the wind, and we would imagine that it was uprooting itself and coming to get us? I was also afraid of those two yeshiva boys in *Two Kuni Lemel*, it was when you were still a baby. Daddy took me to see the movie, it was supposed to be a comedy, but something there gave me the creeps, and for a long time afterward whenever I walked down the passage I imagined two figures in black following me. Walking behind me with dancing steps and laughing and wanting to do something bad to me. I had all kinds of scary fantasies, kids are like that, it's not important, but the point is that all my fear, all the fears, even the oldest ones are gone.

"In the prayer 'Our father, who art in heaven' we ask God to forgive us our trespasses as we forgive those who trespass against us. So you see, do you understand? Now, ever since Sarah was born, I really feel that God has forgiven me.

"And if our father in heaven has forgiven me, what do I have to fear?"

- 6 -

I vowed to keep silent. I vowed not to interrupt, not to push or prompt, to let my sister deliver her speech from the podium of the pagoda without interference.

My old-new sister told a practiced story, but her voice was as eager and alert as if this was the first time she was telling it, and she was only now making the connections as she spoke.

My sister was the heroine of her life story, and who was I to push myself into the feats of her heroism and spoil them?

A transparent cloud does not speak. A squirrel nibbles in silence. May my black tongue cleave to the roof of my mouth lest I ruin this intolerable beauty. Intolerable—yet I would tolerate it. Because it was not for me that a carpet of autumn leaves had been spread here, and not in my honor that a bird flew and a rabbit sprang.

Praise waiteth for thee in silence, and I wait, in silent anesthetized worship I wait.

I am a detail in a still life: a detail bowing my head on my knee beneath a statue of the Buddha. I am an object. I can be an object. Even an isolated object can sometimes survive in a landscape.

Only a bird will twitter. No other sound will be heard. No doubt about it, the whole of creation is united in harmony. There will be no doubt in this place, I won't allow it, and nothing, no word of mine, will mar this triumphant beauty.

In this way, with thoughts along these lines I tried to hypnotize myself. Years after I had collapsed on the watchmaker's doorstep and lost the connection with my legs, I tried as hard as I could to cut the connection of my own free will.

I hypnotized myself until I was a detail in a still life at her feet, until I was almost nothing at all: an object willed into paralysis. And so I remained, still and mute, until my sister said: "Our father in heaven forgave me," and this sentence galvanized me into speech.

"For what?" I begged her, with my soul overflowing and filling the inanimate object with life. "What in God's name did you have to be forgiven for?" My hand wandered to the toe of her shoe, and my fingers pressed the rough cold of the material and fawned on it imploringly.

"First of all for you," Elisheva answered with the slightest hint of a smile in her voice. "For you, and for how I tormented you when you were like an angel. Do you think you succeeded in hiding the price you paid from me? The way I was then I didn't have a choice, but I know that you didn't join the army because of me. That first of all. First of all, you. But apart from that, even before that, before I fell on you, there was that business I'm so ashamed of, what I did when I was still in the army . . ." her voice grew graver. "You know, when I locked myself in with the Uzi, please don't ask me what I intended to, because it's all dark. I only know that it's something that happened, that I threatened to do something with the Uzi, and only God, who watched over me then knows how it could have ended."

"And because of that you believe . . ."

"Wait a minute, please, give me another minute, because I have no idea. These are things that neither I, nor any man, things only God can know, because only he knows how sick I was. I was so sick and so weak then, and mother . . ."

My sister fell silent, and I sat up to see the tears that I knew were coming. "Mother was always sick. And for a long time I never stopped thinking that if only I were a little stronger, if only I were a little more capable, perhaps she would have, that is to say maybe, maybe we'd still have a mother. And then Sarah, and your sons . . . I'm sure she would have loved Sarah. It was her heart, you know, you know what she was like. And everything that happened to me, everything I told them, it was too much for her heart, obviously it was. Only I couldn't, and because of that, because I couldn't . . . but how could I have? How?"

The sobs overpowered her voice and threatened to choke her.

"You didn't do anything to Mother," I cut her short. "You can't think that, you can't. It's something he put into your head. I'm sure it comes from him. I'm sure it was him who frightened you so that you wouldn't tell her. I know where this comes from. I know. But everything he tried to make you think, everything he said would happen to Mother—I know exactly what he said to you—get it into your head, at least now, it was all just a threat." My sister blew her nose, and I didn't stop.

"Get it into your head that our mother was an egoist. An egoist and a narcissist. Who wrecked her own heart on purpose, without any connection to us. That woman couldn't stand having any other sick person around apart from herself. Whatever anyone tried to tell her—if it wasn't about her, she simply shut her ears." I didn't have to harden my heart. I was ice and I was a chisel, and the chisel cut the ice so I could breathe.

"No, don't say that, please don't. A mother is a mother, and it's a fact that her heart couldn't take it. At first it could, but after she found out, after she heard about my abortion . . . I think about you every year, I want you to know, every anniversary I think of you alone at the grave. How you have to do it alone. One day, I promise you, I'll come to Jerusalem and both of us, together . . . Our mother should have been a princess. She wanted you and me to be princesses too. And she worked so hard. Her life was really hard for her. And nevertheless, even though she was sick, you remember how hard she tried to make us happy with the dresses and everything? And if only Aaron hadn't come, perhaps then . . . I don't judge her, because who am I to judge, and now I'm a mother myself. You have sons. But if I even imagine that somebody, that Sarah . . . I don't imagine and I don't judge. But if you want to know what else I ask God to forgive me for—you were my angel and I want to tell you everything— then there's also the fact that I had the abortion."

I stood up. "Are you trying to tell me that God expected you to give birth after being raped? To have the rapist Hitler's baby? To have the baby of your father's cousin—is that what your God expected of you?"

This time she wasn't alarmed. She was prepared. "God is merciful. God is the father of mercy, God is the king of mercy." She answered me quietly and confidently, as if I hadn't raised my voice and towered over her. "But I know why you're talking like that. You love me, and you don't want me to suffer. But it isn't in our hands, you have to understand. God said: 'Thou shalt not kill,' and Uncle Aaron . . . sometimes I wanted to die. There was a time . . . I can't exactly . . . there were times when I believed that I was actually already dead. But nevertheless, nevertheless, however many times it was as if he killed me, he didn't really kill me. He didn't. And I did have an abortion. Because I couldn't . . . So maybe I am guilty, even though how could I have? I'm not saying that a woman can. A woman, a child has the right. So I'm not saying that anyone could, I don't know who in this world of ours could, and that's what our pastor told me too. Leave it to God—he said to me—Elisheva, leave that to God. And so I did. I really did. I left it to God. And after I forgave Aaron and after Sarah was born, I know that God forgave me."

A strange lunar sun glittered on the golden face of the Buddha. My sister looked up at me like a supplicant, praying for the miracle of understanding for her story, which had now concluded. Very far away, at the end of the avenue I saw the men looking toward us. The two of them walked back and forth, and when they saw me standing up they still waited for a sign that they could approach. We were supposed to drive to another little town for lunch. Barnett, who had taken a day and a half off in our honor, was supposed to go back to work. The numbed thumb I had been gnawing came back to life with a pulsing pain. I was growing colder, or perhaps it was the cold that had accumulated in my bones while sitting on the step, and which was beginning to spread through me, to remind me that you can never really part from your body.

But there was one last thing remaining, a "last chance"—I thought to myself—even though if anyone had asked me I wouldn't have been able to say a chance of what.

"I understand that you forgave him. You forgave him, that's what you told me. But apparently I'm too stupid to understand what that means. I just don't get it. Let's say there's a hell. There's a hell, and at this minute, this precise second, God is about to send this Hitler there, to burn. To burn—you know, for all I care not even for eternity, only a hundred days. To roast for a hundred days in the stench and the fire. Now, let's say that your forgiveness is his pardon, and that with this ticket he won't have to spend a single minute there. Let's say that he'll fly up straight from the grave to heaven with you. Will you give him the ticket?"

The frown between her brows deepened. She blinked hard once, and then her face suddenly relaxed, and she clapped her hands in the penguin flap with which I was already familiar.

"But why do you say that you're stupid? You understand everything. You always understood. Because that's exactly it: that's the thing, that I forgave."

There was nothing left. My sister stood up. The good men came toward us, we advanced toward them, and my husband sent me a questioning look. "Everything's fine," I said too loudly, "we're done. The story's over. I told Elisheva. She's not worried." Later he told me that my sister looked to him "as fresh as if she'd just come out of the shower."

"And me?" I asked.

"You looked as if you needed a bath."

We walked toward the parking lot. Oded held my hand. My sister tucked her arm into her husband's. They took the lead down the path and we followed them. More cathedrals of trees, more arabesques of vines, and more natural temples of climbing ferns; and in front of us a woman's stylishly bobbed head and a man's wispy thinning hair. If I hadn't known who they were, if I had just landed up behind them, I would never have recognized those heads and those bodies.

We were already next to the car when four heads rose in unison at the sound of a screech in the sky. A flock of geese flew over us in an arrowhead formation, and pierced me with a superstitious dread that rose in a flash from my tailbone to the bottom of my skull. The wild geese flapped heavy wings, and their screeching seemed to announce some curse to come. One after the other they screeched above our heads. Flapping and flapping and emitting remote, obscure cries, like a distant witness. One tortured screech after the other, never together.

I sensed Oded shudder, he tightened his grip on my fingers, and the flat gray sky closed in over our heads.

"Look, geese," my big sister said, and pointed.

There was nothing left that there was any point in doing together. Because where could we go from here? To the historical museum and the nature reserve with the Indian name? And nevertheless we drove to the next town, because Elisheva and Barnett insisted on us tasting Dutch food. The food was tasteless, and the conversation bubbled with artificial additives. My sister kept touching the back of my hand and my sleeve and saying things like: "But you haven't told me anything yet. Tell me everything about the boys. Tell me about your work. Tell me about Alice. I want to hear everything," and she wasn't put off by the paucity of my replies, as if she didn't notice that I scarcely answered. The geese that had frightened me had robbed me of the vestiges of my strength, and it was hard for me just to sit up straight in my chair.

My sister's story was told, and after it there seemed nothing else to say. She was honest. More honest than I had ever been. She had always known only one way, and had never known how to cheat. The story she told me had not been tailored to suit me, and knowing her it was also clear to me that she had not tailored it to suit any other audience either, but as we sat there in the restaurant over the puréed Dutch food, I imagined her presenting the very same testimony to a beaming group of women, daughters of the congregation:

a partial testimony—I thought—bits and pieces assembled into a fairy tale. An invisible seam sewed up all the ends, and there were no loose threads to continue the tale. I was the only one coming unraveled here, with no closure in sight.

Once she had finished telling me her story, and I had no doubt that she had very much been looking forward to telling me, it seemed that all my sister's expectations of me had been satisfied, and she looked happy and untroubled. She ate with a hearty appetite, praised the dish set before her, and invited us all to taste it.

We said goodbye to Barnett. We took Elisheva home, drank tea, and waited for my niece to return so we could say goodbye to her.

If the child was disappointed by the briefness of our visit, she was too well brought up and too good tempered to show it.

Happy and obedient, the little girl from the little white house kissed her aunt, and skipped out to the yard to talk to Soda the dog.

Nobody mentioned the possibility of another visit, but Elisheva announced that from now on she would not be lazy and she would write to me more often. "And please, please send me your newspaper columns, a few of them at least. I told Sarah that her aunt is a writer, and we're all so proud of you. 'Alice in the Holy City,' what an original idea!"

There were the last words she said to me when she accompanied us to the car. After that we hugged, and a woman with the shoulders of a swimmer, in a red sweater with a reindeer pattern, waved to us from the gate until we disappeared around the bend in the road.

- 7 -

"So how was it really?" asked Oded when my sister's image vanished from the side mirror of the car.

"Fine. There's nothing to worry about, the matter's closed. He has her address, she sent it to him, and she isn't afraid of anything any more," my voice sounded old and tired, as if I were answering him about some distant memory.

"What? How come?"

"As I said. The matter's closed. It's over. She's forgiven him."

"Elinor, please, you can't go to sleep now."

"What's not clear here? She forgave him, she wrote him a letter in which she forgave him, conditionally at least. The condition being that he admitted what he did to her."

"Did a lawyer advise her to do it?"

"Why a lawyer?"

"Because if I was a criminal lawyer, and if I were her lawyer, that's exactly what I would have advised her: to try to get him to confess."

"There wasn't any lawyer, and in any case he didn't bother to reply."

"Obviously he didn't reply. I have no idea what the law of limitations is here in America regarding rape, it's worth looking into, but in any case a man would have to be an idiot to incriminate himself like that in writing."

"She doesn't want a trial. She wants him to ascend to heaven with her, that's what she said."

"You're joking. I don't believe it."

I said nothing.

"It can't be true. I mean, I'm not accusing your sister, God forbid, of lying."

I said nothing.

"There's such a thing as self-deception, you know. Not that a person's lying, God forbid, he's simply unaware: not reading himself correctly."

But I, who had heard my sister, knew with exhausting clarity that there was nothing here to read between the lines. And that if my sister Elisheva had been standing next to the woman who tried to destroy the face of the monster, she would have arrested the upraised hand herself. She would have jumped in and stopped her.

Tomorrow—I thought—perhaps I would be able to take in the full horror of that act of pardon, which at the moment was only a frozen pain in my muscles. Tomorrow, when I thawed out a little, or maybe in the plane, from above. Because down here, on the ground of this prairie where there was nothing to take hold of, it was beyond me.

I wasn't tired but felt a great need to get onto my own private escalator and disappear: my husband wanted to close the events of the day with words, and my husband could wait till tomorrow. Maybe when I got back from my disappearance the right words would come to me.

"Their Sarah seems like a really great kid," Oded tried another tack.

I should say something to him—surely I was capable of saying something, I wasn't sick or paralyzed. A healthy living person should be capable of showing signs of life—so I discovered a sign of life and asked him if he remembered the business with the acid. There was no need to explain what I was talking about, he remembered that "the woman had missed."

"So my sister gives him credit for somehow preventing the attack from coming to trial."

My husband sighed. "Your sister is a fine person, but without really knowing her, I would say that she's a little naïve. The guy had just published his disgusting book. The last thing he needed in the middle of the publicity campaign was a legal confrontation with a Holocaust survivor. A trial like that would have led to his being conclusively identified with Hitler."

I didn't feel tired, but I was overcome by a fit of yawning. The sun was hidden behind a bank of clouds, and it seemed that this gray non-day and non-night would be interminable. Yesterday it got dark. Why couldn't I remember when it got dark here?

"Why all of a sudden a 'disgusting book'? I thought that in your opinion it was a text book for high school students."

"Okay, that's what I said. And I'm telling you again: it's not a serious piece of research. Definitely not. But you know what? Since we talked I thought about it and came to the conclusion that precisely the attempt to present things in a popular way could be dangerous. So yes, it's a popularization, and yes, it's disgusting."

"I see what you mean."

The more my voice retreated and grew weaker, the more loquacious he became. "I'm not a big reader, that's for sure, but if my wife who's a writer tells me that a book is beyond the pale, and my father whose opinion I also respect says exactly the same thing—it makes me think. Let's say I felt the need to make light of it. I felt the need to belittle its importance, don't ask me why. But after you read the book . . . what's going on here? Are you falling asleep?"

"If you let me close my eyes until we reach the hotel, I'll be able to drive to O'Hare afterward."

"I've got no problem driving. I'd prefer it if I drove and you talked to me a bit more, but if you're tired, go ahead and sleep."

"You're an even better Christian than my sister."

"I'm not a Christian at all. Don't say that. If anyone dared to hurt you, I don't want to think of what I'd do to him."

"What would you do to him?"

"Something hellish. I don't know."

"Okay, when you do know what you'd do to him, tell me about it."

"One of the things that surprised me," he said, "was how normal those people are. When you and Elisheva were talking I was walking with Barnett. We spoke a little about his work. I only wish I enjoyed my work as much as he does. Even though it's quite sad, what's happening here. All these farms we're passing—what Barnett explained to me is that they're on their way to becoming extinct. With the taxes that go up all the time, and the dominance of the fast food industry, people are being forced to sell their land. But what I wanted to say is this, that in the meantime with all these processes going on, these Christians are living their lives very contentedly. They enjoy what they do, and the people we met yesterday too, you can see they're happy with their lives, maybe even more than we are. I confess that I expected freaks, and instead I met serious, educated people, connected to what's happening around them. This community seems to me very healthy and completely normal."

"A colorful community," I said slowly. "Broken-winged birds sing again. Dogs bleat in the meadows."

"What are you talking about?"

"Tell me, tell me: encouraging Elisheva to forgive—is that normal?"

"I'm not saying it is, obviously they're got their peculiarities, but that's all they are, peculiarities. On the whole, in my opinion your sister is in an excellent environment. It really couldn't be better."

"Just that in this environment they preach that abortion is murder, and Elisheva has to beg their God to pardon her for terminating a pregnancy from rape," I said and closed my eyes.

"And did God pardon her?"

"He gave her Sarah," I said without opening them.

"Well, so what more do you want? If I believed in miracles, I would say that what's she's done with herself is a miracle. If you take into account what she went through, and it's clear to me that what I know is just the tip of the iceberg, when you think about it, your sister might have been in a completely different place today, completely different, you know. Isn't that what worried you all these years? First of all shows you what tremendous strength she has. And actually I'm not surprised, she's your sister after all. So if somehow or other God helps her a bit, why be petty, and who cares exactly how he helps her? She forgave, she didn't forgive. In my opinion the whole business of this forgiveness is an illusion—self-deception I'd say, without actually knowing. But what does it matter? It's insignificant. The main thing is that what we have here is recovery from ruin on an unimaginable scale. What I'm trying to tell you is that after this visit of ours, I feel as if we can lift a heavy weight from our hearts."

My husband went on lecturing me and setting the record straight all the way to the hotel: he renovated ruins, pointed to tips of icebergs, and lifted weights off hearts like a mythological giant. My husband set the record straight, and I agreed with much of what he said. I agreed and I said nothing, because I didn't know what to think.

Elisheva had found salvation. My fair sister had found more than salvation, she had found happiness that tore the sky wide open. And I, who had abandoned her and fenced off a corner of my own, I, instead of rejoicing in her happiness, felt that a stone was rolling down on me and sealing me into a cave. Let my tongue cleave to the roof of my mouth lest I call her and confound her after she has been set free.

My sister was at peace. Calm and at peace. My fair sister had pardoned me. She had pardoned me and our parents, she had pardoned the Not-man. And the pardon I had not asked for, the pure and horrifying pardon she had pardoned me, was closing in on me.

And I would remain alone, I thought. I would remain by myself in my selfishness, because my sister bore no grudge—not against me and not against him. Now only I, the keeper of the grudge, was left to guard and to remember. Remember what? It was necessary to remember, it was impossible not to remember, and now I was pardoned and erased and dismissed. My sister had told me a story. My sister had rolled the stone. From now on I was on my own.

We stopped in the parking lot of the hotel opposite the swaying plastic figure of Santa Claus. My husband got out to fetch the luggage we had left at the reception desk, and by the time he returned I became sickeningly aware of the fact that I was not as alone as I thought.

My sister had erased me and my sin against her, together with the person of the rapist. And at the same time, as she wiped the two of us clean with her celestial forgiveness, it was as if she had lumped us together and joined me to his person.

From now on to eternity no longer on my own, because from now on only I and the First Person were on our own, because Elisheva was no longer in the world, my sister was now in heaven. She was in heaven, and the person of the Not-man and I were pardoned and left to choke in the dirt of this world together, imprisoned by the pardon.

For some reason the thought of choking was linked in my mind to the geese, as if it was this that the arrowhead was announcing with its screeching as it cut through the sky.

The flight of the geese is heavy and slow—how is it that they don't fall? Barnett said that they migrated from Alaska. Alice the goose also came from Alaska. However hard she flapped her pigtails and screeched her colorful nonsense, the pigtails would not hold her up in the air. Alice fell and she is a sack of feathers on the ground. The screeching geese are gone. My mind is going. I'm going out of my mind and that's why I shall remain alone with the First Person. Because I'm out of my mind and I don't know how to get him out of my mind.

"That's it. Are we awake? Ready to fly to the boys? I'm dying to see what Nimrod looks like without the beard. I never liked that beard," my husband said and closed the door.

After we got home Oded remarked that it seemed to him that I had "worried the boys a little," which was putting it mildly. I could have said that I was too upset to notice, but the truth is that I did notice, and it was even pointed out to me, but I didn't have the strength or the will to stop myself from worrying them.

On the second morning of our stay in Seattle, Yachin took his father for a tour of one of the Bowing plants, and Nimrod, who from childhood had been more interested in heart-to-hearts than his brother, deliberately got up early, and over the first cup of coffee of the morning sat me down for a talk on the topic: "So what's really going on with you, Mom?"

The night before, after returning from the Thai restaurant, I had made the men egg barley from Israel for dessert, but my younger son, after satisfying himself with the comfort food from home, was now demanding nourishment of a different order: "There's a sense here that you're not completely with us," he said. My child wanted his mother "complete," in the innocence of his heart he wanted to taste the root of the poison.

I replied that I didn't know why anyone should feel that way, because actually I was perfectly happy, really. I confirmed that I had missed him and his brother and said that "perhaps I'm just exhausted from the visit with Elisheva."

"Dad says that she's in excellent shape," he protested.

"Dad's right. Everything's fine. It's just that after not seeing each other for years . . ."

"Memories . . ." He pronounced with the knowingness of the young. And what did he know about memories? Memory to my son appeared in the guise of a kind of computer library: click on "search," read, and delete. He knew nothing of the dogs of memory, how they search you out and hunt you down, to stick their teeth into you until things come out that you didn't even know you knew.

"I suppose you remembered all kinds of stories," he said and blushed a little. "I mean from before what happened to her. It's quite unusual to have a mother who grew up in a hotel. There must have been a whole lot of interesting stories, like in that children's book we once had. What was the girl's name again? Eloise."

"There was one old lady, a Yiddish singer. She came back every year . . ."

"And?"

"Nothing. She stopped coming. I suppose she died."

Nimrod had inherited his father's persistence, not to the same extent as Yachin, but nevertheless: "A friend of mine, a girl from Jerusalem who's studying here, came up with an interesting idea. She said that part of your inspiration for 'Alice' may have come from the experiences you had with all kinds of tourists as a child in the hotel."

"Are you still in touch with Tamar?"

"Not on a regular basis. Do you think that you and your sister will keep in touch more now?"

"We'll see. Don't you want to go and take a shower?"

"Because with your father I can understand why you don't want to have anything to do with him. Just leaving your daughter after something like that happens to her . . ."

As far as my father was concerned I had gone relatively easy on the censorship. In the stories I told my son, Shaya Gotthilf was the dust under the radiator. The little bit of dirt that distracts attention from the rest of the filth.

"You know what, if you're not going to shower, I will."

"I just want you to know," my son said and stood up at last, "I just want to tell you that I feel strange that I don't really have any roots."

"You have Grandma Rachel and Grandpa Menachem. Others have less."

"I'm not saying . . ."

"If you're not saying then stop talking. And by the way, if you've already decided to lose the beard, it might be a good idea to get used to shaving every day."

But I didn't behave like that the whole time: I love my sons, I know that we had a good time together, and that we were happy too. After many months of separation, obviously a mother is happy to see her children.

We drove to see forests. We ate together in twelve different restaurants. When the boys sang out of tune in the recording studio in the "Musical Experience" Museum, their father and I kept time for them; when we crossed the bay in the ferry, and went up on the deck, the three men circled me to protect me from the wind.

Despite Yachin's blondness, the two boys look delightfully like their father, and as in Israel, the sight of the matching trio brought smiles to the faces of the passersby. Two handsome sons and the father in the middle. The younger son takes advantage of the picture to flirt inoffensively with the waitresses.

The visit we had paid to my sister on our way had made a breach, and in a moment of privacy Yachin also questioned me about her.

I expected him as was his wont to be satisfied with "she's fine," but this time he surprised me. My stand-offish firstborn buried his hands deep into his coat pockets, drew up his shoulders, and after a moment of angry silence remarked while scrutinizing the horizon: "I can't believe they never even looked for the maniac who raped her."

We were standing on a jetty. One jetty is very like another, and there was nothing to distinguish this one from all the others we had stood on and strolled on during the course of our visit: seagulls and boats and the blue of the sea and the froth of the waves. A green mountain rose from a billow of clouds on the other side of the water, on the left of the picture.

"He was a tourist, you know," I said into the wind. "He left the country, and she didn't talk."

"But after that, after you already knew, it wasn't actually some stranger in the street who raped her after all. I've been thinking about this for a long time: what was so difficult about finding him? That's what I don't get. He was registered at the hotel, you must have had a name, an address, a credit card number . . . you already had credit cards then, no? Your father had all the information. So how come nobody used it?"

"I have no idea what my father knew. Time passed before Elisheva spoke up, and in any event she wouldn't have testified."

"And you didn't try to persuade her that she should?"

A light plane swooped down over the water, for a moment it seemed that the gray body was nose-diving into it, but then it straightened out and plowed through the waves, turned around and slowed down, leaving a frothy white cut in its wake. A seaplane. There are airplanes that can sail on the surface of the water but none that can sail below it. It's submarines that sail on the bottom of the sea, and there is no more terrible death than slowly suffocating in the coffin of a drowning submarine.

"Are you accusing me of something?" I asked my son.

"Mom, no . . ."

The "no" and the sharp movement of the head that accompanied it, warned me. "Stop it," they said, and "What are you doing?" and "Don't ruin everything, Mom," but I didn't stop: "Because if you're accusing me of something . . ."

"Mom, what's the matter with you? You're completely out of line."

"Really? Because if you've got something to say to me, let's hear it."

Oded's son took a deep breath and dropped his shoulders. "I never thought to blame you. I know it's complicated, and with your father abandoning the two of you like that as well. I'm not stupid and I'm not blaming anybody. It's just that the thought of that man going free, never paying for what he did—the thought of it drives me crazy. A person who rapes a child, I don't know what should've been done to him."

"And what do you think should have been done to him?"

"I don't know. Castration, I suppose. That's the usual answer people give. They say that even the most hardened criminals in jail are disgusted by rapists. So maybe that's what I'd like, and that's also what people always say: let the toughest criminals deal with him. The main thing in my opinion is just knowing that this maniac is suffering like you and your sister suffered, because otherwise, you know, the world seems really fucked up."

I was happy to see my son, but these last minutes on the jetty were the only moments of our stay in Seattle when I succeeded in really feeling my happiness. In my mind's eye I saw a heavy-bodied criminal closing the lavatory door and gagging the Not-man—presumably the image came to me from some movie or other—and then my eyes cleared and I was able to see Yachin again. A young man in a checked coat, the most beautiful jawline in the world, authoritative, strict and laconic, tending from childhood to bristle, and only very rarely confused. This was the fruit of my womb. How did I get so lucky?

•

My love for my children was always a given, but already in the car on the way from the airport, something in me seemed to have gone wrong. And after months of feeling the lack of them by my side, and missing the effortless closeness to them—that simple pleasure now escaped me. Nor did what should have been self-evident awaken in me when we arrived at Yachin's tidy condominium, and later too, when Nimrod appeared and beamed at us beardless at the door, and in all the hours when we sat in the twelve restaurants and visited the two museums and strolled on the jetties. The mother's love did not disappear. If need be, the mother would have given her life for theirs. Sacrificed her right hand. Given her eyes. The love had not gone, I knew it was present somewhere beyond my inability to reach for it. But the feeling had stopped moving me and had been flattened into a kind of annoying intellectual awareness: insistent and irritating as an itchy scalp, as the reminder of a fossilized memory.

Seattle is beautiful: beautiful buildings, beautiful people, a city open to the ocean and the forest. On our first day there I apologized for being tired. Afterward I said things like: "How lovely, a sailboat," or "What an exquisite design," but the piercing beauty was unable to penetrate the transparent coat of impermeable insulation tightening around me and cutting me off from anything capable of arousing natural admiration. Because ever since leaving the park with my sister my vision seemed to be clouding, and no amount of blinking on my part could clear the picture.

I stood before the ocean, I knew that the crashing waves were "beautiful," but the beauty remained external to me, like a concept learned in literature classes: these are metonymies, this is irony, and the gray-blue crashing of the waves is called beauty.

Oded and the boys gazed and gazed and rejoiced in the sight of their eyes, and I alone gave voice to empty exclamations in the faint hope that feeling would somehow come and fill my voice.

•

On the evening of the first candle of Hanukkah Menachem and Rachel called to wish us all a happy holiday. A pair of hands peeled potatoes, another pair grated them, and while I spoke to my in-laws, the three men laughed themselves silly by stamping on the wooden kitchen floor in time to shouts of "to banish the darkness we have come." A friend of Rachel's read an old column of mine at the hairdressers: "From that series you wrote about the zoo, the one where Alice rides an elephant all the way to Bethlehem. My friend simply fell in love with your description of how the baby elephant escapes from the convoy and lands up in the square of the Church of the Nativity. She phoned the zoo to ask if the animal trainer really takes the elephants out for a walk on the road, and what nights he does it, but they didn't want to tell her. She knows you don't like telling the public what's true and what isn't in the Alice stories, but she wonders if you might be willing to make an exception in her case. My friend says that if it's true, she has to wake her grandchildren up and take them to see the convoy, especially the little baby elephant marching. So what do you say?"

What do I say? A baby elephant didn't know where to go, and an elephant is liable to trample a child. Elazar the Hasmonean was crushed to death under an elephant, and he wasn't a child.

"Elinor?"

"Tell her to drop it, I made it all up, there's no such animal as an elephant."

"What did you say? I can hardly hear you."

"The boys are making a lot of noise here."

"I can hear that you're enjoying yourselves. We'll talk when you get home. Kisses to everyone and a happy Hanukkah to all."

•

Among the holiday greetings that arrived by email was a flowery one from my sister. "May the holiday candles always light your way" she wrote in big letters, and in smaller ones she added: "Daddy and Gemma send warm regards to you all, and join us in wishing you a happy holiday."

Did she remember our father's amateur painter from her stay in the pension? Did she ever suspect that his meeting with her in Verona was not as accidental as he made out? And perhaps my sister did remember his Italian mistress sitting in the garden of the pension with her skinny, ugly English girlfriend; perhaps she remembered her and forgave him for that too. Because after pardoning the first person, after lumping the two of us together, how could she fail to pardon her father too? And why not bless his happiness too, which was also perhaps thanks to the grace of God? Because perhaps it was none other than the hand of God that had united the broken-hearted betrayer with his Gemma, and our father too was blessed, and only I was cursed.

I did not investigate Elisheva's memory and I was not about to investigate her thoughts. A terrible pardon had corroded everything and there was no point. What was the point? Shaya wasn't important, as far as I was concerned Shaya might as well be dead, and now I alone heard the laughter of the one who had kissed the back of my hand, and bought my sister a potted orchid.

The men fooled around, giggling and nudging each other, as playfully as puppies, while the floorboards creaked under their stamping feet: "Look out, you almost sent Mom flying with the frying pan."

The more I shrank into myself, the more they increased their hilarity, covering up for me with their noise and exaggerated mirth, for my isolation and everything I was unable to provide.

Again and again I said to them that I was "just thinking," but most of the things twisting and turning in my mind could hardly be called "thoughts," and it's only now that I can put them in any kind of order. Odd lines from children's rhymes stuck in my mind and kept buzzing repeatedly in my head, as if I was stuck in a telephone exchange, waiting on the line. I thought: "How sweet is Elisheva / how pretty is my dear / lovely is my love."

I thought: "Two little girls, two little dollies / one called Tzili and one called Gili."

I thought: "My little candles have so many stories to tell," and as soon as the words *ma raboo*, "so many," came into my head I smiled without thinking.

"What are you smiling about?"

"Nothing. Stories . . ." Mom's thinking about stories. Perhaps she's writing in her head. Maybe she's resurrecting the faded figure of a tourist from Verona and soon she'll put her into Alice's adventures in the Holy City. Mom's weaving a plot. Mom's fine. Everything's fine.

But I wasn't weaving anything. I was becoming unraveled. And as I unraveled, the words *"ma raboo / ma raboo,"* so many, so many, kept repeating themselves in my head without rhyme or reason, and at some point it occurred to me that "marabou" was actually the name of a bird. So many birds with curved beaks feeding on flesh. So many birds hovering over the killing fields, laying their eggs in the gaping bellies of the corpses. And from their eggs the parasites of anecdotes are born. Parasites are disgusting, but nobody dies of anecdotes. With them you can live.

On the morning of the holiday I woke at seven o'clock in complete darkness. A story from *Hitler, First Person* had been gnawing at me while I slept and it was this story that woke me. I don't know if it is based on some kind of historical truth, but the story is well told from the point of view of the first person. The late thirties, no exact date is given as far as I remember, the Führer meets someone whose name he doesn't mention in his office, someone he calls "the English Bolshevik." A Labor member of Parliament who had come to Germany in order to try to persuade its leader to stop the rearmament of the country, and carried away by the passion of his mission he quotes from the New Testament, the Sermon on the Mount. The description focuses on the body of the self-appointed missionary: he looks like a squishy pear that has already begun to rot. All you have to do is touch him for your finger to penetrate the skin, into the liquefaction of the flesh. On the fat Bolshevik pear the writer draws the mouth of a frog, and this self-righteous mouth croaks the gospel of Jesus Christ's meek and humiliated in so grotesque a manner that even the Fräulein who brings the coffee has to lift up her apron to hide her sniggers. But it is not only in the Fräulein that the self-righteous pear gives rise to ridicule, the reader too feels an impulse to crush; a kind of desire to pinch the juicy flesh of the sermonizer until he shuts his mouth and opens his eyes.

With this picture I woke up, and with the thought of my sister's letter of pardon and the fact that the First Person did not answer her.

How sweet is Elisheva / how pretty is my dear / a flowered dress I sewed her / exactly like my own.

I got out of bed and made my way to the kitchen in the dark, and to the sound of the gurgling of the percolator I began to collect myself in anticipation of the men about to wake up and another day of fun in the beautiful city of Seattle.

Fortified by the strong coffee, after I had already stretched my skin tight, it occurred to me to crawl back under the covers, and then to whisper in Oded's ear and beg him to save me from yet another day of sightseeing, I didn't have the strength for it, I couldn't stand another day here, and would he please take me away to somewhere else.

"Where do you want me to take you?" my husband would ask me.

"To an ugly place," I would answer him—if only I could.

- 9 -

Nimrod left first for Atlanta, where he was to remain until the end of the academic year. Oded and I took off a few hours after him into weather that grew stormier the farther east we flew.

"So what do you say about our sons?" My husband tried to distract me from the rocking of the plane, but there was no need to do so. Every jolt interrupted a thought, and I was glad of the jolting and interruptions, as if this was exactly what my body needed in order to purge itself.

"So what do you say?" Something thudded. The beverage cart. It was jolted from its place and crashed into the back of the plane, and the riders on the Ferris Wheel let out a groan in chorus. A flight attendant grabbed hold of the cart and hurried to sit down and fasten her safety belt, and someone behind us threw up.

"What do I say? I say that we're blessed," I gasped out loud.

At the beginning of my relationship with Oded, when I was very much in love, I would sometimes imagine myself bumping into him in places where there was no chance at all of coming across him: what would happen if he suddenly walked into the auditorium of the arts faculty? Would he see me sitting there? Would I signal him in the middle of the class?

Say he had been invited to the party too, and at this very moment he was standing in the kitchen with the people who weren't dancing, drinking beer.

Say he had been relieved from reserve duty early, say the whole company had been relieved, and on their way home his mates decided to stop at precisely this bit of the beach, and now he was sitting with them in the shade of that hut. All kinds of nonsense along those lines. That's what people do when they're in love, and it's not completely illogical: coincidences sometimes happen, and why shouldn't they happen to me?

Five weeks after he took me to Mount Scopus, Oded and I were already living together, so that this kind of suspense didn't last long, and turned into a sweet, vague background to our days in the Garden of Eden.

At the Seattle airport I went back to seeing someone who wasn't there, just around the corner, and there, opposite the entrance doors, in a kind of sick reversal, I began to see the Not-man.

I hugged Yachin, who drove to the airport twice that day, first for Nimrod, and now for us. I looked at my husband and my son clumsily embracing in the embarrassment of an emotional farewell, and as I looked at them, one hand on the handle of my suitcase, it occurred to me that perhaps First Person was there.

He lived in America. He was invited to lecture all over the country. There were a number of universities in Seattle, maybe one of them had invited him to give a talk, or maybe he was there on vacation, to ski, and in a minute he would get out of a cab, carrying his gear on his back, like the sun-burnt German couple advancing toward us.

I remembered that there were about three hundred million people living in the United States, I knew that the thought of coming across him, of all people, here, was absurd. But coincidences happen, that was a fact, and a rational person needed to be aware of the facts. Things happened. Events could take place.

It never occurred to me for a second that I might not recognize him, but what did occur to me was the fear that the moment I fixed my eyes on him, he would recognize me. I would have to be careful not to stare, because a gaze that lasts too long is the one that betrays. And so is the one that immediately looks away again. What happened would be determined in the blink of an eye, because the first to blink is the one who goes down. Because eyes that fail to keep guard are the ones that leave the throat exposed.

In the line to hand over our luggage, and in the departures hall, and in the narrow sleeve leading to the plane, I didn't stop looking around alertly, and even after we took our seats I saw fit to peer behind and in front of us, in case he had been among the first to get on the plane. Perhaps he was behind the curtain, traveling business class. Opening his tray and signaling the flight attendant to pour him a glass of wine. Perhaps he was sipping the wine now, nibbling a nut, and studying the menu.

The jolting of the plane did not rid me of the delusion, which continued to obsess me in the New York airport. First Person had once lived in New York, and maybe he still did. Cosmopolitan First Person traveled a lot, he visited many places, and soon he would be in Israel too, in Jerusalem, for the conference.

With this thought and with the darting of my eyes, the awareness that he had a life in the present spread though me like fire.

Not-man was a controversial intellectual. People were curious to hear a controversial intellectual. And a controversial intellectual liked people who listened to him. Perhaps at this very moment he was sitting in a café and dunking a croissant in his coffee—maybe not a croissant, maybe like his hero he had a weakness for cream cakes—never mind, it was nonsense to worry about what he ate—in any case, First Person is sitting in a café and talking to a female student about the Marquis de Sade, explaining how he had preceded "The Penal Colony" in his vision, and how he had foretold the events of the twentieth century. The student sees herself as daring, in anticipation of her meeting with him she wore a black leather skirt, and now she asks him to supervise her doctoral dissertation. In the evening perhaps they would see an art movie at MoMA.

In the evening they would go to MoMA. But now it's morning in New York. Early morning. Too early to have coffee with a student, but not too early for him to wake up. The person who had forced a blinking child to read *The 120 Days of Sodom* to him, is presumably awake already, and now as he gets ready to go out he listens to an old record of Wagner's *Rienzi*. A record, not a disc, because he is no doubt a collector of old records. Yesterday while strolling in the city he bought it, now he listens to it while he shaves. His tiny bristles dot the washbasin, and the wind blows bits of his hair into the air. Hair doesn't disintegrate, even after a hundred years it doesn't disintegrate. For years First Person has been shaving, the air outside is full of microscopic bristles, and people walking in the street breathe Not-man's invisible bristles into their throats. Pedantic Not-man rinses the washbasin, and water carries the black insects of the bristles to the sea, more of them every day.

Bristles don't do anything—I thought—there are no bristles, all this is delusional nonsense, I'm coming unhinged. I'm out of my mind because I breathed in the bristles. My sister's penal colony breathes the air of the city below us, and my sister pardoned him; people breathe in the breath of his mouth.

.

The fire of my imagination spread through me, and as it raged and lit up more pictures, as if at a distance, high above the flames, I realized that I was no longer afraid. The plane leaned sideways, the land slanted below us, Not-man walked the crooked land, and I was not afraid: my imagination was just measuring my strength, testing me with images. There was nothing in the air, nothing microscopic in the sea, I was not a child to be frightened of imaginings. And in reality too, I had the strength to confront the Not-man, as long as it wasn't by surprise—just not that, not by surprise. I wasn't a child, but coming face to face with him in person if he took me by surprise, that was even beyond me now.

Among the various parasites preying on my mind the book I had thrown into the trash in the Chicago airport popped up again. This was already after the plane had steadied itself over the ocean, after the lights had gone off and the flight attendant had asked the passengers to pull down the blinds, when I was feeling a little sleepy at last.

It occurred to me that perhaps one of the cleaning staff in O'Hare had picked *First Person* out of the trash. A woman, perhaps. And presumably she had no idea what it was. She saw a book in good condition, saw the sensational subject of Hitler, and decided to keep it. Before she hid it on her person she presumably removed her rubber gloves. Not a young woman. Her fingernails dirty and painted red, her teeth crooked and in need of dental care she could not afford. She brought her find to her boyfriend, as she was in the habit of doing with all her other windfalls. Many different things can be found in an airport, and this one too she presented to her boyfriend—who was he? A follower of Louis Farrakhan, I imagined. Her boyfriend read it, in the week that had passed since then he told his friends about it, and one night he would order the woman to read it aloud to him. She would stumble over the words, he would snatch the book from her hands and say, "You're so stupid," and when he went to bed with her he would hurt her and look into the gaping void of her mouth and say, "There's nothing there."

And maybe it wasn't a cleaning woman who plucked the book from the trash, but Not-man himself who happened to be passing through the airport at precisely that moment and fished *First Person* out of the bin—so I thought, and with this paranoid fantasy my sleepiness vanished. The thing I threw into the trash was covered in brown paper, Menachem had covered it, and anyone who didn't know what was underneath the paper, even the Not-man himself, wouldn't have been able to recognize it. Why hadn't I removed the paper to look at the cover of the book?

"You never told me what he put on the cover," I said to Oded.

"What?" My husband was sleeping, his mouth was slightly open, to a degree that was not aesthetically unpleasing. My husband was exhausted and asleep, and even in his sleep he did not allow his mouth to sag and gape. The biggest prize of my life. The land of the salt of the earth into which I had come by chance, not by right. Why was I nagging him?

- 10 -

And then we were home. I was always happy to return. I was happy when we returned to our first apartment from our first backpacking trip to Europe, and no less happy on our return from expensive luxury hotels.

Anyone who grew up like I did will always see the room from the point of view of the maid who comes to clean it. And even though I enjoyed the luxuries my husband provided without any pangs of conscience, I never left a hotel room without making sure that our trash was securely bagged, that the sheets betrayed nothing, and that no garments or towels had been left on the floor.

I enjoyed most of my trips with Oded and also the ones in which we were joined by our children, but when they were coming to an end I was always happily aware of the fact that we would soon be going home. To our own house and sheets that were ours alone.

My father would collect old books left next to garbage bins. My mother would buy her fancy-dress costumes from second-hand shops. And therefore, apparently, even in the fanciest hotel it did not escape me that the bed linen covering us was used.

Sheets that had covered us alone, kitchen utensils that no strangers had touched were among the first pleasures of my life with my husband, and on our return home from our holidays I would always spoil the boys by frying real chips or devote the whole morning to preparing a pot of stuffed vegetables. This was also the time when I particularly enjoyed hosting friends. We often invited people to dinner, both real friends and people my husband needed in order to increase our luxuries, and among the latter there were some who became real friends too.

I always enjoyed returning to my chosen books. I enjoyed seeing what was new in the garden—surprises sprouting in the ground even after one week's absence—and I liked knowing that at almost any moment I desired, I could escape to our clean bed and rise from it to the land of dreams. The gates of this land were always close to me, and most of the time they opened easily.

The return from Seattle was different, and both on the drive to Jerusalem and when the taxi was already going down Prophets Street, the happy feeling did not come to me. I said to my husband: "Here we are, we're home," but the fault remained, and the cosmic fault emptied the words and the voice that spoke them.

I had wasted the few days I had with my sons, I had soured and embittered them, and now I felt sour and bitter, and there was bile in my throat. Was it my fault that an evil for which there was no atonement had entered my home with me? My sister had pardoned. And I would remain alone in the prison of the pardon with the sour smell of a Not-man.

It was cold. We turned on the heating. It had rained during our absence. There was no need to water the garden, and Oded only took the pots of grass he had shut up in the shed when we left out into the light.

I threw out a few potatoes that had rotted. I cleaned the muddy prints of a cat that had stolen in and dirtied the marble counter.

We unpacked—we both hate luggage standing in the middle of the room—and while Oded listened to the many messages on the voice mail I crammed the first load of clothes into the washing machine, and sorted out the things destined for the dry-cleaners.

"Emails can wait for tomorrow?" he asked when he handed me a list of my messages. We had already called his parents from the taxi. "I need another hour here," I replied and pointed to the kitchen and living room which were not in any need of cleaning or tidying. My husband rubbed his nose against the nape of my neck and bent down to kiss my tiger face through my sweater. "If you don't need me here I'm going to shower, and if anyone phones tell them we're not back yet."

Oded fell asleep in the light of the reading lamp awaiting me; in the meantime I emptied the vegetable compartment in the fridge and scrubbed it. After that I hung up the washing and, for a few moments in the smell of the laundry softener for babies, I had a sense of normality.

Only after I had made sure that my husband was already asleep, I switched on my computer. The emails could indeed wait for tomorrow, but there was one thing I had to check, and I promised myself that the moment I finished and satisfied the need, I would slip under the goose down and perhaps I would even wake Oded.

I went onto Amazon and located the book. I checked that the same picture appeared on the first edition and on the paperbacks, and then I enlarged what Menachem had hidden.

The face of the first person took up a quarter of the screen, and it was the face of a child. The chin was raised a little, the nostrils looked flared because of the tilt of the head, which stared straight ahead, the eyelids drooping in a way that was too tired for his age.

The arms were folded high on the chest, presumably so they would be seen in the photograph. The way the black hair was plastered to his scalp made his ears stand out. The graphic artist had added a bleeding swastika on the left side of his forehead, and the impression created was that the arrogant child bore his wound heroically, perhaps even defying those who had stamped the crooked cross on his face. *Hitler, First Person* and "Aaron Gotthilf," were written in white letters.

I didn't linger long opposite the picture. The need to see had been satisfied. Enough for now, time to go to bed.

And still I didn't get up, not right away, because there were other things out there that I also needed to know.

I opened Google and ran a search. The globe spun in the upper right hand corner—as it turned I remembered that Hitler had called it "the challenge and the prize." And when the earth stopped turning, the search results showed three hundred one thousand.

Three hundred one thousand links to Aaron Gotthilf, situated in virtual space and leading to—how many people all over the world? There were those who wrote the texts and those who posted them online, because the one who wrote wasn't always the one who posted; and there were those who read and spread the word to others, and not only in writing but also by word of mouth.

An octopus that embraced the world, a world-wide web of tentacles spreading through space. Not one "First Person" but many. A body that multiplied itself.

On page number one the words "mistake" and "my mistake" were repeated: "'My Mistake'—years after the publication of his controversial book about Hitler, Professor Gotthilf explains . . ."; "Although

Gotthilf admits that he made a mistake . . ."; "Professor Gotthilf's great mistake . . ."; "There is no mistaking his new position . . ."

I scrolled quickly through a few of the following links. Texts in English, French, German, and Italian, or maybe Spanish, a text by someone with an Indian name, *Hitler, First Person*; *Hitler, First Person*, the program of a conference at the University of San Jose, the bibliography of a course at the University of Michigan; a link to an article published in the New York Review of Books; another program of another conference; "Professor Gotthilf is the son of scholar Hannah Gotthilf, whose study of . . ."; *Hitler, First Person*—I didn't open any of these links, not yet. I'd had enough for now. The hours of typing and reading, conscious of my sleeping husband, pricking up my ears to listen for his movements, hurrying to close the browser whenever he got up to go to the bathroom—those pornographic nights came later. Because on the first night when I started tracking the cells multiplying on the web, on that night I actually felt the sense of satisfaction that comes from seeing clearly; I'd even say I felt almost calm. When I shut down the computer I didn't send myself straight to bed. I went out into the inner courtyard and stood there without switching on the light until the cold climbed into my bones and cooled the fever of my satisfaction, increasing the sense of calm I had begun to feel. I picked a moist branch of sage and crushed the leaves to smell them, and with the smell of the sage and the penetrating cold my breath opened and a possibility of cleanliness appeared. I didn't know where it would come from, what would bring it, and how it would clean everything. Nevertheless, for a few minutes "cleanliness" was there as something that might be possible.

Penetrated by cold and clear-sighted knowledge, I slipped into bed next to my husband, and in the dark I smelled the sage on my fingers until the scent faded.

- 11 -

We returned to a routine that became increasingly false, and whose falsities both of us in our weakness went out of our way to hide. My husband was incapable of listening. I didn't have the words to explain. I don't blame him or myself, because the spreading infection was stronger than both of us, and like a disease it had to be allowed to take its course until it reached its climax.

Oded was sucked back into the office, and from time to time he complained that he was sick of his work and sick of being at the beck and call of entrepreneurs and landowners. "You read, write, develop, and look at me—I can't even read detective stories any more. Just look at the kind of characters I have to spend my days with. In the end I'll bore you to tears."

Like he used to in the period when we had just met, he spoke of "changing direction" and his wish "to do something completely different," only now he was talking about taking early retirement, after which "I'll finally be able to read something serious, or go and study something for the sake of my soul."

A few days after we came back, he began to get up early in the morning and go for long runs. He complained of growing a paunch in America, that one hour with Yachin in his gym was enough for him to realize how he'd allowed his body to deteriorate, that if he only had the time he would've liked to go back to judo or even to get into some other martial art: "You probably don't remember, but I was once pretty good at that stuff." And in the meantime, until he retired, and until he finished with the mall-owners' case, and until he became a street gang counselor and taught the boys judo, he set the alarm clock for 6 AM.

One evening when I popped out of the bathroom for a minute to get a towel, I passed the bedroom door and saw him standing naked in front of the mirror and examining his body in profile. My handsome husband pinched his belly like a woman, and I hurried away. Love covers a multitude of sins, but I wasn't going to lend a hand to the cover-up any more.

A physical restlessness like Oded's attacked me too. I didn't go for runs, but apart from the stolen hours I spent with Not-man on Google, I had a hard time sitting still. And no occupation, no book I opened, succeeded in keeping me in one place. I gave up the car almost completely, and instead of driving I started to walk. A meeting on the Mount Scopus campus, an upholsterer's in Talpioth, a dentist's appointment on the south end of Hebron Road—I went everywhere on foot; speed-walking, but not for the sake of my health. I walked fast to dissipate the infectious itch that refused to go away and made my skin crawl. All it needed was the touch of a finger for all my thoughts to spill out of me like blood.

The winter was more rainy than usual: a blessing, people said, Lake Kinnereth is overflowing, it's already past the upper red line. The ground water is brimming over. It rained a lot, and I didn't even try to adapt my movements to the intervals in the rain. I simply left the house and started walking, breathing in the air of the Judean Hills together with the stench of exhaust and rotting vegetables in the market, breathing the same air as the First Person, sharing the same sweeping, sickening pardon with him.

My sister spoke in general terms about pictures she labored to banish from her mind, and the pictures she didn't describe haunted me more than the ones I knew about, more than what I gathered during the days of our basement apartment.

At the age of eighteen I was too ignorant to picture things that were obvious, and in any case all I wanted then was to distance myself from the confused vortex of my sister's imagination. But now, all the details she had been incapable of recounting, and everything I had avoided hearing, took on shape, and the shapes moved inside me and hurt like punishment and sent me on punishing walks all over the city.

I won't describe the things I imagined then. My sister was raped, not me. I did not suffer her torture with her, and I won't pander pictures of her body here like some pimp.

Regarding the pictures in which I myself played part, the picture that haunted me most frequently was the one after the first meeting, the one in which First Person kisses my hand. Raises the palm a little, bows his head, lingers for a second, and pecks my skin with his mouth like a clown. A clown making himself ridiculous to make others laugh, and in the meantime laughs at everybody else. Pecks and pierces and laughs.

On the surface, as far as the rest of the world was concerned, things went on as usual, at least in the beginning. I walked all over town, but my walks almost always had an ostensibly normal reason: a visit to the nursery to choose a new tree to plant, to replace the alder uprooting the fence. I returned empty-handed, since it was only once I was there that I realized I wouldn't be able to carry the sapling back on foot, but at least I had gone to check it out, and this too was an activity with a purpose. I went to order new upholstery fabric for the armchair, and I went to a meeting at the Youth Center to discuss the neighborhood parking problems, which were growing increasingly severe. And I went to meet friends.

The truth is that I avoided inviting people over: I didn't stuff leaves from my vine, and I didn't prepare sauces from my figs.

I didn't have the patience for it. But I did spend time with people.

Acquaintances asked after the boys, and closer friends asked discreetly "And how was your sister?" And my answer to all inquiries was: "An interesting story. Elisheva is an interesting woman. Jesus is good for her."

My sister was okay. And I was definitely okay, and the world was okay too.

"Christians or Buddhists, what difference does it make. The main thing is, you say she's happy?"

"Elisheva is one of the happiest people I've ever met in my life," I replied again and again, and I meant it sincerely.

"Good, that's what's important and it's great. The fact that there are all kinds of beliefs in the world is what makes it so fascinating. The way you describe her house and all those Christian types is so picturesque—isn't it a pity it's not like that in Jerusalem? What a waste that your Alice is limited to our Holy City. And with all that amazing nature over there too. You could easily have based a column on the whole thing."

A certain nosy-nelly, who isn't among my close friends and who presumably picked up various rumors, asked if now, after I'd "broken the ice" with my sister, would my sons go and visit her too: "Wouldn't they be able to, with the two of them in America anyway?"

"I don't know," I replied. "What's America? From the point of view of distance, from where they are to where she is, it's like flying from here to Paris. Even farther, because at least there are direct flights to Paris, and my sister's Monticello is buried somewhere at the end of the world, getting there is a real hassle. "And besides," I added, "for young people their age, as I'm sure you know, family relations aren't exactly a big attraction. The last thing they need there is uncles and aunts."

I made the same sort of reassuring noises to Chemi and my mother-in-law: my sister had left me far behind and she didn't need me. She had benefactors of her own, leaving me free to enjoy the benevolence of those close to me.

But Rachel did not seem completely reassured. She asked if I had started being more active like Oded—the two of us agreed that the running did him good even though he wasn't at all overweight. Because he'd been fat as a child, the fear of fatness had remained with him to this day; she asked if I was eating properly; she wanted to know if she was imagining it or if I had really started biting my nails again; if it was very hard for me to part from the boys—when was Nimrod coming home exactly?—in the end she arrived at Alice.

Alice was a problem I was unable to hide. Before we left for America I informed the editor that I was taking a two-week vacation, but soon after our return I discovered that I didn't have the strength to take my tourist out on her weekly excursion.

Like many other newspaper columnists, I had one column in stock, needing only a little polishing and an appropriate ending.

My pigtail-sucker made friends with a lecturer in the Jewish Philosophy department, who let her in on the secret of the man who had taught him Kabala: it appeared that this admired teacher and scholar, one of the founding fathers of the Hebrew University, was a secret practitioner of Kabalistic magic. In deadly secret the professor had tried to create a Golem, and some said that he had succeeded; some also said that on nights of the new moon the Golem could still be seen wandering the labyrinthine corridors of the Mount Scopus campus.

Did Alice meet the Golem? And if she came across him, what would happen to her?

Every day I opened the file and after a minute or two closed it again without being able to write a single word. The Golem devoured Alice. My Alice was eaten up. A Golem swallowed the Golem.

I told my editor I'd returned from America with a virus—it hadn't been diagnosed yet, maybe mono, it could take time—the lie came to me with the naturalness of a fiction writer; and to my in-laws I explained that I was suffering from the kind of drought that periodically attacked writers. "Writer's block. Let's hope I get over it soon," I said and spread my hands in a helpless gesture, as if praying for inspiration to drop into them from heaven.

My writer's block was as a successful alibi for all the eccentricities in my behavior during those days. Our Elinor is coping with a period of drought, it happens to creative people. She understands that such things happen, but it isn't easy for her. The process of creation is a great mystery.

The truth behind the cliché is that in the midst of my feverish rushing about, I did indeed try to overcome the drying up of the wellsprings that in the past had always provided me with an abundance of ideas: I threaded my way through winding alleys, I peeped into narrow entrances, I eavesdropped on the snatches of conversations coming from all-night bakeries, and I opened galleries. But the pigtail-sucker refused to appear, and her delight in the world was gone.

Jerusalem became filthy. The pouring rain had brought the trash to the surface. And I, without my puppy-Alice, nevertheless went walking, on dug-up pavements filled with water and sludge, between wet piles of building debris. Here an old plastic bag floats up and sticks to a shoe, there a shoe treads on a comb and smashes its teeth. A broken bottle threatens to cut the sole, and in the background a radio screams artificial enthusiasm. A curtain of murky mist was coming down and covering everything.

Discordant neighs of laugher and an affectation of vivacious chatter greeted my ears at every function I forced myself to attend. And the artificiality and pretense and the lies and concealment in all this forced gaiety was almost unbearable. It occurred to me that the authorities had introduced some drug of deception into the city's drinking water.

A fawning client sent Chemi a present, a purple orchid, magnificent and aggressive. "Would you like to take it?" my mother-in-law asked me.

"No, thank you. I'll forget to water it and kill it without meaning to."

"I'm sure your writing will come back to you, you're so creative," she dared to console me for what she assumed was making my face fall. "Everything has its own logic, and everything takes its own time. Menachem came up with the idea that, in the meantime, until you recharge your batteries—in the meantime perhaps you should reconsider bringing out what you've written up to now as a book. Menachem thinks that perhaps at the time, when the suggestion came up, you didn't maybe give it enough thought. You're a writer. You're our writer. Our friends never stop saying how delightful they find your writing. One of my friends asked me to photocopy your columns about the zoo for her, she wants to make them into a book for her grandchildren and stick in pictures, too. Why don't you make all Alice's fans happy and bring out a book?"

The thought of having to go over all the delightful nonsense I'd written was more repellent than ever. I didn't have the faintest desire to read all Alice's colorful bullshit, but there were other things I did want to read, I wanted to very much. I went on buying books. The shelf of as yet unread books filled up, but nothing succeeded in catching my attention, and after a few pages they all fell flat.

Reading has always filled a significant part of my day, and the restlessness increased and invaded the new gaps opening in my time. My brain craved the drug of reading, and the same brain rejected the books. Until, in this state of deprivation, the cells started to excrete remnants of matter they had previously absorbed, and to mix them up.

Alone, alone, all alone / Alone on the wide wide sea

>Alone, alone, all all alone
>
>Water, water everywhere
>
>The ship is sick, it rises and falls
>
>And the eye seeks the sailors everywhere
>
>For the pot will boil and the water will roil
>
>Sail, sail my boat
>
>For I am poured out like water.

A woman takes herself for a walk as if she were a dog. She steps out briskly, rhyming rhymes with her lips grimacing pointlessly. And the ship is sick / it sinks to the depths of the sea / thou hast ravished my heart / my sister my spouse. My ravished sister has ravished me, she has done for me by forgiving me. The day is done, Elisheva has won.

Scrambled sentences like these beat time for my steps, and sometimes they made me giggle to myself like a madwoman. You don't know, ha-ha, oh no, you don't know. What do you say? I say, laugh till you're blue, you haven't got a clue, soon you'll be six feet under too.

One afternoon, on the path circling the stadium on the Givat Ram campus, I kicked a rock, because all the way from Musrara I couldn't come up with a good rhyme for "the wicked will rejoice." The kick hurt, but since I couldn't find a rhyme, I had to find an outlet somehow.

Elisheva wrote to say that they were having a winter unlike any they'd seen for the last fifteen years at least. The university closed down for two days. Barnett helped his mother bring the horses in from the meadow, and the poor things were huddled together in the stable now. This morning she went out to clear the snow off the bird feeders, after it had blocked all the openings. Everything was covered in a spectacular blanket of white, and the little birds were having a hard time finding anything to eat. Sarah scattered peanuts on the windowsill, and the squirrels looked grateful. At this very minute, as she wrote, a squirrel was standing and nibbling a peanut on the windowsill.

Only at the end did she add that she had told our father about our wonderful visit, and that he wanted to know if he could have my email address.

I replied to my sister that "even though I wish Shaya nothing but happiness," I could see no point in corresponding with him.

I imagined that the roundabout nature of the sentence came across well in English. Elisheva's computer didn't read Hebrew, and I found that it was easier for me to avoid giving offense in English.

To myself I said that Shaya might as well be dead as far as I was concerned, and that if his ghost was happy in Verona, it was no skin off my nose.

Our father was dead to me, and in any case it wasn't his death that I wanted.

I sent the email and was about to return to Google. A few hours before I had started to read an article by some bigwig at the Jewish Federation. The article I had opened last night discussed the question of whether the members of our congregation in Los Angeles had been right to invite Professor Gotthilf to talk about "My Mistake." Judging by what I had managed to read before Oded got up to have a drink of water, the VIP had found reasons both for and against the invitation. "Although we believe the *mode veozev yerucham* he wrote," and explained the words in English as "a person who admits his wrongdoing and forswears it should be shown mercy," "at the same time it should be taken into consideration"—and here I had to stop.

I brought up the article with the intention of finishing it. In these moments of sickening intimacy opposite the screen, the maddening discordance of all the pretense around me disappeared. But I was unable to sit still and read continuously for more than a few minutes at a time. I brought up the article, and then I heard the front door opening.

It was the second week of February. An ordinary weekday at the beginning of the week. Half past ten in the morning. Outside it was flooding. Water poured down from the sky, welled up from the ground. And my husband was supposed to be at work.

I got up quickly, and before I had time to wipe out the evidence I hurried to greet him. The face that filled the space in front of me for a moment sent alarm bells ringing: it was Oded's face, alien and distorted, the cheeks sucked in with tension. "Okay. I think we need to talk," he said.

I stood confronting him, and the theatrical nature of this confrontation in the middle of the living room propelled me out of the anxiety like the push of a strong hand. One moment I panicked, the next I felt the tickle of ironic laughter: that tone. That dramatic severity. Those clichéd words.

What could happen? What else could happen that hadn't already happened?

"I'd like you to tell me what this is." And without sitting down and without taking off his coat he threw a printout onto the table next to us. A glance from above was enough to identify the column that I had sent my editor sometime during the night. I had sent it, and the idiot had sent it to my husband. Or perhaps he had called my husband first to complain, and my lawyer had asked him to send it to him to read.

"Just a joke, what's the big deal?"

"Elinor, if this is what you call a joke, then I really don't know . . ." his voice petered out, and the hand that had thrown the document down rose to steady his forehead. "Can I ask you to sit down? Can I? Then will you please sit down."

I had composed the story of Alice's last excursion not many hours previously, when sleep continued to evade me. The editor had learned from the heading of the return of the prodigal daughter, and in his delight he sat down to read the text immediately after he entered his office.

In her final adventure, Alice visits the Church of All Nations in Gethsemane. About two weeks earlier my feet had indeed carried me to the church, whose real name is actually "The Basilica of the Agony." This was the place where the fear of death had come upon Jesus and his sweat "fell like great drops of blood to the ground." There he prayed to his God to take the cup from him, and there he said to the priests, "This is your hour and this is the reign of darkness." I know all this because I did the research. Like most of Alice's trips, this final one also enabled me to occupy myself with research.

The story began with a classic joke; a cliché of a joke. Under the Byzantine pillars of the façade—the pillars were designed by the Italian architect Antonio Barluzzi, and their construction was completed in 1924, as I pointed out punctiliously in my column—under the Byzantine style pillars of the Church of All Nations, Alice meets three men: a Jew, a Christian, and a Muslim. The three are standing together in a group, and the pigtail-sucker is delighted to have come across this manifestation of religious diversity: in the colorful tapestry of the city, religious variety is what delights her above all.

The Jew, the Christian, and the Muslim are also very happy to meet a girl from Alaska, and the interesting conversation between the four of them continues until darkness falls, and they set out together to stroll among the olive trees on the higher slopes of the hill. Someone remarks that "It may have been on one of these very tree trunks that Jesus rested his head," but from the story it is not clear who the speaker is.

Alice's body is found the next day—that is to say most of her body. One severed leg is found lying at the entrance to a pottery shop in the Armenian quarter, the other on the fantastic roof of Papa Andreas, a restaurant with one of our city's finest observation points. The torso is discovered in the Hurva synagogue in the Jewish quarter. Another forty-eight hours pass before a fair, red-tinted pigtail comes to light in a bin of cast-off scraps in the heart of the meat market in the Muslim Quarter.

Elisheva my darling, my pretty one! Why they call you lame I do not know / Even if you cannot run / Of the usual pair of legs / you are missing only one.

- ß -

In the end we talked, my husband and I. Rather, it would be more accurate to say that we sat down and my husband talked a lot, while I mainly mumbled that he was right, something was apparently happening to me, and all right, I was sorry.

I really did feel sorry. When he mentioned Seattle, I was sorry for everything that was missed and everything that went sour there—how I had failed to ask Nimrod about his roommate in the dormitories: even when he mentioned his exotic friend and roommate, an original native of Hawaii, I didn't ask a thing. I was sorry for my evasiveness and for my aimless wandering and for the sleep that evaded me—it crossed my mind that I was really very tired, perhaps because of this, too.

I was sorry for my husband's sorrowful face, and for his voice that kept trying to feel me out, and for the fact that part of the time I wasn't really listening to what he said.

At a certain stage when he had almost despaired of me and my replies, he got up and walked around the house, but by the time he passed the computer in my work corner, the screen saver had already come on, and an artificial aquarium with tropical fish hid the First Person.

In the few minutes when Oded was walking around and around like this, I remember that I even felt a certain sorrow for Alice.

Years ago, in my first column, she came to Jerusalem with the intention of learning to paint in desert light. I had invented this detail and later abandoned it, and since I had abandoned it, the girl from Alaska would never, never paint any kind of light, or anything at all.

My Alice would never paint any more—she had hardly managed to paint at all—and I would never learn if such a thing as "desert light' even existed in painting, because without her, what was the point.

"I don't know what else to say," Oded said when he came back and sat down on the edge of the armchair. "I think both of us are stuck here, and that we need some help. I mean psychological help."

My husband said "both of us," and it was clear to me what he was saying. "Both of us" was the hook on which he meant to catch the madwoman and lead her to a shrink. My husband, I guessed, was thinking of the complete collapse of our sex life, he was thinking of its death—and being what he was, in other words, the best of all possible men—it never crossed his mind to put all the blame for what had gone wrong on his wife.

Let me say in short that ever since the twenty-four hours in Chicago, this pleasure too had vanished from our lives, and the almost continuous presence of this absence had made all our movements awkward and clumsy. How pathetic and insulting is the choreography of avoidance. Here I am, hurrying past my husband wrapped in a towel, averting my eyes as he looks at me; trying to look like somebody who has forgotten some chore urgently in need of execution. Here I am scouring the oven and the gas rings, and here is my husband already asleep, wrapped in the bedspread, leaving the blanket for me.

"Both of us" my good husband said. But the problem was with me and in me, because it wasn't Oded who crouched to clean the oven in the middle of the night, and he never avoided my eyes.

Pregnancies and breast-feeding and quarrels and a son in a pilots' course, examinations for the Bar Association and urgent appeals to the supreme court—nothing in our lives thus far had interfered with the flowing current of our sex. It was the city of refuge to which we retreated, it was also open ground. Sex was perfunctory and sleepy, it was wild and anarchic, sweet and boring, but it was always there. Always there—until it was taken from me in the green woods of a little town with a musical name.

Because even before we returned to Israel something went wrong with our touch. Oded's hand on my inflamed skin became heavy and oppressive, and sometimes the opposite—it was light and irritating, as if an insect had landed on my belly and I had to brush it off.

Even in sleep it sometimes happened that he touched me, and I reacted by crying out and recoiling. There was no part of my body left that wanted to be touched.

I was familiar with the usual advice in such situations: close your eyes and think of the queen. Go with it, abandon yourself, pretend, and pleasure will find an opening. Go through the motions and the real thing will come. And in general, all couples go through rough patches, and what can you expect after so many years of marriage?

But I didn't want to. However out of control I was, kicking at rocks and deliberately hurting my toes, one thing was out of bounds. There was one thing at least I would not do: I would not tell a lie with my body.

•

"If that's what you think, then all right, we'll go to therapy," I said. It was clear to me that no Freudian interpretations would give my husband the right touch back. But he laced his fingers, propped his elbows on his thighs, and pressed his knuckles to his forehead. And even after there was no point left, I could not deprive Oded of hope.

"I'm glad," he said and removed his hands from his face. "Thank you. One of the things you learn in my problematic profession is when to call on expert assistance, and that it's nothing to be ashamed of, it's what intelligent people do. The important thing is to find ourselves a good guy, someone we can both respect. I don't really know how to go about it, it's not exactly a field . . . you know. But maybe one of your girlfriends, someone whose opinion you respect, can give us a name." Even in stressful negotiations my husband is adept, as he puts it, in "maximizing his achievements."

I undertook to find us a therapist, and my responsible Oded got up to go back to work, leaving behind him a partner who had become a little more responsible. Like a guest I accompanied him to the door, and we both lingered a moment on the threshold, he rubbing his cheeks, I playing with a lock of hair and tucking in my shirt. For a moment he seemed about to kiss me on the cheek, and then he controlled himself and left. Only as he turned to go I noticed that he had cut himself while shaving in the morning. Once, an eon ago, when he cut himself like this, his wife would have licked the blood from his neck.

A wave of sardonic malice rose in me to the sound of the car driving away, and with this wave the idea of looking up the "expert" soul doctor in the Yellow Pages I had promised to find. I even opened the phone book. "Spiritual psychotherapy"; "Expert clinical psychologist, therapy by hypnosis available"; "Short-term power therapy"; "Dynamic short-term therapy"; "Depression, anxiety, sex"; "Hypnosis and workshops'; "Relationships, dreams, and anger'; "Mid-life transitions."

Who presumed to know when life ended and when it was at its middle?

Power therapy—I said to Oded in my heart—let's not pretend at least, because you must see that this will only work by force: perhaps by hypnosis combined with drugs in the water. In any case, no workshops, and we haven't got the time for "dynamic therapy" because it's impossible to carry on like this, because how long can we go on suffering like this? You understand—how long? Don't you understand that an affliction like this can only be eradicated by force?

And yet, I didn't pluck a magician at random from the Yellow Pages. I was fair, I behaved like a good sport, I gave it a chance.

I called a girlfriend, a child psychologist, and told her about some friends of ours "who were experiencing a mid-life crisis in their relationship." And in order to be even fairer I added that I happened to know that the man—I deliberately avoided saying the woman—"had experienced some sort of trauma at an early age."

"In your opinion would they prefer a male or a female therapist?" she asked.

"Does it make a difference?"

My friend gave me the name of a psychologist "who is both professional and human." And after checking my husband's schedule with his secretary, I made an appointment for the two of us.

At noon on the day we were supposed to meet our therapist, my feet carried me to circle the Old City walls again. When I passed the Church of All Nations, I did not cross the road to admire the Byzantine-style pillars on the façade. Antonio Barluzzi had designed them. An eminent architect. A half-rhyme. And Barluzzi went with Monticello, even though it didn't rhyme at all. Monticello reminded Oded of Limoncello and the only thing it rhymed with was cello. How did a little town in Illinois come to have an Italian name in the first place? Another pretense, another fraud—if not an outright lie.

I climbed as far as the Zion Gate, and went inside with the intention of taking a shortcut home. In one of the streets I came across a ladies' hairdressing salon: the façade was of an old established business, I must have passed it many times before without noticing it. I had time to kill before the meeting in the evening, so I went inside, and in the air perfumed with the scent of roses, among the gleaming posters of foreign singers and dancers and actresses with painted faces—I had my hair cut so short that it stood up in bristles.

When I first met Oded my head was almost shaved; not a lock of hair to take hold of, and Oded, in my opinion, thought it was sexy.

But with the passage of the years he seemed to take credit for every centimeter of hair I grew, and he would run his fingers through the results with an air of self-congratulation.

My mother-in-law remarked on more than one occasion that "with your face anything would look good, but long hair really is more feminine," and I was happy to let myself be persuaded and to let my hair grow down to my shoulders.

I was the only customer, and the tiny hairdresser—bright as a bird in her blue polyester trouser suit—tried to bargain with me. "Why don't we wait until the summer to cut it shorter? Perhaps for now we'll only cut it up to here?"

She demonstrated by pulling my hair up to my ears, and her eyes, heavily fringed with artificial black eyelashes, looked at me suspiciously in the mirror, as if I was setting a trap for her with my outrageous request.

Alice would have milked a jug full of stories from this colorful creature. I could have thrown her head into the hairdressing salon instead of the meat market. But it was too late now, one of her pigtails was already sticking out of a heap of butchered meat, and "after the first death there is no other."

In the end I compromised: the perfumed heat made me feel faintly dizzy, the massaging of my scalp lessened the constant itching a little, but even so I was too impatient to haggle over any further inroads. I declined the tiny hairdresser's offer to spray my hair, thanked her, and paid. She looked happy to see the last of me, and I walked out of there with my hair a little longer than it had been at my mother's funeral.

When I picked Oded up outside the office, it was cold, five degrees Celsius inside the car. And so it was only when I took off my hat in the psychologist's clinic that he saw my old-new hairstyle. Saw it, and refrained from reacting, since any reaction in this situation would have seemed out of proportion, against the background of a décor unsupportive of any deviation from the norm.

The clinic in Abu-Tor was a perfect example of correct proportions. The ceiling was just the right height, a little lower than ours at home. An appropriate wooden table, half-way between office and domestic furniture. A single, flourishing potted plant, recommending the good care of its owner. Two original still-life paintings, containing nothing to distract or remind. A soft wool carpet in shades of golden-brown and cream.

Had we found the place easily? Were we cold? If we were, she could switch on the heating.

In another era, I would probably have liked her. Even as I sat down next to Oded, I acknowledged this. Appropriately feminine jeans, a white linen blouse creased to precisely the right degree, undyeds graying hair, and a face that had rounded and matured in a dignified manner, without a trace of sentimentality. The eyes too, I noted to myself, looked intelligent.

She could have been my husband's older sister. She could have been his older wife, because a glance was enough to establish that she belonged, with inborn naturalness, to "the upstairs people"—at the top. The nice-looking daughter of a professor from Rehavia, or perhaps from Beit Hakerem. Academic success achieved by dint of hard work and perseverance, but never at the cost of crushing effort. In the course of her professional training she had paid thousands of pounds in order to complain about her parents, who were by all accounts perfectly satisfactory. Had her father paid for her analysis or her husband?

An obscure sense of guilt—I thought—drew her to occupy herself with human suffering. Her sympathy for her clients was sincere and so was the attention she paid them. But of the other side of suffering, of evil, she knew nothing. People like her didn't have pictures proliferating in their heads. They didn't know.

Would we like to tell her what had brought us to her?

The husband leaned back in his chair and crossed his legs, giving his wife the stage.

Did all the soul-doctors only know one opening into the hell of the mind?

Before I finished with Alice, I would devote a lot of thought to the opening sentences of each of my columns. Did these people not have the imagination to accommodate more than a single opening? It was possible, for instance, for her to tap her pencil on the table and say: "Name please, address, and serial number," in which case I would be able to tell her why I failed to serve in the IDF, even though all my friends had joined up and I wanted to too, only at exactly the time in question my mother had killed herself and my sister had been released from a psychiatric hospital.

•

The land of those who know no evil has habits of its own. My husband shifted uneasily on my right, and I said to myself that since I had been asked it was up to me to honor the customs of the land.

"My sister suffered sexual abuse, continuous abuse," I stated. "She became pregnant as a result. This was when we were both in high school, and ever since then, the person who did it to her has been walking around free. Do you think you can help me with this?" I was quite proud of my clear pronunciation of the words, because it was quite hard for me to pronounce them.

"I'd like to hear more, if you can tell me."

"Not only is he not suffering, he's a well-known personality, three hundred one thousand hits on Google. Tchernichovsky has less, just to give you a sense of proportion," I explained, and I was even prouder of myself for the "sense of proportion," something the inhabitants of this land hold in high esteem.

"And since this terrible thing happened—how many years have passed?"

"Thirty."

"Thirty years have passed. And this is the first time you've considered therapy."

"Are you hinting at a statute of limitation on rape?"

"I'm only trying to understand the timing. Why now?"

"Because if you're trying to hint that I woke up too late, if what you're asking is how I agreed, until now, to let this thing go on growing—because you see, it wasn't only rape, it was an ideology of raping and raping and never stopping because there's no end to it. The Marquis de Sade and Hitler. That's what it is. And it grows, because it's there. Because for thirty years it was ignored, as if it didn't exist, as if it could stay this way, for someone to suffer such torture, and the person who did it to her . . . as if it can't be cleaned." All at once, without any preparation or intent, I'd been swept away by a torrent of words, but my tongue couldn't keep up, and I remember that I thought about blood, because as my tongue swelled and stumbled in my mouth, I felt my blood rising and bursting through my skin.

In the face of this outburst, the therapist said, "So many painful things, so many painful feelings," and something else about "inundation," as if I had opened the sewage pipes under her cream carpet. On my left, on my skin, I sensed Oded's tide rising, I sensed it very strongly, but I didn't turn my head.

"I don't know how much this word helps, if it helps at all, but what you're talking about is called trauma. And if I understand correctly, then the far from simple issue that the two of you are coping with is how to live with trauma."

"How to live?"

"How to live . . ." She repeated, and it wasn't clear if she meant to answer or to ask.

"I'm not talking about life, why life? I'm saying the opposite. The complete opposite. I'm talking about the person who has to pay, about payment, that's what I'm talking about, about that twisted ha-ha jokiness of his, about the fact that he's still carrying on out there with his two little girls Tzili and Gili, ha-ha, but also about balance. If I came here in the first place, then obviously I want to be balanced. But for me to be balanced inside, there must first of all be balance outside. That's what I meant when I asked you if you could help me."

"To live with injustice, to accept, make peace, or come to terms with injustice, is a very painful thing."

"Accept? Make peace? Come to terms?" I stood up, recovering my self-respect and my tongue, which obeyed me again. Inarticulateness was never one of my characteristics. "Excuse me," I said, "I think there's been a mistake here. I didn't come here to look for any kind of acceptance/peace/coming to terms. That's not what I came for at all, and if I gave the wrong impression, then I apologize."

"Elinor, nobody here . . . I would very much like to understand . . ."

"I'm sorry." I grabbed my coat and walked out of the tasteful clinic with its correct proportions, leaving my husband to write a check or make inquiries about how to hospitalize his wife. I didn't care. I didn't care, because somehow in the course of this farce something inside me had clarified, leaving me with an unexpected sense of relief, and the social embarrassment I knew I should feel didn't even materialize once I was outside.

I circled the car, crossed the street, and walked up to the promenade a few buildings higher up, where the view of East Jerusalem lay spread out below me. The sky was cloudless. The strong light of the stars overcame the lights of the city, and a wind blew and dispersed the clean vapors of mist. For a moment, the movement of the wet air dimmed the lights reflected in the stone, and then it once again revealed ancient views—valley, severe wall, inhabitation.

The city found favor in my eyes, and as I stood there with squared shoulders, I had a strange sense that I too found favor in its eyes, that even if there was no one else in sight, I was not alone. Jerusalem that knew no peace. A city of blood and wrath, jealousy and war, hunger and wild beasts and plague. A city whose stones cry out for vengeance. The price will be paid, and the guilty will not be cleared. Whoso sheddeth man's blood, by man shall his blood be shed. And I will bring this evil upon you, and I will send a fire and cut off man and beast, and break the heads of babes on rocks.

All the weight of the rocks, the stones, and the destruction tilted the scales in my favor to bring balance to the world again. The city was with me in the place where I stood because it could not be otherwise. Supported by the hard, still Jerusalem, I felt steady for the first time since I had parted from my sister. Ever since we parted, I had felt a sense of exile, and now a great city spread out in the darkness before me and spoke to me in my language, and with all the force of its presence it said the things that my tongue, swollen until it was black, had been unable to say. A God of vengeance is the Lord thy God. And He will never pardon the guilty, for the Lord hath a dispute with the inhabitants of the land to rid it of radioactive pollution.

I don't know how long I stood there before hearing Oded's footsteps behind me on the pavement. I don't think it was more than a few minutes before he was at my side.

"So that's what's been occupying you all this time. Him? That's what it's all about—him?" His voice was free of complaint, surprisingly relaxed. I considered the word "occupying." A hobby occupies you. Your business affairs. Your job.

"So it seems," I said.

"Okay, so now I understand a bit better what's going on. Accepting injustice is a very painful thing," he said, and for a moment I thought I was mistaken, but I wasn't mistaken, I had heard right: my husband was teasingly, flirtatiously mimicking the psychologist's calm, deliberate tone. "I haven't had a chance to tell you how much I like your haircut," he went on quickly before I could take in what was happening here. "Can we go to the car now? I don't know about you, but I'm going to freeze if we keep standing here."

I accompanied him to the car and we drove home, and so it happened that we began to talk again, my husband and I, thanks to our brief visit to the soul-doctor.

We didn't talk about everything at once, and we didn't talk about everything: but there were bits of conversations at night, and in the morning before he left the house—exchanges that meant something took place between us.

And there were longer talks as well, on the Saturdays when he joined me on my walks. Because the restlessness that propelled me didn't go away, only now it began to seem to me like something that was necessary, and its existence troubled me less.

Volatile Jerusalem changed its face all the time, sometimes it supported me in its clarity, and sometimes it covered itself in a filthy film of pollution. And not for a moment did I forget: First Person was arriving in the spring.

BOOK THREE
HITLER, FIRST PERSON

- 1 -

"So you didn't save that email . . ." I'd gotten up from the computer a few minutes before in order to greet my husband in the way I once did. I no longer needed the screen saver to hide my occupation, nor did I need to explain which email I was asking about.

He had deleted it. "Sorry, it was foolish of me. I would have fired myself if I did something so idiotic at work. I should have saved it in case of the extremely improbable event of his deciding to bother us again. I think I felt a childish need to simply delete it from our lives."

"And you're positive he didn't mention exactly when he's coming or for what conference." Oded shrugged his shoulders. He had already answered this question before.

None of my web searches came up with an announcement for a conference in Jerusalem that could conceivably have invited *Hitler, First Person* to attend, but I assumed that the information must be somewhere in one of the three hundred one thousand tentacles, and that I couldn't find it because I wasn't doing the search properly.

I couldn't keep away from the computer for more than a few hours, but I also wasn't capable of sitting in front of the proliferating cells for more than fifteen minutes at a time. I sat down, got up, sat down again: Not-man slipped through the holes in the web, and sometimes I had the strange illusion that "Mr. Gotthilf" was not a singular but a plural. I couldn't find a proper biography, he didn't have a website of his own, but in different contexts he was represented as professor at six different universities. The last of these was the University of Indiana, where he had written "My Mistake." Taking into account the frequency with which he changed his place of employment, he could be anywhere.

I thought that perhaps there was no conference, that this too was a lie meant to mislead us. And perhaps he wasn't arriving in spring either, but earlier. And what do people mean anyway when they talk about spring? Some people claim that there aren't any seasons between winter and summer in Israel. Passover is also called the "Festival of Spring" but it often takes place in a heat wave. He has a son in the country, and maybe he's already here with him.

"In November he's giving a lecture in Frankfurt," I said. "'Is to understand to forgive?'—that's what he calls it. There's nothing about Jerusalem."

"Maybe he's dead," said Oded. "What do we know? Maybe he was run over by a truck, or even better: maybe he had a stroke, and now he's lying drooling in some hospital."

"Nothing like that happened," I said.

"No?"

"I just know." I couldn't explain to him or to myself how I knew that the pollution was still alive, or how I felt its existence like a presence. But I felt it and I knew, and somehow it was clear to me that when it left the world—I would know. How? Perhaps I would simply get up in the morning and discover that our rapist uncle,

Uncle Aaron, the ha-ha uncle had disappeared and I could breathe.

"Good, at least let's take comfort in the fact that at his age he isn't capable of raping anyone any more, and it doesn't look as if he's going to write another book about Hitler either."

"And if he was?"

"Capable of raping?" Oded studied his hands. "I imagine that in that case I might think of all kinds of things that aren't exactly within the bounds of the law."

"And what about what was?"

"What about it? Go on, Elinor, explain yourself. Don't run away from me."

But I didn't know how to explain that to him either: that there was no such thing as "was," that everything that was is, and that the past tense was simply a convenient grammatical lie. Nothing passes.

I didn't know how to explain, but I no longer wanted to run away from him, and so I backed myself into a corner and banged my head against the fridge, over and over again.

"Elinor, don't." Oded stood up and took hold of my shoulders.

At this stage we were already touching again, but circumspectly. We embraced, but carefully, avoiding hip to hip contact, the way my husband hugged our sons. Early in the morning, when the heat evaporated from the house, it sometimes happened that one sleeping body wrapped itself around the other. And all this time Oded went on waiting patiently for a sign I did not give. He was patient and respectful and dignified, all anyone could wish for, but the situation made him tense and wore him out; I know very well how tense it made him.

It isn't my fault, it wasn't my fault that we had been deprived of all our desire, all our delight, because I was the first to have been robbed, as if something had invaded me and taken my life away. Oded at least went on wanting, and wanting means being alive.

•

"Tell me what you want." I stood with my back to the fridge, my husband protecting my head and the back of my neck. "Talk to me. At least that. Tell me what I can do. You're not going to bang your head again. I won't let you."

"I don't know," I said, "I can't. You don't understand." Over his shoulder, without any connection to anything, I counted nine wine glasses—there were nine on the shelf, we had originally bought twelve, where had the other three disappeared to?—and when I finished counting the answer came out of its own accord, rising in a childish wail: "Make him be gone—that's what I want."

We went on standing there for another moment: I with my back to the fridge, and my bodyguard stroking my hair, against the direction of growth, like you do with a child. The caressing hand was confused, and I knew that it felt the absence of the locks it could sink its fingers into.

The weakness, the idiotic, childish weakness was intolerable, as was the disappearance of the control and of everything I had worked so hard to acquire. And after that shameful incident with Oded, it even happened that I thought of Erica and her games with the Digoxin in a new way. Because, but for her desertion, but for who she was, I might have been tempted to put an end to the weakness the same way she did.

It occurred to me that thanks to my mother, the medicine cupboard and the carving knives did not tempt me and that, not only for this reason, I might very well visit her grave one day and clean the dust off it. Elisheva believed that I did so every year, and I let her believe it.

No, the medicine cupboard did not beckon me, and as far as harming myself was concerned the furthest I went in my fantasies was getting another tattoo. I remembered almost with longing the concentrated, draining pain with which my tiger-face appeared on my arm, and I thought that exactly this kind of pain was capable of providing some kind of relief: a burning fire on the calf, or maybe a big one on my back could cool my head.

But I didn't get a tattoo either. Maybe because it would require me to sit still for a long time, maybe because I hadn't really gone back to being nineteen, and I hadn't lost everything. My ability to feel love had gone into hiding. My telephone conversations with the boys no longer brought me joy. But the memory of love had not disappeared, and even though I didn't feel anything, I still knew with a kind of intellectual knowledge that there were people I loved, even if they weren't there.

Two weeks after I had asked her not to give our father my email address, Elisheva sent me another message. She reported on the snow, which had not melted but only hardened on the ground, on a field race in which Sarah was supposed to take part and which had been postponed because of the snow hardening on the ground, and at the end she wrote, "Don't worry your head about Daddy. He's in a good mood and he's started learning to play the harmonica. At his age—don't you think that's sweet?'

As always, I knew that she was sincere, that she had no demands and bore no grudge. And I had already realized that the moment she finished telling me her story, her interest in me had waned considerably. The robber of her birthright continued to figure in her life, but now she had been sentenced to stand still in one place, like an ice monument.

At this stage I seemed to have two sisters. One in a red sweater, sending emails in English from a town with a musical name and listening to the sound of a harmonica in Verona. The other, plagued by loathsome torments about which my sister never told me. Because every cruel, vicious spectacle I had ever heard about rose up in my mind to haunt me, with my sister in the middle of it: images of rape that went on and on endlessly, because it had no point. Because the boot that set itself directly down on the stomach and trampled it was itself the point. The boot and the laughter.

Images instilled in me during the course of my life merged with one another to spawn new nightmare births, and sometimes in the company of others I was attacked by the fear that the things I saw in my mind's eye were seeping out of me like sweat, like a radioactive odor. I didn't want them to see what was happening to me, but at the same time I wanted people to open their eyes and see.

How could I make Oded understand without defiling him with the filth, especially since the filth—something I didn't forget—was the product of my own imagination? How was it possible to talk at all, without polluting the land of the salt of the earth?

One Saturday I told him something that had happened. We were sitting in the car in the parking lot of the Armon Hanatziv Promenade. My husband told me that if I felt the need to walk, at least let's walk on the promenade, which was intended for walking. But when we set out, the wind blew so strongly in our faces that we found it difficult to breathe, and we returned to the car and went on sitting there for a while.

My husband talked about Nimrod and his vague plans for the future, and when I was miserly with my responses, he went on to talk at length about himself.

He asked with a certain coyness if, in my opinion, he had been a good father to our sons, and immediately announced that in his estimation "he had done quite a good job with them." He had actually particularly enjoyed the boys during the period of their adolescence, which was supposed to be so difficult. The sincerity of their seeking, their rebelliousness, the totality they had possessed then—in some strange way it appeared that he found it easy to connect to the mindset characteristic of this age: which led him to think that one day, when he retired from the firm, he should work with adolescents. It could be fun. When he was still doing reserve duty, he had never complained when he was sent to command young soldiers. At the age of fifteen, he picked up playing sports and lost more than ten kilos. The guy who had influenced him then—I probably remembered—was a substitute biology teacher, biology of all things. Every teacher, it seemed, could have a decisive influence. And this was why he was coming around more and more to the idea that perhaps his true vocation was to be a high school homeroom teacher. He was also beginning to think seriously that, in a few years time, he might even go ahead and check out this possibility.

I told him that my sister had always hated school, that she hadn't had the good fortune to come across an influential educator there, and then I added that I didn't know what things were like during the period of the abuse. I wasn't there to see what was happening to her. I was in boarding school, and there, far away from her, I actually did come into the orbit of a number of impressive teachers—but perhaps at that time school actually served as an escape from the things he was doing to her, because school could be a kind of refuge.

"I know that he turned her into a piece of furniture," I said, without having clearly decided to tell him. From his reaction I understood that he thought "furniture" was simply a metaphor I had thrown out instead of saying "object," and so it came about that I explained to him: he wiped his shoes on her. He put a suitcase on her and remarked that in every normal hotel room there was a special stool provided for this purpose.

And he once explained to her that everything he did was a kind of experiment, only she was too stupid to understand what he was talking about.

While I was telling my husband this, the potted plant he brought her came into my head, and the final significance of the orchid became clear: that flower was like the banana offered to the monkey after the rubber gloves are removed at the conclusion of the experiment. But I kept this insight to myself.

"So tell me, is there some article in your law book, is there some punishment that covers a situation in which a high-school student is turned into a stool?"

Oded's face twisted. "I don't know about the law. Personally, I would castrate him, and I'm not talking about the chemical variety."

"Is that what you would do? Really?"

"I think so. And I would give him time, too, enough to think about what I was going to do to him."

His mouth remained twisted. I touched the corner with the tip of my finger. "What do you think?"

"I actually thought about a cage. I would shut him up in a glass cage and then would put the cage somewhere where people could come and look. Look at him until he died."

"A glass coffin or box," he said without turning to face me, as if absent-mindedly. He stroked my bare neck. "Armor-plated glass. That man should be stuck standing up in a glass box where he can't move: not sit, not bend down, nothing."

Our car was the only one standing in the parking lot. Our breath covered the windshield with vapors, and Oded wiped them away with his sleeve so we could go on seeing the hard, gray city below us. I think that the sight of the city supported him like it supported me, because the Saturday after that, when we left his parents' house after lunch, he again suggested that we drive to the promenade.

Writers are not in the business of sticking strictly to the facts, and the scenes I've chosen to describe above could give the impression that there was nothing but contention, strife, the Not-man between my husband and myself. But there were other things too, and there are also other images: a woman vacuums, and a husband and wife carry the carpet outside together and hang it on the clothesline to air out; a gardener comes to dig up a tree, and the couple visit various nurseries together to decide what to plant in its place; a father and mother look at the photographs their younger son has sent them from a trip he took to a pueblo reservation, and speculate about the bespectacled young woman with the yellow backpack who appears in most of them.

Oded rolls his Sabbath joint. I make popcorn. I smooth and straighten his eyebrows. We sit together on the sofa, our legs parallel on the coffee table, and watch a movie. We watched quite a lot of movies then, and my husband chose them all, because during that period when I had a hard time making him happy in other ways, I learned to enjoy the movies he liked with him. Aliens, germs, terrorists, a comet, a storm, or a volcano—something threatens to wreak destruction on the world. A good man finds himself in an intolerable situation, and in order to rescue whoever needs to be rescued, he sets the place on fire. He does what has to be done.

I discovered that blood and fire and columns of smoke calmed my feverish imagination, and when we sat like brother and sister and watched Oded's guy flicks, I had no difficulty sitting still in one place for even two hours at a time. The cinematic adrenaline was an efficient antiseptic, and I occasionally fell asleep on the sofa when the movie was over.

- 1 -

I don't know what other people thought of me during this period. I have no doubt that my concerned and observant mother-in-law, keeping a watchful eye on her household and loved ones, heard the seething of my inner ferment, and that she went on hearing it even after her son and I started meeting each other's eyes again.

It's clear to me, and in fact it was clear to me even then, that after a while she no longer accepted my "Alice crisis" as a cause, and began to see it as part of a syndrome.

Personal temperament, family culture, and the hidden but rigid rules that had been laid down between us from the day we met prevented any direct interrogation, but they did not stop her from buzzing discreetly around the subject.

One Saturday she launched into a long monologue about two of her friends who suffered from "empty nest syndrome" after the last of their children left home.

"When the children are in the army it's different, as long as you do their laundry they're still your babies. When Oded moved into his first apartment, he went on bringing me his laundry, and I'll tell you honestly, even if it's anti-feminist, doing his laundry for him gave me a good feeling. They say that the telephone and the computer cancel out distances, but in my opinion, and from the experience of my friends, there's simply no substitute for being face to face. It's only natural for a mother to want to see her child's face, and also to know if he has holes in his socks."

A woman who didn't want to see her children face to face was beyond the bounds of her imagination. If she had been compelled to acknowledge such a possibility she would have been outraged, and she would have regarded me as a monster. But I wasn't a monster, not at all.

I remembered the times before the spoiling, the days when it was enough for me to imagine one of my sons—Yachin kicking his legs in his bay carriage as if he was already in a hurry to run, Nimrod learning from his brother the correct way to lace his army boots—these memories were enough for me to brim over with a great joy at the mere fact of my beautiful sons' existence in the world.

I missed those accessible waves of joy, I missed the joy, but I didn't miss my sons themselves. There is a time for embracing and there is a time to desist from embracing, and I was responsible enough and balanced enough to know that this was not the time to embrace.

The pictures my sister had in her head seeped into me, and the smell of my sweaty visions began to stick to Oded. The sound of the ferment that reached my mother-in-law's ears was the sound of the sights crowding and seething inside me, threatening to overflow and spill out. Sights that I didn't know existed rose up in me and clamored loudly. And I could only be thankful that Yachin and Nimrod were far from the poison, which could burn holes in socks too. The harm I had caused in Seattle was enough.

At another Saturday lunch my mother-in-law showed me an article she had cut out of the newspaper about the various advantages of eating tofu, especially for women of a certain age. She even started cooking it for us, the white stuff that "constituted a natural source of estrogen and calcium. Many studies show that Asian women do not suffer from the change-of-life syndrome, and exhibit a very low incidence of cancer of the uterus and the ovaries. Isn't that interesting? The Asians, it says here, eat tofu all the time, even children and young people like you eat it. The Japanese and the Chinese put a big emphasis on preventative medicine."

The white stuff did not prevent anything or rid her daughter-in-law's system of the dirt, and soon afterward she began to refer mysteriously to "experiences that take time to digest." As much as I loved her, as much as I remembered that I loved her, these metaphoric ramblings about "digestion" only enflamed my rage: as if I needed some mental castor oil to accelerate the exorcism of the vileness from my twisted bowels. As if the vileness had no poisonous life outside my bowels. As if its pollution was only a metaphor and not something real.

It occurred to me to tell her that her son and I had tried psychotherapy, but I didn't want to give her any opening. And in the end my good mother-in-law dared to ask me directly if I thought a lot about my meeting with my sister, because it was only natural for such a meeting after so many years to give rise to all kinds of memories, and it was only natural for me to think about it.

"I never asked you if your sister felt the same as you do, you know, about your parents."

Of all the emotional problems I had brought with me as a dowry, the only one that really worried her was my undisguised hostility toward my mother. She regarded the enmity as an armor with which I covered my wounds, and even more, as the result of a regrettable misunderstanding: a hot-headedness that might be expected to cool down and disappear with the onset of maturity.

"At my age, Elinor, we understand that in our relations with our parents, and definitely with our mothers, there is no black and white."

When Yachin was a baby and suffered from colic, and Oded

and I were suffering from a lack of sleep, my angelic mother-in-law would come by almost every day to allow me to rest. And when she cradled her screaming grandson in her arms, I could see how she was secretly cherishing the fantasy that my motherhood would help me understand my own weak-hearted mother, and to make peace with the dead.

Once, out of the blue, she asked me when exactly the anniversary of my mother's death fell, and whether I never felt the urge to visit her grave.

I tried to brush it off by saying that in general "graveyards didn't mean anything to me," but she, with uncharacteristic stubbornness, persevered: "I can tell you that for many years Menachem was in the habit of declaring that he was going to donate his body to science. With all his modesty, and he really is modest, you know he can sometimes be a bit of a show-off too. So for years he would boast to us about how rational his attitude was, but he never put it in his will. In any event, I'm surprised to hear such intellectualism from you. I'm not judging, God forbid, or telling you what's right, but if you ever feel that you would like to visit the grave, just remember that we'll all be with you."

My new motherhood did indeed give rise in me to various thoughts about my own mother; mainly, it finished off any hint of understanding I might have felt for her desertion.

Rachel, in her womanly way, gave in to me without really giving in. She went on cherishing a sentimental fantasy about reconciliation with the past, and after we returned from America and the contamination flared up and silently threatened us all, she got it into her head again that for me to find peace of mind it was necessary for me to make peace with my dead mother. Not everything was black and white, there were also pastel shades and nuances, and the way to heal both body and soul was to come to terms with your ghosts.

I was burning up in the loathsome intimacy of my knowledge of the vermin—for the pot will boil and the water will roil—and she, in her pastel ignorance, wanted me lukewarm.

'Does your sister feel the same as you do, you know . . . ?"

I swallowed and spat out that my sister had always been a better person than I was and so, apparently, she was in this case too. I saw how my mother-in-law's eyes clouded over in sorrow, I think because of the coarseness of my tone more than my words, and I made haste to add: "Look, I imagine that we both experienced our parents a little differently, that happens with a lot of siblings. But all that's over and done with, and as far as I'm concerned, at least, it's fine for us to feel a little differently."

Quick to take fright and quick to retire graciously from the field, my mother-in-law agreed that "everyone is entitled to feel what they feel. You were sent to boarding school and your sister wasn't, so it's natural for you to feel differently. Being in boarding school probably isn't so simple. Just don't say about yourself that you're not a good person, because if you run yourself down like that in the end I'll tell Oded on you."

Good intentions, only good intentions were behind the following scene:

We sat around the lunch table, the same heirloom wooden table to which an eon ago a young man had brought a tattooed girl to horrify his parents.

"This week Menachem received an interesting invitation"—it was exactly the same tone my mother-in-law would use to say to her grandsons "Let's see if there's something here for you," before she set her bag down in front of them and invited them to open it and look inside. Only this time it was Menachem who opened it.

"It seems that a week after Passover, in less than a month's time, a big international conference is going to be held here in Jerusalem, on 'Representations of the Holocaust in Art.' I understand that they've been working on it for some time already, because a good number of institutions in Israel and abroad are involved in the project. A friend of ours, Mordechai Kushnir—I think you met him, Elinor, on my birthday, Hanita's husband—he's in charge of most of the logistical aspects. Artists and scholars from all over the world are coming, at one stage they even thought that Spielberg was going to come, and Mordechai is responsible for hosting them. To cut a long story short, on Tuesday Mordechai calls to tell me that among the participants is Professor Aaron Gotthilf. Let me say that your controversial uncle is not among the guests of honor, he's apparently paying for his own flight and hotel expenses, but in any case he appears among the list of speakers. One of Mordechai's initiatives, one of the things he's in charge of, is the organization of informal meetings between the scholars. Most of the forums of the conference will be open to the public and will take place not only at the university. The opening, I understand, will be held at the International Conference Center, and among other things they're planning some kind of marathon at the Cinematheque. What my friend refers to as a 'multifocal event.'"

Chemi stirred the noodles into his soup, and laid the spoon down next to his bowl. Menachem Brandeis was not a man to be hurried, and in any case it was impossible to hurry what had already happened and was now a fact in the present. As he was speaking my ears seemed to fill with water, and the rising tide slowed everything down and made me very passive. I felt as passive as after a drunken *hamsin* night. The river flowed and I was borne along in it, there was no point in swimming.

"So Mordechai remembered—actually Hanita reminded him—that we have a Gotthilf in the family—Gotthilf isn't a common name—and he phoned to ask if there was indeed a connection between us, and if Rachel and I would be interested in attending a dinner to which your uncle is also invited."

I sent Oded an S.O.S. No, I didn't even look at him. I concentrated my gaze on the steam rising from the soup and Oded came to the rescue without being sent for: "I thought we had all agreed that the man is beyond the pale. I still remember how you said so yourself, in Spain, about the book. I can't understand how they could've invited someone like him in the first place, his book wasn't even considered worthy of being translated into Hebrew. How can an apologist for Hitler be invited to Jerusalem?"

"Oded, listen to what your father has to say."

"Good, so I hadn't forgotten *Hitler, First Person* either, and I didn't spare Mordechai my opinion, which is no different from yours. But then he told me that Elinor's uncle has completely renounced that abomination—begging your pardon, Elinor—he signed his name to has devoted the last years of his career to what Mordechai called "a campaign of self-condemnation." It sounded quite interesting to me. To repent of something you did, to admit your mistake, is certainly not common, not in our academic life or in our political culture, and in my humble opinion it's definitely something that wouldn't do us any harm to adopt. But to return to the matter at hand, since I was still skeptical, Mordechai sent me a long essay in which the man presents his main points of criticism of his book. I haven't finished reading it yet, I admit that not all his arguments satisfy me, I see some sophistry there, but the bottom line is that there's something to discuss. That's to say that, if in the past, Elinor, I defined your uncle as 'beyond the pale,' as far as I'm concerned that no longer applies, and as I said to Mordechai, an informal dinner isn't out of the question."

The patriarch gave his wife a questioning look—I had no doubt as to who had written the script—and when she sent him an approving smile, he picked up his spoon and started on his soup.

Years after he had taken me to task because of my relationship to the First Person, my mother-in-law had found an opportunity to prompt him to make up for the distress he had caused me then: Something's upsetting the girl, Oded says so too, and whatever it is, we now have a chance to do something to make her happy. And Menachem didn't even have to admit that he had gone too far back, in Spain.

There was no appeal against the favorable sentence that had now been passed on me, and in any case the truth was impossible to pronounce: at the heirloom wooden table there was no place for my sister, who had been turned into a stool.

But Oded still tried, and from my superior vantage point at the apex of my scalp I didn't miss a word: "And I wonder exactly why he set out on this so-called journey of self-condemnation. My guess is that he must have realized it was the only way to save his career."

Now my mother-in-law sent her son a look of rebuke, and Chemi looked at his wife and at me, and they all looked at me to measure the movement of the mercury. But there was nothing to see. I was empty and silent, a unit isolated in space—what would be would be, and the serpent would always be a serpent. Only a kind of laughter stirred and rose on the margins of my passive mind, because I knew, because all the time I knew that a serpent was creeping, and the movement of the heads and the looks around me looked ridiculously slow and exaggerated.

"If we start examining personal motivations, we'll open up a witch hunt that has no end," Menachem announced. "Everyone has his own interests at heart. That's true in politics, it's true in academic life, it's always true, even at this table. So I say that with regard to Elinor's uncle, 'he who admits his wrongdoing and forswears it should be shown mercy.' It's enough for me that he's admitted he was wrong, and that he travels from one university to the next to present this new position. We're not going to start checking up on his motivations, because let's not deceive ourselves, intellectuals are no better than anyone else. People are people, none of us is pure and we are all influenced by considerations of personal interest."

"Except for George Orwell," I piped up, because the main course was still before us and after it the dessert, and only an utter boor would consign so much generosity to the trash.

They knew hardly anything about Orwell, and from my point of view this was fine, because it was very important to know Orwell and important for me to make him known to them. And with my ears full of water I was very eloquent and I explained everything to them at length and in order: how Orwell had fought both the Fascists and the Bolsheviks, and how he had been censored because he hadn't beautified any aspect of reality and hadn't covered anything up, and how he had seen what others preferred not to see, and how he hadn't ignored or concealed, and how he had always been able to recognize Satan in all his disguises.

By the time I was finished Rachel had already served the cake.

"Thank you, Elinor, that was very informative," said Menachem.

- 3 -

"I'm sorry," my husband took a deep breath once we were standing outside the door, "I had no idea . . ."

"It's all right," I replied, checking my exalted sense of calm.

"What I say is: imprison him in a box of armor-plated glass . . ." he said when we got into the car, giving me a gift, or perhaps checking my temperature.

The sun shone brightly. Families of Jews in their Sabbath clothes strolled past us, walking slowly, carrying aluminum trays. April is the cruelest month. It wasn't April yet. When did spring begin? Not yet. Soon.

"Room number 101," I said and started the car. "That's Orwell too. *1984*."

Numbers are a beautiful thing, real, more precise than poetry. Flight number. Date of arrival. Hotel room number. The sound of the typewriter came from the second floor room number 22. For over a hundred days it typed there. Room 22 was my sister's 101. No, that's not right. Things happened in room 22 that no young girl could have imagined in her nightmares.

The sun, as already mentioned, shone brightly, and I went on expounding on Orwell. "Room 101 isn't simply a torture cell," I explained to my husband. "It's the lowest level of the private hell. It's the place where everyone's most private nightmares come true. Because everyone has his own worst nightmare: being slowly burned, slowly suffocated, being buried alive. You don't read pornography, so maybe you don't know that there are some people who are into asphyxiation. But that's not the point. That's not what I'm talking about. Not about the perversions that perverts enjoy. I'm talking about the victims of torture, about Orwell's tortured. Orwell's hero, Winston's worst nightmare is rats, and so that's exactly what his torturer prepares for him in room 101: he puts a famished rat inside a mask and fastens it to his face. And before he fastens the mask to his face the torturer gives him the benefit of his experience by explaining that the rat will gnaw his eyes, but that sometimes it prefers to start with the cheeks."

About what happens afterward, about Winston's betrayal, about how he pleads for his beloved to be tortured instead of him, about the monstrous passage when he screams "Do it to her," about the chapter where it says in so many words, "I'm taking the photograph. Take my sister as my ransom, take her instead of me"—about this I said nothing. This chapter was forgotten for the moment.

This chapter was forgotten, and maybe it isn't important. In the end it turns out that Winston's lover underwent the torture too, that she would have undergone it anyway, without any connection to his betrayal and what he screamed.

Saturday afternoon, people walk with measured steps, pious Jews on their way to visit their families.

"Let's go for a little walk."

I drove my husband to the place where I had refused to take him during the time when we started living together. Jerusalem is small, but it's easy to avoid the end of a street that was once on the outskirts of the neighborhood of Beth Hakerem, but no longer. I hadn't been there on my own either since my father got into a taxi with my sister and me to accompany us to our basement apartment and our *folie à deux*.

In my memory I see that taxi driving away in a cloud of loose pages. The developer who purchased the property from my father conditioned the purchase on its immediate evacuation—so Shaya explained to us—and under the pressure of the haste and the mourning there was no time to find a buyer for the library my father had collected over the years. Works in French, Russian, Polish, Serbian, Romanian, piles of books he didn't know how to read—"my foundlings" he called them—were hurriedly parceled up to be sent to the shredders. Jamilla, the cleaning woman, sympathized with the three of us—for Elisheva, I knew, she had always felt a measure of affection—but Jamilla was already too old to climb up a ladder, and I was the one who climbed the ladder and threw the volumes down to Shaya. There were no fond farewells, books hit the floor and sent up clouds of dust. Covers split apart. Parts of books were trampled. Pages came out and flew about the room. But, as should be obvious to any person of sense, the pages couldn't possibly have flown into the street and remained floating of their own accord—it was my literary imagination that sent them flying around the taxi and left them suspended in the air. Ever since I can remember myself I have attached an exaggerated importance to books.

My parents met when the place was still called "Palm Pension." The young employee took the heart of the owners' daughter by storm. The student who came to support himself while he studied was snared in the daughter's net—with the Gotthilf family you can never know what the truth may be.

But wherever the truth lies, after Shaya had become a partner in the business, and once he realized that his wife would never allow him to sell their common property, one day he decided to make his fate his choice, and in a flamboyant gesture of commitment he changed the name of the place to his own: Pension Gotthilf.

"The truth is that there was never a palm growing here," I said to Oded. "But this fact never bothered anyone, certainly not my parents."

The developer who bought the property demolished the hotel and put up a new building in its place: four stories with balconies for Sukkoth booths and a thin coating of industrial stone. The garden was turned into a parking lot. Residents on the third floor had grown cascading geraniums in planters on their balcony: white, red, purple and mauve.

The demolished hotel was a Jerusalem palace whose stones had all been hewn by hand. Each stone with its own shade of rosy pink. Lovingly cultivated, luxuriantly leafy trees spread their shade from the swing in the garden to the upper windows. In the cool summer evening the guests would sit outside around little tables set with Armenian tiles. A glass chandelier, the sole survivor of European elegance, twinkled at them from inside the house, and the smell of the coffee on the copper trays mingled with the scent of the jasmine.

With the dying down of the fever of my impatience, the spirit of literary imagination rested on me again, and for a moment I was tempted to lie to my husband like a tourist guide or the pigtail-sucker. The destruction of the old hotel prepared the ground for the sprouting of any fancy that came into my head. Because the truth is that not only was there no palm tree, there weren't any Armenian tables or copper trays either, and the uniqueness of the pink stones was a blatant lie too. Pension Gotthilf was a perfectly ordinary building, and the air was not scented by anything except for the dust of the cypresses that clung to the chandelier, which was never cleaned.

But even though there were many things I had kept to myself and never told Oded, I had never lied to him or prettified anything. I had been taken into the land of the salt of the earth from an insignificant and pretentious nowhere, but it was nevertheless the place that for many years, all the years of my childhood, I had called home.

Does Satan's evil begin with his attack on the "downstairs people"? The insignificant people with their foolish pretensions? Because he was elegant, the First Person. He drank his coffee elegantly, declined the cake made with margarine elegantly. "Elinor and Elisheva, Eli and Eli," he said and kissed my hand.

Oded has to understand without my dragging Armenian tables and copper trays into the picture.

"They gave him the corner room on the second floor," I said. On the end of the North side, at the back. He insisted that he required maximum privacy. He even prevented Jamilla from coming in to clean on the grounds that he was busy with his research in the mornings. It was supposed to be a quiet room, but from downstairs, especially from the garden, you could hear the noise of the typewriter."

"Trash," said Oded. "Just stinking trash and not a human being. You know what I think I would do to a creature like him? What I would really do with that trash? I would bury him in the Ramat Hovev landfill in the Negev. Let him choke there under the mountains of garbage. That's the best thing for him."

The new image he offered me caught my fancy and I lingered on it. A bulldozer trundles up. A blade turns the garbage over. Another bulldozer approaches and covers it up. Something twitches in the mound, something stirs among the garbage, or perhaps not. Garbage covers a multitude of sins. The camera moves away, and now we see a clean, arid desert. The noise of the bulldozers fades. In the distance they look like two upturned yellow scorpions. There is no sound.

As my husband said, that would be good. Better than room 101, considerably better than a mask and rats. Dirty things get thrown out in the garbage, and the imagination has no need to fasten the mask to the face and at the same time look into the face of the trash.

In Ramat Hovev, the imagination does not drown in the picture and the throat does not choke.

"So your parents are going to sit down to dinner with him. Okay. I knew it. From the beginning I said he'd find a way to get to us in the end."

"I'm sorry," my knight repeated, and refrained from questioning my logic. "But there's still some time before it happens, more than a month in fact. Let me see what I can do."

I opened a window. "I'm not saying that he initiated or plotted this dinner, I'm not completely crazy, so you needn't look at me like that. I'm just saying that he's not coming here for nothing. Nothing's changed. He wants something. I'm sure. This isn't paranoia on my part, I just know."

"Don't you want to get out of the car? To see how the street has changed?"

"What for? There's nothing to see here. Even before they built this thing there wasn't. Just another ordinary house."

"Still, isn't it a shame they tore it down? Developers. They could have built additional stories on the existing ones. Houses are history."

Isn't it a shame? I carefully considered the alternatives, as if my opinion counted and I had actually been called upon to choose between them: the building would stand. The building would be torn down. The building would go on standing and new stories would be built on the old foundations. Tour guides would be able to pass here with their flocks, point to the old and tell their tales: the lower floors belong to what was once Pension Gotthilf. A pension was here. Gotthilf was here.

"I don't know," I said in the end. "You're the one who knows about real estate and urban planning. In my opinion at least, there was nothing here worth preserving. It's probably better this way."

When we got home I went straight to the computer, only now that I already knew exactly what information I required, there was no need to search: Menachem had made haste to send me the program of the conference. "You'll find your uncle on the evening of the second day, on a panel at the Cinematheque. Rachel says to tell you that to her regret we won't be able to make it, the daughter of friends of ours from Nahalal is getting married. I'm sorry too. The program looks interesting."

Professor Gotthilf of Queen's College would be the third of four speakers under the lengthy heading "Popular Portraits of Evil—the Borders and Limits of Representation." Later on in the evening the film *The Night Watchman* would be screened in the small hall, and *The Bunker* in the big hall. The title of the Professor's presentation was also long, taking into account the twenty minutes at his disposal: "*Hitler, First Person* as a Test Case: Regrets and Errors in the Exploration of the Roots of Evil."

The last speaker's subject was "Education versus Vulgarization— the Test Case of Oprah Winfrey"; I don't remember what test cases the first two speakers were going to discuss, I wasn't paying attention, because the date of the only test that concerned me was already more or less clear.

"I'm sorry," my husband repeated, looking over my shoulder. "My mother has gotten it into her head that we all need to start relating to your family with respect, because that's what will make you happy. I'll find a way to change her mind somehow."

"Your mother is too good for this world. The Brandeis family is too good for this world," I replied unemotionally.

"It's a terrible shame that we can't go there and simply shout the truth, so people will know who that man is and what he did."

"Because what would happen then, exactly?"

"I don't know. He'd be lynched."

"Do you really think so?" I inquired politely. I moved my chair back so that I would be able to look at my husband when he replied.

"But it's inconceivable that they're letting him get away with it, making a second career out of a so-called admission of guilt! What, are they all idiots? It's intolerable how stupid people are. How can they let someone profit from an admission of guilt?"

I went on sitting, watching him contort himself above me in rising rage, as if the snake writhing inside me had escaped and entered into him. "That's the way of the world," I fanned the flames in a tone of indifference. "There are a lot of things that people don't understand."

"My father does somehow smell a rat, of that I'm certain, only he doesn't know. He doesn't know. If he had the faintest idea . . ."

"Elisheva's okay," I said. "My sister's happy, isn't that what's important? She's been born again. She's forgiven him. If she has any ambition at all, it's to save Hitler from hell."

"Your sister can forgive until the cows come home. Let her forgive. It's her right, but I don't forgive."

I closed my email, stood up and gave my husband a non-committal kiss between the eyebrows. And this time it was my turn to imitate our single-session therapist: "Accepting injustice is a very painful thing," I said.

"Shit," he groaned as I withdrew my face from his. "Shit, shit, shit."

Cursing and scowling demonstratively, he looked very much like our Yachin when he was a teenager. And for a moment, like then, I felt like ruffling his hair, and like then—I refrained. Nobody likes having his hair ruffled.

"Okay, but what shit are you talking about?"

"Everything. That a person like that exists at all, and that he's coming here, and his colossal nerve in getting in touch with us. Just the thought of him walking the streets here makes me sick. I know you can ask how come I woke up all of a sudden, but try to understand that your sister and brother-in-law and all that Limoncello—somehow it didn't seem real to me. A place like that, people like that—I know we were there, but somehow it's as if it weren't real."

"So you're claiming again that my sister's a fake."

"I'm not claiming anything. Apparently I'm a simple person, so perhaps your sister is beyond my comprehension. Perhaps she's too great for me, your sister. But it's precisely because of that, I think, precisely because of her greatness that I can't even comprehend, precisely because of this greatness everything suddenly seems utterly loathsome to me. So you can say that I just woke up, and it's true, because it's only now that it's suddenly become real to me: what happened, what he did, that man who's traveling the world now. All the ruin and destruction, the extent of the impudence of evil. I don't know. Maybe I should've seen where you grew up in order to realize how close it all is: where you, where the two of you were while I was playing games in the scouts. You know that I once took my troop there for a camp fire in the valley, five minutes from you? You were still a child then, and so was Elisheva. You still had a few years before the real shit arrived."

Years of maternal self-restraint helped me suppress my smile. Because I was so relieved, and the joy of the relief succeeded in rising to the fortress at the top of my scalp, from which I looked down on everything: inferior families, inferior childhoods also had a right to exist. I didn't need to offer my husband copper trays and wrap my childhood up for him in scents of jasmine for him to understand this. My husband increasingly understood as well as any outsider could, and when the day came—I thought—the day of the deed, rapidly approaching, maybe he would understand then as well, and would not hate me and be revolted by me.

"Look," I said, "look, what happened happened. At his age he isn't going to put suitcases on any more little girls. The main thing is that Elisheva is better now. She's balanced, the world is balanced. The good God saved her. End of story. It's all over."

"What's over? Nothing's over. The good God . . . you know what I feel like doing? What I feel like doing is taking a truck full of dynamite and driving it into your sister's god and blowing him up."

I kissed him again, this time on his lips, and when I retreated he looked a little ashamed.

"Good. As far as this dinner that my parents are supposed to eat with him is concerned, you can stop worrying about that at least. Because it isn't going to happen."

•

A Jerusalem restaurant. Menachem didn't say which one. Perhaps it hadn't been decided on yet. But I needed to know even if it hadn't been decided on. Taking into account the fact that the people invited to the dinner were not among the important guests, it wouldn't be a luxury restaurant. If it was only visitors from abroad we were talking about, the choice may have fallen on one of the tourist restaurants that boasted of their authenticity, for example the one in the first alley on the left, immediately after entering the Old City from the Jaffa Gate. But people like Menachem and Ruth had also been invited, who would not want to walk down the first alley on the left after the Jaffa Gate. And on top of everything else, the place would probably have to be kosher.

I looked at the program again. There was a long list of speakers, most of them had Jewish names, although not all of them, and from the few lines written about each, it was impossible to guess which of them, if any, kept kosher.

My new, exalted calm was grounded in fact, and required facts. On such and such a date, the Not-man would deliver his lecture. On such and such a date he would eat dinner with my father-in-law and mother-in-law. Where? Where? After racking my brains and conjuring up the façades of various restaurants in my mind's eye, the choice fell on one of three restaurants on Keren Hayesod Street. All three were popular, and not only with tourists, all three offered big tables and what was called "atmosphere," and the prices were reasonable.

I was unable to decide which of them would be the venue of the meeting, and after going in and out and in and out again, my imagination agreed to compromise, and without further ado it merged the three into one.

My in-laws would arrive on time, and together with their friend the host they would take their places at the middle of the table, which had been reserved in advance. The waitress would light a candle for the sake of atmosphere: the lighting in the place was dim but adequate. Wine? A drink from the bar? We'll wait for the others. For the time being, only water for everyone.

In the meantime, until everyone arrives, Rachel would enter into conversation—with whom? Perhaps the woman who was going to lecture on the "Test Case of Oprah Winfrey"—What is the case? she would ask. A program Oprah did with Elie Wiesel, the professor would explain. The professor is in her late fifties, she teaches in the Department of Communications at the University of Pennsylvania, a pleasant, friendly woman. Nevertheless my mother-in-law will feel a little embarrassed by her far from perfect English.

I do not dwell on their conversation with the intention of postponing the entrance of Not-man. Not this time. I am already prepared to look at him, but he is late and the last to join the table, around which how many are seated now? Seven. Seven people stand up to shake his hand when he comes in.

"Did Mordechai tell you that we are related?" Rachel will ask and send him a sunny, welcoming smile. But she won't ask right away: my mother-in-law is the soul of tact, and she would never, God forbid, give him cause to feel that he was being ambushed. First of all, they will consult the menu and talk about the media coverage of the conference. Its contents will presumably not be discussed, the Holocaust and Hitler not being suitable dinner table topics.

Not-man will sit at the head of the table, on Rachel's right, his legs sliding out uncomfortably. My mother-in-law will address him in English, because to put one over her and his hosts, Not-man will hide his knowledge of Hebrew.

"My daughter-in-law's name is Elinor," she will explain, because the expression on his face will show no sign that he heard what she said or understood her words. "She is the daughter of Shaya Gotthilf, he had a pension, Pension Gotthilf . . . ?" Her voice will gradually peter out. She will grope for her handbag and press it to her body. Is her English so unintelligible? Or perhaps she has embarrassed him by mentioning something unmentionable? The candle will flicker on the table, and someone on the other side will remark that the Israeli wine has nothing to be ashamed of.

"Elinor," the Not-man will say to Rachel after a long pause. "I met her once, I remember her as a child. Elinor and Elisheva. Eli and Eli . . . so you're her mother-in-law . . ." And then he will clink his glass with hers in a gesture that will be only half-mocking "*Lehayim* . . ." And her freckled hand will hesitantly raise her glass.

My imagination will reach no further than the expression of confusion on the innocent face of my mother-in-law. There are too many questions which may be asked or not asked. The moments after the clinking of the glasses spawned too many possibilities. Notman changes his faces and his attitudes, and in any case there is no point in thinking about something that isn't going to happen.

Nobody could say that I behaved nervously in the days after Notman took on a date and a body. Reality slowed down. I slowed down. I went on wandering the city, but now I wandered slowly.

Sometimes when I walked past a display window I would see an ancient Chinese Mandarin reflected in it: a wise figure on rice paper, proceeding patiently with its hands in its sleeves. Water stains shadowed my forehead and the hollows under my eyes, and the lines running down the sides of my mouth darkened into a moustache.

Sometimes I would find myself a bench, sitting on the wet wood in lotus position, and emulate the gilded example of the statue of the Buddha. But I never sat for long.

I also remember a kind of popping sensation in my ears, as in a rapid descent, but this sensation of a difference in pressure did not bother me. A monument to patience, I would stand and watch the kettle till it boiled, and like an old man I would wait for the road to empty of traffic before I crossed.

Only the thought of the clinking wine glasses went on echoing loudly, and it widened in me like a crack in insulation.

"Did you talk to your mother today?"

"Yes, in the end she went to the dentist. He said she didn't have to have the tooth out."

"Did you talk to your mother today?"

"Do you mean that business with the dinner? I thought about it a lot. It seems to me that it would be best to deal with it at the last minute. At the last minute it'll be easier for me to find an excuse to prevent them from going."

I understood the difficulty and felt no indignation toward my husband. Elinor would prefer you not meet her father's cousin. Why? Because we know that he's no good. All of a sudden she remembered that she heard bad things about him from her parents.

My well-known hostility toward my parents militated against the possibility of my attorney quoting their attitude toward someone or their opinion of him in arguing his case.

I understood and I felt no bitterness. And the sun rose and sank, the chariot of the sun proceeded along its predetermined path, and the river could only flow along the course ordained for it.

"You know, I thought . . . did you ever think, maybe you're prepared to think about . . ." Oded played with a pencil: first he balanced it on one finger, then he rolled it on his thigh. I observed him with interest. This was out of character for him. He was never one of those people who need to handle an object. "Maybe you'd be prepared to consider what would happen if we simply told them. If we told them who and what he is."

"Your parents aren't exactly young. Believe me, you don't want to do that to them."

"You know them. They wouldn't . . ."

"Have you noticed," I interrupted him, "have you noticed that your father calls him 'Elinor's uncle'? 'Your uncle's coming,' 'Your uncle's giving a lecture.'"

"That at least I can easily correct."

"Yes you could, only it wouldn't correct anything," I explained patiently. Oded tapped the pencil on his knee as if he wanted to check his reflexes, and when I continued he went on tapping and poking himself. "Your father knows very well that he's my father's cousin. He took the trouble to check the exact degree of kinship with me, and don't tell me that he simply got mixed up and forgot, because your father never forgets facts. Just remember how he reacted in

Spain after he read the book. Remember how he went berserk at the very thought of having Hitler in his family. Your father will be eighty soon. We're not going to do it to him, and certainly not to your mother. There are some people who deserve to remain clean."

"My father sometimes gets carried away, that's true. Lately in the office . . . but that doesn't mean that in relation to you he . . ."

"And besides, after all these years, you know, it's a little late to come down on them," I said and leaned over to gently take the pencil from his fingers. Because I felt gentleness toward him in those days. All kinds of gentle feelings popped up again, sometimes accompanied by a sensation of déjà vu and sometimes the opposite, in a kind of anticipated nostalgia.

One Friday noon, after three days without rain, I stood and watched him diligently scrubbing at some invisible stain on the door of the Jeep, and my heart went out to his childish concentration.

Another time I saw him beheading a wilted anemone in the garden, and it seemed to me that I had already experienced this very moment, my man and the white, wet, wilted, beheaded anemone, before. He turned his head toward me over his shoulder, and I felt a pang at the knowledge of how I would one day remember this exact movement, this smile of his, and this beautiful shoulder.

Like an old woman full of experiences I rose above time again and again: I mourned the passing of the moment even before it passed, and I tasted the past and the future in the present.

When the consciousness of the conductivity of time broadened, and events increasingly poured through the insulation of the tenses, I sometimes brimmed over to our sons too. One night after Nimrod called and told us about some trivial matter of etiquette in which he had failed in relation to one of his teachers, I sent him a mail whose lines I would prefer to forget. "Whatever happens and whatever they tell you, remember that your mother will always, always love you more than anything in the world"—this is the kind of thing I wrote. Such outpourings were not our style, certainly not since the boys had grown up, and presumably it only embarrassed him. It was a letter that a sentimental drunk might have written, and I wasn't drunk. And long before morning broke I knew that it was a good thing that Nimrod was grown up and living safely in Atlanta, far from my cloying convulsions.

I didn't behave like this all the time—Oded testifies that I looked "disconnected and detached," and so I apparently was for most of the time—but every few days the picture of a particular moment would begin to vibrate inside me, and all of a tremor I would shower people with out-of-place emotions.

I bought a girlfriend an expensive antique alarm clock, even though her birthday was two months away.

I baked a pecan pie and took it to the neighbors, "in honor of the fact that we finally uprooted the Ailanthus tree and it won't be undermining our fence any more." This was the kind of thing I did.

•

One afternoon I dropped in on my mother-in-law without letting her know in advance.

"That haircut really suits you, but tell me, don't you feel cold? I remember when I was a little girl and my mother made me get my hair cut, I was cold all winter."

I put down my cup of tea and got up and kissed her on the top of her head. Since the day that Oded had brought me to their house her hair had gone completely white, but it still felt to me as if this were that very first time, and that this good woman was now stroking my tiger face and asking me if it didn't hurt.

"You always ask the right questions," I gushed, and as if this wasn't enough I added tastelessly: "You should have had a daughter. If you'd had a daughter, I'm sure she would have been the happiest woman in the world."

In the moronic fantasy world I was now inhabiting, my mother-in-law would have kissed me back and said: "But I have a daughter, you're my daughter," but instead of this Rachel gave me a suspicious look and asked: "So what are your plans for the rest of the day?"

It was obvious that she wanted me to finish my tea and leave.

The question of what I was planning to do kept coming up, with my husband returning to it almost every morning.

The liquidation of Alice left me with a lot of time on my hands, not only writing time as such. Alice had been regularly invited to cultural events in the city, and ever since her disappearance the invitations, which I had no desire for in the first place, had dried up.

My family used to joke about my ability to fall asleep and dream at will, but this ability had abandoned me.

I fell asleep only when I was exhausted. I slept lightly. I would be awoken by sounds that fell silent the second I opened my eyes, and I could remember only snatches of my dreams.

Oded, who loved my dreams and the wife who dreamed them, was worried, but what worried him even more was the fact that I had completely stopped reading books.

"What are you reading now?"

"Nothing interesting. The truth is, nothing at all."

I went on buying books. The books piled up next to the bed, but ever since *Hitler, First Person*, the interest I had in fictional worlds had simply vanished. I would read a paragraph, see no point in it, and immediately forget it. *First Person* had deprived me of my ability to read.

Everyone around me thought that I would have a problem "filling my time," but as far as I was concerned time was brim-full of itself and in no need of filling. Everyday activities, when I paid attention to them, swelled with meaning, and each and every one of them thrilled and moved me in its own right. One day I sat down to write a check to the electric company, and I remember how the check and the account focused my mind as intently as the finest of the poetry I had read.

Two monthly account

To: Oded and Elinor Brandeis

7 Bat Yiftah Street Jerusalem

Pay to the account of: The Electric Company

Amount, date, signature.

And at the top right of the check, too, Oded and Elinor Brandeis and our home address.

Like a new bride from some earlier century I signed "Elinor Brandeis," full of gratitude for the new name that had been given me. Gotthilf, as my father-in-law had pointed out, was not a common name. Gotthilf was a rare name, and it could become extinct.

"Elinor, are you listening at all to what I'm telling you?"

"What?"

"I was talking about the possibility of getting an adjournment in the case . . . oh, never mind."

"But I want you to talk." And indeed I did, for there was something uniquely beautiful about my husband when he explained legal matters to me. I was eager to see him talk: only listening presented a problem.

"I was going to say that my father interferes for nothing, and that if the judge agrees to an adjournment, there'll be a possibility . . . forget it, it isn't interesting: legal nonsense."

"But why do you say that? I want to hear. You know, I had an idea about that dinner, maybe the best solution would be for your father to organize an invitation for me, too."

- 5 -

The seder that year was the first that both Nimrod and Yachin didn't come home for, and in the days before Passover this thought saddened their father: "Up to now we've been really lucky, at the last minute at least one of them was always able to make it. Just because a person realizes how lucky he was doesn't mean that he's prepared to stop being lucky."

My husband missed our sons; I didn't, but in my increasingly warped mind the thought occurred to me that the sadness everybody assumed I was feeling could serve as an excuse for my strangeness: April is the cruelest month. Passover is the hardest holiday. Overnight it became very hot, and in the sudden heat the swollen moon turned orange, and the wolves bared their teeth and howled with longing.

All families were tested by this gathering of the clan under the full orange moon, and it was only natural for the mother wolf to grieve the absence of her sons.

Passover is also the family Day of Atonement, of the mutual settling of accounts. And it seems that there is no better time than this for the plot to take a turn. Isn't it obvious that the Brandeis family seder should provide the setting for a dramatic turning point?

Here sits the family, reclining around the table, the grandfather at the head and the grandmother opposite him. Old conflicts seethe beneath the surface of the conversation, gradually the conflicts heat up and the tension rises and boils over. Dark secrets are revealed. Forbidden feelings burst and come violently to light. Father against son. Son against father. Daughter-in-law against mother-in-law, fighting in possessive fury for the soul of the only son. Everything held back for years breaks out.

Will anyone believe me when I say that there were no secrets or darkness in the Brandeis family except for mine? That these good people had succeeded in achieving the no-longer-believable: a happy family?

The land of the salt of the earth was clean, and I was cleansed in the sunshine of this land, until the filth came back to infect me.

The natives of the land that adopted me were not foolish or naïve, they knew about the existence of evil. But they had never known it as I was forced to know it, and they never carried it in their guts.

So no family turning-point took place at the Passover seder, I succeeded in damming the darkness, and the only change that took place that night was that I almost stopped talking.

Our movements appeared pleasant and relaxed. Oded wore a blue shirt he had bought in Seattle—for him white shirts belonged to the daily grind of the courts—and I got up from the computer to undo his top button.

Elisheva sent holiday greetings with the usual decoration of deer tracks, and added in Hebrew in English letters: "Next year in Jerusalem."

"What should I answer her? Happy holiday to you too? Amen? Hallelujah?"

"Whatever you say will make her happy. Come on, let's go."

The radio was on, my husband hummed along with "sheaves of wheat standing in the fields" and the newscaster announced that "preparations for the holiday have been completed throughout the land." I remember that I became a little obsessed with the word "completed"—what was complete here, what had concluded?—but I got over it quite quickly.

I was wearing sandals for the first time since the winter. I took the *haroset* out of the fridge. Oded carried the salad bowl. When we were already standing at the door, Yachin called, and his father told him we would talk later from his grandparents' house.

Determined not to let the absence of the boys cloud the occasion, Rachel and Menachem had invited another couple whose four children were abroad or in the army, and a distant relative of Menachem's who had come for a visit from Argentina with her youth movement, and whom they referred to incorrectly as their "niece." At the last minute one of the legal clerks in the office had also been invited, after it transpired that he was on bad terms with his parents.

Grandfather sat at the head of the table, Grandmother opposite him. Grandfather rose to say the blessing. We answered "Amen" and read the Haggadah with the businesslike seriousness of people fulfilling a not unpleasant obligation.

Until "blood and fire and pillars of smoke" I sat quietly and behaved normally. I even noticed how the clerk's expression softened when the Zionist niece read "How is this night different from all other nights" syllable by syllable. Her face was bright red from the Masada sun, and as she read the four questions—which aren't really four questions at all but only one nagging question—her lowered face grew even redder.

I waited for the reading to be over, for an opportunity to ask if the date for the dinner with the conference guests had already been fixed. It was important for me to know, but the Chinese Mandarin who had taken up residence inside me went on guiding me in the path of patience, and I went on being patient.

Reality descended on me when we dipped our fingers in our glasses to sprinkle blood and fire and pillars of smoke and the other ten plagues, one drop per plague. From the house of the neighbors who had begun the ritual early rose sounds of singing, and with "Once we were slaves" in my ears and the drops of wine that had merged into a red puddle on my plate, all the seders in the country merged into one in my mind, and suddenly I knew with a certain knowledge that the Not-man was also sitting at a seder table, and it seemed that he too was sitting with us and he too was dipping his finger into his glass opposite us. And I also knew that he was already in Israel and I was not yet ready, not ready at all, my preparations had not been completed.

I had not taken leave of my senses: he had an ultra-Orthodox son. Those people, as Erica said, were scrupulous in obeying the commandment to honor their parents, and if the father was coming to Israel anyway, they would certainly have invited him to join them at the seder. So it was only logical to conclude that at this very moment he was sitting with a skullcap on his head and dipping his finger into his wine, perhaps singing. Not singing—I corrected myself—not singing yet. With the religious the reading went on forever, so at this moment he was still reading the Haggadah in his hard-to-place accent.

Soup was served and I ate. A conversation developed and I was silent. At some stage, when my husband was helping his mother clear the soup plates from the table, the Zionist niece asked me: "What do you do?" What did I do? I considered the question seriously. "I think I'm busy going crazy." Nobody heard me but her. And from her nod it was clear that she wasn't sure she had heard right. Immediately after that she resumed her conversation with the clerk, and I went back to being quietly driven mad by reality.

•

The opportunity to ask what I wanted to ask came with the roast and green beans and potatoes.

Because of the holiday, and in honor of the Zionist niece who had come to Israel to study and deepen her identity, the conversation turned to the Jewish destiny. And I, from where I was sitting at the archetypical seder table together with all the rest of the House of Israel, went on listening: Rachel mentioned her uncle who had been murdered by the Arabs in 1929. Her friend mentioned a large family lost in the Holocaust. The Zionist niece said something enthusiastic about "the uniqueness of our history." The clerk said that perhaps the uniqueness lay not in history itself but in the ability to turn it into a story, just as we had done now.

"So what do you say to a Jew, a professor, a survivor of the Holocaust himself, who chooses of all things to tell the story of Hitler?"

Menachem's voice promised his guests that he was about to serve them a conversational delicacy, and he kept his promise. He set it all before them: the First Person and the professor's retreat from the First Person, and also the fact that they were going to meet said professor in person. "That professor" Chemi called him, without mentioning his relation to "our Elinor."

I was given the opportunity and I failed to take advantage of it. The women directed the conversation into less fraught channels: Israeli Prime Ministers, the increasing frequency of allergies in the spring season, the importance of using sun screens, and such matters. And plates were cleared and bowls were brought, more wine was poured, and dessert was served.

I must point out that I had not been struck dumb by hysteria. When I was addressed I replied "yes" and "no" and "apparently," I went on following the conversation and I can remember every word. My abstinence was voluntary, I retired of my own free will because I had things to do.

Suddenly I realized how close the day was when I would have to act and how unprepared I was, and therefore I removed myself in order to enable myself to prepare.

There was no point in asking Chemi exactly when they were going to meet "that professor," because the date was no longer important. Because already with the "blood and fire and pillars of smoke" and the puddle on my plate, I had grasped that the dinner with the conference guests was only one of the illusions I had allowed myself to harbor: Not-man sowed confusion, and I in my fear and foolishness had become confused and wasted my time on fantasies of some imaginary restaurant on Keren Hayesod Street.

There would be no meeting between my family and First Person, and even if there were, I could not permit myself to waste any more time on restaurants, because it was not there, not in a restaurant, not in the presence of my loved ones, that I would finish him off.

When did I know that I would have to kill him? On the Saturday when he phoned and invaded my home? During our stay in Seattle, when I realized how he was robbing me of my family? And perhaps long before that, in the days of the basement apartment when my sister told me things, or even before that, when a thumb had been poked into my breast, or perhaps when I called the gynecologist and confirmed that the abortion had taken place, while the orchid in its flowerpot still stood on the counter of Pension Gotthilf.

Even now I can't say when it became inevitable. But after Monticello and after Elisheva's pardon, ever since I had remained alone with the First Person, ever since then—you could say that I knew.

When a normal human being, a normal woman, begins to think about how to kill someone, her first thoughts naturally tend toward art and fantasy. One day it came into my head that I would follow Menachem and Rachel into the restaurant in Keren Hayesod Street, and poison him there. The first image I saw was of a cyanide capsule bursting between his teeth. Did such capsules still exist and if so, where would I find one? Because one was enough, that was what was so good about cyanide. I remembered reading somewhere that cyanide had a "pronounced smell of bitter almonds." A smell of bitter almonds—a pronounced smell of bitter almonds would therefore rise from his open mouth. And what if somebody identified the smell and tried to bring him back to life? Cyanide kills instantly. And I didn't want it to be quick, and I also didn't want his body twitching and convulsing in front of Rachel and Menachem. And I was also afraid of the resuscitation attempts on the part of some paramedic sitting at the next table, rushing to breathe into a mouth full of cyanide.

It was important to me to protect Rachel and Menachem; I feared for the young paramedic enjoying a long-awaited date.

And then I went on to think of other substances, the kind that kill slowly: gold dust, copper, lead, which in the opinion of certain scholars destroyed the Roman empire. I once read that the Romans believed that copper protected the body from the effects of lead poisoning. Was it possible that the water in the restaurant was served in copper jars? Could the copper neutralize the effect of the lead?

•

Digoxin, which is prescribed for cardiac patients and destroys the healthy, was a much surer bet, and also readily available. It would be easy enough to find a doctor who would prescribe digoxin without a second thought.

These were the amazing fantasies that came into my head, but I don't blame myself for them. I was prevented from serving in the army, I had never held a weapon in my hands, and almost everything I knew about killing I had learned from works of art.

•

For many years the roof of the Jewish Agency building in King George Street had prominently displayed a sign that read: "What to do? Do!" At some point during the course of the seder, it was when we were already eating dessert, I suddenly remembered this sign, and its words silenced the turmoil of my thoughts: What to do? Do! And after a moment I think I giggled, because the observer inside me observed that you can never know what will calm the troubled soul: a poem, a philosophical saying, or a silly slogan on the roof of the Jewish Agency.

The Passover seder came to an end. The guests thanked their hosts and dispersed. The two couples whose children were abroad kissed the hostess. And the clerk offered to drive the niece to the hotel where her group was staying. Three couples got into three cars and drove off in three directions.

No plot twist took place on that night. And no secret was revealed. The only change that took place was that as I sat at the table together with all the House of Israel and the First Person, I returned to reality and was able to once more distinguish between a plan and a fantasy: time was short, and I needed a plan.

eavy with wine and too much to eat, Oded went straight to bed. If he noticed my silence that same night he probably attributed it to a physical condition similar to his own. My husband fell asleep; it was close to midnight, and I embarked on a thorough spring-cleaning of my house.

From the day that I moved in with Oded I became a house-proud woman, and the traces of the cave-dweller I had been till then disappeared. Even when we could afford to hire a maid, I refused to allow a stranger deal with our dirt like most of our friends did, and for the most part I found a measure of unfashionable satisfaction in keeping our territory spick and span.

The house was clean and tidy, which somewhat eased the complicated task of making it kosher for Passover. Cupboards were opened. Files were stacked on the table. Papers were packed into one big garbage bag, worn out kitchen utensils in another. Shoes were consigned to a third. There's something sad about old shoes, and when I closed the bag I thought that I would at least not leave this sadness of worn out shoes behind me.

There were thirteen days left to the official appearance of the First Person on the scene, and I was determined to leave a clean space behind me: this was the least I could do for those who had been my Garden of Eden.

I was about to end it, and even though I still didn't know how, it was clear to me that however much I thought and planned, the chances of my getting away after the deed was done were slim. I didn't have the strength to consider what would happen afterward. I assumed I'd go to jail. I assumed that I would be interrogated, and I assumed that I would say nothing. Because what kind of discourse could there be with a world where a god exists who expects a rape victim to forgive, what could you say to those who duplicate the First Person three hundred one thousand times, who fly him from country to country, give him a life, work, and an audience, and set cream cakes in front of him?

Come what may, I thought, I would not hide behind the inarticulate little girl who was turned into a reader aloud of the works of the Marquis de Sade. Her, that little girl, I would not give them. I wasn't that little girl. And in any case now, I too was alone and locked up and suffocating, and those outside didn't hear, and even if they heard they wouldn't understand, because from outside it's impossible. It takes two to understand.

What to do? Do! Because in the beginning was the act. What would happened afterward was out of my hands.

My vision of after-the-act was patchy and full of holes. I saw myself silent, I realized how the sick world would interpret my silence, and in one of the less-faded patches of my imagination I heard a smug, self-satisfied male voice explaining:

"We have before us a case of a morbid obsession regarding a book. According to our information, it appears that Elinor Brandeis believed that she was destroying not the author of *Hitler, First Person* but Hitler himself. This kind of confusion between author and narrator is not uncommon among unsophisticated readers, and a learned writer such as Professor Gotthilf was no doubt aware of the risk he was taking when he chose to speak in the devil's voice."

I didn't expect understanding, but I admit that a flicker of anger flared up in me at the thought of some idiot presenting me as a primitive reader. I suffered no confusion as to the facts: Hitler died on the 30th of April, 1945. He shot himself, apparently at the same time biting down on a capsule of cyanide.

And what about my loved ones? someone will ask. Didn't you think about all the sorrow and shame you were about to bring down on your loved ones? Didn't you take them into account?

I thought—I reply to the rebuking questioner—I thought, and the more I thought and took into account, the clearer it became to me that my dearly beloved would be better off without me, because even if they don't know it, a quick, clean cut is best.

On our visit to Seattle I was a cause of grave concern to our sons, my husband told me so, and even without him I'm not blind. And when we were in Seattle, the gangrene inside me had not yet spread. A mother is not supposed to frighten her cubs, cubs are not supposed to be afraid for their mother, and what happened to us was against nature: the corrosive corruption of Not-man has reached as far as the land of the salt of the earth, and the most faithful of men is already suffocating in its stench.

If my dearly beloved had known what I knew, if they had seen, they themselves would have understood that this was the humane thing to do. I would end it, and afterward I would be locked up and removed. Anyway, it makes no difference if I don't exist in any case. And in leaving them like this, at least I will leave them a better world.

Is there a prosecutor in existence who would dare to argue that a world in which Not-man draws breath is preferable to one in which he no longer exists? If anyone deserves to suffer, to suffer in agony for far longer than a hundred and twenty days, it's him, and I only intended to put an end to him quickly and allow myself to breathe. A humane sentence according to any human logic.

At four o'clock on the morning after the Passover seder, I carried six securely tied garbage bags to the bins outside. On my desk I left a stack of files that required patient sorting. My clothes closet demanded more deliberation than anything I was capable of producing during the course of that night; the kitchen, on the other hand, gave me satisfaction. Twelve days until the official appearance of the First Person; at some point during their course I would have to remember to replace the microwave: a man without a wife to cook for him needs a reliable microwave oven.

The streets were deserted, exhausted in the aftermath of the holiday. The streetlamps were still on, and in the rustic quiet I heard a donkey bray in the distance.

My husband was sleeping in same position as he had fallen asleep. And with the nagging thought about the microwave—maybe I should write myself a note so as not to forget—I took a blanket out of the linen chest and collapsed onto the bed in what had once been Yachin's room, and in recent years had been at the disposal of both boys on their visits.

Ever since I had moved in with Oded, apart from his reserve duty in the army and his business trips, we had always slept together. Is that strictly accurate? Writers tend to round corners for the sake of elegance and beauty, and here too I have rounded a little. Once in a while when I had a bad cold and realized that I was snoring, I'd retire to the living-room sofa. Once in a while Oded fell asleep in the armchair opposite the television and only woke up in the morning, and once when we quarreled . . . I enjoyed the privilege of living in the Garden of Eden, on that I insist, but it doesn't mean that I was an angel.

"Him again?" When my husband paused in the doorway to the boys' room, to examine the rumpled evidence that I had spent the night there, I was already busy with the coffee. I shrugged.

"I know I haven't solved the problem of that dinner yet. I promised you, Elinor, I'll deal with it. But in the meantime, do me a favor, make an effort and just try to put it out of your head."

The understanding I had reached during the seder had made the meeting between my in-laws and Not-man what my husband called "irrelevant," and I shrugged again.

"Don't you trust me?"

"Yes."

"Yes you do or yes you don't?"

"Yes I do."

"Elinor?"

"Yes."

He stood next to me and blocked my way to the sink. "The landfill in the Negev?" he suggested lamely. I looked at him, a nervous, empty smile distorted his face. If only because of that foreign smile, if only because of the way I had distorted his face, I had to remove myself from him.

After it's all over, I thought, perhaps he'll find somebody else, better than me. Of course he'd find another woman, or more likely she would find him, but one way or another she would very soon be found. She would have bigger breasts than me, the kind all men like even if they don't admit it. Without a doubt she would be an intellectual, because this modest husband of mine admires intellectuals. An artist. Perhaps a painter, come to Israel to capture the desert light.

I don't want to go into details about what happened in the next twelve days, and it seems there's no need to, because what had already happened only went on happening. "Are you going to sleep there tonight too?" "Yes." "Do you want to tell me what's going on?' "Not now."

My husband watches me as I sort out newspaper cuttings, old receipts and photographed texts from my student days. "What are you doing?" "Spring cleaning." "Don't you want to go out for a bit?" "No." "What's that photograph?" "A poem."

Robert Lowell to Elizabeth Bishop: I myself am hell/ nobody's here/ only skunks . . .

. . . I didn't crumple up the page, simply added it to the pile to be thrown away.

The weather suddenly turned dry and blazing. The desert invaded the city. Penetrated the houses and covered surfaces with sand. Asthmatics had difficulty breathing. And my husband, who had planned a jeep trip with friends, was reluctant to leave his wife on her own. He came back after only one day and returned to the office, and was still reluctant to leave his wife on her own.

My husband on the phone: "What's happening?"

"Nothing."

After a few days I stopped answering the phone and ignored the messages he left me. At some point during the intermediate days of Passover I drove to electrical appliance stores to acquire a new microwave, and there, in Givat Shaul, as I was putting the parcel into the trunk, like a presence behind my back and a kind of intensification inside me, I sensed the presence of Not-man, and then I knew that he was coming closer and that he was already in Jerusalem. I knew—just as I had known before that he had arrived in Israel, and as I knew that he lived in New York even before I saw the program of the conference.

Professor Gotthilf of Queen's College. According to the college site he taught two seminars to third year students there. One had the complicated name of "'Abandon hope all ye who enter here':

The Realities of the Marquis de Sade, Friedrich Nietzsche, Heinrich Joder, and Franz Kafka," while the other was called simply "Stalin and the Jews."

I did not feel threatened by the closeness of his person. I was going to meet him. For a moment I was even eager for it to happen right away. I only wanted to avoid being taken by surprise, and so in the few days remaining, I seldom left the house. I didn't miss going out, because with the clarification of reality and the progress of the plan, all traces of the old itch to keep moving had melted away.

My husband on the phone: "Elinor isn't feeling too well. It's nothing to worry about. She'll call you back."

My husband to his mother on the eve of the second Passover holiday: "I'm afraid we're not going to make it. Elinor's caught some bug . . . no, not at the moment . . . I think it's best just to let her sleep."

But I didn't sleep, or I slept very little, and it occurred to me that it was a good thing that I'd spent so much time sleeping in previous years and stored up reserves: now my thoughts no longer escaped me or turned to pointless fantasies.

My abstinence from small talk also intensified my ability to concentrate on reality, and from day to day it became clear to me how I would do the deed: no more vain thoughts of cyanide and nonsensical fantasies about gold dust.

There were no weapons in the house ever since the boys had completed their army service and Oded had been relieved of reserve duty, and in any case, since I myself had been prevented from serving in the army, even if I had known how to get my hands on a gun—I wouldn't have know how to fire it.

My black-belt-salt-of-the-earth, my worried love, was capable in principle of breaking someone's neck, while I couldn't even imagine myself using a knife.

The only realistic weapon available to me was the car, and from the moment it occurred to me I wondered how I hadn't thought of it before, it seemed so obvious.

In order to run him over I would have to somehow get him to place himself in front of the wheels, because a scenario in which I lay in wait and ambushed him was far from obvious, and in fact improbable in the extreme. In order to place him in front of the wheels I would have to see him, meet him, get into conversation with him and entice him to some lonely place: the edge of a cliff? Not realistic. More realistic to think of a deserted street or a parking lot. In any case, I would have to meet him, and I would meet him, this would present no difficulties, since he wanted to meet me. At the end of the meeting I would see to it that he accompanied me to the car. I could offer him a ride. I could ask him to guide me out of the parking lot. Or maybe I could ask him to get out and check if the headlights were working: but in order to send him out of the car I would first have to get into it with him, and for this I would need to prepare myself. Stepping on the gas, on the other hand, was a routine activity, that would be the easy part, even easier than pulling a trigger. I would sit high up in front of the steering wheel, he would be opposite me but low down, opposite the silver front of the Defender. Because from the moment I began to see the picture, I saw myself in Oded's 4x4 and not in my dilapidated little Toyota.

My husband, who is far from any kind of ostentation, bought the 4x4 less than a year before, after a long hesitation centering round his self-image, not the price of the vehicle. "Tell me honestly, at my age, with my way of life, doesn't it seem pathetic to you?"

"You're a man, men are pathetic, enjoy it at least."

And he did enjoy it, even though the Jeep left the parking space no more than twice a week. Oded walked to work, but occasional drives along dirt tracks and the religious polishing of the vehicle were enough for him to delight in his acquisition.

"Do I make you laugh?"

"You bet you do. Take me for a drive on Saturday—or are you cleaning it on Saturday?"

I assumed that I would find some pretext for explaining to my husband why I needed his car. I didn't worry too much about finding one in advance. And only a few days after the plan was born, I realized that I was going to stain my man's precious toy so that he wouldn't want to touch it any more. Oded wouldn't touch it and he wouldn't touch me, and his next woman, the artistic woman with the big breasts, he would take out for drives in a different car.

I was sorry for what I was about to do to him, but no other possibility and no other weapon was available to me. I would befoul my husband's car, but a greater foulness would be wiped out as a result.

In the shock of his sorrow my husband would not sense the difference—perhaps he would never sense it—but after the deed was done, the ground would be more balanced, and everybody's air, not just his, would go back to being something breathable.

•

On the last night before Not-man's appearance in person, I went to look at my husband in his sleep. To be more precise, it was early in the morning, and to the best of my recollection, in the moments before I did so I thought again about how he would be robbed of his pleasure in his car. The thought came back, and presumably it made me sad, because I wanted very much to give, not to take away.

I stood in the bedroom doorway like a ghost. It was very hot, the *hamsin* was closing in without any relief. The light in the garden shed, which we left on at night, came in through the window and cast a faint light on his face. My husband had fallen asleep exposed on his back, in a trusting position that touched my heart, one arm bent above his head, the other stretched out at his side, his limp palm turned upward. Very soon, when I was caught, he would no longer sleep like this. And if I wasn't caught? This thought was forbidden. There is nothing more weakening than the scent of happiness seeping through the wall of time and threatening to disappear, dimming the eyes with longing. There is nothing more weakening than the smell of my husband.

Will he miss me? Perhaps only in his sleep will he remember how it was between us, because the shadow of the act I was about to commit would fall backward and darken all our past for him. He would divorce me and I would accept it immediately, without any arguments I would agree to the divorce, and this moment and I would be cast out of his life forever.

I came closer to the bed, my dreaming love let out a long breath between closed lips, and I bent over and pulled down his underwear and wrapped my lips around his sleeping penis. The member woke up immediately. The rest of him a moment or two later.

At first, still half asleep, he sent a drowsy hand to my breast, and I instinctively removed his hand and returned it to the side of his body. I wanted to make him happy, with all my heart and soul I longed to give him pleasure, but I couldn't let my love give me anything. It was enough. He had given me enough already.

But the hand I removed refused to lie still, and again it rose to underneath my jaw and moved over my throat in the dark. Again I removed it, and this time it made no more overtures, but reached for the switch of the reading lamp as soon as I laid it down.

The light went on, and a man looked at his wife. He sat up, touched my chin and took it in his hand, and without taking his eyes off me pulled up his underpants.

"Not like that," he said, his voice hoarse and hostile.

I thought that if only he agreed to turn off the light I might be able to explain. What could I explain to him? From the look in his eyes I could see that there would be no exemptions. It was a rare expression that I knew from the rare occasions on which one of our sons crossed the line not to be crossed. "You'll have to talk to me," he said.

I played with the strap of my nightgown and kept quiet. There were too many things clamoring in my head: pictures, snatches of words, and what all that clamor produced in the end was: "Tomorrow night, that is, tonight, can I take your car?"

"Take my car . . . and for that . . . ?" Judging by the disgust on his face you would have thought that I had already done the deed. This is how he would look at me from now on, if he looked at me at all. This is how he would look whenever he thought of me, and why shouldn't he? I came from another land, and he and I were a mistake from the beginning. How I had deluded myself when I took him to Beth Hakerem. How I had let myself go on and on, talking and explaining. Just as with the foolish fantasies of gold dust and lead, I had been wasting my time. Now he was looking at me as if I were a whore.

•

"Of course you can take the car. You can take whatever you like, no problem, just don't try to pretend that you're not all there, because it won't work. And now please tell me why you need my car."

What had gotten into him? He was quicker than me. I had always been the quick-witted one, and he the thorough one.

This was the spirit, if not the exact letter, of the exchange between us: I was blindsided, and my husband, who had just woken up, was quick and focused.

What did I need the car for? To run him over and end it? In any case, I didn't think that I would have an opportunity to do it this evening. But nevertheless, the Defender was very important to me.

"There's a lecture this evening," I said.

"And to listen to a lecture you need my car."

"Yes."

"Good. That makes a lot of sense. I told you, Elinor, you can get away with pretending to be crazy with other people, but not with me."

"I'm not crazy."

"No, you're not, and you don't need the Defender tonight either." Oded got out of bed and turned off the alarm clock. "We won't need the alarm this morning. In any case I was going to go for a run before it gets too hot. Where are you going?"

"Nowhere."

"Right. You're not going anywhere. And you know why you don't need the car? You won't need it because you've got a driver. I happen to be going to the Cinematheque this evening too."

Going to the Cinematheque. He knew.

"So listen up, my dear," he leaned with demonstrative ease on the iron headrest of the bed. He had never, ever, called me "my dear" before. "So listen: my first thought was that if I went to hear him talk, perhaps it would give me an idea of how to stop my parents from going to that dinner. Now I realize that that was only an excuse."

He fell silent, obliging me to ask him "What do you mean?" and then he outflanked me again, forcing me to speak: "An excuse. You know, an excuse."

"An excuse for what?"

"My curiosity, let's say. The guy's going to talk about 'Questions and errors in pursuit of the roots of evil.' It appears that I too am interested in the roots of evil."

I hugged my knees, and the bed floated and swayed on the sea. I felt as if I had spent hours under a blazing sun: the liquid in my brain was shifting from side to side, my eyes were deluded into seeing land in shadows on the water.

"Only you won't understand," I blurted out, without knowing exactly what, out of everything, I was referring to.

"And why won't I understand? Because I'm not clever enough? Because he's too intellectual for me? You think I might be confused by some child rapist? Do me a favor . . . I can see what that swine is doing to you, and I think it's about time I know what he looks like. I have to know."

The raft went on swaying, and words rolled about and escaped me.

During the deliberate silence in which I had immersed myself I had lost the old confidence in my ability to make myself clear to my audience.

"What did you think? That I wasn't aware of the date of his lecture? That I wouldn't find out when it was?"

"There's a problem with facts," I said weakly.

"Yes, and what exactly is the problem? It's clear to me that what I know, what you've told me, is only the tip of the iceberg, we've talked about it more than once, but even so I think I understand quite well. You know what? Why don't you tell me something you think I'm not capable of understanding? Go on, tell me, try me, at least. I think I deserve that at least—for you to try me. So here I am, and I'm listening."

His wish to know was loving and pure, untainted by any appetite for sensational thrills. He was not a glutton for suffering. But being who he was, he could not but believe that understanding is acquired by a comprehensive knowledge of all the facts. He sincerely wanted to understand, but what could I tell him? All the facts seemed as hollow as headlines in a newspaper. Talking wasn't the thing itself. In order to understand something you need to be immersed in it, you need the *folie à deux* in a three-and-a-half room basement apartment, you need images that seep through your skin until they change the composition of your blood. And as for the jangling facts—I myself didn't know them all: he did, she cried, what exactly did he do? When did she cry? Perhaps she never cried at all.

"Elinor? Talk to me."

Oded was coming to the lecture. He was going to prevent me from laying my trap and maneuvering the First Person to stand in front of the Defender. I knew that talking to him would only tie me tighter to the bed. But he looked at me as if he was pinning all his hope on me, and if only because of the hope, if only for the sake of the memory of this night, I could not keep silent or leave.

"Okay, here's something," I opened slowly and paused a moment. "Okay. You remember how my parents didn't really believe it, and how I tracked down the gynecologist he took her to, and confirmed it all over the phone, so they didn't have any option but to believe it."

Carefully my husband stroked my tattooed tiger face, a gesture of encouragement to the woman telling the story and an expression of appreciation for the resourceful young girl she had once been.

"Okay," I said for the third time and switched off the reading lamp. "So that story with the gynecologist—it happened, but not exactly the way you know . . ."

Writers fantasize and round corners, and the first time I told my husband this chapter I didn't exactly lie, but I shortened and skipped, let's say for beauty's sake.

It's true that Elisheva remembered more or less where the clinic was, and it's true that I searched the Yellow Pages and found a gynecological clinic in Hahovshim Street in the vicinity she remembered. It's also correct that I phoned the gynecologist's secretary and pretended to be Elisheva, but nothing was verified in that conversation. The idea of getting confirmation over the phone simply never occurred to me, and all I did was to make an appointment for the person pretending to be Elisheva Gotthilf.

I went to the clinic. It was early evening. There were about ten women in the waiting room, some of them pregnant. More women arrived and we all waited for a long time. That doctor let women wait. About two hours after the hour of my appointment, I was told to go in. On the desk was a gray cardboard file with the name Gotthilf, Elisheva written on it in a black marker.

"How can I help you?"

At this point I could ostensibly have left, since the existence of the file was enough to fling the truth in my parents' faces. But I had already taken a seat in the chair facing the doctor, and a normal person who walks into a doctor's office and sits down doesn't suddenly stand up and walk out. That would be very impolite, and I was very young, and I didn't have the courage to be abnormal and impolite.

I stammered that I was having problems with my period. "I thought that perhaps it was because of the abortion, probably not, but I wanted to be sure that I can get pregnant one day." Until then I had never thought about my womb, and certainly not about fertility. Nor did I think about such things for years afterward, at that age you think about all kinds of things but not about your womb— apparently the thought popped into my head because of the pregnant women in the waiting room.

Since entering the room I hadn't dared to look the man opposite me in the face. If I had met him in the street two day later I wouldn't have recognized him. I was sure that he was about to unmask me as an imposter and then . . . I don't know, maybe he would call in the police, even though he was actually the one who should have been afraid of the police, not me, but that didn't occur to me.

It turned out that there was nothing to fear: apparently the good doctor was not in the habit of looking at the faces of the women on whom he performed abortions, or maybe he just had a lousy memory. The first thing he said was that everything was in order after the procedure, and that if a problem existed it was certainly not connected to the procedure. I don't remember how many times he repeated the word, procedure, but that was the word he used.

"Let me examine you anyway."

There were a thousand things the girl could have done: told him who she was, threatened him, said that she didn't want to be examined and she only came for a consultation, asked him if he was in the habit of performing abortions on girls brought in by men old enough to be their fathers.

She could have done a thousand things, but she didn't do any of them. She neither confronted him nor found a way out. She stood up and obeyed his instructions, went behind the screen, took off her jeans and panties and put them on a stool, sat in the chair and parted her legs. That's what she did. Because that's what he told her to do, and she was Elisheva, and before she could think her feet were already in the stirrups, and a hand in a rubber glove was rummaging inside her.

"That's it, that's all. A gynecological examination," I said to Oded. "And if you want to know, I wasn't a virgin either. I wonder if he would have noticed if I was. Never mind, people pay a far higher price when they're fighting for the truth. And in the end, what price did I already pay? A medical examination, that's all. Women have them all the time. It just happened to be the first gynecological examination I ever had."

If I had any clear wishes as to my husband's reaction, I would have said that he fulfilled them all.

He didn't ask "But why? Why did you let him do it?" He didn't question me at all, or try to caress me, or comfort the child I was then from the heights of the present.

"A bad business," he said shortly after I had finished, "a very bad business, but I'm glad you told me."

He went to make coffee and after he put the cup in my hand, he spoke about "trained and experienced fighting men' who were overtaken by paralysis. He mentioned a case involving one of his commanding officers, and another involving a well-known lawyer suddenly struck dumb in court.

I needed to hear his voice speaking, and he gave me his voice, and so we lay side by side while he spoke to me of this and that: about Nimrod's new love affair—was it true love or simply the product of loneliness? About his father who kept announcing his intentions of winding down his activities in the office, and in complete contradiction to his declarations had started to interfere in his son's cases to an extent he had never done before; and again about his old dream of teaching school: "It's just a dream, I don't think I'll ever realize it, but lately I've been thinking that if I could only find the right place, maybe I could teach for a few hours on a volunteer basis. To teach judo, for example. Maybe I'd just teach girls. What do you say? You think something could come of it?"

And I listened to my husband's soothing chit-chat, I really did listen, and I even replied. Only when the light in the shed vanished into the light of the rising sun, his voice departed from its gentle, everyday tone and took on an exaggerated casualness. "So I'll pick you up at home tonight and we'll go to the seminar to see and hear. And two other things: one, the dinner my parents aren't going to attend is supposed to take place the day after tomorrow. And two, if you're interested, I assume you're interested and that you've already found out for yourself: he's staying at the Hyatt."

"How do you know?"

"So you didn't check it out. Good, then you have to admit that there are a few advantages to being married to a lawyer. Even though it wasn't something I needed a detective to find out. I simply phoned the university and asked the spokeswoman."

"But what did you say to her? Did you give her your name?"

"Certainly not. I gave her a false name and said that I ran a book club. And that we wanted to invite him to speak to us."

The question of the First Person's location had been preying on my mind for the past few days, but why did it concern my husband? I didn't know.

It was a morning of surprises, and worn out by surprises I could only surmise that he had located the predator in order to minimize the anxieties of his preyed-upon wife.

The hands of the clock approached the hour when the alarm was supposed to go off, and in the moments remaining we said no more.

I remembered the arrowhead of the wild geese in the sky. For some reason it occurred to me that after reaching its destination, whenever it did so, perhaps even now, the slow, screeching arrow would turn around and return to the country from which it had departed.

I imagined geese and clouds and saw continents from above, I sailed with them in the sky. I must have dozed off, and when I woke Oded was already dressed in his jogging outfit and busy tying his shoes, and I was covered with a sheet.

With the pale satin material covering my body, I went on lying there and thinking about what could never be.

I thought that if I could only do what needed to be done and live to see more mornings like this, I would go down on my knees and wash the feet of all the gods.

And I vowed that if only it could be, then I would never, ever again want to get into some car bomb and blow myself up in the role of some god or other.

- 1 -

Evening started to fall, and the terrible heat did not abate. My husband picked me up at the house and we drove to the Cinematheque, and parked the Defender next to the Scottish church. In the dusky light we crossed the narrow bridge leading to the Valley of Hinnom and went down the steps to the Cinematheque, and at ten past six I saw the First Person.

I heard him speak to the audience, and no doubts entered my mind: I knew with a certain knowledge that the past, the present, and the future would be better without him, and that I had to erase him.

But that's no way to tell a story. There are details without which the truth does not become a story, and the truth does not become a story without cold shivers running down my spine, and hairs standing up on the back of my neck, and my heart beating faster as the hands of the clock advanced. Heart beats are imperative, because the heart creates credibility, and without it nobody will believe me.

My wrist watch has no hands, but my heart definitely beat faster: here is my heart, pounding at an ever-increasing rhythm as we cross the bridge—who is that walking behind me?—my heart pounds in my ears, and here I am opening it, revealing all.

There was indeed a dark red pounding in my ears, but at the same time I should point out that I didn't miss a word, and that I heard every sound that the First Person uttered. Because from the moment he started to speak my thoughts no longer strayed: no images of loathsome tortures invaded my mind, I had no sister, nor did I imagine a body in front of the car. Everything that had haunted me went away now that I was face to face with the haunter.

He took the stage and spoke, he had been invited to lecture, and I was present at his lecture, in full possession of all my faculties, and therefore I am competent to bear witness. So to hell with the cardiology report. The increase in the rate of my heartbeat is only a marginal symptom.

I intended to arrive exactly on time for the beginning of the panel. In places like the Cinematheque, there are always people you have to wave or nod to, and I wanted to avoid waves and nods and definitely from having to reply to "What are you doing here, research for Alice?" or "Where did you disappear to? We heard you were in America."

A late entry, on the other hand, can lead to the turning of heads, and even though I assumed that he would not be able to recognize me, this logical assumption did not put my mind at rest.

We wanted to get there just in time for the opening of the proceedings, the gods of parking were on our side—bless them—and so we succeeded in entering the hall on time after sitting in the car for less than ten minutes.

I mentioned "the audience" before. The big hall of the Cinematheque was about three-quarters full, which means about three hundred people. Three hundred people had assembled to view "popular portraits of evil." The tickets cost thirty shekels, Oded and I paid sixty together, and took our places at the back of the hall, close to the exit. Two lecturers spoke before the First Person took the stage, and if we count the host of the panel as well, then he was preceded by three speakers.

What they spoke about—I don't remember. I started to pay attention only when the host approached the podium for the third time and introduced *Hitler, First Person*. Until then my eyes were busy searching the front rows for him. My ears were increasingly deafened by the drumming inside them. My nose was dry from sniffing.

As the host reached the podium for the third, time Oded bent down to his bag at my left, took out a yellow legal pad and placed it on his lap, as if about to take notes.

Oded set a pen to the paper, and my eyes no longer searched for Not-man. He rose from his seat in the audience only after the host said: "many publications," "a range of subjects," and "a book that gave rise to mixed reactions and a controversy which will no doubt be of interest to us all."

Hitler, First Person rose, and now there is presumably no option but to raise him up in person.

Evil needs flesh to be incarnated, and who will believe me unless I portray him in the flesh?

The bottom of the portrait shows spider legs so long as to be out of proportion to the rest of the body, the top a coif of wavy hair unaffected by the passage of the years, no doubt further proof of his satanic nature. Before he began to speak he took a pair of narrow reading glasses out of his jacket pocket and set them low on his nose . . . and that's enough. Never mind what the rest of him looked like. He was there, standing on the stage below us, he was there and nothing had changed.

It was evident that most of the audience had no idea of what to expect. A generation had passed since that book first came out, and it never came out in Hebrew at all. People's memories are short, and in any case they don't want to remember and they don't want to know.

Even before he opened his mouth he began to draw attention to himself, sucking it in and gobbling it up: seducing the audience to look at him as he unfolded the arms of his reading glasses, riveting their gaze as he produced a page and smoothed it out slowly on the lectern.

Evil is deceptive, and I was not surprised by the failure of the spectators to recognize it in its present incarnation. And in view of their failure, it occurred to me that I should put an end to him in public, because only thus would a great cry go up—instead of this gullible silence in which they watched him smoothing out his sheet of paper on the lectern.

But I wouldn't end it in a minute. First he would scream, and shouts would rise from the audience, and at some point I would ask the screaming mouth if he agreed with Schopenhauer and others that pain was more real than pleasure.

We were there. Not-man was close at hand. The possibility was at hand, and until he started to speak I imagined a great shout deafening a different scream, and after that silence. A sentence would wipe out a sentence, as if it had never been pronounced.

When he opened his mouth it spoke English. Then I thought again that it amused him to hide the fact that he knew Hebrew well and understood what people around him were saying. Now I think that perhaps he chose English in order to benefit from the politeness with which strangers and guests are treated.

The mouth opened and shut and opened again. Shall I allow it to make itself heard?

I heard it all, I took in everything from beginning to end, there was never a more attentive listener than me, and even if by doing so I will serve as his mouthpiece, I think that the story obliges me to give an account of his words.

First of all he thanked the moderator for introducing him and the conference hosts for inviting him, and he didn't simply thank them but tugged his humble forelock, bowed his head, touched his long vulture's neck, and cooed as modestly as a dove. The imposter thanked, and then he explained that he was going to talk about a grave mistake that he had made, and for a variety of reasons it was important for him to come and admit his painful error here in Jerusalem.

In order to clarify the personal and intellectual background to his fall from grace—he said—he should first explain what he had sought to do in his writing, and what was the nature of the trap into which he had fallen. In his humble opinion, the temptation in question was almost as old as the human race itself.

He had always believed—many people here would no doubt agree with him—that the preeminence of man could be described in one simple and wonderful word: "Why?" A whipped horse does not ask "Why?" A dog—a doubtlessly intelligent animal—when it is kicked will only try to escape from the next kick. A human being expresses his humanity when in confronting the greatest of horrors he insists on demanding "Why?" When Faust seeks to know what holds the world together he does not expect a reply from the field of quantum mechanics or string theory. Faust seeks meaning. He wants to understand.

A human being expresses his humanity in insisting on his need for an explanation.

I could describe how the audience hung on his every word, and say that what I did later on that evening was aimed at liberating all those gullible souls who were seduced and led astray. But the truth is a little different, and the truth is that the more he progressed in his lecture, the less spellbound the audience as a whole became, and I could sense their attention gradually wandering. There were some who leaned forward to catch every word. But there were also not a few who dropped by the wayside: they didn't understand his English, they had come to see one of the films that were going to be shown later on in the evening. They were impatient to see Magda Goebbels poisoning her children in the bunker, and they had no patience for philosophizing.

Are there some things for which we should not seek an explanation? the mouth asked. Is it wrong to seek an explanation for Hitler? Was this the fateful error he had made? Some see Hitler as a demon, a monster—not in the metaphorical sense, but literally. There are those who see him as a phenomenon originating in the world of darkness, whose meaning or explanation, if they exist, should be sought in the fields of mysticism and theology.

"While I respect this approach, I don't agree with it," said the First Person. "Hitler was a human being. He belonged to the human species and, therefore, in principle at least, he can be understood by other human beings. I am not referring, God forbid, to the vulgar notion that claims that 'there's a little Hitler inside every one of us,'" the rich voice dried with scorn as it drew out the syllables of a "lit-tile Hit-ler." Even if it had been incarnated in a different body I would have recognized that mocking voice, pouring scorn on those who don't understand and all the "downstairs people."

"Mother Theresa is not Hitler," he said. "And to say that there is a 'little Hitler' inside her, too, is meaningless. But even Mother Theresa, even Janusz Korczak are capable, in principle at least, of understanding who Hitler was. Because no human being is an angel, the boot that tramples and crushes is not beyond the horizons of the understanding of any one of us. Moreover, it is tremendously important for us as human beings to understand what motivates the boot and what lifts the foot to trample a human face."

The mouth coughed, First Person withdrew a little from the lectern to cough, he straightened his reading glasses on his nose. He moved at his will and uttered whatever sounds came into his head, and I saw every movement and heard every sound. The pounding in my ears died down, and no fire alarm or invitation to the most delight-ful pleasure imaginable would have uprooted me from my seat: more than anything in the world I needed to see and hear.

He spoke about others who had preceded him in the attempt to solve the dark riddle of Hitler, right from the beginning of the Führer's career. Any library worthy of the name possessed books on the sub-ject. Some of the explanations they provided were cheap and sen-sational, not worth commenting on, others gave food for thought, but he would not dwell even now on the serious attempts to come to grips with the subject. There were thousands of such texts in existence, he had not read them all, but let's say he had read quite a few, and some of them he had even had the opportunity to teach.

After years of studying and teaching, after all the explanations, he felt that we were left with a black hole, with an unsolved riddle, and that all the explanations, even the most profound, were only words, words, words . . . that every explanation and every theory collapsed into a black hole of surpassing evil, supreme evil, pure and distilled.

This awareness, this growing despair with words, gave rise to the idea that in order to crack Hitler a completely different way of thinking was required. And this led to the conclusion that what was required in order to plumb the depths of the abyss was not the rational vision of a man of science and theory, but the vision of an artist, the intuitions of an artist, and the courage of an artist.

The speaker bowed his head for a moment in silence, and massaged his cheek with his index finger, as if to pause for reflection before he continued:

When he embarked on this ambitious—today he would not hesitate to use the word "presumptuous"—project of writing about Hitler in the first person, he sincerely believed that only art had the power to plumb the depths of the most evil of souls, and investigate its contents. Scholars and scientists could tell us about Hitler, but only art could make Hitler present to us.

Various accusations had been hurled at him with regard to the book. He agreed with most of his critics, and he was even prepared to add self-criticism of his own to their criticism of him. But of one sin he stood accused of, at least, he was innocent: he had not taken the heavy burden of writing the novel upon himself lightly, and not out of any lust for fame or provocation. Since he had come to confess his error, he would say frankly that from the outset it was clear to him that some people would not understand, and some people would be hurt. In this sense at least he embarked on his project with his eyes open: in the clear knowledge that both art and truth were ruthless.

As far as the criticism of the book was concerned, he was his own harshest critic. As we could see for ourselves, he was no longer young, and he had devoted the last years of his life to the single purpose of exposing the error of his work. He had made a grave mistake in the assumptions he had made, but one thing he could say for certain and in all honesty was that the author had undertaken the writing of the book as a sacred task. The author believed with all his heart that if there was ever anything worth doing, it was writing *Hitler, First Person*.

His voice. I should describe the elusive quality of his voice, without which this report would be lacking. I have already mentioned the unidentifiable accent, but an accent is not a voice. His voice aspired to pathos when he spoke of art, but at the same time it held a note of parody, as if he were presenting us with an imitation. He sounded like a kind of clown mimicking himself—a clown mimicking a clown imitating an imitation, an imposter pretending to be an imposter—until the listener felt lost and foolish, because he had no idea what was at the bottom of the voice and what it intended. One minute he sounded sincere, and the next he seemed to be mocking the very notion of sincerity. I remembered well the effect of this voice of his, but this time I no longer waited uncertainly for his next sentence in the hope that it would reveal his intention to me. I already knew who he was. And I already knew better than to expect any meaning.

The passing of the years, or perhaps the fact that he was standing on a stage, had intensified the ambivalence of his tone to the point it actually jarred, and I could sense an undercurrent of unease in the audience. On my left, Oded kept rubbing his wrist against the arm of the chair, as if absent-mindedly scratching an insect bite.

The voice dropped to a tone almost of complaint when he went on to review two of the writers who had crossed the line before him. Richard Lourie, a professor of literature, had written a novel called *The Autobiography of Joseph Stalin* which, as the name implies, tells the story of the Soviet Czar in the first person. If we judge the degree of evil by the number of the tyrant's victims, then Stalin was even worse than Hitler, but nobody accused Professor Lourie, who was a candidate for the Pulitzer Prize for another of his novels, of doing anything outrageous, and nobody identified him with the subject of his novel or called him "Stalin."

George Steiner, an outstanding scholar and intellectual, gave Hitler the right to speak and argue in his provocative novella *The Portage to San Cristobal of A. H.* Steiner came in for a ton of criticism—he himself thought the text very courageous—but in his humble opinion, Steiner didn't go far enough in looking into the abyss. Steiner's Hitler was a polemical Hitler, not a personality in the full sense of the word, but rather a collection of bold claims regarding the role of the Jews in history, the author's argument with himself and his identity.

In writing *Hitler, First Person* the author strove to advance beyond what Steiner, for whom he had the greatest admiration, had done. He aimed at plumbing the depths of Hitler's soul, his soul and not his arguments. He wanted to present Hitler not as a series of arguments, and not as a case study under a psychiatric label of one kind or another, but as a human being who experienced reality in his own unique way.

How did this human being experience reality? asked the voice, and his finger rose to massage his cheekbone again.

What conflicts created his stormy stream of consciousness? What did he dream about in his sleep? What images were seared into his mind as a child? These were the questions that would not let him be, and his need for answers, his prayer for answers, he addressed to the muse of literature. More and more he came to believe that only there, only in the realms of art, only under the trance-like inspiration of Mnemosyne, might he come to understand.

In a little while we were about to watch the movie *The Fall*. What had made us leave home in the heat of thirty eight degrees Celsius, and come here? A purely academic interest in the last days of the Third Reich? Curiosity about the way in which contemporary Germans tell the story of those days? Let us be honest with ourselves. We came here because secretly, in our hearts, we wanted to see Hitler. We came to see Hitler, and we need not feel ashamed of it, because the dark riddle of Hitler still holds us spellbound after all this time; it calls to us and will not let us be until we succeed in solving it.

Steiner's novella was made into a play. A very talented English actor played Hitler. A no less talented actor plays the Führer in the film we are about to see. We should consider the immense spiritual resources these good people had to bring to bear in order to get under the skin of the character and to understand it. In his opinion, regardless of what we thought of the play or the film, we should respect these two artists for the spiritual sacrifice they were called to make in order to bring Satan before us. Let us consider the possibility that by means of their art and through the personal sacrifice they made—and under the mysterious trance of the muse—these two actors came closer to solving the Hitlerian riddle than a thousand professors with their theories.

The lecture ended abruptly. The mouth fell silent, and Not-man folded the sheet of paper at which he had hardly glanced. Later on I wondered if the members of the audience who were less alert than me had noticed that the speaker had failed to describe the "error' he was supposed to talk about. The applause was rather weak: neither more nor less enthusiastic than that which had greeted the speakers who had preceded him. And nevertheless, about eighty people clapped their hands for him, in other words a hundred sixty hands moved and struck each other in his honor; in other words, the voice moved hands.

●

The moderator said that there was time for a question or two, and a dwarfish little old lady with hunched shoulders in a sleeveless dress stood up in the third row. Her English was poor and bad, but "Auschwitz" is not an English word, and there is no need for any great linguistic powers in order to say "mother," "father," "grandfather," "grandmother," "other grandmother," "little brother," and "six sisters."

Her language failed her only when she insisted on trying to say something about each of the relatives she had mentioned, and the incoherent rush of words had to be taken apart and put together again in a sentence that made sense: Manya played the piano. Father believed in the progress of humanity. The little brother had connections with certain elements—even after the deconstruction and re-assembling it was impossible to know who they were—and when the Germans marched in he tried to contact them.

A murmur of impatience gradually spread through the hall. "She didn't understand a word he said," a young man complained in front of me, without lowering his voice.

The moderator came to the podium again, and stood to the right of the First Person in a demonstrative waiting position, but two or three more minutes passed before he interrupted the woman and asked her to come to her question, if she had one.

Only then she shifted to Hebrew and said: "I didn't read the book, but in the newspaper it said that the esteemed professor lost his family in the Holocaust, and I would very much like to understand how a Jew . . . how a Jew who went thought what you, sir, went through, can speak in the name of the Nazi monster and spread his propaganda."

A sigh of disdain rose in front of me. And I thought: if only she had known English better, if only she had worn a more suitable dress, a dress with sleeves, if only . . . it wouldn't have made any difference.

Without losing his composure First Person waited for the moderator to translate the words he understood. He took off his reading glasses, put them in his jacket pocket, and in the patient and emphatic tone of a person obliged for the umpteenth time to reply to the same childish question, he replied that the horror affected all human beings insofar as they were human. And therefore, while in this case what was written in the newspaper was correct, he would say that his personal closeness to the subject was irrelevant to how the book should be judged. At the same time, he was also prepared to say that precisely because of his closeness to the subject—and such a closeness did in fact exist—precisely because of this, he possessed a particularly burning need to understand what—paraphrasing Faust—"what it is that holds evil up from inside." And it was very important to him too, to point out that in opposition to the facile conclusion of a certain Hollywood movie to understand was not to forgive. A person could understand and not forgive, and sometimes people forgave only because they did not understand.

"I imagine that if I had succeeded in what I attempted to do, I would be judged differently. But when I myself look at the text today, it is clear to me that I failed miserably: the muse did not choose me. And I have no choice but to admit that in the end all my efforts and sacrifices resulted in a trivial work. I failed to solve the secret and added nothing to what my learned predecessors had already written. It appears that I am not the kind of artist I thought I was, and the limitations I refused to recognize, the limitations and the original sin of hubris, are the basis of my mistake. The task I undertook was too great for me. I still believe that one day a greater artist than me will enter the little breakthrough I achieved, and shed light on one of the greatest of human mysteries. But this evening I stand here before you and openly confess: I wrote a mediocre work, I wouldn't hesitate to use the word "banal," and this is without a doubt my fault, mea culpa." He raised his hands and in an ancient, sickeningly familiar gesture he beat his breast. "Mea maxima culpa. This is my greatest fault."

Not-man descended from the stage and took his seat in the first row. The moderator rose to introduce the next speaker, who asked us to watch with her part of the popular television program hosted by Oprah Winfrey: an interview with Elie Wiesel. But perhaps the Professor would like to say something beforehand? The speaker rose briskly to her feet, a plump, energetic young woman: not at all like the lady professor my imagination had sent to have dinner with my in-laws in that kosher restaurant on Keren Hayesod Street.

I took the yellow notepad, on which Oded had not written a single word, and wrote: "I'm going up to the Baradanshvilis. If you love me, please tell him that I want to talk, and bring him there."

I was in desperate need of oxygen, but when I was already getting up I lingered for a moment more, and crossed out "if you love me" with two lines, and only then gave the pad back to Oded. The air was thick with First Person's presence, my lungs urged me to leave, and I was in a hurry, my redaction was slipshod. He could still read what was written underneath it.

- 8 -

The Baradanshvilis gallery had opened a few months previously on the hillside opposite Mount Zion, right above the Cinematheque. I had met Lilly and Shabtai Baradanshvilis, a sculptor and a painter, during my research for Alice, and but for the demise of my pigtailed heroine I would have written about their place, and presumably succeeded in attracting a few more visitors to it.

They had a studio in Tbilisi that also served as a gallery and a club for the discerning. Artists and poets, students and members of the diplomatic corps—the Belgian consul himself accompanied by his mistress—would come and stay till morning: drinking tea, wine, and vodka, eating pastries and fruit whose taste surpassed anything to be found in Israel, and arguing about art and ideas. The finest artists had their first shows there, the best known were exposed to criticism. Those who had the money paid, those who were short of cash paid another time.

Lilly and Shabtai had succeeded in opening a gallery in Jerusalem, but their dream of renewing the nights of Tbilisi had not yet been realized. Optimistic, they cleaned the little inner courtyard adjoining the building, built a small pond for goldfish, planted orange trees and ferns in pots, and installed lighting, and when their preparations were completed, they returned to their sculpting and painting without losing heart, and kept on hoping for guests to arrive and make their dream reality.

There was not a hint of desert light in Shabtai's abstract charcoal drawings, but when Alice was still sucking her pigtails, I planned to connect their studio to the monastery in the Valley of the Crucifixion, and to give the beautiful Lilly a secret relationship to Shotha Rusthaveli, who had composed his great epic there.

I intended to read *The Man in the Panther's Skin*. I got hold of a copy, but everything that had happened, and what had happened to Alice, sentenced it to remain unread. And so the gallery-studio of the Baradanshvilis was doomed to remain in its desolation. As I climbed the steps leading from the Cinematheque, I noted this loss too.

When I entered the gallery the only person there was Lilly and Shabtai's oldest son, busy sorting a pile of photographs into envelopes. He apologized for the disorder in the gallery and the fact that the courtyard was full of stuff: they had cleaned the place out today and not yet managed to put everything back. I said it didn't matter, I felt quite at home, he could carry on working and I would take care of myself.

And so I did. I went to the fridge, took a bottle of vodka from the freezer, and poured myself a double shot. I didn't forget to leave a banknote in the box, and with the brimming glass in my hand I went out to the courtyard, which, as he said, was not arranged for guests: the iron chairs were collected in one corner, their cushions stacked on a table, the other three tables were loaded with painting equipment.

I put a couple of cushions on one chair next to the ornamental fishpond, and dragged up another chair, set it next to the wall on the other side of the table and measured the distance between the two. Two chairs. Oded would have to take the hint. And what if he insisted on ignoring it and stayed?

Of all the events for which I had to prepare myself, I fixated on this foolishness and wasted the little time at my disposal contemplating it.

The last and only time I had asked Oded to go away was in the delivery room at the Hadassah Hospital, two hours before Yachin saw the light of day. Now too I had something to do, and I needed to concentrate all my strength and prevent it from dissolving under an anxious look and a tender touch.

But what could I say to him now, what exactly was I going to say to my husband? "Go away now, please be good enough in your great, your tremendous, your incomprehensible and incomparable goodness, to go away and leave me alone with this thing?" How would I say it? I was indeed alone with this thing, that was the truth and had been the truth since Monticello. So why tell any more lies? Elisheva had forgiven, and only I was alone with him, forced to be alone with him. And in a minute face to face. On my own. Myself and Not-man. Enough deception and pretending that it wasn't so.

The enclosed courtyard stored the heat of the day, and the heat closed in on me like a dense physical entity. I hadn't eaten all day, it was a long time since I had drunk vodka neat, and my guts, weakened by being treated so delicately, reacted instantly to the icy liquid setting them on fire.

The woman who had taken the stage to discuss the case of Oprah Winfrey was the last of the speakers, and I estimated that I had about half an hour to wait, no more, before my husband arrived on the scene and brought me the First Person. The possibility that he would decide not to bring him or that he would fail in his attempt to bring him didn't occur to me; in fact, nothing much occurred to me at all. It was hot. The vodka went to my head. The goldfish darted nervously above the gleaming pebbles. One of the fish leapt out of the water and dived back again. Another one leapt in a mute suicide attempt. The pond was small and the water was overheated. The deep boils over and the cauldron hisses unappeased. Fish don't hiss.

I thought of going to the fridge and bringing ice to cool the water down, and then I thought, "Fuck it," and "Enough, enough already." And I thought "Stop it, what are you thinking," and "You're so dumb," and "What is this? What's going on here? Don't you understand? I'm not being photographed, I'm taking the photograph."

And then they were there, my black belt and the spider legs about a meter behind him, and already opposite me: my husband in front, separating me from them, preventing any attempt to shake hands, gesturing Not-man to sit down and only then picking up a chair for himself and carrying it into the pool of light around the pond: carrying it, not dragging it.

"I told Professor Gotthilf that as a result of his lecture you've changed your mind and you're prepared to talk to him. The professor realizes that it's not a simple matter."

"Aaron," the voice corrected him courteously, "Aaron."

The relative darkness under the wall blurred the deep furrows under his nose. What emerged in the relative darkness was the wavy crest of hair, the skinny vulture's neck, and the movement of the lips.

"Family, as you say, Oded, is not a simple matter. Sometimes people make do with correct relations, but polite formalities in the family circle, and among Jews what's more . . . With my two sons the relationship is far from simple, but neither of them calls me professor." Now he spoke in Hebrew.

"Aaron," I pronounced, tasting the poison in my mouth.

"Thank you," he said.

I was aware of the fact that I was sitting up stiffly in a theatrical manner, but even when I shifted my position slightly and unobtrusively, my limbs continued to arrange themselves in a self-conscious pose. I looked in silence at the stone wall opposite me, as a chatty voice—very different from his voice on the stage, but still, always the same deceptive, buffoonish voice—launched into a monologue about his sons.

His eldest—"who is in fact your second cousin"—his eldest was Orthodox, and not simply an Orthodox Jew but an important rabbi in Bnei Brak. He was said to be a great Torah scholar, and perhaps he was, to his regret he was not competent to judge. This son had given him nine grandchildren, and he had celebrated the Passover Seder with all of them: his son, his son's children, their husbands and wives, and their children. A big family.

Did we too tend to regard Orthodoxy as Judaism in its purist form?—the lips chattered. Because it was his impression that many Israelis held this view. And at the same time, it would not be a mistake to say that their attitude toward the ultra-Orthodox smacked of more than a hint of anti-Semitism. We would agree with him that this was a fascinating phenomenon. He himself was of the opinion that it was connected to Zionism, connected—but not entirely dependent on. Had we read Otto Weininger? Every Jew should read Weininger once. His passion, the passionate eloquence of his self-hatred . . . Hitler, by the way, said of him that he was the only decent Jew who ever existed. Decent? That perhaps not. But the authenticity of the emotion cannot be denied, however infuriating. To be honest, he was ready to confess to us that although he was of course grateful to his son and daughter-in-law for hosting him and observing the mitzvah of "honor thy father," there were certain aspects of the ultra-Orthodox way of life, unaesthetic aspects that—how should he put it?—jarred on him. No doubt we understood what he was referring to . . .

·

I glanced at Oded. He neither nodded nor shook his head, he never moved a muscle. Illuminated from the side in the hazy orange light of the garden lamps, he looked like the character of the bodyguard in one of the movies he liked, not any particular bodyguard but all the best ones put together: still, holding himself in suspense, but fully present. The voice that had moved an audience to clap its hands did not move my husband.

Three times in the past we had slipped away together here, when the Cinematheque café was crowded. That was in the distant days whose sweetness was liable to befuddle and weaken me even more than the heat. We would not sit together again.

The irony of fate—the voice continued—his younger son was in many ways the complete opposite of his brother: that is to say an American Jew, in other words an ignoramus. And perhaps it wasn't the irony of fate but simply a typical Jewish fate. With this son too he has difficulties, but in his case the reasons are different. This son lives in Texas, and from him he has one granddaughter. She was born a year and a half ago, and to the grandfather's regret he has not yet seen her.

There was a moment of silence. The talkative grandfather took out his wallet. The being disguised as a boring old grandfather opened his wallet, took out a little picture and held it out to the light: whether to look at it himself or to show to the others. The bodyguard sat still as a statue, the hand retreated and withdrew the picture.

"Fathers and sons . . ." The voice sighed. "You too, so I hear, have sons. They must be grown up now . . ."

"Elinor . . ." said my husband, the perfect gentleman, opening the door for me.

"I have a question," I croaked. And immediately my throat cleared and the continuation flowed as if of its own accord: "I have a question, which is actually the reason we asked you to come. I wanted to know: how many women have you actually raped?" I hadn't planned this question. The way things turned out, I didn't plan anything.

A hand reached for the table, picked up a purple pastel crayon and rubbed it between its fingers. A hand spotted with freckles like that of an old man turned upward and balanced the crayon on its palm. A hand that was not that of an old man gave itself away and didn't tremble. The orange lighting illuminated a steady hand weighing a purple pastel crayon in its palm.

When it began to answer, the voice was as steady as the hand and the chatty tone was gone.

He appreciated my directness, and more than that, he thanked me for it. They said that directness was a characteristic of native born Israelis. Some saw this characteristic as indicative of a lack of culture and sophistication, but he thought otherwise. He remembered that even as a young girl I was very direct: in my speech and especially in my eyes, a very particular look I had in my eyes.

His difficulty in answering my question was related to the presumption of guilt it contained. There was a lawyer sitting with us, and he would no doubt confirm that such a startling question belonged to the stage when the so-called criminal had already admitted his guilt and the counts of the charge were being negotiated. We weren't children, and it was clear to us all that the only direct answer he could give would make it impossible to continue this conversation. Speaking for himself, he would be sorry, since the reason he had contacted me a few weeks ago was that he was eager for a chance to do something else. When my charming husband had invited him to come up here, he imagined that I—with every right—was going to ask him for explanations for all kinds of troubling questions, such as for example why the relations between my father and himself had been broken off. In this as in other matters he did not see himself as free of guilt, certainly not, human life by its very nature involved guilt. But things were complicated, very complicated, and they could on no account be summed up in the shallow medium called "an admission." He had been told that Elinor wrote a literary column for the newspaper, and as someone close to literature she had surely taken note of the fact that while there was a literary genre of confession, there was no genre of "admission." The admissions extorted by the police in the course of their interrogations never amounted to a text worth anything.

He was a professor, the habits of a lifetime were hard to uproot, and therefore we would allow him to further remark that questions to which the answers were "yes" or "no" would accomplish nothing in furthering the understandings of any one of us. Did Stalin have signs that the Germans were about to invade? Yes. Were there Jews in key positions in Stalin's terror apparatus? Yes indeed. The problem is that this "yes" does not really enrich our understanding, and it will not help us to prevent any tragedies in the future.

As he had mentioned in his presentation, which he was very grateful to us for being kind enough to attend, the great human question is "why?" and to this "why?" there are not, and cannot be short two- or three-letter answers.

In any event, it saddened him greatly to think that two wonderful young people like us, two of his own relations, should regard him as a hardened criminal. He wasn't complaining, he understood that in the light of our partial information perhaps it was impossible for us to come to a different conclusion, but he had not yet lost hope of trying to correct our impression.

Did the name Hannah Arendt mean anything to us? If so, perhaps it would interest us to know that she wrote that the Eichmann trial was an indescribably low and repulsive event. Whatever we thought of him—the voice smirked—he wasn't Eichmann, and none of us would gain anything by holding a show trial for him here in this courtyard.

•

The shadowy profile of the mask turned toward Oded. Even when he was addressing me he avoided turning his face to me. Perhaps he thought that the debate should be conducted with the man, and perhaps it was one of his parodies of politeness: not to look a woman in the eye in the presence of her husband.

So the head was turned to Oded. One spidery leg was crossed on the other. One sharp knee rose above the table. A dark wave of gray hair crested over a huge head. The hand that had weighed the pastel crayon came to a satisfactory conclusion and returned it to its jar. And the voice that had fallen silent in order to assess our silence saw it as confirmation and continued into the enclosed space of the courtyard:

If we were ready to do without the show trial and listen to him, he would like to tell us about a certain text, a novel, in fact, which he had been working on for over two years now. It could be argued that after the mistake of *Hitler, First Person* he should have abandoned literary writing, he understood this argument, but sometimes, and there were a number of examples of this, great achievements grew precisely out of what on the face of it seemed a failure, out of the strange joy that seized hold of a man when his back was to the wall.

In any case, it was about this novel that he wanted to talk to us when he tried to make contact with us that time. We were family, and as such it was important to him to clarify certain things with us before the book came out. And since he was going to be in Israel anyway he thought that he would take advantage of the opportunity.

As we may have already guessed, his novel contained certain biographical elements, but it was on no account an autobiography or a *roman à clef* in the usual sense. That is to say, it did not present events as they had happened, or seek to portray real people in disguise. In the words of the poet, the best of the poem is its fabrication, and the same holds true for prose. While the book enlarged upon issues he had already touched on in his essay, "My Mistake," it was important to understand that it was basically a work of fiction, and should be read as such.

Reducing a work of literature to its plot was doing it an injustice. In time to come perhaps we would do him the honor of wishing to read his book, but in order for this happen he had no option but to do himself and his book this very injustice, if we would have the patience to listen.

The plot takes place in the present day. The hero, whose name is Albert, is the French cultural attaché in Phnom Penh, a far from simple challenge considering the history of France in the country. But this, of course, is something the average Western reader knows nothing about. He himself, who knew a little history, had to do a lot of reading in order to create a convincing factual foundation for his novel. The research, by the way, was highly instructive, but this was a matter for another conversation. He didn't want to digress too far from the subject. Up to now we had shown extraordinary patience, which he appreciated very much, and he had no wish to impose upon it any further.

Albert, the hero, is a European intellectual of the old school, a little like himself: a graduate of the Sorbonne, not exactly the type commonly found in the foreign service, and his present post is the last before his retirement. The special situation in which Albert finds himself gives rise in him to a sense of freedom—a consciousness of his personal freedom, perhaps—and thus, more than occupying himself with the dissemination of French culture, the consul devotes himself to the local culture.

At first he broadens his knowledge of Sanskrit, and also tries to learn Khmer. For a certain period he explores the roots of Buddhism. His journey begins with the ancient Khmer traditions, and shifts to the horrors of the history of Cambodia in the second half of the twentieth century.

Do we know, by the way, what the Americans called their carpet bombing of Cambodia? These murderous daily flights were referred to in the American air force as "breakfast," "lunch," "dinner" and "snacks." Two hundred thousand people were slaughtered in this manner. To remind us that the jackboot comes in different colors. But to get back to the book.

Phnom Penh, as we know, is surrounded by mass graves. And the proximity of the murderous hell oppresses Albert. The terrible past seems more real to him than the present, and he is increasingly repelled by the pleasures of the new life of the city. It is important to point out that we are talking about a serious-minded person here, an intellectual with no hedonistic inclinations, who sees the pleasure-seeking life around him not as frivolous but as sinful: as a denial of the horror and the truth.

The hero's research becomes increasingly focused on the four years of Khmer-Rouge rule.

Opinion is divided on the question of how many people were liquidated by the regime of Pol Pot. So divided that the estimates vary from less than a million to two million. A similar confusion, a shocking confusion concerning millions of human lives, can be found in the research into the Stalinist terror, but he is straying from the subject again. The crux of the matter is that Albert is increasingly absorbed by Pol Pot's penal colony, and the more the subject absorbs him, the greater his need to understand the mind that came up with the idea of the slave labor camps and strewed mines around them.

Albert is a bachelor. Apart from one sister, an old maid who lives in Lyon, he has no family, and he has hardly any friends. The diplomatic way of life combined with a difficult character make him a solitary figure and turns him into a stranger wherever he found himself. From his earliest youth he has kept a diary—the novel in fact consists of Albert's diary—and in his diary he documents his growing disgust with the official banquets, ceremonies, and other vanities of the empty diplomatic life.

The crux of the matter is that the empty space in his life is increasingly filled with thoughts about the Pol Pot regime, his diary is increasingly filled with these thoughts, to the point where they could be described as an obsession.

Like one possessed he returns again and again to the killing fields of Chvang Ack, and stands before the thousands of skulls in the memorial sepulcher. Albert visits and revisits the skulls, the dry bones, but his thoughts are mainly on the mind. He feels compelled to understand the living mind that smashed the heads of infants only because they were born into the wrong class. He has to understand. And this sense of inner duty gives birth in him to the realization that it is his mission to write a book: he understands that he must write about Pol Pot.

From the point of view of class, the consul belongs to the urban intelligentsia, that specific urban race which Pol Pot described as the root of all evil. And nonetheless he has two things in common with the mass murderer: they had both been educated in Catholic schools, and they were both graduates of the Sorbonne. At the beginning of his research, the naïve scholar believes that with these keys in his hands he will be able to penetrate the layers of ideology and get inside the brain. And only gradually, in the fourth and fifth parts of the diary, does he come to realize how empty his hands are, and how far he is from understanding anything.

To sum up, in banal terms: Albert goes mad. Since he was a child Albert has never experienced a need so absolute, a drive so lacking in doubt, and the thought of giving up the most meaningful project of his life—on what he sees as his vocation—is equal in his eyes to the embrace of death.

In the seventh part of the diary, which is perhaps the most important, Albert has a vision. This happens in the month of May, at the beginning of the monsoon season, when the hero goes to visit the lost towns in the depths of the jungle and returns home burning with fever. There is no clear diagnosis. Different doctors provide him with advice and medications, but he is not healed. In the middle of a restless night of delirium, Albert leaves the house without knowing why, and gets on a plane to Angkor. And there, among the ancient temples of Angkor, under sheets of torrential rain, Satan reveals himself to him.

If this sounds like nonsense to you, please remember that the man was educated as a Catholic. And even though he has lost his childhood faith, and in spite of his philosophical atheism, in utter contradiction to his intellectual convictions—Satan still exists in his mind as a real entity.

So Albert meets Satan, and the Prince of Darkness laughs at Albert. He mocks the insignificance of his life, and throws at him that an urban intellectual will never be able to understand even the least of his representatives. The King of Horrors—he tells him—is not a butterfly to be stuck on a pin and examined under a microscope. There is only once way to understand the acts of Satan, and Albert is too weak and cowardly to embark on it.

The provocative apparition is about to disappear, and Albert, on the point of losing consciousness, understands the choice before him without the need for explanations. This is, of course, an archetypical choice: he must choose between knowledge and the Garden of Eden, between his creation and the immortality of his soul.

Albert falls to his knees and implores Satan not to leave him. He is ready for any sacrifice. And a moment before he loses consciousness he hears Satan instruct him: seek me inside you.

The voice changed its tone, quick and agile as a monkey: one minute it was intimate and engaging, ingratiating almost to the point of parody in its eagerness for our belief; and distant and dry the next, clipped in its pronunciation, as if cynical, and as if flattering our disbelief as if insolently asking us to enter into a clandestine alliance of shared mockery. A liquid voice seeking a crack to seep into. A voice evaporating around us into gas. And not a single, solid word.

Every summary of a plot sounds superficial, says the voice. Like questions demanding a "yes" or "no" answer, a summary too sins against the spirit, and when he was required to send a summary to a publisher, he struggled with the task more than in the composition of the book itself. We had to believe him that the book was far from being as superficial as it sounded when he described it like this.

And so, as we had no doubt guessed, Albert recovers his health, there is no need to go into the details now, but the words of Satan will not leave him be. He understands that evil is not an object, and certainly not an external object to be examined with surgical gloves behind the masks of theory. In order to get to the bottom of the mind that refers to burning people with napalm as a "snack"; in order to mine the depths of a brain that empties an entire city of its inhabitants, a man must expose himself to true and honest contact. He must have the courage to penetrate the abyss of the soul of evil and to be truly penetrated by it.

Albert's serious difficulty, his problem, is that in every accepted sense of the words he is a good man. And however much he examines his mind and his past, he cannot find any dimension of Satanic evil in them. A miserable affair of a broken engagement, the firing of a secretary for no good reason: the only reason he fired her was that he couldn't stand the silly way she laughed—it was all as petty as a child stealing apples. In order to understand the workings of pure, distilled, inhuman Satanic evil, you had to experience it in action. And this meant that Albert would have to get rid of humanist sentiments and become evil himself.

Months of mental agonies follow. He falls ill again. He thinks of suicide. His nerves are exhausted. The diary grows more and more confused. But to cut a long story short—Not-man suddenly started talking very fast, as if in a show of self-contempt—the long and the short of it is that in the month of October, at the end of the monsoon season, Albert defiles himself with a terrible act. Nothing could be more foreign to his soul than the crime he commits, and it is precisely for this reason that he believes he must commit it.

He seduces his maidservant's daughter, he forces himself on a child of ten.

- 9 -

Oded suddenly moves. For a moment it seems to me that his movement is directed toward the figure in the shadow of the wall, but no: he signals to the Baradanshvilis's son who peeks into the courtyard. My bodyguard is sitting with his back to the entrance, and nevertheless he senses his presence, as if he had eyes in the back of his head, and now he signals him that we're fine, we don't need anything. The lad asks if it's okay with us if he goes out for a few minutes to load some paintings into the car, and Oded signals his agreement. Only when the son leaves does my husband open his mouth and addresses the First Person:

"So that's it, that's your story?"

"Actually we've only reached as far as two thirds of the novel, and I must emphasize again that it is a novel, in other words, a work of fiction. What happens in the last third of the book, which I haven't finished writing yet, is that Albert comes to realize that he has fallen victim to a Satanic trick. The great work that Albert thought he would write does not get written, and all that he succeeds in producing despite all his efforts is a confused, childish text. There is a philosophical concept called 'moral luck,' and Albert in a certain sense is unlucky, a man with no luck. The victim of a mistake in evaluation. If he had been lucky and succeeded in writing a work of cultural significance, something that would really have enriched his fellow man, then perhaps, I say perhaps . . . with thoughts like these he tortures and flagellates himself. But Albert's tragedy is that he is a poor, mediocre writer, and from now on he will have to live with the knowledge that he defiled his soul for nothing. The book is not yet finished, but as intelligent readers it must be clear to you how it ends. Albert has to die, the only question is how. How will he die— this is not yet clear: by a human hand or by the hand of providence; the intervention of what we might call force majeure; what could be interpreted as divine intervention, seen as the intervention of a higher power. As potential readers, I would be glad to hear your opinion."

"And this is the book you're going to publish," my husband says as if weighing the words in the balance, and the voice replies, "A superficial summary of it," and adds the name of a publisher unfamiliar to me.

I'm holding something in my hand: a metal can. And the metal doesn't cool my hand. The voice had gone on forever, like a nightmare, and stopped in a second, like a nightmare, and at some point I had started to play absent-mindedly with the painting gear on the table. There was a moment when I caught myself playing with a piece of chalk, only to return it with disgust to the jar. Now this metal object: wet with the sweat on my hand, resisting my attempts to crush it.

"I'm quite an unsophisticated reader, so explain to me," says my husband, "explain to me: did Pol Pot rape children?"

A moment ago he was alert enough to register a movement behind his back, and now like a blind child he steps right into the filth in front of him. In a minute he'll touch it, in a minute the pus will infect him.

Red shame, red rage, something red flares and spreads over the nape of my neck: I should have found the strength to tell Oded to go. Go away, go, go now—soundlessly I implore the good man innocently asking and sincerely wanting to know.

And already the tongue clucks, pouncing triumphantly on the obtuse student, and the mouth replies in the same patronizing tone of weary disappointment with which it replied to the hump-backed old lady in the Cinematheque.

"Pol Pot engaged in social engineering, not rape," the voice says, "but in the eyes of Albert, as in the story as a whole, this crime has an obvious metaphorical meaning. Because what in fact is rape, if not pure metaphor? The Marquis de Sade did not write erotic literature. And it is not by coincidence that Hitler spoke of the rape of Europe. It is only by metaphor that we can construct the monstrous meaning of this act, which is a degree higher than ordinary torture. Torture is usually justified as a means to an end: the whip and the vice are intended to achieve something of benefit. Rape has no purpose apart from symbolic expression. Rape is the universal symbol of the relations between master and slave. It is the most distilled metaphor for de-humanization, for turning people into objects, for treating a human being as something no different from a table or a stool."

I stand up. At some point I removed the lid from the metal receptacle. Now I circle the seated Oded, still in the pool of light, the lamp shining directly on me. How can I describe the beauty of my movement?

Among the yogis there are some who achieve perfection in the art of archery only by constantly enacting the drawing of the bow and the shooting of the arrow in their imagination. There are some who develop the body of a wrestler only by the imaginary flexing of their muscles—so I have read.

My sister practiced this movement in her mind and practiced it until she dropped the weapon from her hand; I, who never practiced, caught the dropped receptacle and aimed at the face, as if I had inherited her spiritual exercises. The movement is perfect, and I am completed, perfectly fulfilled in making it.

I spray. The eyes close instinctively, but the foolish mouth gapes, perhaps to scream. He doesn't scream. A gleaming dark void absorbs more and more of the spray, and a smell like that of acetone fills the air. The gaping mask is covered with moisture and the moisture evaporates fast. The body recoils, the back of the iron chair hits the wall, hands go up to protect, in an instant both hands and mask are wet and dripping, and I go on pressing, and the spray is constant and quicker than it takes to evaporate. The space between the hands is mute. My head spins a little, and the spinning too is the perfection of movement. Only when the hissing changes its sound and the can is already light do I lower my hand, and only then does Oded say with a strange quiver glinting in his voice: "Elinor, my God, Elinor, how careless you are."

My husband is standing by my side. He takes the empty can from me, and I feel the laughter tickling me when he holds the can up to the light, away from his face, as if he's reading a book.

"Fixative," he reads and immediately afterward pronounces the words: "an accident," "sir," and "emergency room."

The mask coated with the fixative spray moves crookedly. The gleaming hole mumbles, closes and opens and closes again, in a moment it will vomit its guts up. Lips move and try to say something. Around the hole more moisture drips, now from the eyes. "*Wasser*," croaks the voice behind the mask, and again: "*Wasser*," and then: "Water."

Oded grabs hold of a garment and lifts the slumped body, and walking backward in a strange kind of slow motion, he drags it step by step to the fish pond and drops it on the edge.

"Can you drive?"

On its knees, the body stretches its hands to the water.

"Elinor, I'm asking you, can you go and get the car and bring it here?"

"Yes. What?"

My husband puts both hands on my shoulders and brings his face close to mine. "Ramat Hovav. The garbage dump," he says with a crooked smile, "the garbage dump. Now go, bring the car. I'll meet you outside in five minutes." And then he almost pushes me to the door.

When I come out into the street, accompanied by my husband's condolences, the heat closes in on me again, and my feeling of completion is shattered by a crushing realization. Ramat Hovav. With absolute clarity I realize that from now on there would be no retribution, nothing but miserable condolences such as these. Because I would never succeed in getting the First Person to confront the Defender.

I had one chance to lay my trap and I failed to take advantage of it: I wasted it childishly, and my punishment from now on would be the consoling words intended to mollify a foolish child.

At the top of the road, at the entrance to Emek Refaim Street, they were repairing the street for the umpteenth time. A bulldozer trundled, the air was steamy and reeking of tar. Behind my back, beyond the Valley of Hinnom, the Old City was illuminated by a lighting display, and the ancients mocked me from inside the walls. No fire burned. No famine arose. No heads were smashed on a stone. I was given a single opportunity, and I sprayed fixative.

My husband would clean up after me, the way you clean up the mess made by a wild, wayward child. He would take him to the Emergency Room, and say "an accident," and "hormonal imbalance" and "vodka." He would talk and explain until Not-man forgave me. "My wife this and my wife that," he would say. My lawyer would undertake to see that I went to therapy on condition that no charges were brought. And Not-man would go on walking the land, and Not-man would forgive me, and no charges would be brought.

I climb the two hundred meters to the Scottish church. With great difficulty I climb. The metastasis of the abomination had not been excised, and it would only go on growing inside me. And as I climb I think: I'd be better off dead, and I know that Oded remains behind me, and that I won't die and leave him there, behind me. Five minutes, he said.

- 10 -

Five minutes later my husband opens the back door of the car. "I'm sorry," he says over the recalcitrant bundle. "I'm really sorry, but I have no option but to take you to the hospital. Both as a human being and as a lawyer I must insist." And then he guides or pushes the bundle onto the seat behind me. From the way he talks it's clear that he had started this prattle earlier, and perhaps he had been keeping it up throughout my absence.

Until Oded gets him into the car I register an image: First Person's eyes have narrowed to motionless slits. The bouffant crest of hair around the huge mask of his face looks as if it has been set with hair spray. The front of his jacket is wet.

Oded slams the door, and through the open window for the second time this evening he brings his face close to mine, and for the second time he asks me: "Can you drive?" I nod, and again he says: "The garbage dump," and only then, so quietly I can hardly hear: "Ramat Hovav is quite far. Take the road to Mishor Adumim. You know the way. I'll direct you from there."

For a moment I am alone in space with First Person and his wheezing breath, and then Oded circles the car and gets into the back seat next to him. His movements are exaggerated, as if directed at the eyes of distant spectators; every movement is a gesture, and in a magnified gesture of a routine action he fastens the safety-belt around him. "Here, allow me . . ." another click. And the seatbelt on the other side is locked as well.

I step on the gas. I sit high up in the Defender. Behind me Notman is half blind, motionless, making queasy sounds of nausea, and Oded who doesn't stop talking to him confirms in an exaggeratedly loud and emphatic voice that I understood the unbelievable correctly. "Hadassah Mount Scopus, the ER," he says. "Just to be on the safe side, so we can all have peace of mind. We'll go in and get it over. An unfortunate accident. In any case it's better for all of us to have documentation. According to what's written on the can washing with water should be enough, but nevertheless . . ."

A wind blows in and snatches away some of his words. The car is blazing hot. And I can't bring myself to close the windows and turn on the air-conditioner.

After the Jaffa Gate the road enters a tunnel and comes out on the south side of the Old City wall with a split-second view of the Dome of the Rock in all its glory. Only ten minutes walk from here, in a parallel universe, is our house. And we drive ahead, into the distance. Oded babbles on about "the pace of the infrastructure construction, even the people who live here get lost. The city must look very different to you from your last visit." And the road takes us on, to the south.

The First Person, as I said, is half blind. The fixative presumably makes it difficult for his eyes to move. Even Jerusalemites lose their way on the roads. But a few minutes after the car drives past the Hyatt Hotel and the turn off to Mount Scopus on the left, as we approach the traffic lights, the mouth behind me whispers: "I want to go to the hotel. To the hotel. Please be good enough to take me there."

Another spate of talk from Oded. Whenever we stop at a traffic light he increases the volume. And I no longer listen to the words, only to the artificial tone that once again confirms that I was not mistaken, that it's true: we drive on.

"Pay attention. In a little while at the intersection. Turn right."

We pass a police roadblock. We don't stop. And when the car starts to descend the Ma'aleh Adumim road I marvel at the breadth of the road, which I haven't traveled on for a long time, at the number of the vehicles, and at the fact that my ears remain open on the descent. On almost every journey to Tel Aviv my ears are blocked by the difference in the pressure, and now, on this steep descent, they remain open. It occurs to me that this may be the effect of the vodka, since alcohol dries, and it's lucky that I drank vodka.

"Hail me a cab," the not-voice requests.

The lights of the town dwindle, and soon they are behind us. The streetlamps draw a bridge in the desert. A blazing wind closes my pores, and my skin has resumed its function and again separates me from what is outside me.

A dark night. The bridge of light slides between the curves and hollows of the clean desert darkness. My two hands on the unaccustomed steering wheel. My foot on the gas pedal. A Muslim moon, a slender sliver of a moon, appears in the east beyond a hill.

Not-man says "Hail a cab for me," and again, "a cab." His breath wheezes and creaks. His mouth breathes heavily, and then he says something long that I don't catch.

"What did he say?"

"He says that he can cancel his contract for the book. That he only wanted to hear our opinion."

"Tell me," I almost shout at Oded, "do you also think that suffering is more real than happiness? That happiness is only a momentary relief from suffering? No more than that?"

"After Mitzpe Jericho take a right. There should be a sign for Nebi Musa."

"As if you put something heavy on someone, say a suitcase, and then lift it," I say.

"Or as if someone is dying of thirst and then you give him water," replies my husband. "Pay attention now, here's the sign."

There's a certain movement on the back seat. I don't look in the mirror. My eyes are on the road. A turn right, and we're on a dirt track. We pass a white-domed building. A big pothole yawns in the road, the Defender takes it in its stride. The headlamps illuminate a black tent, the sliver of moon right over it.

"You know how to distinguish the new moon from the moon at the end of the month?" our tour guide asks in a loud voice. "I'm sure Elinor knows, it's a trick for people who know Hebrew. You add a little line at the top, if it comes out like the letter '*gimmel*,' the first letter of the word '*gorea*,' diminish, it means it's the end."

The car jumps over bumps in the ground. The road is becoming more and more rocky. Our car is big and strong and high. It skips over mountains and leaps over hills like a roller coaster. The movement is liberating, and only the bundle in the back oppresses.

A jackal runs across the road. Not a jackal. Probably a dog. Another dark animal emerges from nowhere, a meter in front of us, and freezes. I brake, and the second dog disappears in the wake of the first. The dirt track twists and turns. The path disappears for a moment and then appears again. We cross some kind of bridge. Pass concrete huts. Suddenly a clear desert plain in front of us.

"Not good. A military training ground. Turn around here," says Oded, and we go back a little. "Take a right. Now left." My salt of the earth in the middle of the desert. "Give it more gas." We're almost at the top of the ridge, opposite us, a little to the left is an escarpment. "Okay. The Kidron River. We can stop here."

I turn off the ignition and leave the lights on. Whistling sounds of breathing spoil the silence. "Thirty six degrees tomorrow in Jerusalem, forty at the Dead Sea," says Oded, and the artificial sentence is swallowed up in a genuine yawn. The whistling breather swallows all the oxygen in the car, and others have to yawn in order to get their share of air.

"Okay," repeats Oded, this time as if to himself. And then again: "Okay, I think we've reached the emergency room. Elinor, you stay in the car."

Not-man says that he doesn't need the emergency room, he doesn't want the emergency room. "Your sister," he says, "your sister Elisheva forgave me. She wrote me a letter. I can show you. I have it in writing."

Oded gets out of the car, leaving the door open, and from outside he opens the other door. "Come on, professor, out."

Once more there are sounds of movement in the back, and I am still holding the steering wheel when the voice pleads: "But there's no need: I understand that it was an accident. I won't complain."

"Out."

My husband and Not-man stand in front of the Defender. I get out of the car. All the police procedurals I've ever seen go into action fast. "Empty your pockets," says my super-cop. "All of them, please." A handkerchief, notebook, cell phone, hotel-room key and old-fashioned leather wallet are piled on the hood. Oded wraps the handkerchief around his hand, picks up the cell phone, and throws it like a pro into the wadi.

"But listen to me, I swear by all that's holy to me . . ."

"Calm down, we're only going to talk. So just relax and put your things back in your pockets. You really think I would harm my wife's only uncle? Does that sound logical to you?" I'm sure I heard something similar in a movie. Where did I hear it?

"I swear to you that I've forgiven . . ."

"Let's go. It's time to talk."

My husband guides him in the direction of the escarpment of the wadi. He keeps a few steps behind him, without touching. "Go on." A winding goat track, hardly a path at all. A stone is dislodged when Not-man begins the descent, and he lets out a hoarse cry.

"Keep going."

The beam of the headlights catches a bush and stones and a body sinking slowly, step by step, into the wadi. The legs, the torso, and finally the head.

Only when the First Person has completely disappeared, Oded begins climbing down after him. Again the sound of tumbling stones, this time a lot of them: one stone dislodging another. I go closer to the edge. The silhouettes creep with unreal slowness. At moments they seem to be standing still, but at no moment does the figure bringing up the rear send out its hand to touch the one in front. And all the time I watch to make sure that it is not sent. The pounding in my chest cries out for the movement to be speeded up. The pounding that rises to my ears refuses to adapt itself to the slowness of the scene, but I am patient and even my accelerated heartbeat does not urge Oded to hurry: to speed things up and bring them to an end he would have to touch, and come what may, on no account do I want my husband to touch him.

When the silhouettes vanish behind a dark fold in the ground, I remain where I am, and only when Oded reappears, climbing up easily toward me, do I return to the car, because at last it's okay to hurry.

- 11 -

"Should I drive?"

"No, let me."

Risen from the darkness, bending forward, my husband directs me back to the main road. Even though I didn't have a clue about the way, I anticipated most of his directions, as if I had heard them even before he opened his mouth, and at the same time I was glad of every word he said, simply because of the fact that he was speaking. He was sweating as if he had been running, but he didn't smell strange, and his clipped instructions, "pay attention, right turn coming up," or "straight ahead," sounded normal. Oded is always short and to the point when he's giving directions, and like our sons, he too doesn't tolerate being spoken to or distracted when he's concentrating.

If there had been any other vehicle on the road we would have seen its lights from far in the distance. We didn't see any lights, and there was no reason to imagine that any of the Bedouin we passed would be interested in our doings, yet it was obvious that our first priority was to get out of there in a hurry.

A new time was born. Events were still too pressing and urgent for my mind to take in the breadth of the grace, but even as I hurried forward I knew with a certain knowledge that there would be time for the two of us to talk: even if a shadow had coiled itself around us, I would not rest until I had undone it knot by knot. Limitless expanses of patience would be granted me in the new time.

Oded didn't make a single mistake. Even before the air-conditioner had time to cool the car we were at the junction, and I negotiated it with the greatest possible care. I hadn't driven so carefully since our sons were small and everything dear to me was inside the car. I was careful of myself too then, when they were babies, simply because they needed me so much. From the minute I started driving back from the wadi, I became aware that the frightening feeling of the fragility of the body had returned, and that I could no longer take any pleasure in the capricious leaps of the car.

When we reached the bridge of light of the expressway, Oded leaned back. "Good, so he won't be publishing his novel now. I don't want to think about what that book would have done to your sister." His voice sounded hollow under its armor, and that boastful, contemptuous sentence—"so he won't be publishing his novel now"—still seemed like something I had once heard in a movie.

I allowed a truck to pass us, and after it receded into the distance I dropped my hand from the wheel and took hold of his hand. With only my left hand on the wheel, I needed to concentrate even more on the traffic, now I leaned forward, but I didn't take back my right hand, and Oded linked his fingers in mine.

"They won't find him," I said.

"Alive? Not a chance. In this weather no one hikes in the desert, except perhaps for a couple of yeshiva boys who decide to get lost in the wadis. Even the army has cancelled their maneuvers. No, in this weather there isn't a chance."

"But they'll find a body."

"That's doubtful too. I don't know what will be left of him."

"Maybe the dogs will eat him?"

"Maybe."

"A wild beast," I persevered, and my voice sounded like that of a child listening to a bedtime story. "A wild beast will eat him."

"Maybe in winter, with the floods, the bones will be washed into the Dead Sea, that's possible."

I thought about bones and the sea, and I didn't want him to die slowly. I hoped he would died quickly, as quickly as possible, for him to be dead already and for the wild beast to hurry up and pick the bones clean.

"You understand that it's not about the book or the possibility that he would have sued me for attacking him," I said, because it was very important for him to understand, and in the new time that was opening up, he could understand everything.

"It isn't relevant . . ."

"No it isn't. Not at all. It's got nothing to do with anything like that; with anything else he was liable to do. It has to do with cleaning. Erasing. Think simply. We erased, that's all. Now I'm clean. Free. It's erased."

Oded raised our linked hands, and put them on my thigh. For a few minutes we drove like this in silence, and then he said in a thick but slightly more normal voice: "So do you think that you'll start wearing dresses again?"

"I—what? What did you say?"

"Nothing, just that it's already summer and you haven't worn any of your sexy summer dresses yet. It just came into my head. I'm allowed. Stop it, don't laugh . . ."

The house was amazingly close, and as soon as we entered the dazzling lights of the city its presence became very concrete: first we have to look for a parking spot, maybe I'll let Oded direct me, at this hour the street is full of revelers going out on the town, and the Defender really isn't suitable for the city. The key to the front door is in my pocket, it isn't hot inside the house, inside the house it's pleasant, and this time we have no bags and parcels to carry in.

But then, when the car was already rolling as if of its own accord down the familiar path, when the miraculous everyday actions were only a few minutes away, an idea came to me, and when it became clear I realized that I had to postpone—if only for a little while—the miracle.

"Elinor, what exactly are we doing?"

The same cunning antic spirit that had taken me many years before to the gynecologist in Hahovshim Street, now took me in the direction of the Hyatt. Back then, at the doctor's, the spirit betrayed me and abandoned me and I failed: like a sheep I gave in and mounted the stirrup chair when he told me to. This time, sitting high next to my husband in the Defender, I knew that I wouldn't fall down, that the spirit wouldn't desert me, and that one more thing remained to be done.

I drove right up to the hotel entrance and stopped.

"Let's wait a bit. It won't take long."

We waited more than a bit. I almost gave up on the ingenious present with which I intended to surprise my husband: in another minute I would have answered his questions that grew more and more stressed, I was close to surrendering to the impatient drumming of his fingers on the seat—when the security guard came up to us. He looked exactly as he was supposed to look and said exactly the words he was supposed to say: "Excuse me, ma'am, you can't stand here."

Before Oded was the player, now I could play too, I wasn't going to leave him alone in the game. Jerusalem's a small town, Oded had left the Cinematheque with Not-man. There was a good chance that someone who knew him had seen them leave together and that he would remember. It was my turn to look after him. My turn to look after both of us, and according to the rules we both needed an alibi.

Conscious as a wayward girl of my husband's fascinated gaze, I said to the security guard: "Sorry, we just let someone off here, one of your guests. He's supposed to call me from his room and tell me if he's coming down to give us something. It will only take a second."

The security guard stood his ground, and I stood mine with all the exhibitionism of an insistent drunk: "Come on, show a little flexibility, we're in a hurry, we're late already, we're not blocking anyone's way here. He'll call in a minute, be nice, do me this favor . . ." And I carried on as long as I could, debating with him face to face about my right to stand there, and when I was convinced that the conversation was etched in his memory I gave up gracefully. "Oh all right, we'll move. In any case it's taking him too long," I threw demonstratively at Oded, and started the engine.

"Okay, okay, I get it," said my comrade, prodded into muscling in on the act. "In the movies the immediate suspect is always the last one to be seen with the victim. But if we're already doing it, then tell me what he was supposed to be bringing us from his room."

"I have no idea." My scene was concluded, I felt that it was perfect, the wind had gone out of my sails and I had no desire to go on with the game.

"'I have no idea' doesn't cut it, it's not good enough," boasted Oded in his commando voice. "How about for example a chapter or a synopsis of his book? Let's say that's what he was supposed to be bringing us: the synopsis of *Pol Pot, First Person*."

"You weren't listening. There is no first person of Pol Pot."

"Too much literature for me. I told you the first time we met: I hardly managed to get eighty for literature in my finals. You can't accuse me of failing to come clean. How about turning down the air-conditioning? It's freezing in here."

"My Mistake," I said in a tired voice.

"What?"

"That's what he was supposed to bring us from his room: that article of his, 'My Mistake.' He said that he would check to see if he had a copy. In the end he didn't come down."

"'My Mistake' is good. And in the end he didn't come down and he didn't call. Just so you know: tomorrow my father isn't in the office, so my plan was to tell Hodaya to call the hotel and leave a message that I was looking for him and ask him to get back to me. I'm just wondering whether it would be best to do it tomorrow or to wait one more day."

"It makes no difference. In any case he isn't going to get back to you."

"No, he isn't."

"Because what was never there can't come back. It's as simple as that."

"Right."

We reached the street next to the house. In the end it was me who maneuvered the Defender into the parking spot. We parked close to the house and went on sitting in the car, like when the boys were still living with us and we would stay in the car to conclude our business.

"So we attended the lecture and met him and gave him a lift to the hotel," Oded insisted on getting things straight. "He said he would call us and for some reason he didn't come back. Didn't it seem a little strange to us, weren't we worried by him disappearing like that?"

"We weren't worried. He was a drag and we were rid of him. What was there to worry about. It's only out of good manners that you called him the next day."

We seemed to have agreed not to take this conversation with us into the house. But although I was already ready to get down from the high seat, my husband went polishing his act in the darkness. I was already itching to shed the part of my character in the movie, but he still needed her to stay with him.

"I'm texting Hodaya to ask her to type me some document first thing tomorrow morning," he said to her. And I was jarred and stumbled on the erratic rhythm of his speech: one minute blustering, with the words gushing out thick and fast, the next slow and arrogant.

"All right."

"And you should get in touch with someone too, some girlfriend or someone, so it'll register with someone somewhere that you were going about your usual affairs this evening."

The past weeks had distanced me from all the people I could have called up spontaneously. I needed a minute or two to think, and then I did as he asked.

"It's a pleasure doing business with you," he delivered himself of this cliché when I was done. "Now let's see: he had the key on him, and if he had it on him, then on principle he could have returned to his room."

"I know. I already told you, I took it into account."

"You're a panther, you are. Next time I think we'll rob a bank."

The moment had arrived to go into the house, into the new time opening up: to be with the real Oded who would get off the screen already, with my three-dimensional man, with him—and not with the role.

"Stop it, that's enough. It's enough. This is me, and I don't want you to talk to me like that." I put my hand on his cheek, and it was dry and cold. "Oded, what's going on?" He clamped his lips and took a deep breath and breathed out slowly—for a long moment he sat next to me empty of oxygen and emptied of himself—and then, like light floating up from below I saw, I actually saw, his soul returning to him, and his skin sunk under my hand coming back to life. He pressed my hand to his cheek, and then moved it away and looked intently at the palm as if he wanted to read the lines in the dark.

"What's going on? Tell me what's happening."

He raised my hand and slowly kissed the center of my palm, and slowly closed my fingers over it like we used to do with our sons when they were babies, so the kiss wouldn't escape.

"It's not that simple. Not quite so simple. I think it will take me a few days to get used to it, but whatever happens—I want you to know that I don't have any doubts and I won't regret it," he said in his normal voice.

And only then we went back into the house.

BOOK FOUR
ONE SWEET SABBATH

- 1 -

When the two of them enter the house they fall on each other voraciously. The man kicks the door closed behind him. The woman presses her loins to the loins of the man leaning against the door. There is the sound of a tear when he pulls of her blouse. Articles of clothing are scattered on the way to the living-room carpet: jeans, a black lace bra, a skirt. The man's violent grunts of lust mingle with the woman's screams of ecstasy.

The next day the breach opens. A brief item on the morning news says that a mortally ill man of about seventy was discovered by an IDF patrol in the Judean desert, in the vicinity of the Kidron River. The man whose identity was not known was in a coma, the police were investigating how he got there.

Days of fear. Sleepless nights of terror. The breach widens. Will the patient wake up? The woman's nerves fail her and she accuses the man of not being man enough: a real man would have finished what he started, she says. And the man curses the day he met the woman.

The phone rings. It's the police and a polite detective comes to meet the couple. The victim has been identified, and the investigators already know about the meeting in the gallery. The man pours himself a whiskey and his face sweats. He is afraid that his wife is about to betray him and make him take the blame. After the detective leaves, the woman says to the man that they have to go to the hospital and finish him off. She tries to seduce him. She sits on his lap and licks his lips, and he goes on drinking and ignores her. The woman gets up, sweeps glasses off the shelf and smashes them. In general, this character has a habit of breaking things, and when the couple go to visit the man's parents, and the white-haired mother starts talking about the mystery of the uncle's disappearance—the heroine drops the dish she was about to put on the table. Red spaghetti sprays and stains the mother's respectable dress. A meatball rolls and touches the bare foot of the heroine. Her mouth gapes in a silent scream.

When Alice's ghost appeared and brought me this scene, I was so surprised that it took me some time to recognize her. Alice had undone her pigtails. As befitting a ghost she was dressed in a white kaftan, apparently picked up on her way out of the Old City. And only when she came closer to me in a wild cascade of auburn hair—when she became truly manifest—I finally recognized her, and understood that she had disguised herself as Nemesis.

But not only the appearance of the tourist from Alaska, also the narrative voice which preceded her manifestation took me time to identify: during all those years, on all our expeditions, the teller of my tales had happily blown soap bubbles in the air. Under the protection of a rosy Providence which for some reason favored ignorance and naïveté, the little pigtail-sucker had been oblivious to sex, and any hint of violence had slid away from her like water off the feathers of a goose.

And now all of a sudden my little Pollyanna was strewing items of clothing from the door to the carpet and giving voice to shrieks of ecstasy.

Her rude sexual awakening embarrassed and confused me. If she feared for me and my safety and thought that I needed a cover story to sign off on, why was it necessary for her to strip me of my clothes in this story? What was the point of stripping me naked if the intention was a cover up?

Her crude violence was as new to me as the cunning with which she tried to satisfy it. Presumably these characteristics had been latent in her before, but she had somehow succeeded in concealing them even from me.

Alice's ghost was lying for me again. The fictions she was trying to weave into my plot were intended to protect me in case I decided one day to tell it. But the content of the fiction also exposed an opposite wish: a clear desire to see me punished.

Despite my embarrassment, this sly wish was actually easy for me to understand: I had done what I had done, and deeds have consequences. Which is as it should be.

Which is presumably as it should be, but at the same time I noticed that my red-haired goddess of vengeance was not demanding blood for blood. Her kaftan looked as if it had been taken from a school fancy-dress box, and the flush of anger did not hide the freckles on her nose.

The more I thought about the ending she proposed, the more convinced I became that she had no desire to smash my skull and shed my blood. My little Nemesis was satisfied with smashing a dish and spraying spaghetti sauce, and these symbolic acts did not disturb me unduly. I didn't smash a dish, but in the days preceding her appearance I somehow succeeded in dropping and breaking three wine glasses from the set standing on the kitchen shelf, and one precious Wedgwood plate. I was a little sorry about the plate. It was part of a set I had received as a gift from my mother-in-law for my fortieth birthday. I accepted my distraction and temporary unsteadiness, accepted it and understood it. Deeds necessarily have consequences, and until their effects wear off, what you need to do is take a deep, mindful breath: count to eight with the in-breath, count to eight with the slow out-breath—and wait patiently until the panic subsides, in the certain knowledge that the terror has passed and this is nothing but a simple panic-attack: a transient symptom like the chicken pox that are still visible after the patient has already recovered. The main thing is to leave them alone and not to scratch.

There was one thing and one thing only that I was on no account ready to accept, and this was Alice's attempt to make trouble between me and my husband with her scorpion stings. I rebelled against this sabotage of what was most precious to me. And after I had scrupulously examined myself, Oded, and the slanders of the narrator of clichés, after days of examination, I decided that I had to talk to him about it. If only in order to make sure that the virus of punishment had not settled in his bloodstream, and that it was not about to break out and lead him to curse the day he had met me and followed me into the desert and the darkness.

I could not see any signs of the virus, but in the situation in which we found ourselves then, what could be considered normal and what abnormal? So I needed my husband to confirm my diagnosis: to verify it in words.

When I approached him I didn't mention Alice. Alice only confused the issue. And I have to admit that in spite of her weakness, her reappearance had somewhat undermined me. Apparently I was quite undermined already—yes, I was definitely a little undermined. And therefore I, who never approached Oded in roundabout ways, approached him one evening with a story-telling expression, and taking the coward's way out told him about these two people who had started to hate one another.

"Let's suppose," I asked, because this was the only way I dared to ask, "let's suppose that somebody wrote our story, and that the writer decided to end it like this. What do you think?"

"You're not going to write it?" he recoiled.

"I'm just wondering."

My good husband rubbed the cleft in his chin and said that with all his ignorance of literature, the story I had described sounded to him more like a movie than a novel, and that, as I was well aware, he wasn't a fan of film noir. In any case, he wasn't turned on by the particular fantasy I had outlined—except perhaps by the black lace bra, the bra was okay, even though it was a bit pornographic—but altogether it was hard for him to believe that any audience would enjoy this scenario, and he was sure that he wasn't the only one who would be put off by it.

What do we need art for? said my husband. For wisdom and pleasure. But what kind of pleasure and what kind of wisdom is there in your characters fighting each other? Why should they be punished? For what? In accordance with what logic? And according to what justice and what kind of psychology? These two people loved each other, that was the main thing, and in the circumstances I had described it seemed to him that their love would only grow stronger.

"When you think about it, Elinor," he toughened his voice, "when you think about it, then as a soldier in Lebanon I probably killed people who did a lot less harm than that scum. I liquidated people I didn't know and whose lives I knew nothing about, and as you know I sleep very well at night. So tell me why your guy, who only wanted to save his wife, wouldn't sleep soundly?"

For a moment it seemed to me that I was listening again to the character bragging to me on a movie screen on our way back from the desert. For a moment it seemed to me that the character my husband had put on in order to save me and taken off afterward in order to be with me fully, had stolen into the house again.

He'll never hate me, I thought, not that, definitely not that. But perhaps the price and the punishment is that this is the only way we'll be able to talk about ourselves and about what happened: indirectly, putting on fictional characters, in a language that isn't ours. Hadn't he just said to me "Why should they be punished, for what?" Because that's what he thinks, that's what he really thinks. "Why should they," he thinks in the third person . . . and says. And I too don't see myself as deserving of punishment. I don't deserve it, I don't, and Oded definitely deserves only good. We'd suffered enough evil. And we had done no evil—uprooting evil isn't a sin. So why was it impossible now to speak directly? It didn't make sense. Not us. So why?

Oded went on expressing his opinion to me, according to which most of the audience would probably find a proper degree of satisfaction in "the hand of cosmic justice," and also volunteered to offer me what he called "a theoretical alternative script":

Your two gave Gotthilf a lift to his hotel, he explained to me, fluent and prepared as if he had been waiting for the opportunity to explain. The two of them took him to his hotel. Before that they had hauled him over the coals, but still, he was an old man, and in the heavy heat they didn't like to send him to look for a cab. Decent people didn't do things like that, and we're talking here about a respectable couple—that goes without saying. You can also add that before that, when they were still in the gallery, the swine

told them that he was sick: let's say he complained of visual distur-
bances and dizziness. So they gave him a lift, and after that, it's not
clear when, he simply disappeared. Months later, in winter, let's say,
a group of hikers discovered human bones in some wadi near the
Dead Sea. And a pathological examination confirmed that they were
the remains of the missing man. Who knows what happened to him?
Anything's possible. Perhaps in some attack of senility he decided
to go for a hike in the desert in the middle of summer. Perhaps he
was the victim of a terror attack, and perhaps he simply got on the
nerves of his taxi diver. In any case, cosmic justice did its work, and
the sadistic swine got what was coming to him.

"Unconvincing," I said emphatically. "You can't rely on cosmic
justice. You yourself don't believe in it."

"You yourself," I said. I succeeded in saying "you."

He looked into my eyes, up to then he hadn't looked straight at
me, and I felt an unexpected warmth flooding my face. My husband
was looking at me and I was blushing—the awareness that this was
happening only deepened my blush.

For a moment we sat like this, him looking and me blushing and
not lowering my eyes. This went on for a moment, until he smiled
faintly and shrugged his shoulders, and said that he trusted me.
"You . . ." he said. "If you ever decide for some reason to write
that fantasy, I believe that as an artist you'll find a solution." His
living voice sounded almost laughing. As if he was laughing with
me. There would be no punishment. There should be none and there
would be none, because Oded and I wouldn't allow it. There was
nothing to be punished for.

Oded said that he trusted me. My husband smiled at me as if at a
young girl. "Their love will only grow stronger," he said to me. But
the rubbing of his chin that followed immediately betrayed anxiety
over my thoughts about writing. And thus, in the same breath as he

expressed his belief in me, he suggested bringing Alice back to life and renewing my walks in our city with her. "Think about it. Just think about it. In fact it isn't even a question of bringing her back to life like in all kinds of rubbishy serials, and you don't have to explain to anyone how come she isn't dead. Apart from your editor and me nobody knows what happened to her in the last column you wrote, because in the end they never printed it, and you can relate to it as if it never really happened."

•

My husband was always stubborn, but ever since the incident in the desert he had shown a new kind of self-assertion—anyone who knows him will confirm this—and things reached such pass that last month he went head to head with his father in the office. Oded abandoned the way of quiet diplomacy, and from the secretaries I heard about the shouts coming from behind the door. Menachem, I imagine, did not raise his voice, but afterward, for four days, the two of them didn't exchange a word, and my husband, who was calm and resolute, made it clear that if his father refused to back down and or stop interfering in his cases this time, he would walk out.

My mother-in-law called me every day with soothing small talk, as if I was the one who had to be appeased. But by the time our usual Friday night visit came round, Menachem had already surrendered unconditionally, with patriarchal dignity, because his son refused to be satisfied with less.

The men came to whatever agreement they came to. In response to his father's surrender, my husband conducted himself with ironclad politeness—for the first time since we met I noticed the resemblance between the two men—and when we all sat down at the table Menachem put his arm round Oded's shoulder.

"My son has beaten me," he said to me, and his son did not bow his head or raise his hand to touch him. He looked straight ahead, his face was hard to read, in those days it was hard even for me—I can only say that he looked reflective.

Deeds have consequences. Necessarily so, but was this a late development leading from our actions? Was it the events of that night that had brought about a change in my husband's personality? From the point of view of the plot it could be presented like this: one thing leads to another, until everything is made plain. But the truth is that I don't know what led to what or how my husband was affected, just as I don't know what exactly led me in the end to visit my mother's grave. There are never any definite reasons for such things, neither in life nor in truth, and my immediate and apparent reason was Elisheva.

The anniversary of our mother's death was approaching, it was clear that she would ask me, and I didn't want to be evasive or lie to her.

I didn't want to disappoint her; at this stage I already felt stable and I knew that I had it in my power to please her. And once I had decided to fulfill her wishes, I realized that going to the cemetery was not going to be a sacrifice or a forced concession made for her sake. I understood this when instead of the resentment I expected to feel, I was actually seized by a kind of curiosity; a wish to reassess myself at the graveside of the mother who had deserted us. I had not undertaken such a fundamental self-examination since I gave birth to my first son, when my motherhood was still new to me. A lot had happened since then. I did what I did, I made an end, I removed a Not-man from the face of the earth. I had no alternative, the earth could not bear him, and neither could I. Had this act of removal somehow softened my attitude toward my mother? Perhaps she too could bear no more, and therefore she made an end.

Once I had made my decision I had to find out where the grave was located; I had simply forgotten the dead woman's address, and when we got there, Oded and I—not on the date of her death but two days before it—could hardly recognize the place. The trees on the slopes had grown tall. New roads cut through the mountain, and the whiteness of the graveyard had spread far around. It was dusk, and from the spot where we were standing I counted five bulldozers parked in the area.

The view awoke nothing in me, no tender forgotten memory, but I did what was expected of me: I got hold of a pail, filled it with water, and washed away the yellow dust that had accumulated on the tombstone.

There was no sense of reconciliation in this act, no purification, and I point this out because I could actually have concocted a catharsis out of this scene: mixed the water of purification with the amniotic fluid of birth, and holy water with tears at the end of a drought.

Alice had retired. Ever since her attempt to stir up strife between me and my husband I no longer heard her voice or saw her. Perhaps she had despaired of me when I failed to respond to her Nemesis act, perhaps she had gone to look for another disguise. Perhaps she had gone to join the dead whose place of burial is unknown. One day I will have to give her a proper funeral. In any case, wherever she may be, Alice had not put in an appearance these many months.

Alice had retired. But even without her, even now that my winsome little charmer was gone, the impudent symbolism of many waters went on paying court to me and seducing me: the tourist had departed, but apparently she had not packed up all her seductions and taken them with her.

The deceptive symbolism winked at me. Symbolism likes to wink, inviting the writer to cheat and prettify the picture, to inflate the nothing I felt into something. Because the truth is that I hardly felt anything at all: no feeling of symbolic uplift visited me as I lifted the pail and poured tepid water over the gravestone of the woman who had been my mother. No ceremonial uplift and no blurring tenderness either. I was very well able to differentiate between water and water, and above all between mother and daughter. My mother deserted and abandoned and I, when all is said and done, did the opposite: I did not desert my beloved and I did not abandon the world to the serpent. For all my sins against my beloved this was the end of the matter, this was the end, and in the end I did not abandon.

This is the thought that came to me at the gravesite, but it too did not come as a sudden revelation. The verdict had been delivered and upheld before. I had been aware of the great difference between us before, and therefore the awareness did not strike me, so to say, but simply concentrated itself there. For one concentrated moment I measured myself against my mother. For a moment more I stood there with the empty pail in my hand, but already when Oded took it from me I looked down at my toes, which had been a little muddied, and immediately started to think about the lamb I would prepare for my son Nimrod in honor of his homecoming. The day after tomorrow, I thought, the day after tomorrow would be a good time to go to the butcher. The weather was reasonable, the walk to the Nablus Gate into the Old City would be pleasant. But for the root vegetables I would wait till Friday morning, because roots dying in the fridge spoil the pleasure.

So that's it, that's the story as it was: we drove to the cemetery and returned—during the entire visit I did not splash with my mother in a bath of reconciliation, and wellsprings of consolation did not well up in me—but as soon as we got home I wrote an email to my sister, because it was mainly for her sake that we had gone there in the first place.

I informed her that we had visited the grave, and explained that because we were so busy and because of Nimrod's imminent home-coming, we were unable to go on the actual date of the anniversary itself. "In spite of the hard summer we have had here the trees in the cemetery look good. The plants are flourishing in our garden too. We watered them a lot and it seems that the combination of the heat and the water encouraged the plants and made them think that they were in a tropical country."

The next morning the reply was already waiting for me, and the letter that opened with an expression of sorrow trembled on the screen with more than the usual emotion.

Elisheva had sad news for me: their good friend Martha, dear Martha who had visited us in our apartment in Talpioth and whom I had met in their home, had passed away this week after a long illness. When I saw her I must have noticed how sick she was. And exactly yesterday, perhaps exactly when Oded and I were at the cemetery, they had accompanied to "Mount Hope" the woman who had been like a mother to her since she came to America. Wasn't it strange that Oded and I had been obliged to visit our mother's grave before the anniversary, and that we in Jerusalem and they in Monticello—had visited cemeteries on the very same day?

Martha will be sorely missed by us all, wrote my sister, but it was important for me to know that up to the last minute she was very brave and continued to be an inspiration to all who loved her.

"Tell me," I said to Oded, "do you remember any mountain in the area where my sister lives?"

"Mountain—what mountain? Where do you get a mountain from? There isn't even a hillock there." He was busy organizing his briefcase for the office, leafing through some documents or other, and had no inclination to chat.

"I don't know, Elisheva wrote about some funeral, and I'm trying to understand what kind of people call a cemetery situated on a plain—'Mount Hope.' It's the same deceit as calling a town where there isn't a single Italian Monticello. 'Mount Hope.' What hope is there exactly in death?"

My husband wasn't in the mood for wondering and didn't answer me. But after he left the house, I thought that I would like to be sure that there was no hope and no eternity. Because if there was hope in death, then what had been erased wasn't erased. And the serpent still existed, and I had to believe that he had no existence. Not even in hell.

After the first death, there is no other.

Years and years after I had read Dylan Thomas to my sister and been appalled, an entire era afterward, I understood at last that this was a sentence of consolation: there was no eternity in which I and Not-man could dwell together. There was no eternity in which we would breathe the same air. There was no eternity—and therefore none either for "two little sisters, Eli and Eli" and a pointing finger, and "Ha-ha, said the uncles, this one or that one?"

After the first death there is no other. The First Person would not be reincarnated. What was dead—was dead, and only the living existed. My sister had survived the Valley of the Shadow of Death, she was fine with her life, and I was here, and I had mine.

Here I was washing dishes in the kitchen, turning the tap right and left, enjoying the control over the jet of water as if I had made a new discovery. Here I was rubbing cream into my hands and breathing in the smell of camphor, lemon, and lavender; the vapors of the camphor deepened my breath and tickled my nose.

And here in two and a half days' time my arms would embrace Nimrod and Nimrod would embrace me back without embarrassment, because my youngest knew how to embrace. Cleansed, I would drive to the airport with Oded to meet our son, and clean and free I would sit here with the two of them afterward at the table: if I spread a tablecloth over it, would the festivity seem exaggerated to Nimrod? After I had pulled false sugary faces at him, and after I had ruined the trip to Seattle I could not burden him further with any exaggerations: it was important for everything to be ordinary, quiet and normal, it was important for us all—and that's what it would be, quiet and normal.

Quiet and normal because there were no more images clamoring for attention and spawning nightmarish litters.

Quiet and normal because everything I had been dragging after me, all that vociferous, metastasizing abomination, had been cut off and cast into oblivion.

That's how it would be, yes, as quiet as it was now, because after the first death there is no other.

●

I didn't know what to write to my sister: I hardly knew her friend Martha and I had never seen her Mount Hope. So instead of a reply I simply sent her an up-to-date photo of Yachin; it was a beautiful picture, a really beautiful picture of my handsome son, with a clean sea and boats in the background.

- 1 -

The narrator has jumped the plot months forward: skipping smartly over certain difficulties and solving them without any problems. Now all is well with the couple who were saved and returned to the Garden of Eden, and soon their son will be back too.

I jumped the plot months forward, and this acrobatic act, which no doubt did not escape the notice of the reader, may perhaps give rise to the impression that I have something to hide:

For what happened, what actually happened after we came home from the desert? Is it conceivable that we simply wrote off that night and went back to our old routine? That we put the lid on the past and hardly spoke about it? That our actions had no effects or that the consequences were all beneficial?

That's not possible, things by their nature happen differently: you can't put a lid on the past so easily and that's no way to end my story.

Silence hints at a secret, and if so—what is it? Is there really a secret that I'm keeping quiet about? Am I pulling an Alice and directing the eyes of the observer to the dust bunnies so they won't notice anything else? I don't think so, but to remove any doubt, let me pick up the story where I left off:

We came home. Oded, who was sweating profusely, went into the shower first, and I went in after him. While he was showering I prepared iced tea. We emptied the jug quickly, I prepared another one, in case one of us grew thirsty in the night, and in the meantime we talked a little, saying things that sounded almost routine—"Are you going in to the office tomorrow?" "Will you be okay? What will you do all day?"

The fridge chugged loudly like it sometimes does. Oded gave it a shove to shut it up like he sometimes does. We said that we would try to sleep.

According to Oded he slept like a log, and I dreamt a surprising dream whose details I didn't remember in the morning: I only knew that it was full of brilliant color and sweetness perfumed with rose water. This was the first in a series of Oriental dreams that came to me in the following weeks: dreams flowing in shiny brocades and silks. When I opened my eyes I would smile in wonder—and almost in embarrassment at the memory of the tickle of their peacock feathers. No actual pictures of these fantasy trips remained with me, but their sweetness seemed to seep into me gradually, and gradually it padded and rounded me.

The heat wave broke in the early hours of the morning. The next day Oded cut his hours in the office short, and I spent most of the day weeding the neglected garden. Approximately every hour I went inside to check the news sites on the internet, but nothing relevant to us came up.

On his way home Oded stopped at the video store and took out two thrillers, which we watched one after the other.

"I still can't take in just how warped he was, it's simply incomprehensible," he said to me between one movie and the next, and for a moment it seemed that he was referring to the main villain we had seen on the screen. "So many words he had. Do you think that all that intellectualism simply provided him with an excuse, or that he really believed . . ."

I put a warning finger on my mouth. "Don't start with that. Just don't start with it."

"With what?"

"With trying to understand. Don't even try to get close to his head, and don't ask about that thing, what it was. There was nothing there. You saved me from what there was, and now there's nothing."

Then we watched another movie. And in the coming days, many more.

In those days of the beginning of our return, I caught myself keeping a fearful eye on my husband, assuring myself that he was doing his work, keeping to his schedule, sleeping enough and eating what

I cooked with a reasonable appetite. I knew that he wouldn't fail me and that he wouldn't crack, but I still couldn't stop myself from keeping an eye on him—but secretly, so he wouldn't sense that he was being tested. After he fell asleep I would examine his face, trying to guess his dreams and watching for signs of disquiet. His features looked calm. He slept uninterruptedly and rose early as usual. Early in the morning in my dreams I would hear him busying himself in the kitchen, going out to the garden and after that a silence, in which I wrapped myself in my dreams again. Only several days and many dreams later I realized that he stayed in the garden and that he had stopped going out for his morning run. And when I realized, I got out of bed and went out into the air of the new day to join him and asked him why.

Leaning forward in his chair, Oded rested his chin on his thumb and rubbed one eyebrow with the tip of his forefinger. "Look, it's like this: running empties your head, it's a physiological thing. When you indulge in intensive physical exercise—you can't really think. Often this is helpful. But for me at this moment in time not thinking would be like running away." I licked my finger and tidied the wayward hairs of his eyebrows, but a moment later his hand went up to push them out of place again. He looked impatient to me, and somehow it was clear that his impatience was not directed at me but at himself.

"So at the moment your exercise is getting up early in order to sit here in the garden and not run away," I said.

"You should know that I don't have any new thoughts or perceptions regarding what happened, believe me, that's for sure: no new thoughts and no new conclusions. Only without any thoughts my mind somehow insists on going back and replaying the film. It simply runs the scenes over and over, and at this stage it seems to me that I have no option but to let it. In any case my idea is that if this is what needs to be, in other words if I already have to let the film run, it's better to try and do it in an orderly way: to get it over first thing in the morning, before I begin the day.

"Don't worry. I'm okay. In the end everything will be fine," he added, and I crouched down in front of him like a Bedouin and peered into his eyes.

"In the end?"

"It's already fine. And as soon as I'm finished playing the movie I'll go back to exercising."

"You'll do exactly the right thing, always, I have no doubt," I said eagerly. For some reason I was ashamed to tell him what he would probably have been happy to hear: that I was not haunted and that I didn't see any pictures. That with me it was perhaps the exact opposite. For a considerable part of the day I still felt shaky. But within this shakiness it happened that I sometimes stopped with a sudden sense of wonder, and with every stop I needed a moment to grasp the thing that filled me with wonder was the new cleanness of my mind. Perhaps it was also because of the novelty of this cleanness that I felt shaky. I needed to rest. I needed time to get used to the existing restfulness. But somehow I knew too that soon, really soon, when I recovered my strength, my eyes would be cleared to see whatever I wanted to look at, and I was already beginning to feel a little curious about what things I would see when I went out to look: the garden was big and there was much to see in it.

"Everything you do is right," I said to my beloved, whose suffering I did not share. Because what could I say that had not already been said? And who would I help by repeating to him what he already knew? I knew very well that no words and no arguments would help against pressing pictures. "Would you like me to make us an omelet? To put on more coffee?"

I believed him when he said that he was okay. I believed what I said to him too, that he always knew the right thing to do. I believed, and at the same time for a certain period I went on watching him for signs of any subcutaneous wounds. I knew that the blue-black of subcutaneous bleeding does not appear at once. And I thought that if there was indeed an injury, I had to make sure that the dawn watches to which he had sentenced himself were not making the bleeding worse. Oded went on sitting in the garden until almost the end of summer, but no blue-black bruises made their appearance. And all this time he remained clear to me.

In my concern for him, watching over his sleep and food, and showering him with positive reinforcements, I was close to becoming a mother and sister to him. For moments we came close to it, it almost happened, but my husband wouldn't permit it. My husband wouldn't permit it, and even as I worried about his well-being, he insisted on behaving toward me with a gentle and slightly weary authority, and as if he had appointed himself to be my big brother he would repeatedly say things like: "Are you eating lunch?" "Let me, I'll peel it for you," and "Careful with that armchair, it's heavy"; to which I would reply in sentences like: "What's the matter with you? It's not at all heavy and I'm not an invalid."

And so we worried about each other until, in time, reality showed us that all our worries and concerns were superfluous.

Eight days and nights passed until two newspapers printed brief items on the disappearance of the professor, and almost a week more until one of the weekend papers ran a longer article: about eight hundred words under the headline "The Mystery of the Missing Professor." Not-man was described as an "enigmatic figure" and once more presented as "a controversial figure both among historians and in the

Jewish community in the United States." One historian interviewed anonymously defined him as "a intellectual with bold intuitions tending to over-hasty conclusions" and another said that he was "an impetuous charlatan and dangerous populist." The police, the article said, were still groping in the dark.

Oded and I had heard abut the disappearance even earlier. We heard abut it from my mother-in-law, after she and Menachem returned from the dinner which took place in the steak house at Ramat Rachel and not in a vegetarian restaurant on Keren Yayesod Street: "The meal was excellent but your uncle didn't come. Mordechai says that he didn't even get in touch with him to say he couldn't come. It's a pity we didn't get to meet him."

No dish fell and smashed, and no red sauce splashed on my mother-in-law's dress. Oded folded his arms on his chest and without blinking an eye said "Maybe it isn't a pity at all. In the end Elinor and I went to listen to his lecture and both of us felt that he wasn't the kind of person we would want to have any connection with."

"May I ask why?" inquired Menachem.

"He was disgusting. The whole thing was nothing but a piece of self-advertisement. He didn't even come close to understanding his mistake."

Accustomed to treating the sensitive subject of "Elinor's family" with kid gloves, and somewhat shocked by the rare tactlessness of their son, my in-laws let the matter drop, and the conversation turned to other participants in the conference, serious and interesting people, who had come to the dinner.

I have no idea when Not-man was officially recognized as a missing person. Perhaps when he was supposed to check out of the Hyatt.

Presumably he had other appointments for which he failed to show up: encounters of one kind or another with people who saw him as a "bold intellectual," coffee with a journalist writing up the conference, meetings with other lecturers; perhaps his son came up to Jerusalem to put a note in the Western Wall and took the opportunity to try and get in touch with his father. Perhaps on his way back from the Wall he passed the hotel and left a note there too. In any case, the First Person wasn't important enough for anyone to search for him in earnest. Messages like the one Oded's secretary left for him presumably piled up at the reception desk of the hotel, in the pigeon-hole where there was no key to the room; but the addressee was no longer there. He had vanished into thin air.

Alice had once investigated the fate of notes fallen out of the Wall, and on one of her first expeditions she had accompanied the sacks of these fallen notes to a dignified burial on the Mount of Olives. My computer contains no trace of this column, but people read it and I still remember. And this, in short, is the story:

As she stands and watches the burial of the sacks a faded note flies straight up to Alice, and when she dares to open it she discovers a letter from a little girl with cancer. Without knowing why, she puts the decorated exercise-book page into her pocket, and only on her way back from the cemetery an inner voice tells her to return the lost wish to the Wall. Someone who landed in our city to seek for desert light will always follow her inner voice. And she does so this time too. And as the sun sets and Alice stands on tiptoe to reach for a crack in which to insert the letter, a little girl comes up to her and offers to put the note in one of the relatively empty cracks lower down. The child says that this is what she did with her own note a moment ago, and adds that she came to thank God for curing her of leukemia. She completed her last treatment a week ago.

Even the constantly thrilled and amazed Alice understands that she will never know if the little girl she encountered at the Wailing Wall is the same one whose prayer flew up into the air opposite the grave. Perhaps there were two sick little girls—she reflects at the end of the story—and perhaps there was only one. But if there were in fact two, all we can do is wish: if only this miraculous encounter was a sign from the cosmos, a cosmic sign that both of them were cured.

If only it wasn't me who had written this transparent tale. But I did write it, and I wrote it without the faintest idea of what and who I was writing about. It was so forced and affected that on the Friday it came out even Menachem refrained from calling me to give me his reactions, but I was so obtuse then that I didn't even wonder about his silence. Was I transparent to him? Or perhaps Rachel read me between the lines? I think not, I would like not to believe it, and in any case it's not important any more. Not important, no, only disturbing. Two sick little girls, I wrote. If only they would get well, I wrote. Unthinkingly I faked this bluff. Unthinkingly I faked, because that's what I was like and it didn't bother me a bit. And for years for a large part of my time I definitely enjoyed wandering the city in pigtails.

Later on I'll give it my attention. I have to, it's impossible not to think. Later on I shall certainly give it attention, a lot of attention—but not now, not at this minute, when there's something else entirely on the agenda and when there's another truth I have to tell:

Notes that fall from the Wall are indeed given a respectful burial just as I wrote, whereas as notes with messages left behind by hotel guests are thrown into the trash.

It occurred to me, it definitely occurred to me that the police might well have confiscated the messages received by the missing person and examined them. But weeks went by and nobody from the police contacted us to ask us any questions, or if they did, and I don't think they did—my protective husband, my guardian angel, didn't tell me about it. If that's what actually happened, I'm okay with it, and even now, at a distance in time, I have no need to ask him and to know.

Once we returned home it was clear to me that the possibility of the police tracking us down was purely theoretical, and that the truth was there was nothing more to fear. I did what was necessary to make sure that there would be no deviations from the successful outcome of our plot. I acted according to the rules of the game. But in fact, on our way back, when I was busy preparing our alibi, I already knew, I knew for certain, that all this preparing-for-any-eventuality was superfluous, and that it was only a mental game that Oded and I were supposed to play, as if in obedience to the rules of some genre.

There would be no deviation, because the deviations were over and done, and from now on there was no more terror but only flickers and flashes of panic. My husband and I returned home, we were at home, and in the land of I-shall-fear-no-evil you don't fear evil.

The new time opened out in front of us. The Garden of Eden once more opened its gates, and I was determined not to delay and not to set up a way station on the threshold.

Our relief grew steadily, whether quickly or slowly. In the first days the domestic environment seemed fragile and gleaming, as if everything was made of crystal sparkling with light. I remember myself holding a frying pan with tremendous care—the bottom reflected a ray of sunlight, a spot of refracted orange light danced on the wall—and I held onto the pan with both hands so it wouldn't shatter in pieces.

Carefully I moved between one precious object and another, until the fragility gradually abated and only the gleam remained.

Three or four weeks passed before I started getting in touch with friends and bringing people back into my life, and in a rather vague way I prepared myself for difficulty: decades of reading had prepared me for the feeling that what I had done had set up a barrier between me and the rest of the world. I didn't spend a lot of time thinking about it. Perhaps because I didn't think much, the apprehension didn't swell in me. I felt no real anxiety, but when I started to make contact again I was nevertheless sometimes astonished by the ease of the contact and the absence of any barrier. When I was with people it did sometimes cross my mind that I had a secret, but this awareness when it surfaced was almost neutral, neutral and weightless as the fact that I had brown eyes. Not-man had disappeared, and it seemed that the weight of the secrecy had disappeared with him.

Three or four weeks passed before I got in touch with a girlfriend and suggested that we go to buy sandals together, but even before that, even before I started contacting people, when Oded was still following the news on the internet and keeping his dawn watch in the garden—I had already given myself back our grocer's morning smile. I had already recovered the pleasure of eavesdropping on the conversations of passersby, the surprising charm of an incorrect word, the smell of freshly ground coffee, the smoothness and sweetness left by the taste of halva between my teeth. I recovered the sight of the tender shoot of a fig tree breaking out bravely between the paving stones, the sense of solidity afforded by stone walls, even when they turn pink in the evening. I recovered many things like this.

The relief grew steadily, and the new freedom left more and more space for happiness. After what I had survived, after what we had been through—who would begrudge me my delight in coffee and halva, and who would say that we had no right?

As for books, I confess that I needed time, and that for weeks everything I tried to read still seemed boring, absurd, or trivial. Again and again I bent over the water in my thirst, and each time the water receded and my mouth remained parched.

My road back to reading was completely and accidentally paved once, in groping thirst, I opened the Bible and began to read the Book of Judges. The bible was neither boring nor trivial, and I spent weeks with Judges, Kings, and Prophets.

Like a turbaned Orthodox woman moving her lips in the bus over a little Book of Psalms, I carried the Bible with me wherever I went: I read it in a café waiting for friends, I read it in the hotel in Safed where we went for the weekend with Chemi and Rachel, and I read it almost every night before gong to sleep.

"What is this, Elinor, in the end you'll be like Elisheva."

I ignored the teasing and went on reading. I liked the severe Old Testament God: his passionate temperament and acts seemed more convincing and believable to me than those of many other fictional characters I knew. I understood this fiery God and occasionally, in some strange way, it seemed to me that he understood me too.

For many days I clung to my blue-covered Bible, until in the end—perhaps simply because I persevered in the habit of reading—I found that I could read other books too.

In Zion Square, close to the place where I had collapsed before having my sister hospitalized, a frightening old beggar stands on a permanent spot. Twenty years ago this man had terrified my sons with a smoky voice that seemed to rise from the depths of some enormous sound box, and they were so frightened of him that they would always tug my hand and demand that we make a wide detour around the square. On purpose, I think, he would suddenly hurl this dreadful voice at them to frighten them, and so he continued to do to other passersby in all the years that followed.

One morning, not long ago, I walked past this beggar, and all of a sudden, in a quite low, perfectly normal voice, he asked me to give him a few shekels. I stood still for a moment to ascertain that the voice was indeed coming from his throat. I had already become so accustomed to the terrible voice that it had ceased to frighten me, but that morning, when I dropped a few coins in his hand—his "thank you, ma'am" sounded quite natural and normal.

The bass voice was the same, but now it came from an ordinary human throat and not from a smoky sound box.

Something in reality had changed since the disappearance of Notman. The ground had balanced out, or steadied a little. The air above the ground had lightened. The change was very subtle. Perhaps only beggars and raging madmen were able to sense it, perhaps it was mainly evident in them. But something real had changed, an actual shift had taken place—this I know with sober, clear-headed awareness.

I'm not crazy, and in this matter I am not subject to any delusions: the man we got rid of was not Hitler, and with the elimination of the First Person the world has not been redeemed of all evil. The world is not redeemed, this is clear to me, but it is no less clear to me that it has changed.

Those close to me, with the possible exception of Oded, apparently do not sense the change, and if they sometimes feel relief, they do not know what to attribute it to, or wonder what it stems from. People go out into the street, people walk in the streets and breathe cleaner air—so, what does it tell them? But it's a fact, a palpable fact that the air is lighter.

Small, elusive things have changed their shape and conduct, and I myself, who have not been blessed with a scientific mind, can only rarely catch them and point to them.

The plants, not only in our own garden but also in the public parks, looked stronger and healthier than they have ever been. Our neighbor's dog has stopped howling and wailing at night. Our sons are already grown, but I guess that fewer babies cry now for no defined reason.

Presumably some statistical study exists showing that asthmatics now suffer fewer attacks than before, or that the attacks are less severe. I expect I could find such a study on the Internet, but I'm sick of the Internet.

And I feel no desire to check it out.

In brief: the earth still cries out. Perhaps it always will. But now—of this I have no doubt because I have the evidence of my ears—it cries out less.

- 3 -

One infinitely sweet Sabbath. The fragrance of figs bursting with ripeness fills the inner courtyard of the house. Clouds filter the gold of the sun between the leaves of our grapevine pergola. A short while ago we returned from a visit to Oded's parents, and now, relaxing in wicker chairs, he rolls himself a joint. Lately my husband has been smoking grass on weekday evenings too. He does this only rarely, and according to him he doesn't smoke to calm down but in order to express the calmness inside him.

My husband pours me a glass of wine, and I hold the glass up to the sun while he rubs the cold bottle against my arm. In the past I sometimes considered having the tattoo surgically removed, but with time my doubts disappeared and today it's clear to me that my tiger face is better than a scar.

The golden Sabbath time pervades our surroundings without reference points. A muezzin calls the faithful from inside the Old City, but he is calling to others, not to us. Oded slides the bottle lazily around my nipples. The lust is there, it's palpable, but we have plenty of time.

•

When we came back from the desert we were not sexually aroused, that's clear, and there was no trail of garments leading from the front door to the living room. Anything like that would have been inconceivable.

In the first days we simply treated each other gently, very gently, as if we were recovering from a long illness. Desire, when it existed, was also cautious, and only gradually, movement by movement, step by step, did it come into its own.

"Elisheva sends us regards from my father," I tell my husband, because I have all the time in the world. "She says that if he feels well, he and his lady friend will come and visit them in the autumn. Gemma wants to paint the autumn leaves."

Oded raises his eyebrows questioningly and keeps the bottle on my breasts.

"I asked her to give him our regards too. Why not, what do I care."

"Right, who cares. I adore this dress. Is it new?"

I taste the wine, and before I dive into the glass my eyes seek to capture the scene and I take the photograph: a picture of a garden with me and my husband in it.

Photographed thus in my mind's eye, I take a few more sips of wine, and only then slowly abandon my thoughts and yield to the primacy of the body. A sunlit redness gradually spreads through me, and when I close my eyes, I see the light through my eyelids, playing in our courtyard and giving rise to sparkling spots of color.

A motorcycle drives past in the alley and leaves a palpable silence in its wake. Close to me a bee buzzes, and a purple spot on the screen of my eyelids vibrates to the sound of the buzzing. Inside the house the phone rings, and we don't bother to get up to answer it. Nimrod, apparently: wanting to let his father know that he'll be late in returning his new Jeep to him.

Inside the Sabbath time there is space for everything. There is no early or late, now everything is permitted to me, and permitted too to others.

The skin on my arm tingles. I smell the joint going out and my husband asking "Should I pour you another glass?" I hear the vine growing. And the vibrating purple expands.

A wind, a light Northern wind carries the scent of rose from outside—in our garden there are no roses—and I see the wind and more: I see the points of the compass rose. In the East the desert, in the South the basement apartment—it must still be standing—in the West there was once a pension. Puffs of wind move the petals. The four petals of the compass flap like wings. The wings of the earth slowly rise and fall, and our garden is planted in the center. One of my bare feet is on the ground. The earth beneath me is firm and still. The garden will not move.

The purple tide rises and separates into shades, and the tide covers and the tide opens to see an infinity of purples opening out and spreading through space. The purple spreads and flows, an infinity of shades of purple, with a black eye at its center.

"Elinor? My love?"

A wind of words tickles my ear. Now a spark of gold beats in the heart of the eye. I close my eyes tighter, dive into the flickering blackness and make for the gold.

The Garden of Eden. A swooning Sabbath time with a ripe smell of fig and vine stretching immeasurably around us.

The Garden of Eden. The present is the only time.

The Garden of Eden. My body is present in itself and in the garden, and my body is the truth, and all of me in it is one: here I am, and from here there is no other.

G ail Hareven is the author of eleven novels, including *The Confessions of Noa Weber*, which won both the Sapir Prize for Literature and the Best Translated Book Award.

Dalya Bilu is the translator of A. B. Yehoshua, Aharon Appelfeld, and many others.

Open Letter—the University of Rochester's nonprofit, literary translation press—is one of only a handful of publishing houses dedicated to increasing access to world literature for English readers. Publishing ten titles in translation each year, Open Letter searches for works that are extraordinary and influential, works that we hope will become the classics of tomorrow.

Making world literature available in English is crucial to opening our cultural borders, and its availability plays a vital role in maintaining a healthy and vibrant book culture. Open Letter strives to cultivate an audience for these works by helping readers discover imaginative, stunning works of fiction and poetry, and by creating a constellation of international writing that is engaging, stimulating, and enduring.

Current and forthcoming titles from Open Letter include works from Argentina, Bulgaria, China, France, Greece, Iceland, Latvia, Poland, South Africa, and many other countries.

www.openletterbooks.org